FAWNESS

My Books

Young Adult Science-Fantasy
Aevo Compendium Duology Series

Isoldesse
Fawness
Companion Novella: The Red Umber Forest

Young Adult Dark Fantasy
Three Shades Trilogy Series

Shade of Light

FAWNESS
Aevo Compendium Series
KIMBERLY GRYMES

Cover Design and Title Page Design by Atra Luna

ISBN-13: 978-1736179352 (Hardcover)
ISBN-13: 978-1736179345 (Paperback)
ASIN: B0BWPVV1H6 (eBook)

P.O. Box 261, Rose Hill, KS 67133

www.kimberlygrymes.com

To Kayla.

*You're not just my daughter,
you're also my friend who listens, supports,
and goes on coffee runs with me.
I love you to the moon and back.*

THE WORLDS OF
ISOLDESSE

EARTH   SENDARA

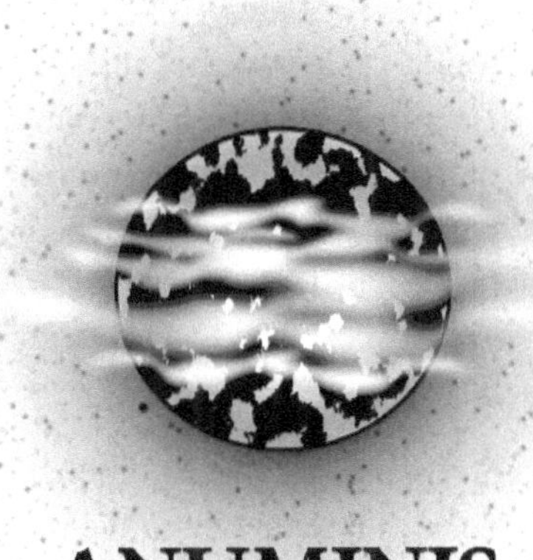

ANUMINIS

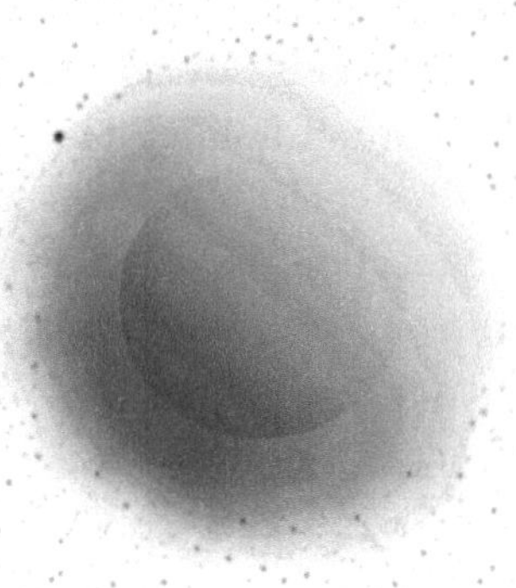

OBARD

ANUMEN
TERMINOLOGY

Amula – (ah-mew-lah) Incantations that involve speaking certain words of the Anumen language that are encoded with instructions to manipulate the energy of the Eilimintachs.

Anumen – (ah-new-men) A race of beings that live on a world called Anuminis. The women of this species have a magical connection to the Eilimintachs.

Anuminis – (ah-new-min-is) The home world of the Anumens.

Arcstone – A powerful stone found on Anuminis that has the capability of holding the essence of a single Anumen woman after her physical life ends. The arcstone can also form a permanent bond, a connection, to a living person, who can then see and hear the Anumen occupying the stone as well as utilize the magic of the arcstone.

Daramum – An Anumen term for *grandmother*.

Eilimintachs – (el-im-in-tocks) Believed by the Anumens to be powerful beings with a connection to the elements who have blessed Anumen women with the ability to cast amulas.

Essence – Similar to a soul, but it's also a form of energy with strings or mechanics that keeps the soul and body alive. An essence is fueled by the elements.

Ittums – (it-tums) An Anumen term for the Hiccum flower.

Iya –An Anumen term for *hello* and *goodbye*.

Obard – A race of hostile beings. They invaded Anuminis, forcing Anumens to flee their home world.

Pioras – (pie-or-us) An Anumen term for unexpected side effects during an arcstone bond; usually because an Anumen casts a secondary amula on the arcstone prior to bonding.

Sèara – (say-era) An Anumen term for a powerful Anumen who can sense amulas, communicate with Anumens in the Unforeseen World, and sometimes get glimpses or premonitions through visions or dreams.

Transessent stone – A smooth white stone, flat and oval in shape. Originally mined from Anuminis. The Sendarians use the stones as batteries, whereas the Anumens use the stones to amplify their amulas.

The Unforeseen World – The place where an Anumen's essence ascends to after their physical life is over, and where they live out their second life before final rest.

Youthen – An Anumen term for *young child*.

SENDARIAN
TERMINOLOGY

Aevo Compendium – (aye-voe | com-pen-di-um) Also called Aevo C; an observation project left to the Sendarians by their goddess, Isoldesse, who instructed them to continue her work observing and documenting the evolutionary progress of the worlds she mothered and influenced.

Anumen Doctrine – Sacred scriptures and charges left by Isoldesse for the council and royal family to use as they rule over Sendara.

Athru – A Sendarian rebellion group who intends to remove the governing forces of the royal family and Elemental Council from Sendara.

Beannaith – (bay-nayth) A Sendarian term for *hello and goodbye*.

EarLincs – Temporary ear translator implants that allow the recipient to instantly hear what others are saying in their own language.

Elemental Council – An overseeing agency that monitors and enforces the consumption of natural resources on Sendara.

The Endless Forest – A thick wooded forest that covers most of Priomh's moon surface.

Essence – Similar to a soul, but it's also a form of energy with strings or mechanics that keeps the soul and body alive. An essence is fueled by the elements.

Giminos – A forest creature similar to an Earth monkey.

Gróntah – (groan-tah) A Sendarian slang word that means *asshole*.

Hegah – (hey-gah) A Sendarian term for *hell*.

Hiccum flowers – Small green flowers found in Hiccum trees, and when you pick them, they instantly turn a bright yellow color.

Imperilment – A Sendarian term for when someone is acting beyond the means of being helped or arrested. The only way to stop them from harming themselves and others is to use force by whatever means necessary. Only a Rhaltan Enforcer can call Imperilment.

Khal – A Sendarian alcoholic drink.

Lasher – A Sendarian weapon. Similar to a baton but longer and with a tapered, more flexible end that whips your opponent.

Lead – A supervisor of departments within a community. She or he reports to the Leadess or Leader of that community.

Leadess/Leader – An overseer of a designated community. Assigned by the Queen of Sendara and reports directly to the queen, the Elemental Council, and the Rhaltan Enforcers.

Live InterNeural Connection – Also known as a **Linc**, is an artificial assistant implanted into a Sendarian once they've entered the predult stage of their life. Lincs are wired directly into the nervous system and become a part of the Sendarian. Lincs are more like personal assistants as well as resources for information, as they are all connected to the Sendara Main Network.

Loggie – A Sendarian slang word that means *idiot*.

Mount Nocholus – (mount | nock-oh-lus) A lone snowcapped mountain on the Priomh moon.

Paralytic restraint – A snug, semitranslucent silicone device fitted around the neck like a collar. When it's activated, the brain and muscles of the wearer can be controlled through a plac.

Pinship – A special, and secret, transport spaceship that uses space-pinch technology to travel between worlds.

Plac – A portable computer device used by the Sendarians. It has the ability to morph into a soft, pliable silicone material for convenient storage.

Predult – A Sendarian term that describes the years that come after the teen years and before adulthood.

Priomh – (pre-ohm) Sendara's third-largest orbiting moon. It's a habitable moon and is home to the research community also called Priomh, which is dedicated to the Aevo Compendium.

Rhaltan Enforcers – (rawl-tan) The Sendarian military/police force.

Scout – A Sendarian term for *spy/assassin*.

Sendara – The home world of the Sendarians.

Sendara Network – The main online Sendarian computer network.

Sendarians – A peaceful race of humanoid beings. They have advanced technology and are capable of traveling through space to other worlds.

South Sendara – Also known as the Isle of Awry, or the land of the lost. Sendarians believe those who've lost their faith in Isoldesse reside on the isolated island. The Sendarians there have broken away and declared independence from the royal family, Elemental Council, and Rhaltan Enforcement.

Spiaire – (spy-ir) A Sendarian who lives a double life on an alien world during an Aevo Compendium trial. There are four total Spiaires assigned to four different regions of whatever world is undergoing observation. A Spiaire's job is to befriend the subjects without revealing their true identity and prepare the subjects for extraction to Priomh.

Tarais – (tar-ess) The main transport spaceship that travels between worlds, bringing Spiaires and subjects to and from the many worlds observed.

Taut – (taught) A Sendarian slang word that means someone extremely annoying and selfish.

Transessent bracer – A metal wristband that monitors an individual's health and tracks their location. It's powered by a transessent stone.

Transessent stone – A smooth white stone, flat and oval in shape. Originally mined from Anuminis. The Sendarians use the stones as batteries, whereas the Anumens use the stones to amplify their amulas.

The Waking – The procedure in which the Sendarians on Priomh wake the subjects from deep-space sedation.

PART

ONE

PRIOMH

1

Meegan had never been a runner. On rare occasions she went for a jog, but the idea of it for sport or fun seemed boring. There was nothing but running and breathing, and more running and breathing, and lots of sweating. Though, this time as she cut through the night air, something felt different. Her legs moved with a speed she didn't know she had as she leapt over fallen logs and bulldozed through low branches. All without breaking a sweat.

Ever since she'd unlocked the power of the Fawness during yesterday's encounter with that murderous Sendarian man, she'd felt a constant surge of power coursing in her veins. Not being able to sleep, Meegan decided to try and exhaust some of the energy with a midnight run.

Two full moons lit up the night sky to her left. To her east, the top of Sendara peered above the treetops. It seemed so close, yet she knew it was millions of miles away. She wondered if the Athru rebels had escaped to the Sendarian home world or if they were still hiding somewhere here in the forests of the Priomh moon.

Weaving between trees, she recalled the events of yesterday at the abandoned building. That oversized thug, Quaid, had held them against their will. He'd killed Nick and would've done the same to her best friend if she hadn't stopped him. Killing him was the only option. She had no regrets. She only wished she could've saved Nick.

I'll save his essence. I swear to that, Meegan silently promised.

Sprinting out of the forest, she continued through a meadow. Bright moonlight cast over the clearing, and she was tempted to stop to admire the view but decided to keep going. She was enjoying the combination of power humming beneath her skin and the rush of running faster than she'd ever run before and wasn't ready to stop. Even the wispy tips of tall grass barely tickled her skin as she ran to the opposite end of the meadow. Then, with a wide stretch of her leg, she leapt over a boulder and into the next section of forest.

Not wanting to get lost, she kept a straight path so she could find her way back to the Priomh compound. She knew there would be questions specifically aimed at her come morning. Everything her parents had drilled into her head about keeping her identity a secret surfaced, but it was too late for that. Meegan had used her abilities, revealing she wasn't human.

No more hiding. No more lies, Meegan thought. *Not only will these Sendarians learn the truth about who I am, they'll also learn the truth about who their so-called goddess is. And when we find those who took Kenna's mother and the others, I'll be happy to show them the same end their leader met.*

Breaking from the forest again, she sprinted through the meadow. Even without the moonlight, her heightened sense of sight spotted the coming ravine. It was wide, but that didn't stop her. She increased her speed, and without hesitating, she leapt off the cliff's edge and commanded, *"Teacht gohaf luhte balla."* The bottom of her foot landed on a large disc of condensed air. Another appeared, and then another, allowing Meegan to run across the top of the ravine. When she landed on the other side, she released the amula with a single word. *"Déanta."*

Continuing forward, she entered another section of forest full of Ittum trees. Though here, the Sendarians called them Hiccum trees. The familiar floral scent given off by the tiny green flower that bloomed at the base of each leaf reminded her of her childhood back on Anuminis. She didn't remember the flowers specifically, because she'd been only a youthen at the time, which was basically equivalent to a young human child, but she did recognize the fragrance floating in the air. When touched or grazed, the flowers released microscopic particles into the air. These particles, Meegan had read in one of her parents' old medical journals, had the ability to heal injuries. That was the reason the Anumen people had such long life spans. While Meegan was happy to have the sentimental reminder, it also fueled her anger toward Isoldesse. That traitor had no right to alter the natural way of the Sendarian world by planting Anumen-born trees.

Coming upon a winding creek, she stopped at the edge and sat on a rock surrounded by green grass and moss-covered stones. The gentle current gurgled a peaceful ambient sound as it flowed downstream. Meegan watched as a dead leaf, traveling along the current, got caught in a small pool in front of her. There was something relatable about that poor leaf, stuck spinning in one spot and going nowhere.

She was about to reach out and push it from the pool when a white light illuminated beneath the water's surface.

"Fawness," a voice called to her through her mind.

Looking up to the night sky, Meegan answered, "Where are you?"

"We are everywhere," the collective voices responded in her head again as a ball of water the size of a soccer ball emerged from within the creek. The leaf spilled over the edge of the pool, continuing its journey along the current. The glowing sphere of water rose up until it was eye level with Meegan.

This time when it spoke, tiny vibrations rippled across its surface. Its voice resonated in the night air. "We've waited a long time for you to acknowledge our presence."

A strong gust of wind blew by, momentarily drawing Meegan's gaze up to the swaying treetops. When the wind died, she asked, "Are you the Eilimintachs?"

"We are." The white light dimmed, allowing Meegan to see more of the clear water wavering along the surface.

"Why haven't you ever spoken to me before?"

"You denied our presence."

"True. My parents only told me about the responsibilities that come with being the Fawness. I never imagined I'd feel so powerful."

"What you call power is what we call responsibility, and you haven't been very responsible." The rippling water around the sphere stilled, and the whole ball looked like a solid piece of glass. A blurry image appeared on the surface, and when it came into focus a familiar scene played out like a movie, recapping yesterday's events. It was Meegan, standing before Quaid. Her eyes were white and filled with black smoke. One arm was outstretched with her fingers splayed open as she lifted the man from the ground. The man smiled at her, as if he were amused instead of scared.

"That man was evil," Meegan whispered. "I did these people a favor."

The Eilimintachs didn't respond; they only continued the scene. Quaid narrowed his orange eyes and said to Meegan, "You must be what they're coming for."

"You must be what they're coming for! You must be what they're coming for!" the Eilimintachs repeated over and over again, louder each time. Their voices resonated up into the trees.

Meegan shouted, "Let the Obard come!" as she got to her feet. The ball of water rose, matching her eye level. With her palms facing outward at her sides, she gathered her power, its energy coursing through her essence into her hands. White electricity formed at her fingertips. "I am not afraid of anyone or anything. Not anymore."

The scene on the water's surface shifted to Nick lying on the floor. Blood poured out from his chest.

"It is unethical to obliterate an essence."

"No!" Meegan cried, ignoring the Eilimintachs. Her eyes teared up. Seeing him like that again filled her with an overwhelming sadness and…and guilt. She could've prevented it all if she'd only done something sooner. Not wanting to relive the moment anymore, she swiped one hand through the side of the floating ball of water. It burst open, raining over the creek.

Tears streaming down her cheeks, she yelled up into the night air, "I know he died because of me! I don't need you to remind me of my mistakes." After a short pause, she wiped her face and then added, "I can promise you this. I won't make the same mistake twice. There's no more holding back or trying to be someone I'm not."

"Tread carefully, young Fawness." The Eilimintachs' words floated through her mind.

"You could've saved our world when the Obard attacked. But you didn't!" She stared up into the forest, waiting for them to answer, but the only response she got was silence. "You and the Fawness back then could've stopped them from attacking and killing our people… BUT YOU DIDN'T!" She was about to turn and head back when she stopped and said, "Let the Obard come, if that's what Quaid meant. I will do what you should've done centuries ago!"

She didn't wait for a response this time. Instead, she took off running, back toward the Priomh compound.

It had been her first encounter with the Eilimintachs, and all she could think about was how they'd told her nothing about who they were or what role they played in her life as Fawness. One thing she did decide was that the Eilimintachs knew nothing about loyalty, friendship, or the lengths one would go for love.

2

Kenna had woken before sunrise, and unable to fall back asleep, she'd decided to check on Meegan in the next room. When she found the bed empty, panic immediately set in.

"*She's fine,*" Ulissa said in Kenna's mind. "*She's far, but near. Nothing to worry about.*"

"You're sure?" When her bonded companion didn't answer, she grabbed one of the spare blankets from the end of the bed, wrapping it around her shoulders. Quietly, she slipped out through the common area and onto the balcony.

A chill lingered in the morning air as the sun peeked over the treetops. Kenna hugged the blanket tighter over her shoulders as she settled down on one of the upholstered lounge chairs.

Ulissa's form materialized in front of her, standing by the glass railing. With her back to Kenna, she stared out at lone mountain in the distance. As always, the old woman's golden aura coordinated with the color of her gown—a beaded long-sleeve top with a floor-length skirt, layered with sheer fabric the color of clouds at sunset.

Her black hair was braided and pinned up into her usual flawless updo. When she faced Kenna, the soft glow surrounding her body briefly flickered and dimmed. Her movements were slow—even the smile she offered Kenna seemed to take a lot of effort.

"Are you okay?" Kenna asked, adjusting the blanket over her shoulders. The early-morning air was much chillier than she'd expected.

The older woman's expression shifted, releasing any signs that she was fine. Kenna knew things like gravity and air didn't affect Ulissa, who existed as purely energy—an essence residing inside the arcstone around Kenna's neck. Yet her features were drawn and weary.

Slowly raising one hand and nodding, Ulissa said, "I'm doing as well as can be, but the boy's essence is taking a toll on the arcstone's capacity."

"We'll figure it out. I'm sure Meegan will come back and know exactly how we can save Nick's essence without harming yours." Guilt tailed her words because it was highly unlikely her best friend would return with an answer on how to save Nick's essence. Had they done the right thing, capturing his essence from its path to the afterlife, or wherever human souls went after death? This got her thinking. "Do you know what happens to a human's essence after death? Do we go to a place like your Unforeseen World?"

Tilting her head to the sky, Ulissa closed her eyes and took in the cool breeze that swept across the balcony. When it'd passed, she smiled and lifted her shoulders as if the wind offered a small boost of energy. Opening her eyes, she explained, "The Eilimintachs are a wonderous presence on any world. They only communicate through Fawness, and she only shares what they allow."

"What does that mean?" It wasn't exactly the answer Kenna had hoped for, and it made her think of a whole new list of questions, specifically about this Fawness title Meegan now held.

Ulissa lowered herself onto the end of the lounge chair. "Every world has a different name for that entity who they believe creates and sustains all life. My people, the Anumens, were fortunate to have a direct connection with that force through each Fawness. That is how we know about our second lives in the Unforeseen World after our physical deaths. But what happens on other worlds…to other beings…may be different from what happens to those on Anuminis."

It made sense, but it didn't ease any of Kenna's concerns about what could happen to Nick if they couldn't relocate his essence. Would he continue on his original path to a peaceful place, or had they inadvertently altered his afterlife? She hoped Meegan would be able to speak directly with the Eilimintachs and get some solid answers—for Nick and for her own curiosity.

The thought of getting answers reminded her that Breyah, Holt, and Bennach could walk in at any moment wanting an explanation of yesterday's events. She imagined most of their questions would be directed at Meegan.

"Have you heard from your father?" Ulissa asked, hands clasped together in her lap. Even sitting, the old woman tried to maintain her graceful posture, though it was noticeable how her shoulders sagged slightly. They really needed to find another arcstone and fast.

"Your father, have you spoken with him?" she asked again.

Kenna shook her head. "Sorry, my mind is all over the place. But I did speak with him briefly last night before going to bed. I guess when a banished prince returns home there's a lot of catching up to do, or something like that." It had excited her and confused her to see her dad yesterday, especially when she realized his brown eyes weren't really brown but a bright orange. All this time, he'd been pretending to be human.

And my mother too, Kenna thought. *How did I not realize that both of my parents are aliens?!*

"If my father is from Sendara and my mother is an Anumen, what does that make me?" Kenna asked, but the old woman's attention was focused out onto the forest again. Giving the old woman a moment of peace, she too stared out at the forest. After a few moments, Kenna asked, "What is it? Is it Meegan? Is she okay?"

"She's getting closer." Ulissa stood, her aura fading in and out. Her words were laborious, but she continued, "You're a good friend, and she'll need your help over the next few days. I can't imagine what she must be going through. To have all that power thrust upon her under such an unfortunate circumstance. It's important for her to keep her emotions in balance with her surroundings. Denying her birthright means she was probably never properly trained or educated on the responsibilities of being the Fawness, and I worry she might feel overwhelmed."

Ulissa completely disappeared for a few seconds before returning. Kenna leaned forward, letting the blanket slip from her shoulders. "Ulissa!" Worried that her elderly friend was slipping away, she pulled out the slender golden crystal-shaped stone from beneath the collar of her shirt, pinching it between two fingers.

When Ulissa reappeared, she said with a sigh, "I'm tired and need to rest. And you must speak with Fawness. She must decide about the boy, and soon."

Kenna nodded, and just as Ulissa began to fade again, she asked, "Did we do the right thing? Stopping Nick's essence from…from going wherever it was going?"

Ulissa's distant voice filled Kenna's mind. *"What's done is done. We can only move forward and learn from the past."*

Leaning back in the lounge chair, she got comfy and waited for Meegan. The list of things Kenna needed answers to kept growing. She hoped that her mother, Julianna, and anyone else taken captive weren't in the hands of rebels like Quaid. If they were, Kenna feared the worst. And after yesterday, she didn't know if she could handle losing anyone else. Even worse, she wasn't sure what another death might do to her best friend.

3

With a single word, "*Déanta*," Meegan released the amula she'd cast to open a hole in the energy barrier doming over the entire Priomh compound. The power of the Fawness would've come in handy back on Earth when the Sendarians initially trapped her, Kenna, Ally, and Xander with a similar barrier in Prue's backyard. But there was no point in dwelling on what could've been. Thoughts like that might drive her mad with regret. For now, she enjoyed her newly acquired power. She especially liked the endless knowledge of every amula ever known, instantly downloaded into her brain the second she accepted her destiny.

While running through the woods, her mind focused on her encounter with the Eilimintachs, she hadn't noticed the bright morning sky until she reached the Priomh compound. She took her time, walking across the lush grass toward the three-story cylindrical building that was situated some distance from a much larger and taller building. A single enclosed glass bridge connected the two.

Meegan continued to the back side of the smaller building, toward their guest quarters.

Using the same amula she'd used to cross the ravine, she made her way up and over the glass railing of their balcony. To her surprise, Kenna sat waiting on one of the outdoor lounge chairs.

"I've been out here for over an hour. How about a note next time you decide to take a midnight stroll? If it weren't for Ulissa sensing you, I'd probably have called the Sendarian security or Breyah or…or Ben! What if you were taken by that rebel group? Held hostage by another psycho—"

"I can handle myself," Meegan cut in. And she could. Things were different now and she was ready to handle whatever dangers came at them.

Kenna stood abruptly, gripping her blanket tight around her shoulders. She marched across the open balcony to where Meegan stood next to the glass railing. The two faced the forest, shoulder to shoulder. It wasn't only concern laced in Kenna's tone, but empathy too, when she said, "You know you can talk to me, right?"

"Of course. You're, like, the only person in the universe I *can* talk to."

"Because what happened yesterday—" Kenna started to say.

Meegan pushed away from the glass banister. "Was something that needed to be done."

"Are you sure?" Still leaning on the edge, Kenna faced her friend. "You killed someone. That's not an easy thing to live with."

Meegan walked away and headed toward the balcony door, but then abruptly stopped and spun to face Kenna. The ends of her black hair twirled outward from the sudden motion. "He threw a knife at Nick's chest, killing him! And he was going to kill *you* too!"

"And I'm beyond happy that he didn't, but…" She paused, chewing her bottom lip. Meegan knew her friend was pondering whether to continue or not. At this point, Meegan didn't care about anything except losing Kenna's trust. That was something she needed to hold on to.

"Just spit it out!" she barked.

"Fine!" Kenna marched over and stopped with their faces inches apart. In a low tone, she said, "You didn't have to kill him."

Fire radiated inside. How was she the only one who understood that asshat needed to be put down? Meegan stared at Kenna, not wanting to be the one to give in.

After a long moment, it was Kenna who eventually broke away. Her shoulders relaxed and she loosened the blanket, letting it slip slightly down her arms. "Ulissa's not doing so great."

"She's fine." Meegan faced the forest, which stretched as far as she could see in all directions. It was out there she wanted to be, searching every inch of this moon for the Sendarians who'd taken Kenna's mother, Julianna, and Rian. Though, helping the Obard woman was debatable. Regardless, it frustrated her to be locked up in their quarters when she sure as hell knew she was the only one who could saw those taken.

Noting Kenna's concerned expression, she was about to rephrase her response when the balcony door opened. Ally popped her head outside, and said, "There you two are." She walked out, dressed in the standard black three-quarter-sleeve shirt with coordinating loose-fitting pants cinched at the ankles. Her brown curls were tied up with a black ribbon. "The guys are up and were asking where you two were."

"We needed some morning air before the onslaught of questions from Breyah and whoever else runs this place," Kenna said, making room for Ally to join them.

"And how are you doing?" Ally asked, rubbing Meegan's arm.

"Eh, you know, as good as can be." She smirked, hoping it was convincing enough that Ally wouldn't push anymore about *how she was feeling*. Because she felt fine. In fact, Meegan felt amazing. That monster deserved what he'd gotten, and now she didn't have to hide who she was anymore.

Ally didn't ask again, but she did ask Kenna, "And Ulissa. How's she doing?"

Kenna's gaze met Meegan's before she told Ally, "Not well. I spoke with her this morning and she looks exhausted. And her body kept fading in and out." She then looked at Meegan. "I'm worried about her. And Nick."

"I'm working on it!" Meegan snapped.

"And?" Kenna insisted, eyes boring into Meegan.

"Listen, this is all new to me too, you know. I'll figure it out. I just need a little time."

"Maybe we shouldn't have—"

Meegan turned, eyes narrowed as she cut her friend off. "Do not finish that sentence."

After a long, awkward moment, Ally said, "Um, did I miss something?" When no one said anything, she quietly suggested, "Can't we put Nick's soul into another arcstone?"

"Do you have another arcstone lying around?" She didn't mean to sound curt, but Meegan's patience was wearing thin.

"Hey, there you guys are." Liam held the glass door open. "They're bringing in breakfast."

Kenna craned her neck from behind Ally and smiled. "Morning, Liam! We just need a few more minutes. Save me one of those cruller-looking things, okay?"

He nodded, returning the smile before heading back inside. Meegan wanted to shove Kenna after him. To scream at her that she should go and tell him how she felt. Liam had been her childhood crush slash friend whom she hadn't seen in years, and they'd kissed the other night, right here on this balcony! If Meegan could go back in time, she wouldn't have listened to her parents. She never would've broken up with Nick. Act on your gut feelings or move on; that was her new motto. No more waiting or contemplating or wishing something could happen.

She was about to say just that to Kenna when her friend's eyes lit up. Kenna leaned in closer and said, "I've seen another arcstone! Or at least I think it's an arcstone."

The idea didn't seem completely impossible, especially since the Sendarians use transessent stones in those metal arm cuffs. And if there were other arcstones, then there's a good chance they can save Nick. "Okay, we're listening."

"Breyah wears this arm cuff, and there's a golden stone in the center. It has to be one, right?"

"It could be one…*and*…it could also be occupied."

Kenna shook her head. "I don't think it is. I mean, there have been times she hasn't been wearing it. If she was bonded to it, wouldn't she experience pain from being separated from it?"

"Yes, but there could still be an essence inside the arcstone. She might not be bonded to it."

Kenna's shoulders sagged. "True."

"But it's a good starting place," Ally said, offering up some hope in her cheery tone. "Can't you cast a spell or something to see if it's occupied?"

"I guess I could. If I was close enough."

"Perfect!" Kenna exclaimed. "All we have to do is find a way to get you next to Breyah while you do your thing."

"That shouldn't be too hard, especially if her tall blue friend isn't around."

Kenna then reminded Ally, "Rian was taken by the Athru, remember?"

"Oh, yeah." Ally shifted her weight to the other hip.

Meegan wasn't sure she wanted to find the Obard woman, but Kenna's mom—Honnah, who had hidden her identity as an Anumen all these years—needed to be found. "Don't worry. Whatever Breyah and Ben have planned to find your mom and the others, we're going to help."

"What?!" Kenna and Ally responded in unison.

Kenna released the blanket from her shoulders and draped it over one arm. "I don't think that's a good idea. Look what happened the last time we tried to help rescue people."

"Yeah, well, that was before I had all these powers." Meegan held up her hands, flexing her fingers as white electricity arched between each one.

Shaking her head, Kenna stepped away. "Now is not the time for you to be jumping in and testing your new powers."

"Are you going to leave Honnah's life in the hands of these Sendarians? Over me?"

Kenna stood silent, then stuttered her answer. "I-I don't know. But I'm thinking we should let the Sendarians handle this one."

"It's your mom, Kenna!" Meegan snapped. "So, yes, we are going to help rescue the captives *and* find out more about what Isoldesse started here."

"Meeg," Ally quietly chimed in. "We've already lost—"

"We're not losing anyone else!" Meegan shouted, then stormed off toward the balcony door. She didn't want to hear that she'd made the wrong decision about killing Quaid *again*. It was starting to get annoying that everyone was complaining more than thanking her for putting an end to the hostage situation they were in yesterday.

If I have to go alone, then so be it. The glass door shut behind her as she entered the common room. *I swear I'm not letting anyone else we care for die. Even if it means releasing all kinds of hell on whoever stands in my way.*

4

Kenna followed Ally inside to the common space of their guest quarters. The quarters on the second floor overlooked the main room, giving the room an expansive open feel. The polish of the smooth cement-like floors shined from the morning light shining in from the domed glass ceiling. It was a minimal space with lots of room to move. Two semi-circular sofas set closer to the balcony doors while the dining area was set up toward the rear, against the exterior glass wall, curving the right side of the common area. On the other side were eight doors, each one leading into private quarters.

Over by the two long wooden dining tables, three Sendarian women in trapeze-style halter dresses finished setting out a variety of pastries, breads, fruits, and cheeses. Meegan sat at the far end, away from the others, piling food onto a small plate.

Ally reached the table before Kenna. She sat on the long bench, same side as Meegan, but more in the middle. Instead of sitting between her two friends, Kenna took a seat at the opposite end of the table, across from Liam. "Good morning," she said, taking a plate and browsing their breakfast selection.

"Morning," he answered, and then thanked the Sendarian woman as she placed a glass carafe in front of them. A sweet fragrance wafted up from the dark liquid inside. She didn't answer or make eye contact, and only gave the slightest nod before hurrying off with the other women, closing the door behind her.

"They're acting weird," Liam said, staring at the doors to the common room. "Usually they're all smiles and take their time, but not today." He bit into a toasted roll filled with red jelly. Kenna met his eyes before glancing to the end of the table where Meegan sat. Liam picked up on the shift in her attention and followed her gaze. "Oh, yeah, that might be why," he whispered with a subtle lift of his eyebrows.

Kenna nibbled on some fruit and the cruller-looking stick that was sweet like a donut but dense like her mom's homemade biscuits. Thinking about her mom, Kenna asked Brody, who was sitting next to Liam, "How are you holding up?"

When he finally noticed it was him she was talking to, he shrugged and answered her question with a question. "When are they sending us home?"

"They haven't said," Ally answered.

"We can't leave until Julianna and the others are found." Liam twisted on the bench to face Brody. "I'm not leaving her here."

There was no way Kenna was leaving without her mother too. "Let's just hope whatever Breyah and Ben are planning works and Julianna, my mother, and the others will be back here with us soon."

The room fell silent, and everyone picked at their food. Everyone except for Brody, who stared down at an empty plate. Ally tried to offer him some insight into what the foods tasted like, but he wasn't having it. Eventually, he got up and shut himself up in his room.

"He needs time," Liam offered to the group.

"That's understandable." Kenna pinched her arcstone between two fingers. "I can't even imagine what he went through. I mean, we only saw Quaid for what…less than an hour…and he spent days around that psychopath."

"Yeah, well," Liam started, then stopped as if he was rethinking his answer. He shifted his attention to Meegan. "I guess we owe you a thank-you."

Meegan sat up straighter, her stony expression softening. "I did what needed to be done."

Kenna waited for her friend to glance her way and give her the *see, I told you so* look. But she didn't.

"And I'm guessing you're not human?" Liam hesitantly asked.

This time, Meegan did look down the table to Kenna, then back to Liam. "No, I'm not. My people are from a world that was invaded and destroyed. Those who survived escaped to other worlds. My family and I, along with a few hundred other Anumens, have been living on Earth for the past one hundred years."

"That sucks, and I'm sorry." Liam took another bite of the pastry he was holding. When he was done chewing and swallowing, he asked, "And your people have magic?"

Meegan continued eating as well while answering his questions. "Only the women, and to different degrees."

"Cool," Liam said, then in a more hushed tone added, "I wish things had played out differently than they did yesterday."

"We had no idea what we were walking into yesterday," Kenna chimed into the conversation. She lifted a hand to adjust her glasses, out of habit, then lowered it when she realized she wasn't wearing them. She wanted to say they were wrong to have snuck out and taken it upon themselves to try and rescue Darci, but that would only start a pointless argument. Everything that happened yesterday was in the past, just like Ulissa had said. No point in dwelling. Now, they just needed to focus on getting close to Breyah's arcstone and finding out what the plan was to rescue Kenna's mom, Julianna, and the others.

"Do you think you can convince your friend to tell us more about this rebel group?" Meegan asked Liam.

"Why?" Kenna asked.

"Because…" Meegan shifted in her seat, her hand midway to her mouth with a piece of fruit. "…we need to know more about them so we can fight them."

"Fight them? I already told you I'm not going back out there!" Kenna stood, hands pressed to the table. "I almost died yesterday. And—and Nick *did* die. There's no way any of us are getting involved with another rescue mission!"

Meegan also stood from the table and faced the group. Though, her eyes were focused on Kenna. "I don't have to hide anymore! I can save them and punish those who deserve it!"

"Punish them… Is that what we're doing now? Are you some kind of vigilante?" Kenna slowly walked down the length of the table, closer to her friend. Anger butted with confusion about why her friend was acting this way. "We need to let Breyah and Ben handle this. My dad—"

"Your dad," Meegan spat, "told us that we have a destiny to fulfill. That means we need to get up off our asses and do something."

"I don't think Brody's ready to talk about it," Liam said from the table. "He barely said two words to me last night, which is unlike him because he normally tells me everything."

"Brody wasn't the only one there," a timid voice said from across the room. Darci shut the common-room door behind her as she entered. Kenna had mixed feelings about seeing the Sendarian girl. She stood in the doorway of the main common's room entrance, wearing what appeared to be a black training outfit complete with fitted pants and matching top. Darci's strawberry-blond hair, which was usually in a whimsical braid, was pulled tight into a ponytail.

Meegan stormed over to Darci, keeping some distance between them, and with a finger pointed to the door, she said, "You need to leave. Now."

It hadn't been easy to learn that Darci had lied to them. That she'd played a part in their being taken from Earth and brought to this world. But something in Kenna's gut told her she could trust

Darci. "Wait!" she shouted and walked over to where the two girls were standing. "Why are you here, Darci?"

"I wanted to explain."

"No. You don't get to explain anything," Meegan said, putting her face inches from Darci's. "You are the reason we're here. You are the reason Nick is dead."

Tears fell from Darci's orange eyes. She bit her lower lip while shaking her head. "I swear, nothing like this has ever happened." She swallowed and wiped her eyes. "I would've fought every single one of those Sendarians if I could. I would've put myself between them and you." Darci's gaze drifted from Meegan's face to Kenna's. "Right after I left your house, that day we went to the outlets, I was knocked out and taken. I couldn't do anything."

"Oh, Darci," Kenna whispered. When she reached out as if to hug her friend, Meegan swatted Kenna's hand.

"Don't." She faced Darci and said with a peaceful tone, "Maybe you should leave."

More tears streamed Darci's cheeks. "I only came to check on you and to tell you about Prue."

"Prue?" Ally jumped up from her seat, quickly stepping over the bench. Her brown eyes were open and alert, looking right at Darci. "What about my sister?"

"The same Sendarians who took me, my friends Eryn and Grace, and Brody also took Prue."

Ally clasped her hands over her mouth, stopping before reaching them. Kenna hurried to her friend's side, one arm wrapping around Ally's shoulders. With a trembled voice, Ally asked, "Is she okay?"

Darci shook her head, and Kenna felt Ally's body slip from her one-armed embrace. Tightening her grip, Kenna led Ally over to one of the semi-circular sofas. Once they were seated, Darci continued. "Quaid stabbed her, then left her for dead, but"—she moved past Meegan, holding her hands out in a gesture that said *don't panic, there's more*—"they found her and transported her to surgery before that could happen. She's in Medical, resting and recovering. Holt asked me to inform you that she was here."

Ally stood and approached Darci. "I want to see her, please."

"Of course. I can escort you there when you're done with—"

"We're done," Meegan said, not letting Darci finish. "You can take us there now."

"I'm going to stay here and check on Brody," Liam said, coming up behind Kenna.

She offered him a grateful smile. "I know this is a lot to handle. You're a good friend," she said, leaning in to kiss his cheek. While their proximity was close, she whispered, "I was hoping we could talk about the other night…about us." When he didn't answer, she leaned back, meeting his gaze, and repeated her question, "Can we talk—"

"—I think," he cut her off, "you should go and see your friend in Medical. We can catch up another time." Liam pulled her in for another hug. "I promise." Then he released her and walked toward the line of doors.

It was odd, his reaction, but she brushed it off as part of the chaos going on around them. Being taken to an alien moon, a rescue mission gone terribly wrong resulting in Nick's death, and now his best friend was dealing with the trauma of being held captive by that psycho Sendarian, Quaid. She would approach him again, but later. And this time she wouldn't hold back. She would confess her feelings to him, and he would do the same. They would be happy together. Then, any thoughts about a certain brutish Sendarian man wouldn't weigh on her thoughts any longer. She would be with Liam.

Her heart pounded with excitement, and she snuck one more glance in his direction before following her friends out of the common room to Medical.

5

·+⁺+ GEMMA +⁺·

The loud laughter and jumbled voices of the tavern were exactly what Gemma needed to get her mind off of the shitstorm that had gone down on Priomh. She didn't blame herself. Everything that'd happened was because of that gróntah, Quaid. Out of the three Athru leaders, he'd been the worst and was secretly glad the Beast was gone. If that self-centered loggie had only stuck to Anora's plan—to capture the Spiaires and a few humans, forcing the princess to give herself over in exchange for the captives—the Athru would be on their way to winning this rebellion.

Carefully touching the sore spot over her left cheek, she recalled how Anora expressed her disappointment after learning Gemma had left Quaid behind. She'd only done what was asked of her, which was to watch over Quaid during the Earth stage of their mission. It was a huge favor, one that supposedly Anora only trusted Gemma to do. In the end, Gemma only agreed to keep an eye on the Sendarian brute while they were off world because her sister, Cahleen, and brother, Micah, would be accompanying her.

Waving her hand for the barkeep, she finished her drink and waited for a refill. The Beast had had no intentions of following Anora's plan. They'd determined this after Cahleen reported overhearing him in a call while on his ship, making a deal with someone…or something…about letting Quaid have Sendara after they were done. And their threats to attack only stood if whatever they were looking for wasn't returned to them. The whole situation baffled Gemma, and she wasn't sure where her loyalties remained. She wanted the queen and Elemental Council removed from power, but at the same time she didn't want to lose everything that was good about her home world.

Her thoughts shifted to the human girl with long black hair. The one who'd overtaken Quaid, a man twice her size, with nothing more than a look. How her eyes had gone white, black smoke swirling inside them, as the room filled with powerful winds. It all seemed impossible. Too magical. Too much like…Her.

The barkeep refilled her glass. She barely registered his presence or that of anyone else in the tavern. The world around her faded as her thoughts were consumed with the possibility that the human girl wasn't human at all. That she could be an Anumen like their goddess. A divine being somehow living among the humans.

But why Earth? Why not come here and live on the world Isoldesse deemed worthy of carrying out her work? The Anumen gods and goddesses obviously approve of the Sendarian world over that piece-of-shit planet, Earth, because Isoldesse revealed herself to us—trusted us with continuing her work. So, why Earth?

"Now, would ya lookie here." A man slid onto the empty stool to her right, his breath smelling like rancid, warm ale. "What's a dainty thing like you doing in South Sendara? You from the mainland, aye? Did ya sneak over here to roll with a lad your parents would hate? I think they'd hate me, don't ya agree?"

The stool creaked as Gemma spun to face the man. He eyed her over, rubbing his poorly shaved beard. His midsection bulged and his pasty arms were covered in hair. She refrained from gagging when she caught a whiff of his foul odor and noticed the wet stains beneath his armpits. She crossed one leg over the other and leaned away, her elbows resting on the bar.

"Oh, I suppose you and your loggie friends"—she gestured with a nod to the men circling behind—"are interested in showing me a *good* time?" The man's orange eyes widened, and his lips parted, revealing brown teeth. That did it. She couldn't hold in her disgust anymore. "Yeah, that's not going to happen. Have you looked at yourself in the mirror? You'd be lucky if a wild animal would roll with you."

"Why you little—" His elated expression faded. The muscles in his face tensed and he straightened his shoulders. "I don't think you have a choice in the matter," he said and reached for her arm.

This was exactly what she needed to release some frustration. Balling her fists up, she got ready to strike, but before she could swing, someone grabbed ahold of the grimy man's wrist and twisted it, causing him to writhe in pain. Gemma turned to see Cahleen eyeing the bloated man.

"That's my sister," she seethed.

"Sorry, Cahleen! I...I didn't know!"

Cahleen pulled out her blade and pressed the clawlike black edge against his wrist. "Do you like your hand?" He nodded vigorously. She continued, nicking his skin, "Then I suggest you think twice about who you touch in the future." She pressed on his wrist, the bone cracking from the coiled pressure. He yelped and winced from the pain. His outburst had a few patrons to glancing their way.

"Do I make myself clear?" The second he mumbled words of compliance, she freed him. The two sisters stood by and watched as he and his gangly friends scurried between tables and out the front door of the tavern.

"Everything was under control," Gemma said to Cahleen, but without looking at her sister because she'd been watching the men leave. As the mangy group of men vacated, a predult, too clean for South Sendara with his crisp white shirt and groomed hair, strolled into the bar. Weaving between tables and groups of rowdy

Sendarians, he made his way toward the back stairwell. But instead of going upstairs, he continued down the dark hall beneath the stairs. Gemma knew the hall led to a private bar where Anora was probably drinking, but why was the predult going back there?

"Did you hear me?" Cahleen barked, then downed the rest of Gemma's drink.

Gemma faced the bar again, brushing off the strange feeling she'd gotten from the predult. Whoever he was, he wasn't her problem. She had enough shit to deal with.

Returning her attention to her sister, she said, "I didn't hear you, and I could've handled that douche myself."

"Oh, because you've handled things *beautifully* up until now."

"Hey, you know what," she said, her frustration doubling the second she realized her glass was empty, "I did what I thought we needed to do. It's not my fault that gróntah had other plans. He's the one who messed shit up!" Waving the barkeep over again, she added, "And what… You're no longer concerned with whatever deal Quaid was making? The one you and Logan overheard?"

Cahleen shrugged one shoulder. "I don't know what we heard, and besides, it's the queen's problem. Maybe an invasion is exactly what our world needs."

Is she serious right now? I did not sign up for genocide of our people. I only wanted to help take down a corrupt ruling system, not kill innocent Sendarians.

The barkeep eventually moseyed over but didn't refill her glass. Instead, he poured Cahleen two shots.

Cahleen swallowed one of her shots, then said, "Yes, Quaid screwed things over big-time, and that's Anora's problem. But that's not what I'm talking about." She rubbed a hand through her overgrown red hair. She'd gotten ahold of some shears and shaved the sides of her head, and now she looked again like the badass sister she was known as. Something that had gotten away from her while they were stuck on the *Tarais* traveling home from Earth.

"Then what are you talking about?" Gemma scoffed.

"You were one of the Leads on the Earth mission, but you can't let go of your old life. You still think of yourself as one of Breyah's Spiaires."

"I do not! And it was a good call. Breyah's up to something, I know it. That annoying little taut of a Spiaire wouldn't have met with unauthorized humans unless she was told to! We need to ask the human woman, Honnah, why she was meeting with the Spiaire."

"Oh," Cahleen said with a sneer, "we're on a first-name basis with the prisoners now?"

"Shut up!" Gemma snapped.

"And there is no *we*. You've been pulled from the loop. You're to report to your room and remain there until Anora says otherwise."

"You're kidding, right?"

Cahleen shook her head, downed the second shot, and stood from the stool. "Anora's sorting things out right now, as we speak. Starting with questioning your human friend."

Shit. Xander didn't know anything, and she prayed to Isoldesse that whatever torture they were inflicting wasn't too bad. "Is she planning on killing Xander?"

"Xander?" Cahleen's face twisted with confusion, but then she seemed to understand. "Seriously, Gemma?" She bellowed out a hearty laugh. "You think Anora would waste her time with that pathetic loggie? He's about as useful as this stool." She kicked one of the legs of the stool Gemma was sitting on. While turning to leave, she stopped and said, "Listen, just stay out of sight for a while, until Anora figures things out. Biryn will be here soon—"

"Oh, we're finally going to meet the mysterious third Athru leader?"

"No, *we* are not. And besides, I've already met him and believe me, if you thought Quaid was a psychopath, then you don't want to have a run-in with the mastermind of the three siblings. Now, get back to your room and stay put."

Gemma sat there, wallowing in her thoughts about how she'd arrived at her unfortunate situation. If she was going to survive Anora's anger, and supposedly Biryn's too, she needed to somehow win their favor. Standing, she waved for the barkeep. When he glanced her way, she pointed to the black screen along the beveled edge of the bar counter. He nodded, then moved to a long plac haphazardly hung on the wall. The sides of the glass, which should've been embedded into the wall, revealed an array of ports and wires jutting out from the sides and hanging to the floor.

This place may be free from the ruling constraints of the mainland, but that freedom comes with a cost. Everything that is given to the Sendarians over there needs to be stolen or bartered for over here. Is our world to become like South Sendara if the Athru win? If Anora succeeds in overthrowing the queen, the Rhaltan, and the Elemental Council, will our world revert to savagery and greed—like the days before Isoldesse?

Was this what she'd really signed up for? Doubt floated through her mind, leaving her unsure if she truly wanted to win back Anora's trust.

When her tab lit up on the glass strip along the counter's edge, Gemma's attention returned to her orders. *"Get back to your room,"* her sister had instructed. She tapped in the Athru account code and waited. It took more time than she'd like, but eventually the word *paid* displayed in bright green letters along the glass strip. At least she still had access to the Athru account with South Sendarian credits—a monetary system not used on the mainland.

The barkeep continued cleaning his mugs as she meandered her way toward the front entrance. A strange sense that someone was watching her made her turn and scan the tavern. Beneath the stairwell, hiding in the shadows of the corridor, was the predult she'd seen earlier. He leaned against the doorframe, orange eyes staring right at her. With a mischievous smirk, he shot out two fingers from over his right eyebrow like a strange greeting. She wasn't sure what to make of it. Was he flirting with her? Another guy thinking she was a piece of meat to roll with. Blood boiling, she narrowed her eyes at the young man. The second she stepped in his direction, wanting so badly to release the frustration building inside her with a fist to his face, he backed away, disappearing down the dark hall behind him.

Better run from me, you little shit, she thought before turning and leaving the tavern. For now, she would follow Anora's orders. Go to her room like a child and wait to be reprimanded…again. In the meantime, she could use the alone time to plan out her next move, because at this point, she was starting to regret her decision to join the Athru.

6

Kenna stood arm in arm with Ally by Prue's bedside. The Sendarians had set Prue up in a private room. A single twin bed was situated in the middle of the room, facing the exterior wall, which was a single pane of glass, floor to ceiling. The view overlooked the verdant treetops of the forest. Tree after tree, the woods stretched out for miles, butting up against the lone snow-capped mountain.

"She'll love the view when she wakes up," Kenna whispered.

"I hope so." Ally reached for her sister's hand. "I should've gone to her house after telling her we saw that asshat at the outlets. What was I thinking?"

"You were thinking it was late, and that you'd go in the morning. And you did, remember?" Kenna wrapped an arm around Ally's shoulders. "Besides, what's done is done and she's here now."

Wiping her eyes dry with the heel of her palm, Ally said between sniffles, "I don't know what I'd do without her."

Prue had on the same white silicon face mask they'd all worn when they'd first arrived. The pliable shield concealing Prue's face was attached to a wide headband that rested across the top of her head. The ends of the headband covered both ears. Kenna shuddered at the memory of pulling out the plugs that had been burrowed deep inside her ear canals after the arcstone had somehow woken her from sedation.

A Sendarian woman, dressed in a navy-blue medic's dress, stood behind a tall glass panel that extended from the top of the headboard into the white plaster ceiling above. Her bright orange eyes scanned the small display screens spaced out like tiles along the glass panel. Every so often, the woman would tap one of the semiopaque boxes and compare whatever information was displayed there to the info on the tablet in her hand. It frustrated Kenna that the woman's expression never hinted at Prue's progress.

Meegan stood a few feet from the end of the bed, arms crossed and a blank expression on her face as she intently watched the medic. Darci kept her distance, standing across the room by the door. In her hands was a black tablet, similar to the one the medic was holding. Even though Darci rarely looked up from the device, Kenna was happy she was here. She'd known at some point she was going to have to forgive Darci and hoped her friends would too.

"Can I see her face?" Ally asked the medic.

The Sendarian woman ignored Ally and continued reviewing the glass panel above Prue's headboard.

Kenna leaned over Prue's sleeping body and lifted the edge of the mask.

"Leave it be!" the medic scolded. "In fact, don't touch anything in the room. Understand?"

The two girls nodded while Darci lowered her gaze to her tablet again, but not before meeting Kenna's eyes. Meegan stepped closer to the footboard, curling her fingers over the top of the wooden frame. "What kind of medicine are you giving her?"

Good question, Kenna thought. They weren't on Earth and who knew if Sendarian medicine or treatments would end up doing more harm than good.

The medic's hand froze at eye level as she glared through the glass at Meegan. For a long moment, Kenna thought the woman was going to ignore Meegan too, but she stepped out from behind the narrow panel and said, "You don't scare me. I don't care what they're saying about you. You are nothing like our goddess."

A chill ran across Kenna's shoulders. *Oh, geez. This can't be good.* She and Ally both stared at Meegan, as did Darci.

"I am nothing like that traitorous—"

"Meeg!" Kenna interjected. When their gazes locked, she shook her head.

Meegan's attention flicked to the medic, and her posture turned casual. "Honestly, I don't give a crap about whatever rumors you've heard. All I want to know is how you're helping our friend."

The door behind Darci opened and she quickly sidestepped, allowing Holt to enter the room. He didn't look at her, but he did answer her questions. "We have an ample supply of medicine from all the worlds we observe." The Sendarian woman continued scowling at Meegan for a few seconds longer than Kenna liked. Eventually, when the Lead Medic moved in to review Prue's vitals, the Sendarian woman backed away. "Everything appears stable. Surgery went well, without any complications, and her internal wounds are slowly healing." Moving out from behind the panel, he said, directly to Meegan, "Does that answer your question?"

"Can we take the mask off, if only for a second so I can see her?" Ally asked, interrupting the stare-down going on between Holt and Meegan.

"Unfortunately, no. But I can show you her face beneath the mask here on the monitor." He returned to the panel and tapped the glass. Ally and Kenna quickly followed, staring at the live video feed Holt had brought up on the display.

"It's really her," Ally said, leaning in closer. "I can't believe this is happening."

Kenna looped her arm through Ally's again and reassured her friend, "They'll take good care of her."

"That we will," Holt said, sliding two fingers down the length of the panel, deactivating all of the information tiles. Kenna peered through the clear glass to Meegan, who was still gripping the end of the bed.

Holt continued, "We've sedated her, using Earth sedatives, until her wounds have surpassed our fifty percent heal mark. It's too risky to wake her any sooner. We need her to be as still as possible while her internal organs heal from the stab wound."

"I appreciate you helping my sister," Ally said. "She'd probably be dead if it weren't for you and your medical team."

"Um, no." Meegan raised her eyebrows. "It's his fault. It's all of their faults." She released her grasp on the footboard, crossed one arm over her chest, and pointed the other between Holt and Darci. "If they'd just left us alone…on Earth…none of this would've happened. Not Prue being kidnapped and stabbed. Not your mom being taken," she said to Kenna before returning her gaze to Holt and Darci. "And Nick wouldn't have gotten—"

Kenna stepped in front of Meegan, blocking her view of the Sendarians. "That's enough."

Dark eyes narrowed at Kenna. "I'm only saying what we're all thinking."

"You're not wrong," Holt said, drawing everyone's attention to him. "It's all very confusing… For both sides." He looked as if he wanted to say more but ended up shaking his head. On his way to out, he stopped and said, "Oh, I almost forgot. There's a transport vehicle outside. Darci will take you to it. I guess you've all been invited to visit Princess Emmalyn this afternoon. Now, if you'll excuse me, I have other patients to check on." He was gone before anyone could ask any more questions. The medic woman followed, closing the door behind her.

No one moved for a long moment before Darci said to Meegan, "Holt has devoted his entire life to the Anumen Doctrine and Isoldesse, so have a little patience with him… With us all." She pressed her tablet to her chest and added, "Right or wrong, it's all we've ever known."

Kenna was happy Meegan refrained from sharing her thoughts, because at this point, she wasn't sure what her friend would say or do.

"Whenever you're ready, I'll take you to the transport vehicle. Hopefully, Princess Emmalyn will have some news about how they're planning to rescue everyone from the Athru."

Ally moved to Prue's side. "I'm going to stay here."

"What? No. We stick together," Kenna said.

"I can stay with her," Darci said. "I mean, I can come back and hang with Ally after escorting you to the vehicle." She brushed her hand along the smooth strands of red hair pulled tight into her ponytail, then turned to Ally and asked, "If you're cool with that?"

Ally shared a glance with Kenna before nodding. "I'd like that, thanks."

After a few more moments, Kenna and Meegan followed Darci to a transport vehicle waiting for them outside. Seeing this side of the Priomh community, rather than the view of the forest from their balcony, was exciting. Kenna's curiosity about the Sendarians' world feuded with her concerns about the problems at hand.

If anyone could give them some straight forward answers, she guessed it would be the princess. She was a princess after all. Because with everything they needed to figure out—saving Nick's essence and rescuing the captives—Kenna still had her destiny to think about. Whether or not to tell the Sendarians the truth about their goddess was a constant question lingering in the back of her mind. If anyone had experience making global decisions for the greater good of her people, it would be the princess. Or so Kenna hoped.

7

Gemma pressed an ear to the door. A group of men were laughing and talking in the hallway, guarding her room. It was ridiculous that Anora had her locked up like one of the humans instead of enlisting her to help make their next move.

She stormed away from the door, the floorboards creaking, and yanked out one of the chairs and sat at the table. The hot tea she'd been drinking didn't do much to ease her nerves. It would've been nice to have another drink or two at the tavern before being locked up.

In a rage, she threw the teapot across the room. It shattered, leaving a streak of tea leaves and hot water dripping to the floor.

One of the men banged on the door. "Settle down in there!"

Gemma needed a moment with Anora, to explain that she'd done everything asked of her. The only matter she could be blamed for was bringing back an extra human captive—which, in Gemma's opinion, played in their favor, especially if the woman wasn't lying about who she is—Gerard's wife. That meant the banished prince would come for his beloved human wife, which again, in Gemma's opinion, was better than some airheaded princess.

She crossed the room and, trying to keep her anger in check, carefully picked up the shards of white porcelain. "Damn it!" she cried when a piece cut the inside of her thumb. Shimmery yellow blood oozed along her skin. Wishing she had a sink to rinse the wound, she made do with a paper cloth brought in with the tea.

After picking up the remaining pieces, she sat on the edge of the bed, holding the napkin to her thumb, and waited. A few hours passed, and as Gemma felt sleep creeping up on her, someone knocked on the door.

Anora strode in just as Gemma sat up. The woman's thick red hair was woven into an thick braid trailing the center of her head. Her white shirt was crisp and tucked into a wide leather belt. Her fitted pants were baggier around the hips. *The perfect place to hide her knives*, Gemma thought.

"Beannaith, friend."

"Friends don't lock friends up." Gemma stepped closer. She'd always seen Anora as more of a friend than a leader. When Anora and Cahleen pitched their plans to overthrow the queen to her two years ago, Gemma believed the goddess had presented her with a higher calling. A new way to prove her devotion. But after what she witnessed yesterday at the old research facility—the supposed human girl taking on Quaid—she couldn't help the doubts swarming her mind about…well, everything.

The abundance of freckles covering Anora's cheekbones was a mismatch of light and dark speckles. A clash of color that, oddly, made Gemma think it represented the uncertainty of knowing if the Athru leader was friend or foe.

"I needed to separate the group, allowing me to hear everyone's version of what happened." She walked over to the single window in the room and stared out at the road below. "Do you want to know what I've learned?"

Gemma got a whiff of fresh soap as the Athru leader strode by. She also smelled a hint of *hosta*, a small nut local to South Sendara.

The oil from the nut was used to tame unruly hair. It wasn't a favorite of Gemma's, but she also knew the Sendarians in South Sendara were limited in their beauty product options. Regardless, it'd been days since Gemma had showered and she would've been happy to use any bath products at this point.

Pushing aside her thoughts of a bath anytime soon, she said, "Enlighten me, please."

Still facing the window, watching the street below, Anora said, "My suspicions about my brother were correct. He did have an ulterior agenda planned this whole time."

"He wasn't right in the head, and I'm pretty sure—"

"I'm not done." Anora raised her hand, cutting Gemma off. "We're assuming Quaid is dead, based on the stories you and Sabine told me." The tall woman slowly turned and faced Gemma. "Though, the two things I'm trying to understand are one—who the girl that bested my brother is—and two—why the human woman you brought from Earth didn't run when the others escaped."

Anora cocked her head, unwavering from her stare. She stepped closer, making her proximity a bit uncomfortable for Gemma's liking. "Since Sabine, Cahleen, Micah, and Logan have no answer to either, that leaves you to explain. And I guess I'll just have to trust you on these matters."

"I've never lied to you. Why would I start now?" Gemma said, half-hurt, and half-annoyed with the distrust in Anora's tone. It was unlike Gemma to be put off by anyone. She was usually the one making others feel belittled.

Anora sat in one of the wooden chairs that'd seen better days. "Let's start with who is the girl?"

Without hesitating she said, "She's one of Darci's subjects. A human girl."

"Humans are not evolved enough to possess the power that you and Sabine described. So, again, who is she?"

"I don't know." She felt like an utter failure, to Anora and her goddess. Whether she wanted to or not, she needed to tell Anora the truth. "I don't think she's human."

"No. I believe that is something we can agree on." Anora narrowed her orange eyes before leaning back on the hindlegs of the chair. "And what of this human you brought here from Earth? What's her story?"

"I already told you. She was meeting with Darci, which seemed odd to me. A Spiaire going against protocol and interacting outside their assigned subject group was a red flag. I made the decision to investigate more. Micah and Cahleen were only following my orders."

"Uh-uh, and tell me, did you share this information with my brother?"

She's kidding, right?

The only thing Gemma could think was that Anora was testing her. She pushed up the sleeves of her oversized gray sweatshirt and fell into her obedient Athru rebel role. "I didn't trust Quaid with the information since he was showing signs of betrayal. Sabine and I believed Quaid killed Abastian and took his Spiaire, Grace, hostage. We had no knowledge of the Spiaire until we arrived at the docking station on Priomh. He'd kept her in hiding throughout the entire journey on the *Tarais*. Even before that, on Earth, Quaid was showing signs of mental instability. He shrugged off my initial status reports the first few weeks we were on Earth. Over time, our conversations grew heated. He started referring to me as a *bug* that he could squash at any moment."

Anora crossed one leg over the other. "Okay, I can see why you wouldn't want to include him, but you shouldn't have taken her. She's another life lost to this war we're declaring on Sendara's ruling forces."

Another life lost. What does that mean?

"She's dead?"

The leader shook her head. "Not yet, but in due time. None of the captives will ever see Earth again. Their sacrifice is needed to prove to the ruling entities of Sendara that we are not backing down." She stood up, fists clenched tight. "That a revolution is coming."

Gemma had no response to Anora's declaration. She wasn't even sure if being here with the Athru was what she wanted anymore. It was true, the Queen of Sendara was more of a crazed tyrant than previous kings or queens, but maybe it wasn't the system that was broken but the individual. Maybe they didn't need to destroy the entire ruling order.

Anora headed for the exit. "You've given me a lot to think about regarding the mess you've created." Opening the door, she said, "In the meantime, I'll see about moving you up one floor. To a room with a shower."

The mess I created? Gemma seethed on the inside but showed no reaction in her expression. "Thank you," she answered, unsure of what else to say that wouldn't dig her into a deeper hole.

Alone in her room, Gemma paced, trying to understand Anora's game. The leader who had confided in her before the Earth mission had now turned on her, blaming her for Quaid's death.

Twenty minutes went by, and Gemma was still circling the room. She wasn't going to get any answers being locked up—down here *or* upstairs in a room with a shower—which meant she needed to figure out a way to get a message to Micah. To find out what the hegah was going on.

When a sudden *thud* from the adjacent room startled her to a stop. Curious, she moved closer to the wall, pressed one ear to the painted surface, and listened. There were voices coming from inside the next room. Then, when the dresser next to her pushed away from the wall, Gemma looked to the door, waiting for the guards to burst in from the loud sound of wood scratching the floorboards. But they didn't.

Cautiously, she peeked behind the lengthy piece of furniture to see a giant hole. A sly smile spread when a man ducked his head through and asked, "Hey, sis. You ready to get out of here?"

8

Now that Prue was here, Kenna knew Ally would probably remain by her sister's side the rest of their time on Priomh. Her roommate had no interest in leaving the compound yesterday when they'd ventured out to rescue Darci, which was probably for the best.

They'd been driving for almost ten minutes, passing house after house. The top half of the transport vehicle was enclosed in a tinted glass, but Kenna could still make out the boxlike homes, each with a moderate sized yard. She imagined Prue's secluded home, miles inland from the overcrowded Florida beaches and suburbs. From what she's seen, the Sendarians didn't need much to be content, which was nice. Kenna liked how simple their lives were here on the moon. Though, who knew what life was like on their home world. She glanced up at the planet, which took up a third of the sky. Visiting Sendara would be an amazing, memorable trip, as visitors. Not to go and infiltrate a rebel compound. The idea of putting themselves in danger again made her nerves flutter with anxiety.

Anyway, she was fairly sure Breyah would make sure the next ship they'd be on was a return flight back to Earth.

But oh, she thought, *how wonderful it would be to stay and learn more about these people and their ways.*

"Talk about cookie-cutter," Liam said from the seated row behind, breaking Kenna from her daydream about life on Sendara. She was happy he and Brody decided to come visit the princess with them. It might do Brody some good to get out and see a better side of the Sendarian people.

"Every house is the same, with a few minor differences like one or two stories, or mirroring details," Liam said, observing the neighborhood as they drove through.

Kenna glanced over the seat and saw Liam trying to start a conversation with Brody, but his friend's attention was focused outside.

"It's crazy how much these people live like us." He tried again, waiting for Brody to answer.

After a long moment, Brody grumbled, without turning his attention from the window, "It's basic survival. Nothing more. And from that, intelligent life will evolve. Don't overthink the wheel."

"All I was saying is that the houses look like the houses you might find on Earth." Liam snorted, blowing off his friend's gloomy attitude.

Liam is right, Kenna thought. Every house was constructed with the same design—wide, horizontal planks, stained a dark walnut color, covering each side of the home. A few of the designs incorporated glass walls into the exterior frame, coming together at the front or back corners of the house. Home after home, they drove through the suburbs of the Priomh compound.

Leaning closer to the front seats where the security officers sat, Kenna asked, "Does the princess live within the Priomh borders?"

Neither of the men answered.

"I mean, I'm going to assume she's close by and protected."

Again, they didn't respond.

Kenna reached to tap one of the guards on the shoulder, in case they couldn't hear her, but her hand slammed into an invisible wall. "Ow!" she cried, the unexpected pain pulsing around her knuckles. This caught Meegan's attention, and they both touched the barrier between the front and back seats. Blue energy webbed outward where their hands pressed, the surface warm beneath Kenna's fingers.

"It's like the protective shield they've got over the entire place here," Meegan said. She whispered something under her breath, and after a few seconds her hand pushed through the barrier. The driver slammed on the brakes, launching everyone forward.

Kenna's hands shielded her head from hitting the invisible barricade while the guys behind her yelped from the sudden stop.

"Get back!" the guard sitting in the passenger seat yelled.

"Okay, okay!" Meegan said with a cocky smile. She held her hands up in a gesture of surrender. "I was just testing it."

"Well, don't," he snapped. After a long moment, the vehicle started moving again.

"Could you please not get us locked up in our rooms, or possibly somewhere worse?" Kenna quietly asked.

"As if they could lock me up," Meegan snickered.

It was nice that her friend was in a good mood, but at the same time she wasn't thrilled about Meegan's smug attitude. *This "I'm invincible" idea she's got stuck in her head is going to get her in trouble.*

Clearing the area of homes, they entered a stretch of forest. Tall trees canopied above, shrouding them from the blue sky. She didn't dare ask the guards how much longer, so instead she tried to lighten the mood and tapped Meegan's arm. When her friend glanced her way, Kenna said, "Thanks for coming."

Meegan shrugged, as if nothing weighed on her mind. "We need to stick together. Plus, I want to talk to Her Royal Highness about how they're planning to rescue your mom and the others."

"I'm sure they have a plan."

"Well, we need to be included in that plan."

Kenna shifted in her seat, facing Meegan. "Not this again. Seriously, Meeg. Let them handle the rescue mission."

Meegan tucked her black hair behind one ear. "I can help."

"We've got enough to worry about," she said, pulling out the arcstone from beneath her shirt. "Can we focus on one thing at a time, please?"

"We can multitask. Besides, as soon as I see Breyah again, I'll cast an amula to connect me with the essence inside her arcstone. If there's someone inside it, then I'll deal with that—"

"Deal with it? I don't even want to know what you mean by that." Kenna shook her head, unable to believe the words coming out of her best friend's mouth. "And what happens if Breyah's not wearing the arm cuff?"

"Then I'll politely ask her to go get it."

"Politely?"

The corner of Meegan's lips curled up, and she rolled her eyes. "I'm not going to use force, if that's what you're asking." And before Kenna could respond, she added, "Unless I have to." She then slouched in her seat, crossed her arms, and stared up through the glass dome of the transport vehicle.

With Meegan's attention turned elsewhere, Kenna knew the conversation was over, or over for the moment. It was understandable that Meegan was acting different. Losing a loved one was never easy and required grieving. She'd also taken a life. It didn't matter that the man she'd killed was all sorts of evil. Killing someone wasn't an easy thing to live with and could affect…or change…a person. And then, on top of it all, she'd unlocked the power of the Fawness that she'd been suppressing all these years. She couldn't even imagine how Meegan was able to get out of bed each morning because she knew if that were her, she'd be a hot mental mess.

There was no way she was going to let Meegan convince the princess, Breyah, Ben, and whomever else to let them help with the rescue mission. Hopefully, everyone else would agree with her *not* to let them go to help rescue the captives, finally putting the debate to rest, because she was tired of arguing about it. She was getting tired of constantly having so many unanswered questions lingering in her mind, too. Would there ever be a day when things would feel normal again?

9

Kenna stared out the window for the rest of the ride, and soon enough the forest opened up into a small clearing. A large patch of sunlight shone over the gravel road. When the transport vehicle stopped, everyone climbed out. Tall Hiccum trees hugged the sides of the two-story home tucked into the forest. Thick wooden beams stacked horizontally lined the front while colorful flowers and bright green moss sprouted between each beam. Three open archways, rounded along the top, were the entrances into the home. Wide stone steps descended from the home to the gravel road. At the top stood the princess, waiting with an elated expression.

Meegan sauntered around from the other side, and Kenna said, "It's beautiful, though not what I was expecting."

"Not very royal-looking." Meegan didn't stop to gawk and walked past Kenna, toward the steps.

"Beannaith!" Princess Emmalyn said with open arms. "I'm so excited you're all here! And now," she continued as Liam and Brody followed Kenna and Meegan up to the landing, "we're going to have a wonderful afternoon getting to know one another." Emmalyn clasped Meegan's hands. "And I'm especially excited to meet a child of Anuminis."

Slipping her hands free, Meegan narrowed her eyes. "And how many Anumens have you met in your lifetime?"

It might have been a bit forward, but Kenna was curious to hear the princess's answer.

"Let's just say, I've become quite the specialist on your world and your people." Before either girl could respond, Emmalyn twirled toward the house and waved for everyone to follow. The lightweight fabric of her white blouse and matching pants fluttered from her swift turn.

"What the hell did she mean by that?" Meegan quietly asked Kenna as Liam and Brody moved past them and into the house.

Kenna shrugged, and then motion caught her attention. A man, dressed in a white uniform with gold trim, was watching them from the yard by the corner of the house. She turned and noted a second Sendarian woman, also dressed in white with gold trim, on the other side of the front yard.

Reassuring herself, Kenna thought, *They're here to protect the princess, that's all.* She wasn't sure why having so many eyes on them made her uncomfortable. Now that everything was out in the open, she would've thought things would've been easier, less stressful, but no. She couldn't help but worry about what new can of worms they'd opened by revealing Meegan's true identity.

"Come on," Meegan said, then headed inside.

Kenna followed but at a leisurely pace, taking in the architectural details and decor. The second she walked beneath one of the archways, she felt a slight resistance. At the far end of the foyer, a broad-shouldered woman stood and tapped the glass panel embedded in the wall. Kenna spun and faced the arched doorway she'd just passed under. A blue flicker of energy cascaded up the space between the arches. She held a hand to the barrier, and energy outlined her fingers.

"You'd best stay with the others," the woman said in a deep but nonthreatening voice. She then walked away, disappearing down a dark corridor.

Voices from the rear of the home filled the wide, empty hall, and sunlight shone over the group as everyone made their way outside. Kenna started to follow, but then she heard her father's voice coming from nearby. Curiosity got the best of her, and she crept down the hall until she reached the end. Pressing her stomach and chest against the white wall, she peered around the corner into the adjacent room.

"Please, you have to understand I had my reasons for leaving." Her dad's back faced Kenna, and it wasn't until Breyah stepped out from behind his form that Kenna realized whom he was talking to. "I never meant to hurt you."

Were they a thing? Kenna wondered.

"It's in the past, Gerard." Breyah wrapped her hands around her arms and gently rubbed her pale skin. Kenna noted Breyah wasn't wearing the arm cuff. If she'd been wearing it, Kenna probably would've interrupted the conversation, regardless of how intimate it appeared. They needed that arcstone.

Her father approached the Priomh Leadess, and Breyah stepped away from him, holding up one hand. "Don't. There's no picking up where we left off. You have a wife and child now."

"I know," he said, leaning against the arm of a nearby chair. Kenna wondered if her father regretted leaving all those years ago. "My daughter means the world to me, and I would do anything to protect her."

"And your wife?"

"Oh, Honnah can take care of herself, but yes. I've grown to…" He paused, a hesitation in his answer that concerned Kenna. "…appreciate our relationship."

Breyah stared at Gerard for a long moment. Tears welled in her orange eyes. "Why did you leave?"

"I thought you said you didn't—"

"—I know what I said! And *it is* in the past, but I need to know why. Why leave the world you were to rule? Why leave everything behind for a complete stranger? And…and why leave me here, after…" She drew out a thin silver chain from beneath her top, a silver pendant hanging at the end. It was too far for Kenna to see the intricate design etched into the center of the round disc, but she recalled seeing something similar on Ben during one of their dreamlike encounters.

"Why betroth me if you were only going to leave? Did you forget what happens when a betrothal is broken?" When Gerard didn't answer, she asked again, "Did you?"

Kenna wondered, *What happens when a betrothal is broken? Did Ben break his vows to marry someone? Damn, I need to find a Sendarian history book or something.*

"Breyah, I would've never left you if there were another option. But there wasn't. Honnah came here as one of the Aevo C subjects. It was purely coincidental that I was here visiting you."

She wiped a tear that escaped and trickled down her cheek. "So what happened? Why did you leave me?"

Kenna knew she shouldn't be listening in on their conversation, but there were so many secrets that her father had been hiding and she didn't want to pass on the opportunity to hear a few of them, even if it was eavesdropping. He shouldn't have been keeping secrets from her in the first place.

Gerard inhaled a deep breath before he continued explaining. "Honnah approached me that day in Medical after she'd sprained her ankle."

"I remember that day. She'd wandered off from the group while the subjects were being escorted out to the meeting place for their initial test. To see how they react and behave when approached by our hostile actors."

"Yes, exactly. She knew, somehow, that it was all a ruse. That the threat wasn't real. She knew about Isoldesse and the Aevo Compendium."

Breyah's expression pinched as she shook her head. "That's impossible. There's no way a human would have that kind of information."

"Breyah…" He dragged his words out. "Honnah isn't human."

"What?"

What?! Kenna mimicked Breyah's reaction, her knees buckling beneath her. Using the wall to stabilize herself, she forced her mind to process her mother's identity. She needed to hear what else her father had to say.

"Honnah is Anumen. Like Isoldesse and like Meegan." He dragged a hand down his face, over his short beard. "She approached me in Medical. Told me she needed my help. That she was carrying a seed to a child that needed parents."

"What does that mean?" Breyah asked, while Kenna asked the same question in her mind.

"There are two types of Anumen women. One who creates and carries the seeds of life, and one who grows and gives birth. It's the way of their world, and there's so much more involved based on which type of woman you are, but it's not relevant right now."

"The hell it isn't," Kenna whispered.

Breyah sniffled and asked, "So you left to help find parents for this unborn child? Or…or is Kenna that child, and you decided to take it upon yourself to become a father—leaving an entire world of Sendarians behind?"

"Again, there's so much more to the story, but yes. Honnah was looking to do something never attempted. She wanted the baby to be born to a Sendarian father and a human mother. Kenna is that child and her blood…her essence…will be the bridge between all three of our worlds."

"What. The. F—" Kenna whispered with an exasperated gasp. "I have another mother? And I'm supposed to be some kind of bridge?"

"What are you doing?" A man's voice startled her from behind.

Kenna spun to see Ben. His arms were folded across his chest, a fitted blue jacket hugging his torso. Her gaze lingered over his body before she looked up at his stern face.

"You're not supposed to—"

She shushed him, waving a dismissive hand. "I need to hear this." Ignoring him, she returned to listening, but he grabbed her arm.

"You should be outside with the others."

But Kenna didn't move, and when her father started speaking again, she felt Ben's hand relax and slip from her arm.

"Breyah, Kenna is no threat. She doesn't even know who she is."

Kenna glanced over her shoulder at Ben. One brow raised it seemed Ben's curiosity had been piqued too.

"Okay, but the fact is you left. You left your duties as the next king of Sendara. What does that mean now?"

There was a long pause before Gerard's voice filled the air. "I don't know. We need to rescue Honnah first."

"And Rian," Breyah added.

"Yes, and Rian, but, Breyah, there's something you should know about your friend."

Kenna knew exactly where the conversation was going, and she wasn't sure Ben should hear the truth about Rian. Turning to him, she said, "You're right. We should go."

Not budging, he shifted his gaze between Kenna and the doorway, as if he was trying to decide the right thing to do versus the thing he *wanted* to do—which was to hear what Gerard had to say. "Hold on," he finally said, moving past Kenna. "This might be important."

Without arguing, she stepped back, letting him listen.

"What about Rian?" Breyah asked. Kenna couldn't see inside the room anymore, but she could still make out their voices.

Her father answered, "She's not a Sendarian."

"Yes, she is. She told me after she first arrived here that the medics on Sendara tested her DNA and found a rare pigment strain that altered her hair, eye, lip, and nail color to be blue. She explained that life on Sendara wasn't easy and that's why she requested a transfer to Priomh."

"No, Breyah." Gerard's voice was calm. "She lied to you. She's not who you think she is. Though, she wasn't lying about not living an easy life on Sendara. Most of it was in hiding."

Kenna wished she could see her dad's face as he told Breyah the truth.

"She's a being from a hostile world Isoldesse had visited. We think Isoldesse went there hoping to bestow her influence, like on all the other worlds of the Aevo Compendium, but things didn't go as planned. The details are unclear, but supposedly she did something that caught the attention of some very powerful leaders. She fled from their world, and they pursued her. They are called the Obard, and they're the reason Anuminis no longer exists."

"That's horrible," Breyah said, sorrow in her voice.

"It is. The Anumens who survived the attacks and fled to find homes on other worlds are convinced the Obard are hunting Anumen women for their magic and connection to the higher powers they pray to—the Eilimintachs. But Honnah has a different theory. That they're after something else. Something taken from them."

"Like what?" Breyah asked, while Kenna thought the same question.

"A relic of some sort. Honnah had me download and bring a copy of our Anumen Doctrine to Earth with us so she could study it and compare it to the journals her parents had brought with them during their escape from Anuminis."

More questions. A never-ending list of unanswered questions. And now more about her own mother and how Honnah had been investigating Isoldesse all these years. Hearing her father's confession made Kenna wonder, *What happened on the Obard planet that resulted in them traveling the galaxy to hunt Isoldesse and her people down?*

"My sister was never one to hold back when it came to trying to better our world, and the ways of other worlds. So, whatever she

did, I believe her intentions weren't malicious," Ulissa said inside Kenna's mind.

Kenna lifted her chin, glancing up at the hallway ceiling. Silently, she asked, *"Did Isoldesse ever say anything to you about her encounter with the Obard? Is what my father says true? Did she take something from them, or did it have something to do with the worlds she was observing? Did they not want her influence?"*

"She never said. But it appears her good *intentions had unforeseen consequences. One of those consequences being the invasion of our world. Even as a youthen, Isoldesse was never reprimanded or corrected whenever she acted on impulse. In fact, many of my sister's traits stem from our mum. One cannot discipline a child if she doesn't see the same problems within herself."*

"Yes, you're right, and I'm sorry, Ulissa. It sounds like you had a rough childhood." She paused before she added, *"Don't worry, we'll figure it out together."*

"It was a difficult time of my life. One that was forever ago. My life changed for the better after I ran away."

Kenna wanted to know more, but also didn't want to drain any more of the arcstone's energy. *"You will have to tell me more about your childhood after we've restored the arcstone's strength."*

"Yes, I think that sounds nice." The old woman's voice faded. *"Please, hurry."*

"There's a lot more going on here than just a rebel group sabotaging the Aevo Compendium project," Gerard said, drawing Kenna's attention back to eavesdropping on his and Breyah's conversation.

Kenna pulled Ben's arm, moving past him so she could have a turn looking inside the room. Gerard was standing in front of Breyah. The large picture window behind them was tinted, blocking out the afternoon sun.

"So what does Rian have to do with Isoldesse visiting that world…? What did you call it again?"

"I don't know the name of their home world, but they're called the Obard, and yes. Rian is most definitely from there. I don't know why or how she got here, but she's not supposed to be here." He stood from resting against the arm of the chair.

"This is all too much, and I'll have to talk with Rian. Once she and the others have been rescued." Breyah paced along the window.

"I don't think she knows, and if she does, she probably doesn't know the full truth."

"I have to go." Breyah took long strides toward the bare sidewall. Kenna ducked back into the hall, hoping Breyah didn't see her. She carefully peeked through the doorway again to watch as Breyah pressed one hand to the flat white surface. A tall section of the wall flickered, revealing a hologram hiding a secret passage. Standing in the doorway, she paused and told Gerard, "I'll see you tonight at the memorial."

He nodded. "I'm sorry about your Spiaires."

"Yes, well, let's make sure their deaths and the others aren't for nothing." With that, she left, disappearing into the darkness. The hologram returned, concealing the secret doorway.

Kenna quickly spun, pushing Ben down the hall. "Come on," she exclaimed, hoping he understood the urgency. "I can't risk being caught."

Out in the main foyer, Ben sidestepped in front of her, stopping her from continuing to the backyard. "You're already caught."

"You don't count," she said, grabbing his arm and dragging him toward the rear of the house. It wasn't easy, as he was a pretty solid guy. He seemed to be resisting a bit too. But she needed to move away from the hall. She didn't want her dad knowing that she'd been listening.

Ben escorted Kenna to the patio garden where everyone was sitting around a long table, talking and laughing. Well, mostly the princess talking and laughing. Liam was listening intently while Brody stared off into the forest surrounding the yard. For a second, Kenna's heartbeat started to race until she spotted Meegan standing off to the side, away from the group.

As she stepped forward, Ben stretched one arm across her path, blocking her from ending their conversation. They stood at the top of the stairs, overlooking the patio garden. In a low voice, he asked, "Why won't you tell me what's going on?"

"Tell you what? Uh, you heard the same stuff I heard!" she exclaimed while trying to keep her voice low. "I didn't know my mother was an Anumen! And I didn't know my dad was freaking royalty until yesterday!"

He crossed his arms, staring down at her. "Did you know about Rian not being a Sendarian?"

Engrossed in her conversation with Liam, the princess hadn't taken notice of them yet. And by the glare Ben was giving Kenna, she knew she needed to give him some kind of answer. Sucking in her lower lip, she half shrugged and half nodded. "But only because Meegan has this ring that turns a different color whenever there's an Obard close by. We don't know any more than that."

"How dangerous are these Obard beings?"

"Very," she answered truthfully. "I've been seeing them in my dreams…or whatever those mental encounters are…and they're scary."

"You confront them during sleep…like we do?" His face pinched, and he stepped closer. "Are you okay?"

"I wouldn't say *I confront them*, but yeah." Staring up into his orange eyes, she felt a sense of protection coming from him. It could've been his Rhaltan instincts, or it could've been something else.

"Look, I know you have a million questions. Me too. And I'm happy to tell you everything I know, but later. Right now, I need to digest what I overheard and go talk with Meeg." She started to walk away, but stopped and told him, "Oh, and heads up. Meegan is going to want to come with you on your rescue mission."

"How do you even know there is a rescue mission?"

"There better be a freaking rescue mission, Ben!" she said with a clenched jaw. Nervous her outburst caught the attention of the princess, she waited a moment before continuing, "You, my father, and that princess out there…hell, Breyah too…better have some plan to rescue my mother and the others."

"We do, but you and your friends won't be involved."

"Good. I don't want to be involved. But"—Kenna pointed out back to Meegan, who was still standing off to the side, away from the table—"she does. And she's not going to take *no* lightly."

Ben stared out at Meegan, releasing a sigh before nodding. "Understood."

"Finally, something we agree on."

One side of his lips briefly curled up. She would've missed it if she'd turned and walked away, but she caught it. A glimpse of the man she'd met before he knew she was human—back when he wanted her.

Leaving him, she walked down the steps and out into the backyard. Tempted to glance back and see if he was following her—to sit with the princess of course, not following her to where Meegan stood—and when she did, he wasn't. He remained at the top of the patio steps. But they did lock eyes, as he was watching her walk away.

She quickly faced forward. Cheeks flushed and her insides swelling with butterflies. *Liam is the one I should be with. Ben isn't an option*, she silently reminded herself. *It's Liam that wants to be with me—that kissed me. Not Ben.*

10

Meegan's gaze followed the crackle of blue energy trailing from the treetops to the protective barrier surrounding the Priomh community. It hadn't been difficult to penetrate the shield earlier when she'd gone out for her midnight run. This made her wonder if someone wanted to get in, how would they go about shutting it down? Was there a command center or an electrical box controlling the power?

A high-pitched laugh cut through Meegan's thoughts, and she glanced over her shoulder at the princess talking with Liam and Brody. Well, mainly talking with Liam while Brody stared off into the forest. They'd all been through a lot, and it annoyed her that he thought he was the exception. That his trauma was worse than everyone else's. If he couldn't get his emotions in check and focus on what needed to be done, then he was of no use to her or the rescue mission.

"Come join us!" Princess Emmalyn called over.

"Yeah, in a second," Meegan said with the best smile she could muster. Time was ticking and her patience was wearing thin. Looking up to the archways into the home, she wondered where Kenna had wandered off to.

"*Your essence wavers, young Fawness,*" the Eilimintachs said within her mind.

Turning away, she looked out past the colorful flowers circling the patio area to the yard. She counted six guards walking the perimeter in pairs along the forest's edge.

Silently, she answered the Eilimintachs, "*My essence is fine. In fact, my essence has never been more awake and ready to take on the responsibilities of the Fawness.*"

Every now and then, the guards would glance in her direction. Oddly, this made her smile. *Good,* she thought. *Be afraid.* For a brief moment, she tried to imagine how many guards she could take out before they restrained her.

Another loud laugh erupted from the princess. *I'm starting to think this princess isn't as competent as we thought. All fun and games, nothing serious about Her Highness.*

"*Why do you judge her so poorly?*" the Eilimintachs silently queried.

"*Stay out of my thoughts. Haven't you ever heard of privacy?*" Meegan scowled, arms tucked tightly across her chest. "*Seriously, get out of my head!*"

"Hey, there you are," Kenna said, jogging over to her.

"Where the hell have you been?"

Kenna pointed to the archway leading inside the house. Ben stood there, talking with one of the royal guards. Meegan faced her friend again, gesturing to the Sendarian. "You were with him?"

"Sort of," Kenna answered, a smile tugging at her lips, then turned away from the group, pulling Meegan closer to the flowers. "I overheard my father talking to Breyah."

"Your dad is here?"

Kenna nodded. "Did you know my mother was an Anumen?"

Meegan's mouth parted. Her eyes were focused on Kenna, but the world she saw blurred momentarily as her brain processed this new piece of information. *There's no way. She can't be. Aunt Bea would've said something… Wouldn't she have? And my parents… They would've known.* The question kept spinning in Meegan's mind. *All those times I hung out at Kenna's house, with her parents. It was bad enough to learn that Gerard was a Sendarian, but now this—Honnah shared the same blood as me!*

"It's a lot, I know," Kenna said, leaning in closer. "And there's more."

Meegan tucked her hair behind her ear. "Okay, what else?"

"My father thinks the Obard are after something Isoldesse took from them."

Meegan shook her head. "No way. That's not possible. You must've misheard. The Obard are *not* civil beings. They're not searching for anything. They're invaders—conquerors—who travel the galaxy destroying worlds. The only thing they're searching for is power. That's why they attacked Anuminis—for our magic and the power within the arcstones and transessent stones."

"I'm not disagreeing with you, but he and Honnah have a different theory. So, we'll have to ask her once Ben has rescued her and the others."

"Kenna! Meegan!" Gerard's voice called out as he approached them from behind.

Both girls turned and faced him. Meegan couldn't imagine what Kenna must be feeling, now that they knew her father's true identity. But Meegan understood. She knew that sometimes secrets must be kept, even from those you trust and love the most.

"Dad, where have you been?" Kenna gave him a half-hearted smile then an awkward hug. Meegan didn't blame her friend for her reluctance. When their embrace parted, Kenna stepped back a few feet and asked, "And what's the plan to get Mom back?"

"Ben will be leading a small security team to Sendara to rescue the captives."

Meegan stared into Gerard's orange eyes. It was strange seeing him without his chestnut-brown eyes, but everything else was him. His red hair was nothing new to them, nor were the faint freckles slowly being covered by age lines beneath and around his eyes.

"We want to go too," Meegan blurted out.

Kenna immediately argued, "No, we don't. We discussed it." She glared at Meegan. "We'd only be in the way."

"No, we wouldn't. Besides, I can help." Meegan lifted her chin, stood tall, and held Gerard's gaze. She needed to present herself with strength. To show Gerard that she could do this.

"We have other things we need to—" Kenna started, but Meegan quickly sidestepped in front of her friend, pushing her out of the conversation.

"When do they leave?" Meegan asked Gerard.

"What's everyone talking about?" Princess Emmalyn stood from the table and made her way over. She was at least a foot and a half shorter than her brother. Gerard explained how the girls wanted to go to Sendara and assist with the rescue mission. Emmalyn immediately hooked her arm through his and tugged ever so slightly while shrieking, "Oh, that's a wonderful idea!"

"Really?" Kenna asked, her brows pinched. "You want us to go?"

"When else are you going to get to see our beautiful home world?" The princess beamed in elation, as if this were all for her amusement.

"I don't think that's a wise idea." Ben spoke up from the top of the steps, still standing beneath the archway. "I can't watch them and—"

"Nonsense! I'm the princess and I say they go!"

Ben crossed his arms. "And how are you planning to conceal their appearances?"

Emmalyn paused, tapping one manicured fingernail on her chin. "Well, I hadn't gotten that far. I'm sure Holt could do something about their eye color, and the rest is just clothes and hats!"

Meegan waved a hand through the air, calling for everyone's attention. "I can take care of our appearance."

Unfolding his arms, Ben narrowed his eyes at Meegan. "Explain."

Turning to the princess, Meegan asked, "May I have a strand of your hair?"

There was no hesitation. Emmalyn unclipped the oversized pin, releasing her long, wavy red hair that spilled over her shoulders. Tilting her head back, she combed her fingers through the ends, grasping any loose strands in the process. "Is this enough?" she asked, handing Meegan a bunch of pieces.

With one eyebrow raised, Meegan selected a single strand. "That's more than enough, thanks." Stepping away and holding the piece of hair in both hands out in front of her, she searched her mind for the right amula. Mentally, she pictured what she wanted the Eilimintachs to do, and the amula formed in her mind.

Wanting everyone to hear, she recited the amula up into the sky while pinching the strand of hair. "*Tarach amach et essence tao ag olra ogah mise comlac.*" When the last word crossed her lips, she raised her hands, still pinching the strand of hair between them, up over her face. The transition was immediate as her hands moved up, then over and down the backside of her head. Her features changed like magic.

"Meeg! Your hair!" Kenna exclaimed, coming over and grabbing a fistful of red hair. The color identical to the princess's. Meegan opened her eyes, and Kenna gasped. "And your brown eyes!"

"I can pass as a Sendarian, right." Releasing the strand of hair from her fingers, Meegan ran a hand through her hair. Lifting her arm, she turned her hand over. "My skin is so pale!"

The two girls chuckled in amusement. It'd been too long since they'd shared a laugh. But it was short lived. Meegan could feel the weight of everyone's attention directed at her, but she didn't shy away. Actually, she kind of liked the attention. All those years of hiding her abilities and who she truly was didn't matter anymore.

She could be herself, and that felt amazing. If only Nick was here to see.

Thoughts of Nick drowned out her moment of joy. She couldn't let herself fall a part now. Looking weak was the last thing she needed to be in front of everyone. Wiping beneath one eye, she whispered, "*Déanta*," releasing the amula and reverting back to her natural self.

Shaking off the sorrow, she said, "See, we'll blend right in." She shot Ben a smirk, hoping he'd have some kind of comeback, but he didn't. He just stared at her with suspicious eyes.

"I don't know," Kenna said quietly. "I still think we shouldn't go."

It wasn't until Liam stood, announcing he was going too, that Ben reacted. He scoffed, then said, "Oh, for the love of Isoldesse. They can't all come." Ben waved his arm, gesturing to the boys at the long wood table.

"I'm not going," Brody mumbled.

"Of course not. You've been through enough, and I think you should stay here with me," Emmalyn said and moved to his side, wrapping one arm around his shoulders. "You've got some healing to do, and traveling to Sendara might be too much for your essence right now. Plus, I'm dying to introduce you to my friend Matthew."

Matthew. Where is that coward, anyway? Meegan searched the yard in case he was lingering around, out of sight. Too afraid after what he'd witnessed yesterday.

"Where is Matthew?" Kenna asked.

Emmalyn released Brody's shoulders and gracefully looked to her niece. "Oh, he's out at his cabin. He's a little shaken up and needed some rest."

"With guilt," Ben quipped. The princess shot him an eye roll, and he responded with a shrug.

The petite Sendarian woman shook off whatever tension passed between her and the Rhaltan officer, because her smile returned with a vengeance, reaffirming her decision. "Tomorrow morning, come first light when you leave for Sendara, you will take Kenna, Meegan, Liam, and their friend Ally with you."

Kenna stepped around her father and said to the princess, "Oh, I'm pretty sure Ally will want to stay, if that's okay. Her sister is still recovering in Medical."

"Well, I'm sure Holt will enjoy the company," the princess said with a smile.

"I highly doubt that," Ben snapped.

Ignoring the tall, brooding man, the princess clasped her hands together and exclaimed, "Now that we have that settled, I wanted to invite you all to a special memorial we're holding this evening."

A memorial? Meegan couldn't help but wonder if now was the time to be holding such things. They should be planning and getting ready to leave, not having a party.

"The deaths of our two Spiaires, Seph and Grace—"

Brody looked up to the princess from his seat, brushing aside the wavy brown curls from his eyes. "Grace died?"

The princess nodded and rested a hand on his shoulder. "Her internal injuries were too severe, and Holt couldn't save her."

Brody's shoulders sagged and his head dropped. "I'm sorry. I didn't know her well, but she didn't deserve to be tortured."

"No one deserves to be mistreated in such a manner," the princess solemnly said.

"And it's a good thing he's no longer around to do such things," Meegan chimed in.

Ben descended a few steps toward Meegan. "And what gives you the right to decide who lives or dies?"

"You were going to kill him anyway!" she barked out, spinning to face him. "You proclaimed," she said with some exaggeration, "that act of Imperilment, or whatever it was you threatened Quaid with… You were going to kill him too! So, what is it? You're pissed because I did it before you?"

"Meegan," Kenna quietly said, coming up next to her side. "You know that's not what he means."

Meegan didn't break from her stare-down with Ben. "Oh, I think it is. I stole his glory and now he's—"

"You have no idea what you're talking about, and worse, you can't even see how taking an essence has affected you." Ben didn't wait for Meegan or anyone else to respond. He grumbled something she couldn't hear as he stormed off into the house.

Coward, Meegan thought.

"Okay," the princess jumped in, hands clasped in front of her, "there's nothing you can do until tomorrow when the transport ship leaves. So, until then, let's meet later this evening to mourn those we've lost. Our people and yours. The girl, Devaney, who you know didn't survive the waking as well as the boy, Nick, who was killed yesterday. We will honor them all tonight under the stars."

When no one said anything, Kenna finally approached the princess and said, "Thank you. You didn't have to include us in your tradition, or those we lost. It's appreciated."

Nick isn't lost, Meegan thought. If she was forced to attend this party, then maybe she could use it to her advantage. Hopefully, Breyah would be wearing her arcstone. Otherwise, Meegan would have to leave the party early and go find it herself.

11

Gemma stayed low as she followed Micah through the hole in the wall and into the next room. He didn't stop, walking straight out the door and into the hallway. Loud, boisterous voices carried toward them from around the corner. Micah gestured with a head tilt to the door at the end of the hall, away from the men guarding her room. Inside was a stairwell, and at the bottom was an exit, leading out into a narrow alley.

The midday sun was high with no overcasting clouds. It was never too early to drink in South Sendara, and she imagined the tavern would be crawling with Athru. Not a good place to go right now, especially if Anora was there. She needed answers before confronting the Athru leader again.

"Where are we going?" she asked.

"Two buildings down." He took off, walking fast alongside the open field that stretched out behind the buildings lining the main street. "Best to stay out of sight."

Happy to have been rescued by Micah, though she wished it'd happened before she was moved to the room with the shower. Her clothes were starting to smell like that gróntah from the tavern earlier.

He stopped when they reached the second building, holding his hand up for Gemma to wait. Peering around the corner, he checked out the alley. When it was clear, he moved and so did she. To her surprise, Sabine was there, sitting on a rickety wooden bench with Xander.

The second Xander saw her, he leapt to his feet, rushed to her, and wrapped his strong arms around her. She didn't hesitate in returning the gesture. He kissed her hair, ear, and cheek, then found his way to her lips. She didn't push him away.

"Xander," she said breathily, but he pressed his mouth to hers again. She leaned away, pushing his chest with her hands. "I'm fine… And happy to see you too. But we have to get out of here before we're seen."

He snuck in one last peck on her cheek. "I don't know what's going on, but you can't leave me like that."

"I know, and I'll do my best to keep you safe, but we've got to move."

"Anora won't be checking in on you again for a while." Micah handed Gemma his plac and pointed to the screen. "This is how we escape. There's a transport ship scheduled to land in ten minutes."

"Is it Athru?" Gemma asked.

"Yes," Sabine answered, standing from the bench. Her plump cheeks were flushed, and her eyelids were slightly puffy. "Anora wants me to return to Priomh. To give myself up."

"What?" Gemma brushed loose strands of red hair from blocking her view. It didn't make any sense to send Sabine back to Priomh. Nothing Anora was doing made any sense. Stepping away from Xander, she asked, "Did she give you a reason?"

Sabine wiped dust from her pants while shaking her head. Then, instead of offering up an answer, she scoffed and said, "I didn't realize South Sendara was so hot and dry. And why haven't they paved the roads here? Travelling between communities would be much easier."

Sendarians walking the main street behind them while motorized wagons went about their business on the dirt road. No one paid any attention to them down the ally. Shady business is normal business when you're in South Sendara.

Answering Sabine's question, Gemma explained, "Because it's South Sendara, Sabine. They don't have the resources, or the kind of community support the mainland has for any of that. Now, stop changing the subject." Gemma crossed her arms and shifted her weight from one hip to the other. The stretched-out collar of her worn sweatshirt slipped over her shoulder, revealing the strap of her tank top. She narrowed her gaze, and asked, "Why is Anora sending you to Priomh?"

"I'm supposed to find out what happened to her brother, and what's going on up there. She also wants to know more about the Rhaltan officer's status." The round woman opened her hand and showed Gemma a miniature-sized plac. "This is how I'm to communicate with her."

Micah took the device from Sabine, then examined it one last time. "I've bypassed the security and tracking measures for the device, encoding a secure frequency so Breyah's security team or the Rhaltan won't hear any of the communications transmitted." He tucked it into a secret pocket in the back of Sabine's jacket. "If they see you using it, well, that's a different story. I can't help you there."

"So don't be stupid, is what you're saying." Sabine rolled her eyes.

"What other orders did Anora give you?" Gemma asked.

Sabine pursed her lips before straightening her shoulders. "I'm to wait for the *supposed* attack and send word when it happens."

Gemma glanced between Sabine and her brother. "What attack?"

From the main road, Logan appeared, walking toward them. "Something is coming, and whether Anora wants to believe it or not,

Cahleen and I want to know what the hell is going on up there, especially if there's an attack."

"Cahleen said she didn't believe what you both overheard. She said it was the queen's problem now." Gemma rested both hands on her hips. Her sister was up to something, and it sounded as though Cahleen was playing both sides. If Anora suspected her personal Scout was going behind her back, things might not end well for Cahleen.

"Your sister can handle herself," Logan said, guessing Gemma's line of thought correctly. "And in the meantime, I'm to fly this one"—he pointed to Sabine—"to Priomh, shove her out the door, and then make my way back here. *But…*"

"But you're going to take us with you," Micah finished.

"Exactly." Logan nodded.

"Why the hegah are we going back to Priomh?" Gemma honestly believed they'd all lost their minds.

"Because something is coming. And we need to warn them, even if we're not on the same side. We're all Sendarians, and this is our home." Logan's shoulders dropped. The broad-shouldered man pursed his lips and scratched the back of his neck. "I don't want any more bloodshed. I've seen enough for two lifetimes while fighting for Quaid."

"So, Cahleen *is* playing both sides?"

There was hesitance in his response, but eventually Logan nodded. "I already told her things won't end well if she gets caught double-crossing Anora and Biryn."

"Have you met this infamous Biryn?"

"Oh, he exists. I've met the little shit. He's more conniving than Anora and Quaid put together." Inhaling a deep breath, he pointed to Sabine. "You're with me. Let's go." Logan walked over to Micah. Gemma couldn't hear what the two men were discussing.

With her lips pursed tight, Sabine offered a peaceful smile to Gemma. Then, to the group, she said, "Beannaith."

Sabine made her way over to Logan, but Gemma wasn't done talking. "Hey, wait!" She called, then jogged over to Sabine. "Don't trust anyone, and keep your mouth shut. I promise we'll figure everything out and then free you from Priomh's custody."

"I guess you're not such a bitch after all, huh?" Sabine's smirk was full of humor, but Gemma could feel the sincerity and gratefulness woven in.

"Here." Logan tossed Micah a small black box. "I did what you asked and connected it directly to Anora's plac. Whatever she sees, you see. Even the communications from Sabine."

Once Micah had the device, Logan and Sabine turned and walked out of the alley, blending in with the bustle of Sendarians along the main street.

"Now what?" Xander asked.

Micah clasped the ghost relaying device to the top right corner of his plac like a magnet. It wasn't long before the device was activated. He locked eyes with Gemma, and that was all the confirmation she needed to know they were ready to go. Micah waved for Gemma and Xander to follow toward the end of the alley. "Now, we need to beat Logan and Sabine to the transport dock. He left the cargo loading door open for us."

"What about Honnah? And Rian?" Gemma asked, following her brother.

"We couldn't free Rian," Xander explained. "And Honnah didn't want to come." He jogged alongside Gemma. "She said she had something important to do here. I don't know what she meant, but she was adamant about staying."

What is that human up to? She's playing with fire staying here.

"She did ask me to tell you something. A message that she needs you to deliver to Gerard."

Gemma slid to a stop, dust clouding around her boots. "Gerard?" Her gaze darted from Xander to Micah, who had stopped at the next building.

"What is it? Our window to get onto that transport ship is slim, Gemma. Come on!" Micah started running again, and Xander followed.

That means he's actually here. The banished prince has finally returned to Sendara, she thought.

"What's the message?"

"She said to tell Gerard that she figured out what they're looking for, and she's going to destroy it."

"What does that mean?"

Xander shrugged and continued, staying low and close to Micah. Gemma hesitated only for a second before running after them. She recalled the communication that Cahleen and Logan overheard back on Quaid's ship. That grόntah had made contact with an unknown hostile force: *"Be forewarned that if you come between us and what is ours, we will take everything from you and your world."*

Whoever that had been, making a deal with Quaid, was looking for something. And it seemed Honnah had found it, planned on destroying it, and clearly wanted Gerard to know.

Shit. That wouldn't be good for Sendara. She had to find a way to stop Honnah. A problem to think about on her return flight to Priomh. A problem she'd most likely have to tell her old friend about.

12

Back at Priomh, in the common area of their guest suite, Liam and Brody retreated to their quarters to get ready for the memorial. The second the double doors shut, Ally walked out of her assigned bedroom and over to Kenna and Meegan.

"How's Prue?" Meegan asked, truly concerned about how the Sendarians were caring for her.

"Same," Ally said.

If they lost Prue too, Meegan wasn't sure she'd be able to refrain from unleashing her anger, because so far, she'd seen nothing good come from this Aevo Compendium project.

Kenna rubbed Ally's arms. "The worst is over and she's in good hands."

"Is she, though?" Meegan sneered and continued toward the room Kenna and Ally had been staying in.

"Hey!" Ally called out and jogged past Meegan, wanting to beat Meegan into the room. "On a positive note, you have to see this!"

Inside the room, on the queen-sized bed, was a polished wooden trunk with dark metal hinges. It took up the full length of the bed.

"What's inside?" Kenna asked, running her fingers along the top. She and Ally examined the detailing of the carved wood while Meegan stood back, leaning against the sofa.

"It came for you," Ally answered. "The guards who dropped it off said you press your finger here and it opens."

Meegan watched from over Ally's shoulder, curious to see the tech embedded within the wood. The girls watched as Kenna pressed her pointer finger to the black sensor. From inside, multiple *click*s sounded off until the lid popped ajar. Kenna and Ally each took a side and lifted the top up and back onto the bed, revealing three beautiful gowns, folded and lined up inside.

While the other two pulled out the dresses and admired the elegance and simplicity of the gowns, Meegan reached for the remaining dress. She rubbed the fabric of the gown between her thumb and fingers. The ivory fabric felt cool and soft, like one of her mother's expensive satin blouses. Drawing her hand away, she faced Kenna and Ally, and said, "We should be planning the details of the rescue mission, not getting all dressed up and attending some party." She spun on her toes and crossed the room, needing space.

"Meegan, you got what you wanted! We're going with Ben and the others on the rescue mission. Isn't that good enough?" Kenna exclaimed, coming up next to her friend, holding a dress draped over one arm. "People have died. Our people and theirs. If they want to take a minute and hold a memorial, then who are we to keep them from their customs?"

"Kenna's right," Ally said from next to the bed, placing the dress she'd been holding into the trunk. "Besides, the ship isn't leaving until morning. Holt explained everything to me during his last check-in with Prue. He also explained that Bennach is the best officer in their entire police force, or whatever they call it here. We have to trust the Sendarians have everything under control."

Crossing her arms, Meegan objected, "We most certainly do not have to trust the Sendarians."

"I trust Holt in taking care of Prue," Ally admitted.

Kenna brushed her dark hair behind one hear, and said, "And I trust that Ben has a plan to rescue my mom, Julianna, Rian, and the others."

With an eye roll, Meegan scoffed, "It's a waste of time, if you ask me."

"No, it's not," Kenna snapped. "It's an opportunity to get to know the Sendarians and their customs. We could learn a lot about who these people are, their values, and of course this *observation* project they've dedicated their lives to. Which means, it's your best chance…possibly your only chance…to learn more about Isoldesse and her connection to these people. Plus…" She paused, hesitating before she quietly added, "I still think revealing Isoldesse's true identity is a mistake."

Meegan threw her arms out to her sides, palms up. "You're kidding, right? Because if there's anything these Sendarians *deserve* it's at least to know the truth. That their goddess isn't a goddess!"

"I know… I know. But what good will come from opening that door? Once it's opened, and the world knows the truth, what will happen? We need to consider and weigh the consequences."

"They'll get over it! Maybe not right away, but they deserve to know they're worshipping a woman who isn't a god. She was a living, breathing, treacherous bit—"

"Meegan!" Kenna shouted. "Please, stop. We all know how you feel."

"I'm starting to think you really don't?" Meegan wanted to pick something up and throw. To release the anger building inside.

"Hey, let's take a breather," Ally said, stepping between them. "I don't know what's gotten into you two, but get your shit together! We can't fall apart. Not now. I need you," she said, looking between Kenna and Meegan, "and so do Liam and Brody… And Prue. We need to stick together and keep our heads on straight."

When no one answered, Ally asked, "Right?"

"Okay," Kenna and Meegan muttered in unison.

Resting her dress on the back of the sofa, Ally continued, "Now, you both make valid points on the matter. Like how we should consider the consequences of telling the Sendarians the truth." The second Ally said it, Kenna nodded in agreement. Then, when Ally added, "But I also think they have a right to know the truth about who Isoldesse really is," Meegan shot Kenna a narrowed glare. With a hand on each of their shoulders, she said, "There's got to be a middle ground to this problem."

Meegan's insides were boiling. She looked at each of her friends and couldn't believe what she was hearing. "No. There's no middle ground." Then, before anyone could say anything else, she stormed out of the room. "I need some air."

It didn't matter if the truth hurt. The fact was, Isoldesse wasn't a goddess, and she definitely didn't deserve the admiration and loyalty that came with the title.

Following Meegan out into the common area, Ally called out, "You'll be back before the memorial, right?"

Without turning around, Meegan grumbled, "Yeah, yeah." Then shoved open the balcony door and leapt over the side, using an amula to catch herself before hitting the grass. With lightning speed, she took off for another run in the woods.

"*The two girls are not wrong,*" the collective voices of the Eilimintachs said within her mind.

"Leave me alone!"

"*You need to heal. Your essence is in a fragile state. Continuing on this unstable path has consequences.*"

"My essence is fine, and consequences be damned." Holding her palm outward, she cast an amula allowing her to pass through the energy barrier. *I'm stronger than I've ever been. And it's my responsibility to fix the mess that traitor caused.*

"*Be cautious with your thoughts. Your emotions are getting the better of you,*" the Eilimintachs whispered, their voice floating through her mind.

"Stay out of my head!" she shouted into the evening sky. Her voice boomed outward, creating a shockwave of energy, rippling up into the forest. The tops of the trees swayed, and a few birds took flight. "I know what I'm doing!"

13

Kenna walked arm in arm with Ally, following two Sendarian guards along a gravel path lined with shrubs twice her height. Lighting their way were bowls of fire, hanging above their heads on long iron rods that extended from within the tops of the bushes. She felt as if they were being escorted to a secret elite party, like something straight out of a Bond movie.

Trailing behind them were Liam and Brody. Both looked handsome in cream-colored button-down shirts, matching dress pants, and golden sashes tied around their waists. The ends of the wide ribbons hung low along each of their right hips.

Behind the guys was Meegan. It had taken some convincing, but eventually she'd put on one of the dresses Princess Emmalyn had sent them.

The dresses were luxurious yet minimalistic. Kenna's gown had a V-neckline with thin straps over her shoulders and an empire-style waistline that hit just below her chest. The soft ivory fabric of her skirt flowed to the ground, swaying along the gravel. Ally and

Meegan both wore similar dresses but slightly different shades of ivory.

It was a bit odd to be attending an evening garden party rather than a funeral, but then again, Kenna understood that every culture celebrated and mourned life differently. Learning that the Sendarians had lost one of their own during the night, the girl who'd been taken captive with Darci, Brody, and the others, made Kenna realize how everyone, no matter where you are in the universe, experiences loss.

They rounded a wide bend along the walkway and reached the last stretch before it opened up into an enclosed garden area. The shrubs provided that *secret party* feel, circling around the entire space, though only half was being used. The back half sat in darkness beneath the starry sky.

Soft string music filled the air from a quartet off to the right, set up between two long tables draped in white linens and topped with an array of foods and drinks. The gravel path they followed split off to the sides, following the lines of the shrubs, while diamond-shaped pavers covered the center of the garden floor. Circling the center of the space were tall stone vases. Each one arranged with a lush bouquet of white and ivory flowers. It took Kenna a few moments to realize, after seeing a few Sendarians dancing with one another, that the center space was the dance floor.

"You look beautiful," Princess Emmalyn said, approaching the group with Gerard at her side. Kenna's gaze drifted from the princess to Matthew, who stood on the petite woman's other side. They were all dressed in white formalwear, Gerard and Matthew donning gold sashes around their waists while the princess wore a boatneck top with long flowing sleeves. Her skirt wasn't a skirt, but loose pants that mimicked the movements of her sleeves.

"Hello, Matthew," Kenna said, grasping the side of her dress and doing some kind of formal bow.

"Did you just curtsey?" Meegan quietly snickered from behind Kenna.

Kenna only smiled, ignoring her friend's banter. "It was nice of you to invite us, and we're sorry for your loss."

"Oh, that's sweet of you," Emmalyn cooed. She positioned herself between Kenna and Ally, forcing them to break their arm link. "Can I borrow you for a second?" She didn't wait for an answer as she led Kenna away from the group.

Glancing over her shoulder, Kenna saw Gerard and Matthew following them, leaving Ally, Meegan, Liam, and Brody to stand there alone.

"Maybe I should stay with the others," she suggested, not wanting anyone to feel out of place.

"Oh, they'll be fine." The princess tugged Kenna's arm and they crossed the open space to where Breyah was conversing with Holt and a few other Sendarians Kenna didn't know.

The princess shrieked with excitement and insisted Breyah tell Kenna about their earlier conversation.

Breyah offered a closed lip smile to Kenna, then to the princess she said with a hint of uncertainty, "Nothing is finalized yet, and I still need to discuss matters with your—"

"Oh, let's not go down that road. You don't need her permission!" Emmalyn squeezed Kenna's arm tighter.

Gerard, who'd been standing elbow to elbow next to Kenna, glared at the princess. "I believe Breyah has the final say in this matter. And if she wishes to discuss certain affairs with the Queen, then so be it." He raised his brows, and Kenna recognized the gesture. He was testing the princess to see if she would attempt a rebuttal. A look Kenna knew all too well from her childhood whenever her father would lecture her about something she did wrong. He was a convincing man with his assertive tone and thorough reasonings. He was also an impulsive man who often leapt before thinking when it came to those he cared for. But on this matter, Kenna wished he hadn't silenced the conversation. She wanted to know what the princess had been speaking of.

With a pout, the princess grumbled, "I know that Breyah has the final say. I was just saying she doesn't *have to* talk with our mother."

Her smile remained but some unsaid words lingered between the siblings.

Then, after a long moment, Breyah said, "It's fine. I'm sure the poor girl is dying to know, so…" Turning to Kenna, she started to say something, but Kenna's attention shifted to over Breyah's shoulder. Across the event space, Ben had entered the garden. He stood tall, chin up while his eyes scanned over the many clusters of Sendarians mingling. Like everyone else, he was dressed in white and ivory, with a gold sash around his waist. Kenna smirked at the rebellious cowlick sticking up over the left side of his forehead.

"Isn't that wonderful!" exclaimed Emmalyn.

Kenna blinked several times, returning her attention to the conversation. "Sorry, what?"

Emmalyn glanced past Breyah to where Ben stood. Her smile grew wider. She latched on to Kenna's arm and leaned in closer. "Between you and me, the betrothal was never official."

"What does that mean?" Kenna whispered, but the princess momentarily stepped away to speak with Matthew and the moment of passing secrets ended.

Seconds later, Matthew disappeared, and the princess's attention was once again on Kenna. "Now, what do you have to say about Breyah's most excellent news?" Emmalyn clasped her hands together and pointed to Kenna. All eyes from the immediate group were on her, and she had no idea what the princess was talking about.

"I'm sorry, I think I missed what you said," she told Breyah with an apologetic tone.

"I need the final approval, but I was saying how you and your friends are more than welcome to stay here on Priomh for as long as you like."

To live on Priomh would be amazing! Kenna thought and wanted to scream *yes*, but the cautious side of her brain reeled in her excitement. "That would be a wonderful opportunity to consider. Thank you, Breyah."

"Don't thank me yet," the Leadess added. "My request still needs to be approved by Queen Adalyss."

"She'll approve it," the princess gleefully said. "I know she will. And then we can spend all the time in the world together!"

Unsure of how she felt about that, but not wanting to be rude, Kenna said, "That would be nice."

"I was wondering if I could ask Kenna for a dance," Liam said from behind the group.

Kenna turned, beyond grateful for his rescue. She mouthed a thank-you before slipping her hand into his, letting him lead her out onto the dance floor.

A few other Sendarians were dancing together. Their motions were in sync…whimsical and graceful…with their hands held up to one another but never touching. Without questioning how they should dance, Liam hooked his arm around Kenna's waist, clasped one hand over hers, and led them in a simple box-step dance. She rested her free hand on his shoulder and let him lead.

"Good thing our mothers forced us to learn how to dance when we were kids, right?"

She nodded, recalling the old memories of the two of them dancing in Liam's parents' living room back in Kansas. "I think they were plotting to marry us off."

"I think they were too," he said, smiling. Though, his smile faded and he seemed to have something to say.

"About the other night. When we—" Kenna started, but he cut her off.

"It's sad that they lost Grace."

Kenna glanced around the garden area, taking notice of the holographic images displaying headshots of those the Sendarians lost. A man whom Kenna didn't know and Grace, the woman who'd been taken captive with Brody, Darci, Prue, and her mother.

"Did Brody know the woman?"

Liam shook his head while tightening his clasp on Kenna's hand. "Eryn did."

Oh, that's right, Kenna thought. *Eryn was the Sendarian who went to Boston to befriend the subjects up there while Darci went to Florida.* She made a mental note to say some encouraging words to Darci the next time she saw her about how they'd find Eryn too.

"Were Eryn and Brody close?"

This time, Liam nodded. "Yes. I think he's in love with her."

"Even now, after learning the truth about who she is?"

He shrugged. "I think so. He still isn't talking much."

"I'm sorry."

Liam continued to lead her around the dance floor. Kenna felt bad for Brody, especially now that she realized someone he cared for was still being held against their will—and with the same horrible captors that'd taken him.

While dancing, Kenna glanced up to see two more holographic images. One with Devaney's headshot and the other with Nick's.

"Devaney would've loved this place."

"I'm sorry about your friend," Kenna offered, remembering how the poor girl hadn't had the chance to experience this new world. Her death during the waking process had been an accident, but it hurt the same. She was a friend to Liam, Brody, and Julianna. Wanting to offer something positive, she told him, "And I'm sure Ben will find Julianna and the others."

Liam's smile briefly returned. "I hope so." He stared out to his left. She could tell he was looking at Nick's image on the holographic screen. "I don't think I'll ever recover after seeing what happened to Nick."

The knife sticking out of Nick's chest was traumatizing, but Kenna had been so focused on saving his essence, the blade barely stood out in her mind.

"You don't have to come to Sendara with us," Kenna said, not sure what answer she was expecting.

"Of course I want to come. I think you'll need all the help you can get down there."

"I'm not so sure. I think we'll only be in the way."

"Nonsense. Meegan can handle herself, and of course I'm always here for you if you ever need me."

"You know…" she said, then paused to gather courage to open up to him. Her whole life, she'd overthought everything, but right now she just wanted to tell Liam how she felt about him and have him return the sentiment. "I never met anyone who lived up to what we had back in Kansas. I mean, I dated guys, but always ended up comparing them…the relationship…to our friendship." Embracing the boldness swelling inside, she leaned in and kiss him. The second her lips pressed to his, he flinched, quickly leaning away.

His reaction caught her off guard. "Oh, I'm so sorry," she said, stepping away, but Liam held her tight, not letting her escape the dance. Once again, her feet moved in step with his.

"Don't apologize. It's my fault." He adjusted his hands on her back and inhaled deeply. "Kenna, there's something I need to tell you. And…and I should've told you the second we started messaging one another on Instagram."

Oh boy. This doesn't sound good.

"First, you should know that I felt the same. I compared every girl, friend or romantic partner, to you…to what we had. Eventually, I realized that no one would ever live up to what we had, so I let that dream go. Turns out I found someone who's pretty awesome. She's not you, but she's great. And we're engaged."

Oh, no. No, no, no. Kenna's mind whirled at the reality of Liam's words.

"It was wrong of me to kiss you the other night, but so right too. I never imagined you'd be in my life again. Like, within proximity, not just messaging over the internet. I let the moment get the better of me and…and I'm sorry."

There was no *them.* They would never be together. She'd been holding on in the hope that he would want her, but turns out he didn't. No one wanted her. Not Liam. Not Ben. No one.

Forcing her hand free, she told him, "I need some air." She spun away and took off between other dancing couples to the back of the garden. It was all too much. The worldly decisions she needed to make, the pressure of saving Nick and Ulissa, and now the reality that no one wanted her was more than her mental state could handle. Picking up the pace, she hurried into the dark end of the garden, where she could find a quiet spot to collect her thoughts before she had a full-on panic attack.

14

Here they were again... Sitting and hiding inside the small storage closet at the Priomh docking station. Logan had been able to land the transport ship south of the Priomh compound, and since Gemma knew these woods like the back of her hand, it hadn't been long before they were sneaking into the docking station and hiding.

Sabine said her goodbyes and left Gemma, Micah, Xander, and Logan to turn herself in. Logan stepped back from making any further decisions, letting Gemma take the lead from there on, which she was perfectly fine with. She thrived on that feeling of everyone looking to her for direction.

Her first decision was to have Micah hack into Breyah's agenda. Though, Sabine provided the log-in information before leaving them so there wasn't too much hacking on Micah's part. While he logged in and retrieved that, Gemma told Logan, "We'll need to make our way to my old place. It's not far from the Lead building, but we need to be careful no one sees us."

"And if there's someone living there?"

"We'll lock them in a closet or something, I don't know. Obviously, we can't let them tell anyone we're here, so we'll deal with that if the situation arises."

Logan nodded. "Okay, so we get to your place first." He faced the glass window embedded in the door. Again, Micah had disabled the two-way recording feature and visibility, only permitting them to see out and no one to see in. "The dock isn't too busy, but we should wait until everyone heads out for the day."

"Agreed," Gemma said, sliding her back against the cold wall, getting situated on the floor. Last time she'd been here, in this spot, she'd been anxious for two reasons. One, because they'd been waiting for Quaid to return from acquiring a transport vehicle, and two, because Anora's plans to swap out the princess for the captives had still been in motion and working. Things would be going to plan right now if that gróntah, Quaid, hadn't deviated from Anora's well-thought-out scheme for his own benefit. Gemma knew it wasn't easy losing a sibling, and felt sorry for Anora, but at the same time she was immensely glad the Beast was dead.

The next few hours passed quickly, especially since Gemma dozed off for a while. After Micah showed her Breyah's agenda, she knew exactly when and where she was going to approach her old friend.

"Maybe we should reconsider crashing the memorial?"

"*We* aren't doing anything. I'm going alone." Gemma reached up her sweatshirt's sleeve and scratched an itch below her elbow. *Damn, I need a shower.*

"If anyone sees you"—Micah continued his attempts to convince her not to contact Breyah during tonight's event—"we could end up in detaining cells. Or worse, shipped off to the closest Rhaltan interrogation facility."

His logic was right. If anyone other than Breyah caught her, it wouldn't be long before Micah, Logan, and Xander were caught too.

Then again, her old friend might turn her over to the Rhaltan too. She knew she needed to approach the entire situation with caution.

"I won't get caught," she said, handing Micah the plac.

"Okay, I think that was the last one. The docking station is empty." Logan faced the group. Then, to Micah he said, "Let her go. She knows this place better than any of us. Besides, we don't know how much time we have before whoever Quaid was communicating with gets here."

"Do we know where *they* are coming from?" Xander asked.

"No. I want to believe it's another rebel group or faction within South Sendara, but something in my gut tells me whoever they are, they're not from around here." Logan rubbed the jagged scar running along his neck, disappearing beneath the collar of his shirt.

"Invaders from another world?" Micah's orange eyes opened to their fullest. "That's not good!" he breathed while removing his baseball cap. Walking back and forth, he paced the small space. "We need to get out of here. I didn't sign up to stop or be involved with hostile aliens!"

Grabbing her brother's shoulders, she forced him to stop and face her. "I will talk with Breyah. Then we can leave." Gemma locked eyes with him, waiting for him to acknowledge her plan. When he did with a nervous nod, she said, "I'll be in and out. Logan will be flying us home to South Sendara before you know it."

"I can go back to the transport ship and wait for you guys. Plus, if you need a quick exit, I can pick you up wherever you need me to."

"Good plan, Logan. Thank you," Gemma said. She did one more check of the docking station before opening the door. "Stay silent and wait for us to contact you." Logan nodded, then darted out the door. Gemma faced Micah and Xander. "Let's go."

The only thing Gemma wanted to do was get to her place and take a long, hot shower and momentarily forget about all the chaos happening around her, because who knew what kind of welcome she'd get later on from her old friend.

15

The second she'd slipped away from the party to the back side of the enclosed garden area, Kenna searched out a place to collect her thoughts. It didn't take long for her eyes to adjust to the darkness, and she spotted a small nook nestled off in the corner. Situated in the center was a stone bench.

The solitude was perfect. She missed being able to hide away in her bedroom for hours. It hadn't mattered whether she ended up studying for school, reading a book, or gazing at the stars; it'd just been nice to be doing it alone, without the distractions of people's drama. Not that she didn't want to be there for her friends, but she knew how easily her thoughts could get overwhelmed. It was just one of those things she knew about herself and had to work with rather than against. *"We are who we are,"* her mother would often tell Kenna when she was younger and stressed out. *"You have to learn to accept who you are and the way you were created."*

She thought back to what she'd overheard her father saying to Breyah. "What did he mean when he said Honnah wanted *the* baby to be born to a Sendarian father and a human mother? Not a baby, but *the* baby." Staring up at the stars, she continued talking out loud to herself. "How is it possible that I'm that baby? And how am I supposed to bring all three of our worlds together?"

"I'd also like to know the answers to those questions." Ben's voice floated through the night air. Kenna sat up from her seat, the sheer fabric of her gown sliding across the stone surface as she searched the darkness. It wasn't until he strolled into the private nook that she made room for him on the bench. He sat, staring up at the speckled sky. "I wonder what your night sky looks like from your world."

Lifting her head, she admired the stars with him. "It depends on where you are, I guess. Some parts of our world have better views. You know, because of pollution."

"Pollution?" Ben dipped his head, and she caught his quizzical expression in the moonlight.

"Yeah, you know, when you manufacture something, there's a chemical residue or waste that goes up into the air."

"Your world has so much *pollution*"—he said the word as if he wanted to make sure he pronounced it correctly—"that you aren't able to see the stars?"

She nodded. "In some places, yes."

"That's unfortunate, I'm sorry."

"Don't be sorry. It's not your fault. We are who we are." She locked eyes with him, smiling. "I mean, as humans. Which, I already know your feelings on."

He inhaled a deep breath and nodded. "I shouldn't have said those things to you. I reacted poorly, please accept my apologies."

He's sorry? Wow, that was unexpected. She knew, of course, it didn't mean he was ready to pursue certain ways to *alleviate* his stress. She recalled their dream encounter when he tried to be intimate with her. Though, at the time, he hadn't realized she was a real person and that their dreams had somehow become more than just dreams—their essences had formed an interstellar connection, which she was still trying to understand. But in that moment, during one of their first encounters, he had wanted her. At first, his yearning to touch her had disturbed her, but now, after getting to know him a bit more and seeing him in person, she kind of wished he'd pursue it again.

"Apology accepted, but you're not entirely at fault. You're a nice guy, Ben, and I misinterpreted our little encounters for something that's not… Well, let's just say I liked the attention. It's usually Ally who the guys gawk at and want to date. Not so much me."

"Well, it's their loss."

Again, he surprised her. Sitting beneath the night sky saved her from him noticing the heat rising in her cheeks. He might not be able to see how his words made her feel, but she as hell felt the flush rising against her skin.

He pointed toward the party. "I assumed the human boy and you were close. Matched even."

"I was hoping, but no." She didn't mean to answer him so quickly, but something about sitting there and talking with him felt good. The anxiety building about all the *what-to-do*s and *oh-no*s seemed to melt away. At least for now.

There was a slight shift in his posture and she decided to change the subject. There didn't seem to be a point in talking about her love life with him. "Breyah put in a request to the queen, asking if it would be okay if my friends and I stayed for as long as we wanted." She'd hoped to catch a reaction from him about her staying, but nothing. He only continued to stare at the stars.

"Interesting. I doubt Queen Adalyss will approve such a request. But a lot of things are surprising me lately, so who knows." This time, he did turn and look at Kenna. "I wish you and your friend would reconsider coming tomorrow."

Her shoulders sagged and she thought, *I wish we would too.* Then to Ben, she said, "Yeah, I'm sorry about that. I think Meegan needs this, though. Something to keep her mind off of losing Nick."

"How long have you known she wasn't human?" He splayed his hands out along his pants, rubbing his thighs. Kenna got the feeling he wasn't fond of Meegan, or maybe of the idea that being Anumen didn't mean being a divine being. She couldn't help but think about the millions of Sendarians and how they would react to learning the truth.

"I only found out about Meegan just before your people took us."

He nodded, hands still pressed to his legs. "And are all Anumens as powerful as she is?"

"No," Kenna answered. "I mean, I'm still learning a lot myself." She lifted the yellow stone from around her neck. "This is an arcstone"—she waited until his attention was on her before continuing—"and it's a powerful stone from Anuminis…that's where the Anumen people were from…and some Anumens have the ability to ascend their essence into one of these stones when they die."

Ben slid closer, reached out, and held the slender crystal-shaped stone between two fingers. "There's an essence living inside this necklace?"

Kenna nodded. "Her name is Ulissa. I didn't know what the stone was when it was given to me with a piece of paper that had strange words written on it. I read the words and next thing I knew, there was this old woman surrounded by a golden aura, and only I could see."

Ben glanced up and searched the nook. "Is she here with us now?"

"No. She's resting."

"Resting?" he repeated with a concerned tone.

"That's a whole other story—"

"Tell me," he insisted, with a slight turn on the stone bench, facing her. "I want to know as much as possible about what's going on. I can't protect the Sendarians here and you if I don't know what I'm dealing with."

"Ben, you're not dealing with anything. Meegan isn't a threat." But then his words sank in: *"I can't protect the Sendarians here* and you *if I don't know what I'm dealing with."*

He said, "And you."

"Can I ask you something first?" When he nodded, she continued, "Do you think it would matter if the Sendarians of Sendara were told the truth about Isoldesse? That she isn't a goddess and is just a woman from another world?"

He sat in silence for a long moment before he answered, "Hmm, I think there will be denial among some communities, and curiosity in others."

"But do you think telling everyone the truth about Isoldesse is worth it?"

"I thought your father, Prince Gerard, said it was your destiny to divulge the goddess's true identity?"

She let out a frustrated groan. "Well, it's a shitty destiny, if you ask me. How am I supposed to make such a decision for an entire world?!"

He nodded. "It is a big decision."

"Big!" she exclaimed. "It's a massive, life-changing decision! And I don't want to be responsible for starting wars or conflicts."

"What does your friend think? Isn't she supposed to make this decision with you?"

"Oh, she wants everyone to know the truth, but not just the fact that Isoldesse wasn't a goddess… Oh, no. Meegan wants to tell everyone how Isoldesse was a traitor to her people and how she was the reason her world was destroyed. I think she wants to turn every Sendarian against Isoldesse."

"Yeah, that wouldn't be good."

They sat silent, and for a second, she thought he was done questioning her. She did just dump a lot of her baggage onto his lap. He soon stood and said, "We should talk more later, because I do want to know more, but right now we should get back to the party." He held his hand out to her.

Kenna stood, slipping her hand into his. It was the first time they'd touched, skin to skin, in real life. He'd held her twice yesterday. Once to shield her from when Meegan was confronting Quaid and the other out in the open field, after Kenna's mother had been flown away by the Athru. But neither time had she felt the warmth of his skin.

They walked toward the soft glow of fire from the torches lighting the memorial event. He released her when they reached the edge of the party, giving her a slight smile and a nod before excusing himself. She stood there, in no rush to return to her friends, and watched him say something to Breyah and Princess Emmalyn before weaving his way toward the exit.

"There you are," Meegan said. She moved in front of Kenna's view, blocking her from Ben leaving. "Where the hell have you been? You can't lecture me about disappearing in the middle of the night if you're going to pull the same shit without telling me!" Her voice was low but stern.

"Sorry." And she was. She didn't want to upset her friend or cause Meegan to make a scene. "I needed a minute to process everything."

"Everything? Like what?" Meegan crossed her arms over her chest, bunching the silky fabric of her dress beneath her arms.

"Liam told me he's engaged."

Meegan pivoted in the grass, searching among the partygoers for him. When she spotted him, Kenna thought her friend was going to approach Liam and confront him, but she only turned to Kenna and said, "You want me to turn him to stone?"

"What! No!" She leaned closer and asked, "You can do that? Turn people into stone?"

Meegan shrugged. "I could try," she answered with a mischievous smirk.

"Uh, let's not. I highly doubt your new Fawness powers were meant to dish out vengeance because I can't communicate well."

Meegan's black eyebrows pinched together. "Don't blame his lack of communication on you. He should've told you."

Yet another thing they couldn't agree on. A wave of anxiety resurfaced, and it almost got the best of Kenna, except she caught sight of Darci entering the garden space just as everyone started making their way out.

"The party's over," Ally said, approaching Kenna and Meegan. "I asked Holt if I could walk back with him to say goodnight to Prue. Do you guys want to come?"

Kenna's attention was across the grounds where Darci weaved through the crowd of Sendarians over to Breyah, where she whispered something to the Leadess. Breyah then faced Emmalyn and Gerard. Kenna assumed they said their goodbyes because seconds later her father and the princess followed everyone out of the event space. Meanwhile, Breyah and Darci lingered behind, waiting for the place to clear out.

"You go ahead," Kenna said to Ally. "We'll meet you back in our room."

Meegan stared at Kenna for a quick second before following her friend's gaze. "Yeah, we'll catch up later." Before Ally turned to leave, Meegan reached for her arm, and said with a low, serious tone, "Don't go anywhere else. Stay with Holt."

"I promise, I won't wander off." Giving Meegan's hand a quick squeeze, she pulled away and then headed to the exit. Holt was there, waiting for Ally along the gravel path. A few feet behind the Lead Medic were Liam and Brody, standing there with one of the Sendarian guards. Except, the guard wasn't wearing his standard uniform. It was the same uniform, but in a soft ivory rather than the monotonous gray. Liam glanced their way, making eye contact with Kenna, but he didn't hold the connection. He hadn't even bothered to come over and ask if her if she was okay or if they could talk more.

When the guard gestured for them to proceed out of the garden, Liam left without asking why Kenna and Meegan weren't coming.

Why is he making this out to be like I did something wrong? I should be the one giving him scowls and avoiding the conversation. Ugh!

Meegan held on to Kenna's arm, whispering one of her amulas.

"What are you doing?" Kenna quietly asked.

"I'm going to put a veil over us so they can't see us. Then we can find out what they're doing."

When Meegan finished, they cautiously made their way over to where Breyah and Darci stood. Neither paid them any attention, and it was comforting to know that Meegan's amula worked. Once they were within ten feet of the two Sendarian women, they stopped and waited. When the last Sendarian exited the party, Darci turned to Breyah and said, "I don't know why she reached out to me."

"It's fine," Breyah answered. "Where is she now?"

Darci pointed toward the back of the garden. "I told her to wait for us and not make a scene."

Kenna and Meegan snuck behind while listening.

Breyah only answered with, "I'm surprised she listened to you. She rarely listens to anyone other than herself."

This section of the garden was like a small labyrinth, and every so often they'd lose sight of the two Sendarians. It took a few wrong turns, but eventually they spotted the faint glow of light coming out from a path turning left. Meegan squeezed Kenna's hand, and they halted, staying within earshot. Both girls peeked around the tall shrub, into the private nook where Breyah and Darci were standing, talking to someone. The second they saw who the third person was, Kenna grabbed Meegan, trying to hold her back.

"No, Meegan! Don't!"

But it was too late. Her friend charged into the nook, white currents of electricity at her fingertips.

16

Gemma couldn't tell if the look on Breyah's face was happy or angry, but she took it as a good sign since her old friend hadn't called for security.

"I'm probably the last Sendarian you want to see right now," Gemma said.

Breyah's frame, outlined by moonlight and the faint glow of Sendara off in the night sky, moved closer. Her features came into view as she stepped away from the shadows of the shrubs. It had only been two years, but Gemma couldn't help but think how exhausted her old friend appeared.

"I've been waiting for you to return." Breyah reached out to Gemma, as if to pull her into a hug, but Gemma stepped away.

"Please, don't do that."

"Do what?"

"Pretend like everything's okay. Like I did nothing wrong."

The young Spiaire standing behind Breyah kept her distance, staring at the ground. Gemma wished they didn't have an audience, but oh well. And it was nice that her friend welcomed her back with open arms, but at the same time, she wanted Breyah to wake up…to get mad…scream at the world for being so messed up! Anything but this passive, compliant nature.

Gemma pulled out a small globe from her pocket. Shaking it, the inside flickered to life, illuminating the small space between the two Sendarian women. Breyah's expression was clear and exactly as always—composed and attentive to handle whatever situation a Leadess faces. Even a traitor that was once a dear friend.

"Of course, I'm upset with you, but you're one of my oldest friends, and I care about what happens to you." Ripples of night air caught against the sheer long sleeves of her white dress.

Damn it, Gemma silently cursed, then aloud asked, "Did Sabine find you?"

Breyah nodded, then with a slight head tilt, she gestured for Darci to jump into the conversation. Darci obliged, stepping forward. "Sabine showed up at the Lead building, turning herself in. Officer Ganecht—"

"You mean Bennach," Gemma cut in.

Darci looked to Breyah, who answered, "Yes, my brother is still here. And he had Sabine transferred."

"Already?" She didn't mean to sound abrasive but she'd hoped—no promised—to help Sabine.

"Bennach felt her presence would cause conflict among the researchers and community members."

There wasn't anything else she could do for Sabine. Not now. That problem would have to wait until Logan was flying them away from Priomh. Returning her attention to Breyah's brother, Gemma said, "I would've assumed he would've returned to Sendara after yesterday's incident." Though, she wasn't too surprised he hadn't left yet, but playing the naïve card was often the best way to fish for information.

"He's returning to Sendara come first light."

"Oh, back to the royal grounds or the Rhaltan Enforcer command center?"

"It's none of your concern where he's going," Darci snapped. "How about you just get to the point of why you're here so we can get to the 'throwing you in a locked cell' part of the evening?"

Breyah sighed. "That'll be enough, Darci." Turning to Gemma, she signaled with a look that the Spiaire wasn't wrong. "So, why are you here?"

"I came to warn you."

"Warn me? About what? The Athru have all left Priomh, and if you're worried about the Sendarian Quaid, well, he's dead."

It did make Gemma happy to officially hear the Beast was dead. "He deserved everything he got. He was a monster."

"He was your leader," Darci growled.

"No, he wasn't my leader. There are three Sendarians leading the Athru." Then, narrowing her eyes and scoffing, Gemma exclaimed, "Why the hegah am I explaining myself to you? How about you be somewhere else and give us some privacy?"

"Gemma," Breyah said with a hint of warning, "Darci has proven herself more than once since she's taken the vacant Spiaire position."

Ow, that hurt, Gemma thought. She didn't need Breyah pointing out the newbie was only here because Gemma left Priomh. Every day since she'd left, doubt lingered in the back of her mind, waiting to be recognized as either butterflies or regret. Turns out, it was regret.

"Fine, whatever." Gemma ignored the taut and continued explaining to Breyah, "Like I said, I came to warn you about a conversation overheard between Quaid and some outside threat. They're on their way to Priomh, looking for something that supposedly belongs to them…or something taken from them."

"And?" Breyah nonchalantly asked.

"And?" Gemma cocked her head. "There's some kind of threat coming this way. You need to evacuate—get everyone off world."

"This is all based on what? Your word? How am I supposed to trust you?" A long silence hung between them. Gemma wasn't sure how to answer, because Breyah was right. She had no reason to trust what Gemma was telling them. Breyah then added, "I haven't been notified of any incoming vessels by our security team. Nothing is showing up on our long-range satellites."

"I don't know if it's an alien ship or if it's some other Sendarian rebel group. I only know Quaid made some deal and it involves attacking Priomh."

"Maybe you're toying with us. Another ploy to sabotage the Aevo Compendium," Darci said from behind Breyah.

Gemma wasn't sure how to convince either one that she wasn't being dishonest. If she were in their shoes, she probably wouldn't believe her either.

From out of the darkness, two figures approached. Gemma shuffled backward, covering the glass globe with one hand, causing the light to dim within the small nook. Breyah and Darci faced the eavesdroppers.

"The threat isn't another Sendarian rebel group. The threat is from a race called the Obard, and I know exactly what they're coming for."

"Meegan?" Darci shuffled along the gravel, closer to the girl. When the second human came into view, the newbie Spiaire said, "Kenna? What are you two doing out here?"

"We saw you and wanted to make sure you were okay." Kenna sidestepped past the girl Darci had identified as Meegan. "And now we can see things are definitely not okay."

Breyah inserted herself into the conversation. "How are you freely wandering about?"

Gemma kept her distance, zoning in on Meegan—the one who'd killed Quaid—the one she suspected wasn't human—the one who was like Her. Gemma's heartbeat pounded in her chest and up into her ears, muffling their voices.

"Hey, are you okay?" Breyah finally glanced her way, slowly resting a hand on her old friend's forearm. "What's wrong?"

Stepping back, Gemma swallowed the lump that clogged her throat and forced herself to focus. Lifting her hand from over the glowing sphere in her palm, soft yellow light filled the nook.

Everyone stared at her. "I'm fine," Gemma curtly said. Then, taking a step toward Meegan, she asked with a sharp tone, "You're not human, are you? You're like Her—like Isoldesse, aren't you?"

Meegan didn't flinch. With narrowed dark eyes the girl closed the space between them in two long strides. Then, she jabbed a finger into Gemma's shoulder. "I should kill you right here for what you did to Nick. You and every other Sendarian in your little rebel group!" As she drew away her hand, white electricity charged at her fingertips, illuminating the space between them.

"No!" Kenna slid her body to block Meegan. "No more killing! And you," she said, facing Gemma, "you need to tell us more about this message you overheard."

"I don't give two shits about what she heard. I can handle the Obard," Meegan shouted, trying to push by, but the girl, Kenna, persisted in holding her back with a wide sweep of her arm.

"Stop! Seriously, Meeg."

Meegan rolled her eyes and circled back to where Darci and Breyah were standing.

"Just for the record," Gemma clarified, "I never wanted anyone to get hurt! I may be a selfish bitch who enjoys telling others what to do, but I would never purposely kill anyone!"

"Everyone needs to calm down." Breyah spread her arms in a peaceful gesture. The electricity in Meegan's fingertips faded. Breyah faced Kenna and Meegan. "You two need to get back to your rooms. Darci will escort you."

Darci moved to the opening of the nook, ready to walk the girls back to their quarters, but Kenna quickly approached the Priomh Leadess. "There is something we need to ask you before we go."

Curious, Gemma inched closer behind Breyah, wanting to hear what the question was.

"Can we borrow the arm cuff you're wearing?" She pointed to the piece of jewelry beneath the sheer sleeve of Breyah's blouse.

Breyah lifted her arm, rubbing the stone beneath the fabric. "My arm cuff? Why?"

"We need to check the stone." Meegan said, then looked to Gemma. "Can you turn the light off?" There was no please or pleasantries in her voice, and Gemma didn't want to argue. So, she shook the globe and the light inside faded, leaving them beneath the moonlight. The Anumen girl whispered something Gemma couldn't hear. Then, when a small ball of light bloomed from nothing, floating above the center of the girl's hand, Gemma stared in awe. It was small but filled the nook with a warm light.

Gemma couldn't believe it. This girl was like Isoldesse. The electricity from her fingers earlier and now this… She'd created a miniature sun in the palm of her hand. Seeing the magic only made Gemma want to know more.

Her attention shifted from the Anumen girl to Kenna, who pulled out a pendant necklace from beneath her shirt. Gemma recognized the deep yellow color of the stone dangling at the end. She'd been friends with Breyah long enough to know its hue matched that of the one affixed inside Breyah's arm cuff.

"This is an arcstone." Kenna held it up higher.

"It's from my world. Anuminis. And it has great power, as does yours." Meegan gestured to Breyah's arm again. "When female Anumens die, some are given the option to ascend their essence into an arcstone, allowing someone still alive to bond to it—giving them the ability to stay connected."

Gemma couldn't help but want to see the stone hanging from around the girl's neck. "Is there someone inside there?"

Kenna nodded. "Her name is Ulissa, and she's—"

"Isoldesse's sister," Gemma finished.

"How did you know that?" Breyah asked, slowly lowering her arm to her side. "I've never heard anything about Isoldesse having a sister."

"It's not directly mentioned in the Anumen Doctrine, but I was able to put two and two together from little hints here and there."

"Well," Breyah said, more to Kenna and Meegan than to Gemma, "if there's a Sendarian who knows all there is to know about the Anumen Doctrine and Isoldesse, then it's this one. She has every word of our law book memorized."

Gemma didn't acknowledge her friend's compliment. She was more interested in a piece of their goddess's home world right here before her. She wanted to hold it, to treasure it. But she knew there was no way the human girl would forgo it, or Breyah's arm cuff. The cuff was a family heirloom, gifted to Breyah by her mother.

"What do you need my arm cuff for? I mean, the arcstone within it?" Breyah asked, lifting her sleeve so she could remove the cuff.

Kenna twisted the slim stone with sharp edges in her fingers. "Yesterday"—she paused, glancing at Meegan, who gave her a slight nod to proceed—"before Nick fully passed on, we were able to capture his essence and store it in here with Ulissa."

"But," Meegan continued, "the arcstone isn't meant to hold two essences. So we need another one to transfer Nick's essence into."

Breyah handed Meegan the arm cuff. "So, I take it you'll be wanting to keep this arcstone?"

"That depends on if it's unoccupied." Meegan closed her eyes while holding Breyah's arcstone in her hand.

"Wait, you mean there's someone living inside there?" Gemma asked, pointing to the metal cuff.

"Maybe," Kenna quietly answered, trying not to disrupt Meegan's amula.

Everyone stood by, silently watching Meegan. Darci and Kenna waited on one side of Breyah, with Gemma on the other side. The stone briefly illuminated with a soft glow before going dark again. When Meegan opened her eyes, she let out a long sigh, glanced at Kenna, and said, "It's not vacant."

"Well then, who's in it?" Breyah asked before anyone else could.

Meegan handed the arm cuff back to Breyah and cursed. "I can't see them. I mean, I didn't really look. I just felt their essence and… Damn it!" she barked out, turning away from the group.

Kenna hurried to her friend's side and wrapped one arm around her shoulders. "It's okay. We'll find another one."

"Where? Where are we going to find another arcstone on such short notice?" Meegan's voice trembled. It was too dark to see if she was crying, but Gemma was all too familiar with the feeling of losing someone. Wanting to help, and hoping it would earn her some favor among the group, she said, "There's another stone like Breyah's at the temple of the Elemental Council."

"Are you sure?" Darci asked.

Gemma nodded. "Yes. I'm positive. The lead council member wears a headpiece with a golden stone affixed to the center."

"I've seen it," Breyah added, confirming to the others that Gemma wasn't lying. "It's much smaller than these two, but it is quite similar."

Shuffling away from her friend, Kenna rejoined the group. "And how are we supposed to get it? It's on Sendara and we're up here on Priomh."

The human had a good point. But saving the boy's essence wasn't a priority. Gemma was more concerned about the safety of the Sendarians here on the moon. She was about to remind Breyah of their priorities when the Leadess said, "I can speak to Bennach about having someone retrieve the stone for you. Maybe they could get it to you while you're on Sendara?"

They're going to Sendara? Kenna and Meegan? Out loud, Gemma asked with a hint of dread, "Oh, please tell me you aren't going to try and rescue the captives?"

"Oh, we're going," Meegan said, voice full of fury.

"Honnah is my mother," Kenna explained. "I need to bring her back."

Gemma's gaze shifted to Kenna. "Honnah is your mother? And…does that mean Gerard is your—"

"Father? Yes," Kenna answered.

Gemma eyed the girl up and down. "You don't look like a Sendarian."

"Well, I'm still trying to figure out the DNA specifics," Kenna joked, but Gemma caught the hint of exasperation woven into the girl's answer.

Breyah slipped on her arm cuff. "I guess there's no way to tell who is residing inside this arcstone?"

"Not without bonding to it," Meegan said.

"And believe me," Kenna added, "bonding to an arcstone shouldn't be taken lightly. It's for life, and if the arcstone becomes separated from you, there's a lot of pain. Like serious insides-are-melting kind of pain."

"I'll do it!" Gemma exclaimed, not wanting to miss the opportunity to learn more about the Anumen ways. "I'll bond to the arcstone."

"Like hell you will." Meegan turned, waving for Darci to lead the way. But when no one followed, she turned to see everyone staring at her. "You can't be serious?"

Gemma held out her hand to Breyah, who removed the cuff again and set it into her palm. Glancing it over in her hand, she said, "It would be an honor."

"Yeah, an honor you don't deserve!" Meegan snapped.

Breyah shrugged. "Well, it can't be me. I have no desire to add any more responsibilities to my already overwhelmed life, but it would be comforting to know who resides inside the arcstone—and I couldn't have asked for a better volunteer. I trust Gemma to do what is best for Sendara, no matter what happens."

Gemma smiled at her old friend. "Thank you, and I promise I will."

"I don't even know why we're discussing this!" Meegan pointed to the arm cuff. "It's not important to know who the hell is in there!" Gemma held the piece of jewelry to her chest, not wanting anyone to snatch it from her.

"I think if she wants to, then let her." Kenna said, leaning in to Meegan's ear, whispering secrets no one else could hear. After their private conversation was over, they turned to the others.

"Fine. Whatever, it's your life. But just know that I can't guarantee that your body will bond with the arcstone. The stone may reject you, especially because you're not Anumen." Meegan gritted her teeth, obviously not wanting to agree to this.

Gemma wondered what Kenna had said to Meegan that changed her mind, but whatever it was, she was grateful. Clutching the piece to her chest, she told them all, "I understand, and I will listen to whatever you tell me to do." She said the words, and meant them, even if they were strange leaving her lips. She'd never purposefully put herself in a vulnerable position like this, especially with strangers. But Breyah was here, and she trusted Breyah.

Meegan studied Gemma for a long moment, everyone stood quiet, waiting for Meegan's response. She finally broke the silence and said, "Just so you know, the moment we have another disagreement…the second you abuse the arcstone's power…I will end you. Are we clear?"

A smile spread on Gemma's lips. "Understood."

She didn't care that this once-in-a-lifetime opportunity came with a threat of death hanging over her head. She wanted to prove her intentions were good not only to Meegan and Breyah, but more importantly—to Isoldesse.

17

Meegan and Kenna followed behind Breyah and Gemma, with Darci trailing after them. For the most part, the group walked in silence. Every so often, Kenna looked as if she were going to say something, but she never did.

At some point, Meegan thought, *she's going to have to come around and not care so much. These people don't need coddling—they need the truth. And more importantly, they need to separate themselves from my world.*

The back path they followed out of the gardens curved away from the neighborhood. Small glass orbs of light staked into the path's side illuminated as they walked by, then faded a few seconds after they'd passed.

"How much farther?" Meegan asked.

Breyah glanced over her shoulder. "It's up ahead on the right."

Amid a cluster of trees was a home similar to the ones they'd seen earlier while driving out to Princess Emmalyn's house. This one, though, was mainly a single story with a smaller cube-like room on the second floor, set toward the back side. Unlike the other homes, it had no windows on the front or sides, just horizontal planks blending in with the surrounding forest.

"Are we good?" Kenna asked, nudging her elbow into Meegan's arm.

"Yeah, but you've got to stop acting like I'm the villain."

"Uh, you were going to hurt her." She subtly pointed one finger to Gemma.

"Maybe… Maybe not. I needed her to know that I'm not weak. That I'm willing to do whatever to those who hurt the people I care about."

"Yeah, it's the *whatever* part that worries me."

Meegan ignored her comment. "You need to stop trusting them or taking everything they say as truth. They've done nothing but lie to us."

The two girls glanced over their shoulders to Darci, who lingered a good distance behind, giving them some space.

"I know, but that was also before everything that happened yesterday. Now we know the truth about what they're doing and why they brought us here. No one is lying to us anymore. They're trying to figure out what to do next just like we are. Not everyone is against or after you, Meeg."

"And her?" It was Meegan's turn to point to Gemma. "How come we're all of a sudden trusting the lady who was involved with kidnapping your mom and killing Nick?" It pained her to even mention his name. She hadn't let herself get emotional in front of others since his death, but hiding her grief was becoming harder and harder. The only thing keeping her from breaking down was the hope that they could save his essence—get him into his own arcstone. But even that was slowly dwindling now that the closest arcstone was millions of miles away on Sendara.

She'd only agreed to help the vile Sendarian woman bond with Breyah's arcstone because Kenna suggested that the Anumen inside might know of another arcstone, maybe one closer to them. But Meegan saw a different opportunity, one she didn't share with

Kenna. If Gemma bonded to the arcstone, then the protection shield would fall, giving her the chance to evict whoever was in there. Then they wouldn't have to worry about finding another arcstone.

When they reached the front door, it opened before anyone could knock or enter a code to unlock it. The tall man Meegan had spoken to at Prue's house appeared. That day seemed so far from now.

"You?" Meegan asked, remembering they'd seen him running from the old research facility yesterday. "What happened to the sweet guy we met back on Earth? You know, the one who spent the day with Prue, taking long walks and bonding over dinner."

His eyes narrowed, and he stared past Gemma and Breyah to Meegan and Kenna. "Why are they here?"

Gemma walked in without answering the man's question. Breyah, on the other hand, said, "Beannaith, Micah. It's good to see you after all these years."

His attention shifted from the girls to Breyah. "Don't *beannaith* me. What the hegah is everyone doing here?"

Meegan, Kenna, and Darci all stepped inside. Micah shut the door behind them and said, "We're supposed to be lying low."

"Plans have changed." Gemma poured herself a glass of water in the small kitchen area.

Not wasting any time, Meegan scanned the open living space for somewhere to activate the bond. "Here," she said, picking up one of the accent pillows and placing it at the end of the long white sofa. "You'll probably want to lie down for this."

"What's going on?" Xander's voice filled the room as he walked in from the backyard. He pressed a finger to the small black glass panel embedded in the wall. Meegan caught the faintest glimpse of blue energy activating over the doorway leading outside.

"There you are," Kenna said. "Not that anyone was worried about you, but where have you been?"

Xander ignored Kenna and went straight to the couch, glaring at Meegan. "You stay the hell away from Gemma. She had nothing to do with what went down yesterday."

"You need to get out of my face or else," Meegan seethed.

Everyone in the room froze. The sudden volatile attention being thrown at her wasn't helping Meegan keep her frustration in check. Even Kenna, fists clenched at her sides, seemed hesitant to get between Meegan and Xander.

"Or else what?" Xander puffed up his chest.

A smile cracking at the corners of her lips, she thought, *This asshat has a death wish.*

"Xander, it's fine. I asked them to come." Gemma held out a hand to Breyah. The Leadess slipped off the arm cuff and gave it over. Then, Gemma said, "I promise to always take care of it. I know it's been in your family for generations, and it means a lot to you."

Breyah nodded. "I know you will. And I appreciate you saying that."

"All right, come over here and lie on the couch." Meegan then told everyone else, "The bonding process is different for each individual. And because she's not Anumen, I have no idea what's going to happen."

"Bonding process?" Micah and Xander said in unison.

"Shush," Gemma said, then lay back on the sofa. When she was comfortable, she looked up to Meegan. "I'm ready."

Meegan rolled her eyes. "It's your life. Just know that once you're bonded to the arcstone, there's no undoing it." After Gemma nodded, Meegan told her to repeat these words while touching the stone: "*Banna idir dufiur et gohdeo.*"

Gemma did, and the second the last syllable left her lips, her eyes fluttered shut. Her body went limp, sagging into the sofa's cushions.

"Babe!" Xander shoved past Meegan and knelt next to Gemma's head. He stroked her hair. "Is she okay?"

"As far as I know, yes. Her body is in the initial bonding stage." Then, to Breyah, she said, "The bond may not take, and if that happens you get your arm cuff back."

"And if it does?" the Leadess asked, staring down at her friend from behind the sofa. "What happens then?"

Meegan made her way to the front door, the skirt of her dress trailing with a flutter. She was eager to get back to her quarters and get out of this ridiculous outfit. She'd done her part. The damage was done. Now, it was a matter of time to see if the arcstone bond would form. To answer Breyah's question, Meegan said, "Well, if the bond takes hold, then the first thing I'll need is the name of the Anumen residing inside the stone. After that… Well, we'll get to that when we cross that bridge." Without another word, Meegan opened the front door and strode outside.

The fresh night air grazed her heated skin. The only relief she had to ease her frustration of attending pointless parties or entertaining enemies looking for forgiveness was the fact that she might be able to use this situation to her benefit. She didn't care who was in that arcstone, because if it came to them or saving the love of her life, she wouldn't hesitate to choose Nick.

From inside the house, she overheard Darci telling Breyah, "I can walk them back to their rooms." And then a few seconds later, Darci and Kenna were outside with her.

Kenna hurried to Meegan's side as they followed Darci. It didn't take them long to reach the center of the Priomh compound, where the Lead building towered over the surrounding one and two story homes.

Before they reached the front entrance, Kenna finally broke the silence and asked, "So, you're just going to leave like that? Not tell them anything else?"

"Like what?"

"Like about how she'll feel separation pain if she removes the arm cuff or how the Anumen might not be of good intentions…or…" Kenna stumbled on her words.

There was no point in explaining what Meegan had planned for the arcstone if the bond was successful. It would only bring about another argument. But it was their best option—to boot out whoever was in there—to save Nick.

"She's a big girl. She can figure all that out on her own."

Kenna and Darci exchanged concerned looks as they entered the Lead building.

"Listen. I'm tired and I want to get out of this dress." Meegan glared at Darci, then snapped, "Just show us back to our rooms so we can get a good night sleep. Tomorrow's mission is what we should be focused on. Okay?" It wasn't so much as a question to be answered, as she marched off before either Kenna or Darci could answer. Besides saving the captives on Sendara, the only thing that mattered was saving Nick. And the *how* part of accomplishing those tasks was becoming irrelevant.

18

When they arrived at the common area of their guest quarters, Meegan continued toward Kenna's and Ally's room while Kenna stayed behind to say goodnight to Darci.

"Are you coming with us tomorrow? To Sendara?"

Darci nodded. "Is that okay?"

Shrugging, Kenna said, "It doesn't matter to me if you come or not." Then, seeing the girl's shoulders sag, she added, "You know it's wrong, right? What you're doing here? You can't take people from their homes."

Darci's eyes widened as she tried to explain. "But try to understand from our point of view. If a god asked you to do something, wouldn't you do it?" She quickly added, in a Darci way, "I mean, we didn't technically know she wasn't a goddess, per se, but if Superman came to your world and didn't tell you he was from another world *and* didn't correct people when they referred to him as a god…" She inhaled a breath, then continued, "…you can't blame the people for creating an entire faith system around said person. Especially if Superman writes out an entire law book for you to follow *and* builds a research facility on the moon and tells you to continue their work while they're gone—"

"Darci! I get your point." Kenna needed to stop her before she rambled on all night.

Darci closed her mouth and smiled. "I'm trying to process everything too. Separate the truth from what's written in our history books."

It wasn't an easy task, trying to understand the truth of something when your entire world's beliefs were so set in stone. Another reason Kenna was hesitant to tell the Sendarians who Isoldesse truly was. What did it matter where she came from or that she could bleed and die like any other organic being? What harm could come from letting Sendara continue on its current path? Kenna still wasn't sure revealing the truth was the best solution.

"Can I ask you something?" Kenna moved to one of the semicircular sofas. Darci followed and sat with some space between them. "How do you think your world would react if they knew the truth about Isoldesse?"

Darci's expression pinched as she thought about her answer. "I don't know. It's been our way for as long as anyone can remember. And what does telling everyone the truth about Isoldesse involve? Like just saying, *Hey, she's not really a goddess, now go about your day* or were you thinking more like, *Hey, she's not really a goddess, now scrap everything you've ever known and let's start from the beginning, rewriting your entire way of life—what you're to believe and the law systems you abide by?*"

"I see your point." Kenna scootched closer. "So, you can see the predicament I'm in. Supposedly it's Meegan's and my destiny to tell the Sendarians the truth about Isoldesse, but I'm worried that the truth will do more harm than good."

Darci glanced out the glass wall behind her. Then, after a long moment, she looked back at Kenna. "I think you've interpreted what Prince Gerard said with only one option: tell or don't tell. I'm no specialist when it comes to politics or running a world, but I do read a lot."

"Yes, you do," Kenna said with a smile.

"So, don't limit your decision to one or two options. And don't rush into anything, because you get to go home afterward…back to Earth…while we have to live with the outcome of your decision."

Hearing that last piece of advice hit Kenna hard. Whatever she and Meegan decided needed to have a positive outcome. They couldn't start a conflict or create doubt, then wave goodbye and head home. Whatever they decided, they needed to make sure the Sendarians' world wouldn't fall apart. *Does that mean I won't be returning to Earth anytime soon? What would a life on Sendara look like? Would Ben be okay with me staying?*

"It's late, and we have an early flight come first light." Darci stood, rested a hand on Kenna's shoulder, and squeezed gently before leaving the common area.

Kenna eventually, after sitting and thinking more about the decision she'd have to make, sauntered off to her room, where Ally was sitting on the sofa with a mug in hand. "Where's Meeg?"

"In her room, showering," Ally said, pointing to the wall where Meegan's room was on the other side. She got up and placed her mug on the counter inside the small nook. "She told me about Breyah's arcstone, said goodnight, and then left for her room. I'm sorry."

"It's not your fault." Kenna took out some clean clothes to change into. "I'm going to get out of this gown, shower, and head to bed too."

Ally nodded, then after setting her mug on the low table in front of the sofa she climbed into bed, sliding over to the farthest side next to the wall.

"Night," Kenna said to Ally before locking the door to the washroom. Her thoughts were racing with how to solve the influx of problems. The biggest one being how to keep her best friend from harming anyone else.

Once Kenna shut her eyes, it didn't take long to drift off to sleep. After yesterday's traumatizing escapade of facing off against a psychopathic rebel leader and losing one of her closest friends, her body finally gave in, subduing her into a deep slumber.

Though, the moment of sleep didn't last long.

"I thought I might run into you." A familiar voice caught her attention.

Opening her eyes, she sat up. A warm breeze drifted by. Long stems of grass or weeds with fuzzy ends surrounded the blanket she woke on. Tall trees with furrowed brown bark stretched up high, warm sunlight glinting between branches covered in thick bushels of leaves.

"This is close to my childhood home," Ben's voice said.

She shifted her backside, looking behind her to see Ben sitting on the blanket. "It's beautiful here."

"It is. One of my favorite places to go as a predult. I never enjoyed the social life like Breyah and Gemma. I enjoyed coming out here and reading, admiring the untouched part of Sendara."

Birds flew overhead, and Kenna sat still, listening to their songs. "How is it that this feels so real?"

Leaning back on his hands, he shrugged one shoulder. "You tell me. This is all happening because of you and your friend…I suspect."

"I don't know. Maybe."

A hint of something bloomed in Kenna's chest. It felt like warmth—like when you step outside on a hot summer day after being indoors all day with the AC running like an icebox. She looked at him as he stared up into the trees, a small smile forming at the corners of his lips.

He was happy. That warm feeling in her chest came from him.

"I'm looking forward to seeing your world tomorrow."

The hint of a smile faded. "I wish it were on different terms. Going to South Sendara isn't a vacation or sightseeing trip."

"I know. And you know it wasn't my idea to go, right?"

He nodded. "Couldn't you try and convince her to stay behind?"

"I wish. Besides, she might actually be able to help you. She's extremely powerful now that she's unlocked these new powers."

He breathed in deeply, then exhaled and said, "But she doesn't have them under control yet, and that's a liability."

He wasn't wrong. Kenna feared her friend might react before consulting Ben or her. "I'll stay close to her. I promise."

Ben seemed to appreciate her words because the corners of his lips curled up again. "Maybe when this is all done, I can take you here for real, instead of while we're sleeping."

"That would be nice. I do hope we could at least be friends, if anything."

They sat there on the blanket in silence, admiring the woods around them. Kenna wasn't sure how much time had passed when she finally said, "I think I should go. I want to get some sleep before we leave tomorrow." Lying back on the blanket, with him looking down at her, as if he were going to lean in and kiss her, she said, "Goodnight, Ben."

And as she drifted off into the darkness of sleep, she heard his words floating through her mind. "Goodnight, Princess."

19

The air smelled sweet, like Hiccum flowers. Curling her legs up to her chest, Gemma savored the caress of silky sheets against her skin while her head sank deeper into the soft pillow.

"This is how I want to wake up every morning," she groaned rolling over and cracking her eyes open. The first thing she saw was the small bouquet of branches sprouting out of one of her drinking glasses. Coin-sized yellow flowers bloomed at the base of each of the branches' green leaves.

Rolling onto her back, then staring up at the wooden beams crisscrossing the white ceiling, she wondered if it all had been a bad dream. Her leaving Priomh to join the Athru…sabotaging the Earth Aevo Compendium…falling in love with a human…and putting her Priomh family in danger. She prayed to Isoldesse that it had been, and she was waking up to report to work as one of Breyah's Spiaires.

"Babe, you up?"

Gemma sat up in her bed, stretching her eyelids while her bedroom door automatically slid into the wall pocket. "I'm up."

Xander rested on the edge of the queen-sized bed. "Darci stopped by with some clean clothes for Micah and me. A few days' worth, actually."

"Well, isn't she just the delightful Spiaire." Stretching, she slid her legs out from beneath the sheets. "Where's Micah?"

"He's downstairs, doing something about the security in your house. He's complaining that they're watching us, especially now that they know we're here."

"Ah. He must be rerouting all the video feeds within the glass surfaces."

"What glass?"

Lifting an arm, she gestured with a wide sweep of her hand. "Any glass surface has the capability to record."

One eyebrow raised, while looking about the room, he asked, "Seriously? *All of the glass*?"

"Seriously. Now, can I have a minute to get dressed?"

His attention returned to Gemma. Leaning in, nuzzling her neck, he asked, "But what if I stayed and helped you get dressed?"

A soft laugh escaped her lips. "Maybe later. Right now I need to figure out what the hegah I got myself into." The arm cuff felt like a regular old metal band strapped to her biceps. There was no energy or power or magic infusing her body, which made her wonder if the bond had actually taken hold.

Thinking about it more, she wondered, *Would that be such a bad thing? What if I rushed into something that could kill me?*

After kissing the top of her head, he exited her bedroom.

Alone, she stood by the glass wall stretching the length of the spacious room. Her house was one of the more private homes set on the outskirts of the compound. The Endless Forest circled her backyard with Mount Nocholus centered in the distant background. Logan was out there, waiting in the transport ship for them. She'd have to have Micah send word that plans had changed. That they weren't leaving anytime soon. Logan wouldn't be happy about that, but tough shit.

She eventually meandered into her washroom, turned on the misting showerheads, and let the room fill with soothing, hot steam. All Gemma had ever wanted was to prove herself to her goddess. To help Anora take down a hierarchy that twisted the words of the Anumen Doctrine to their benefit. The Sendarians deserved better and shouldn't have been forced to live such monotonous lives with so many limits and excessive restrictions. Earth might've been a shithole, but at least its citizens had the freedom to indulge and treat themselves with high-end luxuries. There had to be a middle ground somewhere between the two worlds. That was what she'd hoped to achieve by helping the Athru, but it seemed that wasn't going to happen.

"Linc," she said out loud.

"*How can I be of assistance?*" the woman's voice responded deep within Gemma's ear canals.

"Portrait-sized mirror."

Within seconds, a section of the dark glass wall transitioned into a reflective surface showing Gemma from the waist up. She rubbed the yellow stone embedded in the center of the arm cuff and silently prayed that she'd made the right decision—that she hadn't bonded her essence with someone who would make her life miserable.

It didn't take long for the misting steam to fog up the mirror, and Gemma was about to undress and enjoy her shower when the faint outline of a woman standing behind her appeared. Spinning, she saw no one else in the washroom. She turned back to the mirror, and the woman became more prominent, surrounded by a soft yellow glow. Gemma stepped aside. Even though the woman wasn't in the room, she didn't like being that close.

"Hello? Are you the Anumen in the arcstone?"

The old woman cocked her head, gaze looking Gemma over and landing on the arcstone. She seemed to be focused on Gemma's face. When she opened her mouth to speak, her lips moved but no sound came out.

"I can't hear you," Gemma said, pointing to her own ear. "Are you an Anumen?"

The woman nodded, her short, straight black hair brushing the tops of her shoulders. The white pantsuit she had on looked like something Rian would've designed, simple yet elegant.

"Can you tell me your name?" Gemma touched a finger to the glass and wrote her own name on the foggy surface.

The woman pressed one hand to the glass, her lips muttering words Gemma couldn't hear. Then on the glass surface, Sendarian letters appeared, one by one. When the woman was done, her reflection faded from view.

Gemma gasped. With one hand pressed to her chest, she read the name on the mirror. *Isoldesse.*

PART

TWO

SENDARA

20

There were no windows on the transport ship, and it was killing Kenna not to be able to see Sendara as they made their descent. Before they'd left, Holt activated the two-way comms feature on their implants he'd embedded deep within their ear canals. So, in addition to being able to translate the Sendarian language, Kenna now had the ability to call anyone within their mission group, which included Meegan, Darci, Liam, six Priomh security guards, and Ben.

Ben walked into the passenger cabin of the transport ship and circled around everyone. Twelve high-back seats were positioned around a large round table. Though, for eighty percent of the flight, the seats were reclined into a curved position, allowing a more comfortable flight during sedation.

Kenna wasn't crazy about being put under again, but Holt reassured her it was nothing compared to the deep sleep they'd been under during the journey between Earth and Priomh. Maura, the Lead Medic aboard the transport ship, also reassured everyone the stasis was meant to be temporary and was required for all Sendarians when traveling between Priomh and Sendara. Kenna worried Liam might experience another complicated waking process, but decided not to say anything until they crossed that bridge. She was still upset with him for not telling her about his engagement.

Now that the majority of the space voyage had passed, and they were all awake and okay, she could focus on their mission of rescuing her mother and the others. All twelve of the passenger chairs were upright and closer to the oversized round table in the center of the cabin. Meegan sat to her right while Darci occupied the chair to her left. When Ben entered the cabin, then walked around the opposite side, she couldn't help but turn her attention from her friends to him. It annoyed her that he didn't glance her way and instead continued over to one of the Priomh security guards.

He needed to get over his issues with non-Sendarians being here on the mission. Still, after they'd talked privately at the memorial, and then again while dreaming—sitting on the blanket out in the woods—she thought she'd gotten through to him. She liked that side of him. The more relaxed and sociable man. She wasn't crazy about this serious and authoritative Sendarian. It was almost as if last night's encounters never happened.

Darci leaned her elbows on the glass surface of the white table. Unlike the muted-blue jumpsuits Kenna, Meegan, and Liam were given to wear, Darci's clothes were similar to those of the security team. Dark brown everything, except the black sleeveless vest over her shirt.

Kenna couldn't help but wonder if her friend's bohemian style all those months on Earth was just part of her act or if she really liked the loose, flowing clothes. Kenna hadn't seen Darci outside of *work* on Priomh. Which then sparked thoughts about what her house looked like. Did she have pets? What did she do for fun on Priomh? Who were her friends on Priomh?

"He's probably double-checking our supplies," Darci answered.

Kenna blinked. "What?"

"You were staring at Ben, and I assumed you were wondering what he's doing."

"Actually, I was thinking about you. What your life must be like on Priomh."

A smile spread on Darci's face. "Your brain never stops, does it? Always thinking something?"

It was Kenna's turn to crack a smile. "I can't help it. One thought leads to another, then another."

Darci leaned closer, and after glancing over to Ben, she whispered, "When we get back, and everyone is safe, I'm going to have to have you over to my place and introduce you to Khal." Darci giggled, and Kenna couldn't help but react as if someone had just invited her to her first college party.

"There will be no Khal on this trip," Ben said, standing behind them.

"Of course," Darci said. She sat straight up in her seat, all happiness wiped from her expression.

Kenna twisted in the chair as Ben continued walking behind. She called, just before he could disappear down the corridor, "If you had asked, you'd know she wasn't offering Khal until afterward, when we were safely back on Priomh."

"Even then, no Khal." He didn't wait for Kenna to respond and vanished down the dark corridor.

Furry burned inside her. *What's his problem?* She only relinquished the scowl crossing her face when Liam asked, "What's Khal?"

This had been the first time he'd spoken to her since last night at the memorial. And since she wasn't exactly sure what *Khal* was, she looked to Darci.

"It's similar to your alcohol," Darci explained to Liam as he strapped into the captain-style seat. "Though, unlike you with a bazillion different options, we're limited to a select few." She then quickly added, in her familiar bubbly tone, "Khal is the popular choice among the taverns and bars mainly because it comes in a range of potencies. Some are much, much stronger than others. I once read this article about how they make—"

"Then Ben's probably right," Meegan cut into Darci's babbling narrative about the popular alcohol. She'd been sitting in a half-reclined position, eyes closed, situated between Kenna and Liam.

Darci shimmied into the cushions of her chair. Kenna leaned over the upholstered arm and pointed out, "Just like old time, right? You getting all excited about something and Meegan shutting you down." When Darci grinned, Kenna added, "That's a good thing, Darci. Don't worry. She'll come around."

Reaching for Kenna's arm, Darci's smile widened and whispered, "I'm still having you over to my place after all this is done. I don't care what Bennach says."

They shared a subtle giggle. Then, Kenna said, "I'd like that." She was about to ask more questions about the Sendarian moon, except one of the security guards strode over and asked Darci to come and look at their scheduled route. With Darci gone, Kenna turned to Meegan. "You should give her another chance."

"I am." Meegan still had her eyes closed. "You should be careful not to trust her too much."

"I am."

This time, Meegan opened her eyes and inclined the chair to an upright position. "Are you? Because it seems like you two are besties all over again. We can't trust them."

"I think we can." Kenna glanced past Meegan to Liam. "I know who I can trust."

"Kenna, I'm—"

"No! We're not doing this here. So, no!" Kenna lowered her hand that she'd shot up to stop Liam from continuing. Looking at Meegan, and wanting to change the subject, she asked, "You sure the glamours will hold?"

"Yes."

"Even if we're there for days?"

"If they don't, I'll release the amula and cast a new one. Stop worrying," Meegan said, her attention focused on Darci and the guards.

Darci finished up and returned to her seat. With an elated expression, she said to Kenna, Meegan, and Liam, "You guys are going to love Sendara. It's a lot like Earth…" She paused, gaze drifting to the ceiling while her brows pinched. "Well, now that I think about it, most of the worlds we observe are quite similar in terrain."

"Really?" Kenna wondered how exactly other inhabitable worlds compared to Earth. A thrill fluttered in her gut, and she hoped she'd get to find out—that's if she decided to take Breyah up on her offer. *Stay or go. Stay or go. Ugh, just another decision needing to be made.*

"Oh, yeah. You'd be surprised. Most of the worlds we've visited have similar ecosystems. There are some variations, depending on the chemical and elemental components, but for the most part oxygen is oxygen, carbon is carbon, and hydrogen is—"

"Are you going to list off every element in the periodic table?" Meegan cut Darci off with a curt glare.

"Sorry," Darci said, cowering into her seat.

"Hey." Kenna returned her friend's glare. "I actually wanted to hear more."

"Why?" Meegan rolled her eyes and sighed. "You're forgetting this isn't an exploration trip to study Sendara. I know you want to get all academic and learn as much as you can about these beings and all those other worlds they observe, but we can't. We're here to rescue your mother, Julianna, and the other captives."

"I know that," Kenna wearily replied. "But afterward—"

"There isn't an afterward, Kenna. We're going home afterward." Meegan abruptly stood up. "You can learn all about the worlds out in the universe at home—on Earth."

Kenna knew there was some truth to this. Going home didn't mean she had to stop learning about the worlds out there. Especially with the knowledge Meegan had and if her dad and mom returned with her. But she also didn't want to miss out on an opportunity to learn more about the Sendarians while they were here. And maybe "while they were here" didn't have to end so soon. What was a year or two? She told herself it would be like going to college for another two years. Like getting her master's degree, but abroad. Breyah did mention putting in a request with the Queen for Kenna to stay on Priomh. Though, maybe now wasn't the time to tell Meegan about that offer.

"Kenna," Meegan said, gripping the top of the chair, "I know you're sitting here trying to weigh which option is the right one, but there's nothing to decide. We can't stay. I won't stay. And neither will you." Then, addressing Darci, she asked, "Where's the bathroom?"

Darci pointed at the corridor Ben had walked down.

Meegan didn't move. She held Kenna's gaze, as if she was waiting for Kenna to agree. Kenna didn't want to but didn't want to start an argument either.

"Whatever. I'm pretty sure my mom will want to leave anyway."

"She most definitely will." Then, without another word, Meegan turned and disappeared down the transport corridor.

When the transport finally landed, everyone stood from their seats. Kenna was eager to get outside and see Sendara. Darci stayed close but didn't say much, not after Meegan had blown up about them not staying on Priomh.

"All right, listen up," Ben called out the second he stepped out from the rear corridor. "You three stay here with Spiaire Darci," he said to Kenna, Meegan, and Liam, "while the team and I bring our supplies to the transport vehicles." He pointed to Meegan. "These are for you." He set a black duffel bag onto the glass table and slid it across the top.

Meegan grabbed the bag and unzipped it, and Kenna looked over her friend's shoulder to see what was inside.

Ben continued, "Spiaire Darci will assist you with those." He turned and waved for the Priomh security detail to follow. Almost out the door, he stopped and turned back to the group. "Oh, and don't forget to"—he waved one hand in a circling motion—"put disguises on before you exit the ship. That's an order." He didn't wait for a response. He just turned and left.

"Which do you want to do first?" Darci asked with a small voice.

"I'll change Liam and myself while you strap one of those transessent stones onto Kenna."

"Are you sure I should put it on?" Kenna asked, inspecting the metal bracer. The patina of the metal reminded her of an aged copper roof. Completely blocking off her connection to Ulissa didn't sit well.

Darci held up a slim metal apparatus with a clear tip. "I'll have this with me at all times. So, if you ever want to take it off, we can."

"Plus, I think blocking the arcstone connection will help with stretching how much time we've got left to move Nick. I promise, she'll be fine," Meegan said with a long, reassuring gaze.

Kenna held out her right arm, and Darci attached the bracer. She slipped the slender tool beneath the bracer's edge, and the cool tip transformed into a smooth gel-like substance. Along the top, the seam sealed, camouflaged in the metal.

"There, all done," Darci said, setting the tool onto the table.

"You don't need one?"

"My Linc"—she pointed to her ears—"has the ability to track my biometrics, and more. The implants in your ears are limited to translation, communication, and basic biometrics like heartbeat and breathing. The implanting process when attaching a Linc to the body is complicated and lengthy, and not worth the time and energy to attach to…" She paused, offering a grin as she finished. "…visitors." Then, after shaking off the uncomfortable silence between them, she continued, "So, a few of the earlier Sendarian researchers created these bracers, powered by the transessent stones."

"They can track our location as well, yes?" Kenna asked, rubbing her fingers over the smooth white oval stone affixed in the center.

Darci nodded. "Yes, but the range is limited, and even then, the location isn't always exact. We don't use the bracers to track…visitors, mainly because there are cameras everywhere and that has always been the most effective way to find people."

"I didn't even think about cameras in our rooms."

Darci shrugged. "Yeah, they're everywhere." She turned and pointed to the strip of black glass embedded in the wall next to the corridor. "Any glass surface, like that one or a window, has the ability to record."

"How do I look?" Liam asked from behind them.

Kenna and Darci faced a transformed Liam. Kenna couldn't help but gawk at his blond hair and orange eyes. She reached out to touch his hair but pulled away, remembering his confession last night.

"I like the brown hair better," she said softly, looking away to find Meegan.

He ran a hand through his short hair. "Yeah, I feel like I should be carrying a surfboard or something."

Darci laughed. "I get that reference! I followed Grace on that Instagram application, and she was always watching the…uh, very attractive…surfers out in California." Her smile beamed with pride, but then slowly faded. Her shoulders sagged and her gaze drifted to the tabletop.

Kenna gently rubbed her friend's shoulder. "What happened to Grace wasn't right, and I'm sorry. That's why it's so important that we find the others. No one deserves to be mistreated in such a horrible way." Darci nodded, and Kenna pulled her into a hug. "We'll get through this."

"Are you two done yet?" Meegan snapped, coming up to them.

Pulling away from Darci, Kenna turned to Meeg, ready to snap back. But she held her tongue and focused on Meegan's new look. Her black hair was now a vibrant strawberry blonde, and her light brown skin was two shades paler, splashed with faint freckles along her arms and cheeks. She was about to comment on her best friend's transformation when Meegan shoved a bracer at Darci.

"Take Liam and put that on him outside. I want a minute alone with Kenna."

Darci moved past them, then stopped and asked, "What about yours?"

"I'm not wearing one. Now, go."

Obliging, she waved for Liam to follow. After they were gone, Meegan lined up the four remaining bracers in a row on the table. She hovered her hands over them and said, *"Liida ag arle."* With a *crack*, the metal of each bracer broke away from the transessent stone. Meegan picked up the four white stones and stored them in a smaller bag that she then slung over one shoulder.

"There. No need to wear them when I can carry them."

"Nice trick," Kenna complimented. Inhaling a deep breath, she faced Meegan, ready for her transformation. "Now me."

Meegan turned Kenna so her back was to her. Then she brought her hands to Kenna's face and pinched a single piece of red hair between her thumbs and fingers. She dragged her hands upward along Kenna's face and over the top of her head. Kenna felt nothing. No tingling sensation or hum beneath her skin.

"Did it not work?"

Meegan steered Kenna over to the corridor that led to the ship's exit. She stopped in front of the glass panel and said, "Linc."

"Yes, how can I be of assistance?" The woman's voice sounded alive, filling the cabin.

"That's not a real person, is it?" Kenna leaned close to Meegan.

Meegan shrugged, then said, "We need a mirror."

Before them, the black wavered, turning into a reflective surface. Kenna's mouth opened and her eyes locked with a stranger. The girl staring back at her looked more as if she could be Gerard's daughter, with her auburn hair and deep orange eyes.

"Wow! That's amazing." She blinked several times, watching her reflection blink. It was like one of those video app filters, except the effect actually applied to a person's physical body. Lifting the ends of her hair, she combed her fingers through, amazed at how real the new color looked.

Staring at herself again, she asked, "And you're sure it'll hold? I mean, we're not going to revert back to ourselves, say, in the middle of the rescue mission?"

"It'll hold. Besides, I have these." Meegan stretched open the top of the smaller bag, showing her the transessent stones, before Velcroing the bag closed.

Ben appeared in the hall and the two girls backed up, giving him some room to enter the cabin area. At first his attention was on Meegan, and when he finally noticed Kenna, he abruptly stopped, mouth gaped.

"You look…"

"Better?" Kenna sheepishly suggested as he struggled to finish his sentence.

His brows pinched. "No. I was going to say *like a Sendarian*." He narrowed his eyes, looking Kenna over, and then cleared his throat and returned his attention to Meegan. "It's time to go. My colleague is here, and he's going to come with us. He has a contact over on South Sendara who will guide us to where we need to get."

Kenna started to follow Ben, excited to be finally going outside, but Meegan grabbed Kenna's arm. "I'll be right out."

"What? Why?"

"We don't have time for this," Ben said from down the hall.

"I know. I'll be quick. I just need to check in with Breyah. Can you please contact her for me?"

Ben returned to the cabin area. "What is this about?"

The two girls exchanged a quick look before Kenna nodded, understanding exactly what her friend wanted to do—she wanted to check on the status of Gemma.

"Uh, we just want to check in and see how our friend Ally is doing." Kenna hated lying to him, but now wasn't the time to enlighten him about the magic powers of an arcstone.

"Fine." Ben huffed and faced the glass panel. It didn't take him long to punch in the information needed to connect with Breyah. He said his greetings to the Priomh Leadess, then stepped aside, allowing Meegan to take his place. "Don't be long," he instructed, then marched down the corridor. Halfway to the exit, he stopped and asked, "Kenna, are you coming?"

"You go with Ben, and I'll be right out. Save me a seat, okay?"

Kenna nodded and then followed Ben. Her insides hummed with excitement because she was finally going to see the Sendarian home world. A world much more complex than what they'd seen on Priomh. Her inner scholar wanted to absorb as much as she could during the time she had, starting with whatever was waiting for her outside the transport ship doors.

21

The rest of Gemma's morning went by in a blur. The world continued on as she tried to process what'd happened in the washroom earlier. Micah and Xander were busy making plans and trying to contact Logan, who'd decided it was best to stay with the transport ship somewhere out in the Endless Forest.

Eventually, she made her way outside for some fresh air. Sitting in one of the lounge chairs, she stared out at the line of trees circling her property. When she and Breyah initially designed the layout for the new Priomh research compound, she'd purposefully had her home built farther out from the Lead building and other homes, knowing how much she enjoyed—and needed—her alone time. Not many Sendarians had the luxury of designing their own home, and having the opportunity made her realize that the Elemental Council shouldn't restrict Sendarians from such an exploratory experience. To have the creative freedom to build a home that suits the individual needs and interests, rather than being assigned a home that was assembled based on approved, regulation home designs. It was ridiculous that the Elemental Council wouldn't consider compromising and allowing Sendarians to design their own homes.

Gemma grazed one hand along the edge of the lounge-chair cushion. The freedom to design and create not only new homes and buildings, but also an independent infrastructure from Sendara's felt intoxicating. It might have even been the spark that ignited her desire to pursue other ways to prove her devotion to their goddess. And after her sister and Anora approached her with their pitch to recruit her, Gemma had done something she never thought she'd ever do— abandon her Spiaire position to join the Athru.

Would she do it again if given the opportunity to go back in time? Honestly, she wasn't sure. She hated dealing with Quaid, and feeling manipulated by Anora, but if she hadn't left…hadn't chosen this path…would she be here now…bonded with their goddess?

Goddess. The word rolled through her mind. What did that mean to her now? If what the Anumen girl had said was true, that Isoldesse wasn't a celestial being, then everything they'd ever believed in was a lie. Or maybe it wasn't a lie, but a way to give Sendarians hope. Thinking back to the Anumen Doctrine, Gemma recalled how Isoldesse had come to Sendara offering their world a way to survive—to redirect the current way of life and extend the planet's sustainability, thus extending the future of its people.

Salvation. That's what she offered, and that's what she gave. She saved us. Lifting her arm, Gemma glanced at the golden stone embedded in the arm cuff. *And now she's here. I guess in a way, even though she's not an all-powerful god, she's still my goddess.*

Gazing out into the forest, where a gentle breeze drifted through the trees farther back, beyond the reach of the protective barrier, Gemma decided right then that she was no longer Athru. She wasn't going back to being a Spiaire either. Change was coming, and she wanted to be at the forefront, to help lead Sendarians into a new future.

Proving her loyalty to her goddess was all she ever wanted, and now she knew exactly how to do that—to keep Isoldesse's good will alive. The truth may come out about Isoldesse, but that shouldn't change the fact that she brought hope and peace to their world. She was still their goddess, no matter where she came from.

Glancing over her shoulder, she spotted Xander through the back sliding glass doors, inside talking to Micah. Xander might have been an annoying loggie on Earth, but she'd grown to love him. Yet, something inside told her she had no right to take him from his world. To bring him here without his consent. Though, a little part of her wanted to force him to stay, but when the time came, she needed to let him go.

"*Status report*," someone commanded within her mind. The voice sounded distant—coming and going with each syllable.

She abruptly sat up, almost falling off the lounge chair. "Who's there?" Gemma scanned the forest surrounding her home, thinking someone was going to jump out from behind one of the trees. But no one did.

This time, a little bit louder, the voice said, "*What of the Black Mountain? Does it still stand?*"

"What black mountain? Where are you?" Slowly, she walked from the lounge chairs toward the back edge of her property, searching deeper into the woods. "Come out here and explain yourself!"

There was a long pause, and for a moment Gemma thought the strange voice wasn't real. But then it returned, trembling with sadness. "*Did I kill them all? Where is— No! Don't let them find her. They'll use her! They'll kill her! That's what they do! Oh, what have I done?*"

Recalling the woman in the mirror and the name she'd written, Gemma realized who was speaking. Though, none of what she was saying made any sense. Looking to the sky, Gemma whispered, "Isoldesse, is that you?"

"*Where am I? I can't see anything.*"

"You're on Priomh," Gemma answered, still eyeing the afternoon sky.

Silence filled the air, and Gemma was about to call out to the goddess again, when Isoldesse said, "*Where's Jasper?*"

"Who's Jasper?" Blue energy from the protective shield surrounding Priomh crackled along the dome's surface. Gemma ignored the streaks of light and continued questioning Isoldesse. "What do you need? And where are you?" There was an unintentional hint of annoyance laced into her words. "Please, talk to me!"

An overwhelming wave of sadness struck Gemma, and she backed up until she reached the lounge chair. Sitting, she clutched the front of her shirt as tears welled in her eyes. "What's happening? Why am I crying?"

A burst of adrenaline shot through her, followed by a hum of anger coursing through her veins. Isoldesse's commands echoed in Gemma's mind: *"Destroy the drive, Jasper! Don't let them find her—"* Isoldesse's voice faded, cutting off the end of her warning.

Regaining control of her emotions, Gemma jumped to her feet. "Who the hegah is Jasper, and who are you trying to protect?" Silence filled her mind and the yard around her. "Isoldesse? Are you still there?"

"Hey, are you okay?" Xander asked, running up to her. He held out a blanket, offering it up to Gemma.

She pushed the blanket away, then pressed her hands to her temples. "Damn it! Answer me!"

"Gemma, seriously. Are you okay?" Xander set the blanket down on the lounge chair, then slowly approached her.

"I'm fine." She wiped her cheeks dry and closed the space between them. "I don't know what's happening. I think something is wrong."

He hugged her. "Okay, well, we should call a doctor or someone to help."

She nuzzled her head into the crook of his neck, letting his warm arms hold her while she processed what to do next. After a long moment, she nodded and said, "Yes, I think you're right. I need Breyah, and…" She groaned, frustration swelling inside, because she needed help from the one Sendarian who would never forgive her. "…and Priomh's Lead Medic."

"Breyah's on her way, or she's sending someone. I don't know, she wasn't very clear." Micah lifted his baseball cap and scratched his forehead. He'd joined them outside after Gemma requested Breyah's help. "Are you sure you want to go see Holt? It's risky."

"Yeah, well, he's the only one who can do a bio-scan and tell me what the hegah is wrong in here," Gemma snapped with a little more venom than intended, pointing to her chest.

Xander wrapped one arm around her shoulders. "It's going to be okay, babe. I'm sure the doctor will scan you and tell you exactly what's wrong."

Gemma shot to her feet and released an angry groan. Storming back into the house, she exclaimed, "No! Actually, I don't think he will, but it's the only thing I can think of until that little pain-in-my-ass Anumen gets back from Sendara—"

"Whoa!" Micah cut in, following her into the house. "What Anumen? Isoldesse?"

Inhaling, she reeled in her frustration and turned to them. "No. I mean, yes and no, but the Anumen I need answers from just left on a transport ship to Sendara!"

Xander closed the glass door and moved to Gemma's side. She didn't resist his closeness. She did, however, wish her brother would shut-up and give her a moment to collect her thoughts. But she could tell that wish wasn't going to happen. Micah paced alongside the exterior glass wall of the living area. His eyes hooded by the brim of his cap. When he did stop to face her, he stopped chewing on the inside of his lip, a sure sign he was deep in thought—probably trying to grasp the reality of what was happening. Crossing his arms, he asked, "So, if you're not talking about Isoldesse, then that means there's another Anumen here?"

Gemma couldn't tell from his tone if he was intrigued or concerned. "Yes. The human girl with the long black hair. Turns out she's not human!"

"The one I spoke to that day you made me go knock on Prue's door—that girl? She's a goddess?"

Now she could tell Micah was surprised from the wide-eyed stare he was giving her, waiting for an answer she still wasn't clear on. "Isoldesse is our goddess, yes, but she's also a being from another world. As is the girl whose name is Meegan. But she's nothing like Isoldesse."

"I'm so confused." Micah lifted the front part of his hat, blondish-red hair peeking out, and rubbed his forehead. "How can one be a goddess and the other not?"

"Because," Gemma said, narrowing her eyes at her brother, "Isoldesse came to Sendara with the intent to save our world from ourselves. And she did. Our planet's ecosystem is one of the best in all the worlds we've observed. She did that—she used her abilities and powers to convince the divided regions of Sendara to come together under one rule. She encouraged everyone to value the planet's resources not for themselves but for future generations. That more of something didn't mean more happiness. It just meant less for those that haven't been born."

"Wow," Xander said after exhaling a deep breath. "Sounds like something Earth can use."

Squeezing his hand, she nodded. "Yes. Yes, it does. And that's why I refuse to let the Sendarian people forget everything she did for us."

"But technically, she's not a goddess, right?" Micah raised one brow. When Gemma rolled her eyes and shook her head, he pumped his fist in the air and exclaimed, "I knew it! Oh, Cahleen is going to love this!"

"Yes, well, we can explain all of this to our pain-in-the-ass sister once we figure out what the hegah is wrong with me." She held up her arm. "I think this thing is broken. The connection comes and goes and Isoldesse is acting weird—confused and asking for some guy named Jasper."

"Is that why you need to speak with Meegan?" Xander rubbed a hand through his black hair while looking over the arm cuff.

"Yes."

Micah sat at the other end of the sofa, elbows resting on his knees. "Is that why she was here last night?"

Leaning back into the sofa cushion, she sighed. "I said yes to something I should've given more thought to, but what's done is done."

"So, what exactly where they doing here? Before I knew what was going on, you passed out on the sofa, then Breyah, her Spiaire, and the two girls from Earth left. No one said anything. Just left us here with you out for the night."

"I brought you upstairs to your bed," Xander whispered, leaning in close. She offered him a smile of gratitude, then turned to Micah. "The girl—Meegan—was using some of her Anumen magic to bond my essence to the Anumen essence inside this stone." With one finger, she tapped the golden stone embedded in the arm cuff.

"Before Breyah left, she told me to stay put and watch you, and that she'd check in with us sometime today."

"*Gemma,*" her Linc softly spoke within her ear.

Gemma held up one finger and shifted her gaze to the hardwood floor. Both men stood by, waiting to hear who was calling. "Yes. Understood. Thank you." Gemma stood, brushed her hands down her pants, then explained, "Someone's at the door."

"Where is everyone?" Gemma followed the security guard into Priomh's Lead building. When he didn't answer, she repeated her question with a little more Gemma-tude, "Um, I asked where everyone was?"

"Leadess has ordered everyone that isn't essential staff to remain in the residential area of Priomh."

Interesting. Breyah shut down the Aevo Compendium. I wonder if the queen approved that order. She couldn't help but chuckle inside at the idea of Breyah going against Her Royal Highness.

As she entered the Centrum of the Lead building, a flood of emotions washed over her. This place held some fond memories since she and Breyah had been the ones to design the place.

The grand space of the Centrum, usually filled with bustling Sendarians, was empty except for one Sendarian.

"Beannaith," Breyah said, approaching Gemma as the security guard took his leave.

"So, you gave everyone the day off?" They walked side-by-side, like old times when they were running things together, toward the rear of the circular room.

Breyah stopped before they reached the entryway to the medical-building skywalk. "I owe you an apology."

Scrunching her nose, a bit caught off guard, Gemma asked, "What for? I'm the one who left you without any notice. I should be apologizing to you."

Breyah shook her head. "No. It's my fault. I should've paid more attention to what was happening on Sendara." Before Gemma could respond, she added, "Though, you could've come to me. We've always talked things out and come up with solutions together."

Gemma continued, entering the glass-covered skywalk. "Not this. This was something I had to do on my own."

Breyah caught up and they walked together, the warm sun filling the space. "Why? Because it involved Cahleen?"

Stopping abruptly, Gemma dropped the hand that had been reaching for the door at the end of the skywalk. "You know about my sister?"

Breyah reached for the door, and as she opened it, she said, "Of course. She's the only other Sendarian that you trust more than me. If anyone could've convinced you to leave, it would've been her."

Gemma nodded, then entered the medical building. "It was her and a woman named Anora that persuaded me to join the Athru."

Breyah stopped walking. She rubbed at the spot where her arm cuff should've been. "I feel like I failed you, and Isoldesse."

"You didn't fail either of us. I should've come to you and told you how I was feeling." Breyah was about to continue walking when Gemma stopped her. "Before we go in there, I need to tell you something."

"Yes?"

"Do you recall how the Anumen girl, Meegan, said there's an Anumen residing inside this stone?" She lifted her arm, holding it toward her friend.

With a nod and a narrowed, inquisitive gaze, Breyah gently touched the yellow stone. "You agreed to bond with whoever's essence is trapped inside. Why, has something happened? Is that why you've requested a bio-scan?" She shifted her position, blocking Gemma's view to the rear of the Centrum.

Shrugging, Gemma said, "I'm not sure yet. But yes, it is the reason I want Holt to run a full medical scan."

"Have you talked to or seen the essence yet?"

Gemma nodded.

Breyah's eyes lit up. "You have?! How exciting, yet how odd it must be to see someone everyone else cannot."

Facing the glass overlooking the gardens below, Gemma said, "It is a bit odd, but that's not what I need to tell you."

Breyah rubbed her friend's shoulder. "Whatever it is, you can tell me."

Inhaling a deep breath, then moving in closer, Gemma whispered, "It's Isoldesse."

Taken aback, Breyah gasped. "What?" With a hand pressed to her chest her gaze darted to the arm cuff. "Our goddess… It's her essence in there?"

Gemma pulled Breyah closer, shushing her. "Hey, let's not announce the big news to everyone, okay?" Yeah, Gemma knew mostly everyone was home, but someone could be watching them through the glass recordings.

"This is huge!" Breyah whispered excitedly, adhering to Gemma's wishes to try and stay quiet.

"I know, but…"

"But what?"

"Something's not right. She's asking questions I don't know the answers to, and she's upset. Almost scared-like."

"I see. Well, I guess we can only take one step at a time. Have Holt run a full medical scan so we can first make sure your health isn't in danger. Then we can address you-know-who's condition. Sound good?" Gemma offered a small smile as her reply. Breyah continued, "Remember, dear friend, we can't change the past, but we can try and fix the future. And I need your help, here with me, to do that."

"You want me to come back? After everything I've done?"

"That is not her decision to make," Holt said, entering the corridor. He held open one of the double doors. "That is Queen Adalyss's decision, and I highly doubt the queen will approve an Athru rebel to have access to highly sensitive Aevo Compendium information."

"Beannaith, Holt." Gemma faced him, uncrossing her arms and resting her hands on her hips. "Did you miss me?" she jested, but inside she was hoping he'd forgive her.

"I did not miss you, nor do I commend your reinstatement." He narrowed his orange eyes at her. Rubbing his beard, he dragged out the silence for as long as he could, but eventually he said, "Breyah tells me you have a delicate situation that needs medical attention. And since the particular help you require just left for Sendara to rescue the hostages you helped capture, I guess that leaves me."

"Yup, that about sums it up. Now, can you help me or not?" Gemma tried to offer him a smirk, but guilt tugged at her insides.

He made a *humph* sound, then turned and disappeared into one of the observation rooms.

"I will return shortly," Breyah said, gesturing for Gemma to continue on.

"You're not coming?"

Breyah shook her head. "I have an incoming call I need to take. I will return when I'm finished."

Gemma nodded, and with her head held high, she followed Holt into the exam room. Even if she didn't want to be here, Holt was the only person who could tell if this magic stone was doing more harm than good—to her own body and essence. Then afterwards, they could focus on figuring out what the hegah was wrong with Isoldesse.

22

Darci hadn't been kidding when she'd told Kenna how Sendara was similar looking to Earth. The sky was blue and filled with fluffy white clouds. The trees in the surrounding forest had thick brown trunks full of green leaves, and the dirt from the back road looked like regular old dirt. Kenna inhaled, taking in the fresh, clean scent in the air. Warm yet crisp, with a hint of that sweet, familiar fragrance. Lingering halfway down the steps, she asked, "What's that smell?"

Ben tilted his head up and inhaled through his nose. "I don't smell anything."

"It's the Hiccum trees." Darci walked over to the spacecraft from where the transport vehicles were parked. "The flowers bloom much earlier down here along the southern regions of Sendara."

"They smell amazing." Kenna sniffed the air again. She was at the end of the stairs, about to take her first step onto an alien world, when thick gray storm clouds aggressively rolled in from every direction. Booms of thunder filled the sky as the encroaching clouds closed in directly over their transport ship.

"What's happening?" Darci stared up into the dark sky, yelling over the increasing winds.

Ben gripped the railing of the ship's step-ramp, gaze fixed to the open hatch of the ship, but Kenna quickly held one hand out to him. "No. Let me go see what's wrong." They seemed to be the only two realizing the turn of weather was coming from the Anumen girl still inside the ship.

"If those clouds don't clear in the next few minutes, I'm coming in."

Kenna nodded, turned, and rushed up the steps and through the open hatch. "Meegan!" she shouted, making her way through the narrow corridor toward the passenger cabin. When she finally spotted her friend, facing the glass panel where the video call had displayed, Kenna cautiously approached. The storm was outside, but Kenna could feel the electricity humming in the air around her friend.

"Meeg, what happened? Are you okay?"

Kenna grabbed Meegan's shoulders and swung her around to face her. It startled her to see Meegan's eyes had gone all white, black smoke seeping from the corners.

"Meeg! Hey, you need to stop!" Kenna tried shaking her friend, hoping to snap her out of whatever emotional state she was in.

She didn't know how to help her friend, so she did the only thing she could think of whenever she was upset or sad. She pulled Meegan into a hug. "Whatever it is, we can figure it out together."

The hum of electricity inside the cabin subsided, and Kenna leaned back. The thunder from outside stopped booming, which told Kenna Ben wouldn't come charging in. Or at least, she hoped he wouldn't. After brushing aside, a lose strand of Meegan's glamoured red hair, she asked, "What happened?"

A single tear fell, trailing down Meegan's cheek. Her gaze found Kenna's and she said, "It's Isoldesse. She's in the arcstone. The one Gemma bonded with last night. It's her. It's actually her."

Kenna gasped the second Meegan said *Isoldesse*. It looked as if the Sendarian goddess would be making an appearance after all.

Ducking out of the aircraft, Kenna saw Ben standing at the base of the stairs, waiting. The second Meegan stepped out, following Kenna, he held out a shortsword at his side. Kenna recognized the blade. It was the same weapon he'd used to fight off Quaid's men.

When a blue current of energy sparked to life along the blade's surface, Kenna yelled, "Ben, put that away!"

"What the hegah was all that about?" he asked, not sheathing his sword.

Glancing up, she saw everyone standing around the transport vehicles watching them. Even the Priomh security team had stopped loading the back of one of the trucks.

"She's fine. Everything is fine."

Meegan pushed past Kenna. "We need to get going. I want to be done with this mission and back to Priomh as soon as possible." She stormed past Ben, waving one hand and muttering words Kenna couldn't hear. But when the electric charge of Ben's sword vanished, she knew exactly what her friend had commanded.

Up above, the last of the gray clouds were drifting apart. As Kenna continued down the steps from the ship toward the vehicles, Ben grabbed her arm. He spun her to face him. His fingers tightened around her arm, causing her to wince.

"Ow!"

Instantly, he released his hold on her, putting a small amount of space between them. "My apologies, but now isn't the time to be keeping secrets. What was that all about? And why is she in such a hurry to return to Priomh? Is everything okay up there? Is Breyah okay?"

A tall Sendarian man Kenna didn't know walked over to them, next to Ben. His shoulders weren't as broad as Ben's, but he stood in the same manner—with authority. She assumed he, too, must be one of Sendara's police officers.

Ben ignored the man at his side and stared at Kenna. *He's not going to move*, she thought, *until I tell him something.*

"Breyah is fine." Not budging, or breaking his focus on her, she added, "She was looking into something for us and, well, what she found wasn't exactly what we were expecting."

He straightened, crossing his arms over his chest. "And?"

"And what? That's all I can say right now because honestly, there's nothing we can do from here. Another problem for when we get back to Priomh. For now, everything is fine. Now, let's go."

With a wide sweep of his arm, he blocked Kenna from continuing toward the transport vehicles. "Everything is not fine, especially if every time your friend gets upset, a nasty storm rolls in over our heads."

He did have a point. That would draw some unwanted attention to them. "True, and I promise I will talk to her about that."

The tall Sendarian next to Ben cleared his throat while Ben sighed. "Fine. But the second you don't think she's in control, you need to tell me." His friend coughed louder. Ben glanced in his direction, then said to Kenna, "Or my friend here." Ben gestured to the Sendarian man. "This is Officer Tiernach. I trust him with my life, and so can you."

"Oh, we don't need formalities for this trip, especially if we're going into South Sendara territory." He held out his hand, open palm facing up. Not wanting to be rude, she slid hers over the top of his, grazing his smooth skin. "You can call me Jordi."

Jordi's eyes were a brighter orange than Ben's were. His hair was more ginger than blond, and Kenna liked his smile. She felt an instant sense of honesty and trust from him. "Okay. Hello, Jordi."

"Hello?"

"It's just another way to say *beannaith*," Ben interjected, then cut between Jordi and Kenna, forcing them to step away from one another. He marched over to the Lead security officer Breyah had insisted come with them for this rescue mission. Kenna couldn't hear their conversation, but she noticed Ben was doing a lot of pointing to the vehicles and to the road.

Jordi walked alongside Kenna as they followed Ben to the vehicles. Because he was a foot taller than Kenna, he leaned down close to whisper, "Don't let Ben's serious mood ruin your time here. He's told me everything about what we're doing here and where you come from. I find it fascinating, and I'm honored to meet you and your friends."

The officer glanced more than a few times over to where Meegan and Liam stood, quietly talking. Or at least, Liam appeared to be doing most of the talking while Meegan searched through the cargo area of one of the transports. Kenna wondered what he was saying to her.

"So, what do you think so far?" Jordi asked, reverting her attention back to their conversation.

"Of Sendara?" When he nodded, she said, "Well, I haven't seen anything that doesn't look like home—I mean, Earth. But when I do, you'll be the first to know."

They continued conversing about the surrounding area while walking toward everyone at a leisurely pace. The Priomh security team took their time loading the supplies while Ben spoke with the Lead Security officer. The two men were discussing something while looking at a large plac.

Keeping a good distance from Ben, Kenna seized the opportunity to know more about the man she now often met in her dreams. "Jordi, is he always this serious?"

"Well, I rarely see him outside of our Rhaltan duties, so I'm afraid yes. Though, there was this one stretch of time when he smiled every day, but that seems like forever ago. And there's only one reason a man smiles that much."

"What's that?" Kenna asked as they approached the trucks.

"Why love, of course."

23

The woman who'd destroyed her home world was alive. Or at least her essence was. Meegan didn't care how Isoldesse had gotten into the arcstone. All she wanted was answers—about her home world, the Obard, this stupid Aevo Compendium, and…and if her parents had known the truth about everything this whole time.

She will be punished for her crimes, she thought while staring out the transport vehicle window. They'd been traveling through a dense forest for almost an hour, and she'd barely registered anything she'd seen outside. Her mind was too focused on Isoldesse.

"And who are you to punish anyone for things you do not understand?" the collective voices of the Eilimintachs said within her mind.

She ignored their presence and turned to Kenna, who sat beside her. Eyes wide, Kenna was darting her gaze from one window to the next, as if she didn't want to miss a thing as they sped through the wooded region. It pained Meegan to know how stressed her friend must be with her mother being taken and her father showing up and revealing himself as one of these Sendarians. *Then, on top of it all,* she thought, *he tells her…us…that it's our destiny to be the ones to reveal the truth about Isoldesse to the Sendarians. What an ass! Does he even know his own daughter—to put such a heavy burden on her? She'll be crushed…devastated…if things take a turn for the worst…which they will. And we wouldn't be in this situation if he and Honnah had just done what needed to be done fifty years ago when she was a subject for the Aevo Compendium! Why the hell did they wait?*

"Can you believe this?" Kenna nudged Meegan in the arm. "There are subtle differences, but for the most part our worlds are quite similar."

"It's a forest," Meegan pointed out. "I'm sure most planets have forests, or plant life."

"I know," Kenna drawled out. "That's the spectacular part." Gazing up through the glass ceiling, she continued, "There's so much to learn, and I'm betting there's an encyclopedia of information up on Priomh about every world they've visited."

"You mean observed and studied."

Kenna shrugged. "They never hurt anyone. They're not like—" She hesitated, not finishing her sentence.

"I know that. But it's still wrong. And we're not staying, remember?"

"Yeah, yeah. I know. But think about it—the observing part." Kenna shifted in her seat, facing her friend. "I guarantee you that if Earth had the ability to travel through space to other worlds, we'd be doing the same thing. Maybe even worse! History has proven that humans like power. Not all, but a good majority of them. They'll invade or conquer other lands if given the opportunity. And even if it's not a hostile encounter, but more like a mission of peace, we still end up influencing or interfering. It's human nature to want to parent things; children, projects, whatever—and sometimes it's a good thing and then sometimes it's not."

"That philosophy class has gone to your head." Meegan ran her fingers through her hair.

"Maybe," Kenna said, leaning into her seat. "But you know I've always wanted to learn more about how an environment affects a civilization—specifically in space."

Meegan stared up into the glass ceiling of the vehicle. "I'm pretty sure if we never ended up here, you would've found a way to make a name for yourself in the space industry. Helping to design a space station or something where families could live."

They sat in silence for a long moment before Kenna said, "That would be awesome." Turning to look at Meegan, she said, "And I think that's another reason I want to stay on Priomh. And," she quickly continued, not letting Meegan cut in, "that doesn't mean you have to stay. I do want to go back home, but I also don't want to pass up the opportunity to learn more while we're here."

Meegan sighed. There was no way she was going to let her friend stay, however starting an argument in the beginning of their rescue mission might not be the best idea either. Learning more about Sendara and other worlds did sound intriguing, but from their apartment back in Florida. Not this far from home. Meegan thought about a way to convince the princess or Breyah to give Kenna some reading material, or a way to communicate…but from home.

From the seats in front of them, Ben driving while the other Sendarian man handled navigation, Meegan heard Ben ask, "And you trust this guy? How long have you known him?"

"Long enough," the man replied. She tried to remember Ben's colleague's name but couldn't. It was something like George or Justin.

Leaning closer to the front, she pressed one hand to the back of Ben's seat and discovered there wasn't an invisible barrier like the one in the transport vehicle that had taken them to the princess's house yesterday.

"Look, normally I meet up with my regular contact, but he's not available. And supposedly my contact trusts the guy he's sending in his place. This whole thing was thrown together on a short notice, so we don't have much of a choice."

Ben pursed his lips. "I don't like it."

No one said anything after that. Though, Meegan wasn't worried, because regardless of if they could trust this *inside guy* or not, she could handle whatever unexpected dangers came their way. And now that she knew Isoldesse was on Priomh, a sense of urgency growing in her core. They needed to get to South Sendara, find the captives, kick ass if necessary, and get back to the transport ship all within a day—two at the most.

"There is an imbalance within your essence, young Fawness," the Eilimintachs said softly in Meegan's mind. *"Mind your priorities."*

She ignored their warnings. Her anger toward Isoldesse wasn't anything new. Her home world had been invaded and destroyed because of that traitor. No one ever knew why, and now she had an opportunity to uncover the truth about what happened.

Kenna continued to gawk out the window, pointing out similarities and things that were different. Meegan reeled in her annoyance. This wasn't supposed to be like a school field trip. People could die, though Meegan vowed to make sure everyone made it back to the transport ship—their rescue group and the captives.

Eventually the SUV-like vehicle came to a stop. Kenna didn't wait for Ben to open her door and hurried to get out. Meegan sat there, trying to ease the growing frustration. *Maybe Kenna should've stayed behind,* she thought. *She's only a liability. I shouldn't have let her come.*

Meegan opened the vehicle door and stepped out, and a cool gust of ocean wind rushed her face, blowing back her strawberry-blonde hair. Kenna's now-red hair also whipped around her face as she stood at the edge of the sandbank, looking out at the ocean. Liam climbed out from the third row and stood by Meegan.

"I know she told you what happened."

At first, she ignored him, but then shot him a quick glance while trying to tuck the loose strands of hair behind her ears. The wind along the coast wasn't letting up.

"And I know I should've told her sooner."

"Yes, you should've." Meegan gave up on restraining the loose strands of hair and let them blow across her face. "But what's done is done, and that's not important right now. Right now, I need you to stay focused on why we're here. We don't know what we're walking into and worrying about how Kenna feels right now is only going to get you killed."

Liam nodded. "I know we're supposed to follow Ben's lead, but whatever you need me to do I'll do it. Just say the word."

She narrowed her eyes at him. "Really?"

"Yeah, really. You know what you're doing. And I've seen firsthand how you can handle yourself. You're powerful, Meeg. And that's what we're going to need when it comes down to it. You over those lasher things," he said while pointing to the Priomh security team.

Liam's words were like logs being thrown in a fire, reviving her confidence. "Thank you." He nodded, then strode over to the Priomh security men and women unloading the supplies from the cargo area. Inhaling a deep breath of ocean air, she felt a surge of reassurance that she could handle whatever dangers where waiting for them on the island of South Sendara.

"Come on, let's go down to the water!" Kenna loudly said, running up to Meegan. She hooked her arm through Meegan's. "I know you're anxious to get back to Priomh and talk with"—she dropped her voice to a whisper—"you-know-who, but we're on an alien world! Aren't you the least bit curious about this place? Oh, come on!" Kenna tugged on Meegan's arm. "There might be some cool shells along the shoreline."

Meegan freed herself from Kenna's grasp. "I have no interest in these people or their world. But you are right about wanting to return to Priomh. I deserve answers as to why I lost my world. That's what matters right now."

Kenna's brows pinched. "And rescuing the captives."

"What?" Meegan said, trying again to brush the hair from her face. The ocean wind whistled in her ears.

"You said that getting back to Priomh is what matters, but rescuing the captives also matters—and I'd say more than you returning to Priomh. You'll learn the truth either way, so why rush the mission?"

"I know that." Meegan hopped off the embankment and landed in the coarse brown sand. Wanting to know why Isoldesse led the Obard to Anuminis has been the unknown for her people for as long as she can remember. And no matter how many different ways she tried to explain that to Kenna, Meegan knew her friend wouldn't understand. "Come on, let's catch up with the others."

Kenna carefully stepped over the ledge, using the grass along the embankment for balance as she climbed down onto the beach. "You know!" she hollered over the wind. Then, when she caught up to Meegan, she continued, "I have questions, too, and not just about Sendara's ecosystem or about their daily lives." Meegan gave Kenna a sideways glance because she only half believed what Kenna was saying. "You think you're the only one who's been lied to?"

That made Meegan stop, her shoes sinking into the gritty sand. "I think I deserve to know the truth about what happened to my entire planet. The Obard invasion ended my world. How does that even compare to one person's questions about themselves?"

Not waiting for an answer, she turned and walked away, trudging through the sand toward the others, who were a good twenty yards from them, waiting by the shoreline.

Kenna yelled over the sounds of the ocean waves, "When did all of this become about you?"

Meegan stopped and faced Kenna. "You don't get it. It has always been about me! This whole shitty mess we're in is connected to me, my people, and that traitor Isoldesse! You're only involved because of that." She marched closer and pointed to the arcstone hanging around Kenna's neck. Meegan threw her hands in the air, trying to reel in the anger rolling through every inch of her body. "I'm the only one who can make things right again! That's what being Fawness is all about!" She paused, waiting to see what Kenna would say, but her friend only stared back with glossy eyes.

"Your father was wrong. There is no *our* destiny." Meegan stood with her face inches from Kenna's. "There is only *my* destiny—which is to undo the damage Isoldesse has done and to figure out how to stop the Obard from hunting Anumens so we can return home! You need to stop thinking you have a say in any of this!" Meegan spun, her feet digging into the sand, and trudged off and left Kenna behind.

"*You're wrong*," the Eilimintachs softly said inside her head. "*You would be wise to reassess your priorities. The truth you seek isn't a simple one, nor is the resolution. As Fawness, you need to have control of your emotions. Otherwise, it is not you who controls the power within.*"

"What the hell does that mean? Of course I'm in control. I know exactly what I'm doing, so back off!" Meegan crossed the stretch of beach. Everyone glanced her way at her final words to the Eilimintachs. She didn't care that everyone was staring. "Are we doing this or what?" she yelled to Ben.

Ben nodded before searching the group. He opened his mouth, about to speak, but refrained the second Kenna joined them. "Stay together," he said, eyes locked onto Kenna's.

Meegan saw Kenna wipe her face. She knew she'd hurt her friend, but it needed to be said. The sooner she understood that Meegan was the only one who could fix the mess Isoldesse had created, the better.

"Jordi, bring up the tunnel," Ben said.

At least now Meegan knew the man's name—Jordi.

Everyone shuffled away from the water's edge, everyone except Ben and Jordi, when a long line of bubbles surfaced, stretching out farther into the ocean. Jordi continued to tap at the plac in his hand as a massive glass tube emerged from beneath the water. Meegan side stepped along the beach, wanting to get the full view of whatever this thing was that was going to transport them across the ocean. When it stopped moving up the beach, coarse sand collecting along the bottom sides, a wide section of glass slid open along one side. Inside the glass tube was a slender open-top tram. Inching closer, Meegan couldn't see any wheels or tracks running under it.

Immediately, the Priomh security team headed to the front, lifting up a large cargo hatch. They loaded their gear while Jordi pointed to the front seats. "You six up front. When we land on South Sendara soil, you exit first and secure the beach." The Lead Security officer nodded, acknowledging their orders then continued to load the equipment.

"Alright, everyone in!" Ben shouted, pointing to the beige upholstered seats situated in pairs down the long slender cabin. "It'll be a few hours before the transit tram reaches land, so get comfortable."

Kenna brushed past Meegan, linking her arm through Darci's. "Sit with me," she said.

Darci stuttered, "Ah, yeah. Okay," while glancing over at Meegan. "You good?"

"I'm great. Let's just focus on the mission, because that's what matters right now," Kenna said loud enough for Meegan to hear.

Meegan rolled her eyes. Whatever needed to be done to get Kenna in the right mindset, she felt it was worth the argument. Climbing in, Meegan occupied the last row all to herself. Ahead, Liam claimed the row directly behind Kenna and Darci. And when he tried to talk to Kenna, she looked over his shoulder, briefly meeting Meegan's gaze. Ignoring Liam, Kenna quickly turned and lowered herself into her seat.

"Can I sit next to you?" Jordi asked, gesturing next to Meegan.

"I'd rather be alone," she answered.

He took the seat anyway. Then, using his plac, he tapped the screen, activating a blue energy barrier over the tram. With a few more taps and a long slide of his finger up the glass surface, the tram lifted away from the tube's bottom.

Trying to look over the edge, through the invisible barrier, Meegan was curious to know how they were hovering inside the glass tube.

As if reading her thoughts, Jordi said, "It's a combination of electromagnetic bumpers keeping the tram up and high-powered air currents that push the tram forward."

As the tram moved forward, the glass door to the transit tube slid closed then retracted back into the ocean. The ocean filled the space all around them. At first, they were gliding along through the tube, but the pace picked up and soon enough they were speeding along inside the giant glass pipe.

Setting his plac on his lap, Jordi hard pressed a button on the arm, reclining his seat back. "So, is it true? You are from the world our goddess comes from?"

Attention focused on the water surrounding them, she nodded. Jaw clenched, she gripped the arms tightly then did as he did and reclined her chair.

"We're perfectly safe in here," he reassured her.

Inhaling a deep breath, she said, "I know. It's just I'm not a fan of the ocean… I mean, I'm not a fan of being so far from land."

The man's smile widened. His reddish hair and orange eyes looked like every other Sendarian. "How about you tell me about yourself? Or where you come from. Ben tells me that you and Isoldesse come from the same world."

Meegan only responded with a curt nod.

"He also told me that she's not actually a god."

Curious, Meegan tried to read his expression. She was a bit surprised Ben had divulged the truth about Isoldesse. "She is not. And it was wrong of her to let your people believe she was."

"Maybe," he said, tilting his head back onto the headrest. "Who's to say if she actually did? The Anumen Doctrine doesn't refer to her as a goddess."

"What's the Anumen Doctrine?"

"It's the laws and ways our people live by, written by the hand of Isoldesse herself."

"I'd like to see that, when possible," Meegan said, hoping her voice sounded sincere.

"Of course," Jordi answered. He picked up his plac from his lap and tapped the screen. "Here." He handed her the device. "It will take us a few hours to reach the other side of the ocean tunnel. Plenty of time for you to browse the doctrine." He leaned back again, closing his eyes, then said, "I'm just going to lie here and relax. But let me know if you have any questions. I'm as curious to know more about you as you are about us and our connection to Isoldesse."

She heard what Jordi had said, but the second she had the doctrine in her hands, her attention zoned in on the words Isoldesse had written for these people to follow. She'd outlined an entire law system for this world.

The opening statement read,

> Take care of your world and each other, and by
> doing so, I will return.

Well, this is going to be an interesting read, Meegan thought, scrolling through the doctrine as the tram sped through the glass tube trailing the ocean floor.

24

Holt cleared his throat, prompting Gemma to open her eyes. It'd been the first sound between them since she entered the room over an hour ago. Sitting up, she pulled off the silicone face mask and swiveled her legs to hang off the bedside.

"Are we done here?"

The Lead Medic inhaled a deep breath, then shook his head without looking away from the plac he held. "I might need to run another scan."

Lying there for another thirty or forty minutes in silence didn't sound necessary, but she was curious to know why he wanted a second scan. "Is something wrong?"

After resting the plac on a nearby counter, he turned to Gemma. "I wouldn't say something's wrong. It's more like something's not right."

She hopped off the exam bed and slipped her feet into her canvas shoes. "Aren't those two interchangeable?"

"Yes and no."

"Holt, I seriously don't have time for your medical riddles. Just tell me what the hegah is wrong."

Sighing, he picked up the plac and handed it to her. The readings looked normal. Her vitals and blood levels appeared healthy. She was about to ask what the problem was when she scrolled to the end of the bio-scan report and noticed a new section. "What's this?" She flipped the plac to face him, then tapped her finger on the two different-colored tracks outlining the image of a blacked-out body.

"That's what doesn't make sense. There should only be one essence outlining your body. But you seem to be registering two essences. Which isn't possible… But there it is!"

He might not have understood, but she did. "I've never heard of a bio-scan analyzing essences."

Taking the plac from Gemma, Holt explained, "Yes, well, it's new."

"How new?"

He scrolled through her results again, the silence eating at Gemma. Barking out her words, she asked again, "Hey! How new is this technology, and where'd it come from?"

Holt cocked his head, narrowing his orange eyes at her. "Why do you need to know? So you can run back to the Athru and tell them about it? I don't think so."

"You are the pettiest Sendarian ever, do you know that?" she snapped. "How about you look beyond your devotion to Her and the Aevo Compendium project for two whole seconds to see that there's something big happening out there! Sendara is being threatened and no one is doing anything about it!"

"And that's what your rebel group is doing? Trying to save Sendara?" Holt shouted back.

"Yes!" She gestured excitedly with both hands, palms facing up. When he didn't argue back, she slowly lowered her hands, letting out an exaggerated sigh. "Or at least, that's how it all started. Now… Now, I don't know what the hegah is going on."

Outside, the late-afternoon sun was starting its descent behind the treetops. Gemma's reflection appeared in the glass. From behind, a faint reflection of a tall woman with short black hair shadowed her. Gemma turned to her goddess, but Isoldesse wasn't there. Only Holt.

"You'll get no pity from me." The Lead Medic turned away from her, focusing his attention on the plac.

"Look, I know you're upset with the way I left. It was wrong. But I promise you I was only trying to prove myself to Isoldesse. To show her that I could be there for her in other ways than traveling the galaxy and spying on Aevo C subjects. You out of all Sendarians should know what it's like to want to prove your devotion to Her."

Holt *hmm*ed. When he didn't turn away, she continued, "The Athru weren't what I thought they were, or what was promised to me when they asked me to join. I swear, I was only trying to help Sendara."

The soft knocking on the exam room door saved Gemma from explaining herself any further. Holt opened the door and Breyah entered. Behind her, Princess Emmalyn and Prince Gerard strode in. Gemma immediately bowed to both royals.

"Oh, stop that! You've never liked doing that before, so why start now?" Emmalyn approached Gemma, threw her arms around her, and squeezed.

"Yeah, well, I'm doing a lot of things these past few days that are out of character." Gemma raised her arms and embraced the princess.

"I'm happy to see you've come to your senses. But"—Emmalyn released Gemma and put some space between them while pointing a finger at the ex-Spiaire—"I believe everything happens for a reason. And you leaving Priomh to join the Athru, then leaving the Athru to come back here…"

"Emmalyn, please get to the point," Gerard grumbled from next to Breyah.

"Right! The point is, you're back where you belong. And you learned a lot along the way, yes?"

Gemma rolled her eyes in a friendly gesture. "I did. Though, it would've been interesting to see how things would've played out if the plan actually worked. Would your mother have stepped down if we dangled you as collateral?"

Emmalyn burst out laughing, and everyone stared at her. "Oh my goddess! You're so funny! No. My mother wouldn't have given up her position to save me." She continued laughing. "Was that the Athru's grand scheme? To use me? I'm honored to be thought of so highly, but no."

Cutting into his sister's fit of laughter, Prince Gerard said, "Gemma, did it work? Breyah told me about the bond."

She looked between him and Breyah. "It did. Did Breyah say anything else?"

"No," Breyah answered. "I thought it best if you told them."

Lifting her chin, she glanced over everyone in the exam room before revealing the Anumen's identity. "It's Isoldesse."

Gerard raised both brows, and Emmalyn cheered with bouncy steps. Holt, on the other hand, cut into the conversation. "What do you mean, it's Isoldesse?"

Emmalyn rushed to Gemma and gripped her arms. Sheer joy lifted Emmalyn's expression. "Oh, I had hoped and prayed to…well, you-know-who"—she gestured with a wide look to the arm cuff— "that it was her! And how perfect is this?"

"Are you sure?" Gerard asked.

Holt stepped around the banished prince, blocking their conversation. "What is going on? Does it have something to do with this?" He held up the plac with the blacked-out body, outlined with two essences.

Emmalyn grabbed the plac and skittered over to Breyah and her brother. "It worked! I knew the technology would work!"

"Of course it works. Everything Isoldesse has left works." Gerard took the plac and scrolled through the full bio-scan results.

Meanwhile, Holt's attention remained on Gemma, so she said, "I assume you know the truth about Meegan. That she's not human."

The Lead Medic nodded. "Breyah informed me the other night, after everyone returned from the old research facility. I was tending to Grace—trying to save her life—when Breyah pulled me aside and explained who the girl was."

Breyah approached the Lead Medic, placing one hand on his forearm. "Change is coming, my friend. That's why I've decided to cease all activities pertaining to the Aevo Compendium."

"That's not your decision to make!" Holt's voice pitched higher as he turned to face her. "The queen would have the final decision on the matter. Your position as Priomh's Leadess is to oversee operations, not to make outlandish decisions like stopping the research."

"I know my position. And I also know when to open my eyes," Breyah explained. Gemma was impressed by Breyah's calm composure. This whole situation was chaotic.

Emmalyn squeezed into the conversation, standing next to Gemma. "My mother isn't exactly fit to rule. She hasn't been for some time. Like, a long time."

"I knew it!" Gemma exclaimed.

Holt shook his head, rubbing his graying beard. "This doesn't make any sense. Why would you think the queen isn't fit to rule? And why would you think you are bonded to Isoldesse?"

Gemma was about to answer the second question when the princess cut her off. "After Gerard left, she had a meltdown. Her pride and joy had run off with a human, or at least we thought she was a human, but anywho… He left and our mother lost it. She was determined to find a way to get him to come home. To lift his banishment. So…" Emmalyn trailed off, hesitant to finish. Gemma had rarely seen the princess hold back when speaking.

"It's okay. You can tell them," Gerard urged his sister.

"She opened the doors."

Breyah gasped while Holt narrowed his gaze and asked, "The Reigning Doors—those doors?" Emmalyn nodded, and he continued, "She opened the door to the next reigning era?"

"No, Holt. She opened *all* the doors," Emmalyn explained.

"What?! Why?"

"Because she wanted something to help her find and bring home Gerard."

The room fell silent. Holt turned away from the group while Gemma said, "That explains what Cahleen and Anora told me when they recruited me to the Athru." Everyone's attention turned to her, even Holt's. "They told me that the queen had abused her power and strayed from the Anumen Doctrine. That she was stockpiling resources and had created a new division—a secret army—within the Rhaltan."

"She would never," Holt barked. "You're a liar."

Emmalyn slowly approached the Sendarian medic. "She's not lying. The queen is preparing for something. She's never said what, but it's why I relocated to Priomh. To search for answers without her knowing. To study the Anumen culture."

"In regard to what our mother is preparing for, well, we have some theories. But they're only theories," Gerard added, rubbing the scruff along his chin.

"We?" Holt asked at the same time Gemma silently thought the question.

"My wife, Honnah, and I," Gerard said, then briefly glanced in Breyah's direction. "She's Anumen as well and one of the Athru captives." He turned his glare to Gemma. "Did she speak with you?"

Gemma barely heard his question as she was too focused on what he'd said before that. "Wait—Honnah is an Anumen?" Gerard nodded, and anger surged through her. "Why didn't she say anything?"

"Maybe because you kidnapped her and were holding her hostage?" Gerard's tone was low and sharp, like a dagger pointed at her throat.

"I didn't know," she whispered. Then, with a little more conviction, she insisted, "I swear. I thought I was intervening in something Breyah was doing outside the Aevo C protocols. I only wanted to serve Isoldesse. That's all I ever wanted to do!" Tears welled and trickled down her cheeks. "And now… Now, she's bonded to me for the rest of my life!"

Emmalyn reached to give Gemma another hug, but Gemma pushed her away. "Don't! I don't want your pity or compassion or praise. I only want answers, and to know what the hegah is going on."

"As do we," Breyah said in a peaceful tone. "And now that you're here, and that you've bonded to the arcstone, maybe we can get those answers. I know Meegan will want to speak with…" Breyah gestured to the arcstone.

"Can someone explain to me why you all keep looking at Gemma's arm?"

"Holt," Gemma said, lifting the arm cuff toward him, "last night Meegan bonded my essence with the essence residing inside this arcstone." He opened his mouth, but she held up a finger, stopping him. "Let me finish. This golden stone is called an arcstone, and it came from a world called Anuminis. The home world of the Anumen people." She paused, then with emphasis repeated the word *people*.

"Anumens are mortals?" Holt asked, his voice wavering as if he was unsure he wanted to hear the answer.

"Yes," Emmalyn responded before Gemma could. "They live and die just as we do."

"Some of their people possess great power—a form of magic—that could be misinterpreted as divine powers," Gerard added.

Gemma pointed to the arcstone embedded in the cuff. "And sometimes, an Anumen's essence is ascended into one of these."

Holt's gaze focused on the stone.

She continued, "This one contains Isoldesse's essence."

Holt stepped closer, reaching for the stone. A look of confused crossing his face. "She's in there?"

"Her essence is, yes. And I can see and speak with her," Gemma explained. She didn't want to overwhelm the Lead Medic any more than he already was, which surprised her. Normally, she didn't care about how her words affected others.

He gently touched the smooth surface of the stone while examining it. After a short moment, he drew his hand away and said, "That is why you have two essences in your bio-scan."

Gemma nodded. Then he asked, "And you can really talk with her?"

Gemma nodded again, but then shifted into a shrug. "Something is wrong. She's not making any sense. She's asking about someone named Jasper, and saying that we can't let *them* find *her*. I don't understand what she means. It's all gibberish to me."

"I know what it means. I know what it all means." Gerard crossed his arms over his chest. "Something is coming. And I believe our mother"—he shot a glance at Emmalyn—"also knows what's coming, especially if she's opened all of the Reigning Doors. Isoldesse must've left information about them behind one of the doors."

"That makes sense," Emmalyn whispered. Then, a bit louder, she added, "It explains the stockpiling and secret army."

"What the hegah are you all talking about?" Gemma asked, stepping away from Holt. She wasn't the only one curious to hear what the two royal siblings were talking about as Holt and Breyah also turned to hear.

Gerard exchanged looks with his sister before he said, "We know who *they* are. They're called the Obard and they're hunting Anumens. What we don't know is *when* they'll come or *who* Isoldesse doesn't want them to find."

Gemma thought the *who* part was obvious. They had two Anumens here: Meegan and Honnah. One or both of them must be what these Obard beings wanted. The *when* part still lingered unanswered and scared the shit out of her.

Gemma looked around the room and said, "Well, I guess we need to figure things out, and we're going to have to do it together."

25

The dark underwater world went on for hours. Thankfully, the Sendarian man sitting next to Meegan had fallen asleep some time ago, allowing her some peace to read through the Anumen Doctrine. Jordi was nice, but she wasn't in the mood to make new friends or answer his questions about her home world.

The doctrine wasn't as bad as she'd thought it would be. Overall, it was ridiculously long, but that was to be expected since it was basically the law book for how the Sendarians live their lives. A simple speed-reading amula and she finished the entire book around the time their underwater tram ascended into brighter seawater. Resting the plac on her lap, she stared up through the glass tube. The tram sped through the glass enclosure at a high speed, but not too fast, as Meegan could still spot passing sea creatures or tall stalks of plant life.

"What did you think?" Jordi asked, stretching his arms upward while yawning.

"Your laws mirror the ways of Anuminis, or at least they are based on the ways of my people. But there are many parts of the doctrine that are specific to your people and how Isoldesse wanted your government to be run."

"Do you not have a government on Anuminis?"

"There is no Anuminis, and no, we didn't have a ruling government. There was a family that oversaw the regions, but they weren't a ruling power."

Jordi stared at Meegan for a long moment. "You've told me much about your world, but you never said what happened. Why do you live on Earth?"

Ugh. More questions, Meegan thought, cringing inside. She handed him the plac, and he tucked it into an inside pocket of his jacket. Glancing up at the ocean again, she said, "There are many worlds out there that aren't kind." She inhaled before continuing, "Or civil."

"We'd be naïve to think otherwise."

His words caught her off guard, and she turned her attention from the passing ocean above to Jordi, looking into his vibrant orange eyes. "You truly believe that?"

"Of course."

"And what of other Sendarians? Do they feel the same?"

He did a half-shrug, half-nod. "I suppose so." Then, shifting in his seat, not fully facing her, he added, "The Aevo Compendium observes and documents the evolution of many worlds. This is a fact. Proof that there is intelligent life beyond Sendara. We'd be loggies to believe the worlds we monitor are the only other worlds out there in the universe, and even bigger loggies if we thought every world out there was peaceful." He paused, then leaned in and whispered, "Though, I believe it's best not to assume the worst for any situation until you have all the details. Even when something unexpected happens."

"That's optimistic and naïve of you."

"Maybe. The second something happens, it happens...or happened. There's no going back. Only moving forward. It's as simple as I cannot control your actions, but your actions can affect me. I can only go forward from that."

His words almost inspired her to feel something for his world and its people. He'd provided Meegan some comfort in knowing that the Sendarians weren't all brainwashed by Isoldesse. Maybe she'd jumped to conclusions about the Sendarians just because they referred to Isoldesse as a goddess. Jordi was right when he said the Anumen Doctrine never specifically referred to or called her a goddess. That didn't change the fact that she was determined to reveal the truth about Isoldesse. These people deserved that, at least.

"Maybe you can tell me another time about your home world or why you live on Earth. It's not my intention to push or dredge up hurtful memories of your past."

She decided to test the waters and see his reaction to hearing the truth of his beloved goddess. "Anuminis was invaded. It was an emotional event that left many of my people dead or homeless."

"What brought about their attack?"

"Isoldesse did. The details of what happened aren't clear, but I'm slowly piecing together the truth of what she did that brought about the invasion that ended Anuminis. Especially now that I know about this Aevo Compendium she started. I'm thinking she visited a world that wasn't receptive to her presence. The beings there ended up being a hostile race, seeing a power in Isoldesse that they wanted. It's believed that she fled their world, and they followed her, wanting her power. Then, for who knows what reason, she traveled home, leading them straight to Anuminis. The invasion that followed almost caused our extinction, but thankfully, many escaped, fleeing and taking refuge on planets like Earth. To this day, our people still do not know why our home world was invaded. We only know it had something to do with Isoldesse. My whole life, I've done nothing but loathe that woman and what she did to our world. I will never forgive her."

He sat quiet for a long moment. "And who might these invaders be?"

"They're called the Obard, and they're not peaceful by any means. They strike without warning and kill without hesitation. What they want is power."

Jordi's face stiffened. His jaw clenched, as did his hand on the armrest. "That's horrible. Isoldesse did that to your world?" Meegan nodded slowly, trying her best to reel in the anger swelling inside. Even talking about the traitor made her blood boil. Jordi shook his head as he faced forward in his seat. "There must be more to the story. Isoldesse wouldn't purposefully allow those beings to follow her back to Anuminis."

"It doesn't matter if it was on purpose or not. She caused it by going there."

There was a long silence between them, and Meegan didn't rush to break it. This was what she wanted—to tell the Sendarians the truth. To make them see that Isoldesse wasn't immortal, but a living being like them. That the Aevo Compendium wasn't an act of kindness or salvation but a science experiment. She didn't want to bombard the poor man with that harsh reality, though. Not yet, at least.

Through her earpiece embedded in her ear, she heard Ben's voice. "We'll be arriving shortly. Stay sharp and be prepared for anything." Jordi must've heard the same message because he glanced over at her and nodded. She nodded in return. The thrill of engaging with the rebels again easily replaced the anger for Isoldesse coursing beneath her skin.

The water surrounding the transport tube gradually became brighter and clearer, sunlight reflecting along the surface. When they finally emerged out of the ocean, the tram slowed to a stop at the end of the glass tunnel along the shoreline of South Sendara. Meegan waited, like everyone else, for the glass dome to retract along the sliding tracks.

The second they were about to exit, Jordi jumped out and quickly turned to Meegan, one hand out to her. "Thanks, but I'm good," she said, brushing off his kind gesture.

He rubbed his hands along his jacket before clasping them behind his back. "Of course, sorry."

"You don't have to apologize." With a high step, she moved over the glass tube's edge and onto the beach. The sand wasn't sand but more like fine gravel, crunching beneath her shoes. Over her shoulder, she heard Darci's annoying voice rambling on about the history of this place.

"The island's original purpose was to be where Sendarians were sent and forced to live on their own without the structure of the communities, the security of the Rhaltan, the resource limits of the Elemental Council, or the overseeing guidance of the king or queen," Darci explained to Kenna as they trudged through the gritty gray sand toward the tree line of the bordering forest. "To prove that life without structure would cause chaos."

"But that's not what happened, is it?" Kenna guessed.

"No. The Sendarians who were sent here built something out of nothing, and they survived. It's said that life isn't easy here, especially because the region isn't good for farming, but there's plenty of food in these waters. That was good enough for the early settlers of South Sendara."

Behind them were the Priomh security officers, carrying oversized packs. Jordi motioned for them to follow. "We need to stick together."

Kenna and Darci meandered along, and when Meegan walked by them, their conversation grew quiet. It was ridiculous and Meegan couldn't care less to know what they were talking about, but deep down inside she did want to know. She hated that Kenna wasn't thinking clear, causing them to argue.

Meegan picked up her pace, increasing the distance between them and her. Liam jogged up to Meegan and said, "I know I messed up with Kenna." He paused, waiting for Meegan to acknowledge his apology.

Not slowing for him, she replied, "Yeah, you did."

That seemed to be good enough for him, because he added, "But we're here to find our family and friends. And I want to help." He ran a hand through his glamoured red hair. "So, don't bench me because I'm an ass."

When they reached the embankment, she spun, narrowed her eyes at him, and put emphasis on her words as she told him, "Okay. But you need to give her space. Hear me?"

Liam nodded. "Of course."

"Good." She turned to the steep embankment, and instead of climbing the side like everyone else, she silently cast an amula in her mind, using the surrounding air to lift her body up to the grassy ledge. At the top, she closed her eyes and let the salty air rush against her face, sweeping her red hair off her shoulders.

Meegan stayed there, waiting until everyone was up the embankment. One by one, they trapsed toward the footpath cutting through the woods behind her. She closed her eyes, pretending to enjoy the ocean breeze, when it was Kenna's turn to climb the embankment. The second she walked by, Meegan could feel her friend's essence, and how she paused for a brief second before continuing on with the others.

She only opened her eyes when Jordi said, "You have a gift." He gestured to the ledge. "That was impressive."

"It's part of who I am."

"It makes you beautiful."

"It makes me powerful," she corrected. They stared at one another for a long moment before he nodded.

"That it does."

She wanted to be alone. Wanted only to think of Nick whenever it involved matters of the heart. "Why are you flirting with me? We're on a mission to save people."

"Flirting? I'm not familiar with the term," he replied, blondish-red brows pinched. His wavy light-red hair with blond highlights blew away from his face in the ocean breeze.

She turned and spotted the footpath the others had taken. When she started for the trail, Jordi moved to her side, walking with her. "If you're implying that I'm showing interest in you, well, I am. And if you're wondering what kind of interest, to be honest, I'm not sure. I just know you fascinate me."

"I fascinate you?"

He nodded. "And I'd like the opportunity to get to know you better."

"To study me?"

"No," he quickly corrected her interpretation. "As a person. But if you prefer me to keep my distance—"

"I do," she blurted out, cutting him off. "I have no interest in making new friends."

Scratching his chin, he offered her a weak smile. "As you wish. I shall keep my distance." He fell back, walking behind her.

Inhaling a deep breath, she forced her mind to focus on the mission. They were in hostile territory, which meant she needed to keep her wits about her. They all did.

When she reached the clearing, three transport vehicles that had seen better days were parked. Everyone gathered around in two groups. One group was the Priomh security team, loading their packs into the backs of two of the vehicles while the other group was Kenna, Darci, and Ben. Liam was helping the security guards sort through the supplies.

Ben stepped aside and stood with his hands on his hips, watching Meegan and Jordi come out of the forest. "Over here," he said, more to Jordi than her, she assumed. But she made her way over, anyway.

"What's the problem?" Jordi asked, excusing himself and moving closer to his Rhaltan partner.

"Is that your guy?" Ben whispered, his back to Kenna, Darci, and the Sendarian man Meegan hadn't noticed before.

Curious, she walked past the two Rhaltan officers and included herself in Kenna and Darci's small circle. "And you are?" she asked, locking eyes with the Sendarian newcomer.

"Beannaith. I'm Zeke." The tall, toned man was slimmer than most of the Sendarian men she'd seen so far. He appeared younger, too, like the equivalent of an older teen.

"Okay, Zeke. And you're going to take us to the Athru?"

"If that's what Jordi wants."

"You don't address him as an officer?"

Jordi approached them, answering Meegan's question. "He's not part of the Rhaltan."

Zeke raised a finger, interjecting, "Not yet. But I'm working on it."

"What does that mean?" Meegan looked to Jordi for the answer.

The tall Sendarian crossed his arms, muscles stretching the fabric of his sleeves. "It means that he, and Ember, are trying to build up their credentials to earn an entry position into the Rhaltan. So"—Jordi narrowed his orange eyes at Zeke—"where is Ember? Why did she send you in her stead?"

"She got called in to handle a situation north of here."

"What situation?" Ben asked, joining the group. "Something we need to be worried about?"

Zeke shook his head. "Nah. But your call was last minute, and she didn't want to raise any suspicions by backing out. So she sent me to escort you to Echerce." He leaned in closer to Kenna and said, "Best to stick close to me. It can get rough in these parts." He ended with a wink, which made Kenna giggle.

Meegan rolled her eyes. *Are you freaking kidding me right now? When did she turn into this boy-crazy girl?! And right now, of all times!*

"We better get going." Zeke's friendly expression shifted to one a cadet might wear when addressing their superior. "The Athru camp you're looking for is five towns inland. It's home to more of the aggressive South Sendarians, so best to stay alert and be ready for anything."

Ben called out to the Priomh officers, "Let's ship out!"

Everyone climbed into the vehicles. Kenna and Darci followed Zeke into the first one while Ben took the driver's seat. Jordi headed to the driver's door for the second vehicle, and one of the Priomh security men drove the third. Meegan wanted to stay close to Zeke, as she didn't quite trust him yet, but she also wanted some space from Darci and Kenna. Walking over to the second vehicle, she caught Kenna glancing at her. The second she saw Meegan look her way, she climbed into the transport, Darci quickly following and closing the side door.

Meegan pursed her lips and shook off the frustration growing in her gut. This was ridiculous. She couldn't understand why Kenna was being so selfish.

This mission would be so much easier if Kenna would just put aside the notion that she's responsible for fixing Isoldesse's mess. Announcing that Isoldesse is an Anumen from another world and not really a goddess will not be enough. When is she going to understand that words won't fix this, but actions will?

"Everyone ready?" Jordi asked from the front.

Meegan and Liam answered, "Yes," prompting Jordi to take off in line behind the first vehicle.

Before Liam could strike up a conversation, Meegan focused her attention out the window, turning her back to him. He must've picked up on her mood because he said nothing to her after that. The drive was long, which gave her plenty of time to plan out which amulas she'd use, memorizing each word as if she were loading her weapons before battle.

"Be cautious, young Fawness, with how you use Eilimintach energy," the Eilimintachs whispered inside her mind.

"I will use my powers however I need to," she thought in response. *"This is a life-or-death situation, and I plan to show these Athru assholes the same kindness they showed Nick."*

"Choose a better path." Their collective voices faded.

"How about you choose to stay quiet?"

She waited for a rebuttal, but none came. Staring out the window again, she continued planning out the best amulas to use as her arsenal.

26

It had taken everything in her not to call over to Meegan when they were getting into the transport vehicles. They'd never fought like this, and it annoyed Kenna that they couldn't put their differences aside and focus on what was important. But then again, Meegan's priorities were askew, being on herself and not those in danger.

All she wanted to do is get back to Priomh and confront Isoldesse, she thought. *And I completely understand why, but rescuing my mom and the others is* more *important. Though, now that I know the truth about Mom being an Anumen, I'm not as worried. If she has half the power Meeg has, then I'm pretty sure she can take care of herself.*

She glanced at the seat next to her, where Darci had fallen asleep. It was nice that she'd come. Not only to keep Kenna company when her other friend wouldn't, but also so Kenna could get to know Sendarian Darci, which she was realizing wasn't much different from Earth Darci.

"You're awake?" Zeke said from the third row.

Kenna shifted on the second-row bench seat to face him but still keep her attention up through the crystal clear ceiling of the transport vehicle. Despite her recent quarrel with Meegan, the mission to find her mom and the others was progressing well. As they continued, they were also experiencing the wonders of Sendara, a beautiful and dangerous world full of new experiences.

"How can I sleep? Your world is amazing!" She couldn't tear her gaze from admiring the forest trees as they drove along the dirt road.

"My world?" He leaned closer, one hand gripping the seat for support.

Lowering her gaze, she stared into his orange eyes. "Oh, I mean, South Sendara."

His smile held more meaning than she wanted to read into. They'd only just met, but she couldn't shake the feeling that he liked her. The way he watched her… His eyes would linger a few seconds longer whenever he spoke to her. Like now. He was staring at her, and she couldn't help but ask, "What are you thinking about?"

"You."

Heat rose beneath the collar of her shirt, and it wasn't from the arcstone. "Me? What about me?" Wanting to face him more directly, she reached up and used the back of her seat to adjust her position. The second her fingers curled over the top, he slid his hand over hers.

"You're not like other girls."

"You barely know me."

One corner of his lips curled up. "True, but I'm an excellent judge of character. Nothing is ever a mystery to me, yet… I cannot figure out your story, and I like that."

Ben cleared his throat from the driver's seat, and Kenna quickly swiveled forward, realizing he was probably watching. After a long pause, he asked, "Where to, once we've reached Echerce?"

Kenna glanced over her shoulder, wanting to hear Zeke's answer. But to her surprise, he was still staring at her.

"Zeke!" Ben shouted.

Zeke's gaze slowly drifted from Kenna to the front, where he locked eyes with Ben, who was glaring at them both through the long rearview mirror spanning the length of the windshield. Zeke answered with an easygoing tone, "There's an old grinding mill on the south end of town. No one will be there until first light, so it'll be safe to hide the vehicles there."

Ben said nothing. He only stretched his neck, rolling it from side to side. He glanced back one last time, briefly meeting Kenna's gaze before returning his attention to the road. Heat briefly fluttered in her chest. And not the romantic sort. Shaking it off, she glanced over at Zeke. His smile was gone, replaced with a serious glower while he stared out the front window.

"I'm not a mystery to be solved," she offered, hoping it would deter him from wanting to know more about her. She reached up and held the back of her seat while looking at him.

His orange eyes stared back at her. "Oh, but you are." He scooted closer, his elbow touching her hand. "And I look forward to spending as much time with you as I can." His smile grew, and he winked at her just before leaning back into his seat.

Tilting her head up, staring at the treetops zooming by, she made a mental note to stay in contact with Zeke after the mission was over. Ben shifted in his seat up front, and Kenna caught him looking through the rearview mirror, watching her. Ignoring him, she turned to admire the outside world. She would not let him or Meegan ruin her chance to make a new friend.

"We're here!" Ben announced, slamming on the brakes. The vehicle jerked to a stop. Kenna's and Zeke's bodies were thrust forward. She raised her hands to brace for an unpleasant impact against the seat in front of her, but she was caught by firm hands grabbing her shoulders. Zeke's hands.

"Thanks," she said, lowering her arms.

"Any time."

Ben was out of the vehicle before she could yell at him for such a sudden stop. The side door slid open, and Ben stood there. "Stay close and don't trust anyone." His gaze drifted from her to Zeke, who was exiting his side of the transport behind Darci. During the newcomer's absence, Ben whispered to Kenna, "I'm serious. Stay close."

"Yeah, I know. I didn't even want to be here, remember?"

"What's that?" Zeke asked, catching the last of Kenna's words. "You didn't want to come? I thought you were eager to see the slums of Sendara."

Loud music played off in the distance. Kenna tried to see through the silhouettes of the trees, but it was too dark. Even the light from the two moons didn't help.

Ben shook his hand, and the tip of a short wand lit up. "Here, use this to help you see. We can't have you tripping in the dark."

"Thanks," she said, taking the pencil-length flashlight.

"Is that a party?" she asked, pointing in the music's direction.

Zeke nudged her with his shoulder. "It is. And you're in for a treat tonight. I promise, you'll be glad you ventured away from the mainland after you've experienced South Sendarian festivities. Come on," he said, grabbing her wrist and dragging her toward the forest.

Ben was quick to block them both. "Whoa! We need to wait for the rest of the company. No one goes anywhere—"

"It's just a party. Relax, okay!"

"We wait." Ben crossed his arms, not letting them pass.

"Fine, fine. We wait. But hurry it up! We're missing all the fun."

Kenna nodded to Ben, silently reassuring him they wouldn't go. When Jordi called out to Ben, Ben reluctantly stepped aside and moved to the second transport vehicle, where the Priomh security team was unpacking their gear.

Darci shuffled to Kenna's side. "Is that a party?" She stared out into the forest. "I wonder what they're celebrating."

Kenna glanced over her shoulder and spotted Meegan leaning against the front bumper of the transport vehicle. Liam was standing with her. Neither said anything to one another. They only stood there, watching the security guards unloading everything from the cargo area.

Catching Zeke's giddy expression, Kenna gestured toward the festivities with a flick of her flashlight. "You seemed excited about whatever's going on over there?"

The corner of his lip curled up. Moonlight from the two moons cast a pale light over them. "I am, of course," he said, placing a hand over his heart, "devoted to Sendara and the Rhaltan, but sadly we don't throw parties like they do in South Sendara."

"Take the vehicles and park them out of sight," Ben ordered the Priomh security team. "Stay put until we've located the captives. I'll call you in if, and only if, you're needed. Keep an open comm and be ready if we need you."

"Leadess gave us strict instructions to stay with—"

"Breyah isn't here, and you're under orders to follow me," Ben sternly explained. "You three," he pointed to half of the Sendarian security detail, dressed in covert dark brown pants and shirts, overlayed with black vests and lashers strapped to their thighs, "take the south side of town. The rest of you," he turned and faced the remaining three men, also dressed in covert attire, "cover the north side of town. Stay low and out of sight. Turn your communications on and wait for my command."

The man closest to Ben sighed and gave a reluctant nod. He then turned to his team and reiterated Ben's orders with more details about their designated locations. Ben faced Jordi and said, "I'll take the lead and you cover from the rear." Jordi nodded and stood back while Ben marched toward the edge of the woods. Toward the music and festivities.

As they approached the outskirts of town, Kenna thought the place resembled something straight out of an old western flick. A single wide gravel road travelled down the center with one and two story buildings lining both sides. Maybe it was too dark to see the rest of the town, but if this was it, then there wasn't much to it.

A few buildings down, the first party tents had been raised. Lights were strung up, crisscrossing over the main road, connecting the tents lining both sides of the street. They illuminated the crowds of Sendarians clustered in groups, talking, dancing, and reveling in whatever occasion called for the celebration.

"Remember, stay close," Ben said to Kenna, Meegan, Liam, and Darci before looking at Zeke. "Which building are they in?"

Zeke craned his neck out from behind a stack of tall wooden crates, then when he crouched back down, he told Ben, "Fifth building, on the right side."

While they talked about routes, Darci tapped her ear and said, "Remember to use your Linc if we get separated. And," she tapped the white stone embedded in the metal bracer wrapping Kenna's wrist, "the transessent bracer tracks your location."

Kenna lifted her hand, examining the wide metal cuff. "I hope Ulissa is doing okay."

Darci eyed the bracer. "Why wouldn't she be okay?"

Ben stood and started out for the street. Zeke waved for them to follow, and everyone filed out from behind the crates. Kenna answered Darci's question as they walked. "The transessent stone blocks the connection between essences." Kenna drew out the arcstone from beneath her shirt. "I have no way to communicate with Ulissa while wearing this bracer."

"Oh," Darci said with a sigh. "I'm sure she's fine."

"Hey," Kenna said, nudging Darci's arm. "I'm glad things are better between us. You know, now that everything's out in the open—no more secrets."

Darci smiled. "Me too. And I'm glad you're staying on Priomh. Especially since change is coming."

Kenna hadn't exactly said yes to Breyah's offer to stay on Priomh. And if Meegan had any say in the matter, Kenna definitely wouldn't be staying. A problem for after they rescued the captives. Ben was still talking with Jordi and Zeke, so Kenna quietly asked Darci, "Does that scare you? Knowing that change is coming."

"Nah. Well, maybe a little. But that's part of evolution, right? To grow and change over time. And Sendara is long overdue for a new era."

This got Kenna thinking that maybe change wouldn't be so bad for Sendara. Maybe announcing the real story of who Isoldesse was and where she'd come from would end up being more beneficial to the Sendarians. Maybe Kenna had been overthinking yet another problem that had a simple answer. She looked over her shoulder at Meegan, who was walking with Liam. He was talking while she scanned the surrounding area. Focusing on the gravel road, not wanting to trip and be the reason they got caught, Kenna thought about how much they'd changed too over these past few weeks. The concerning part was if the changes would ultimately lead to her best friend no longer being her best friend.

As they progressed toward the crowd, the music grew louder, the lights got brighter, and the hurrahs got closer, everything momentarily distracting Kenna from daunting thoughts about her friendship woes. She needed to focus on the mission—save the captives.

The atmosphere was intoxicating. She wanted to rescue her mom, but something inside her also wanted to let go of all the stress and anxiety and just join these Sendarians in whatever they were celebrating. So many Sendarians with shades of red hair and orange eyes filled the street, dancing and singing and drinking. Their movements were all in sync with the music floating in the night air over the crowd. Sendarian musicians beat multiple sets of drums and played an array of stringed instruments, luring Kenna's curiosity toward the clusters of dancers. The movements between these Sendarians were nothing like the dancing they'd done at the memorial on Priomh. It was like an outdoor club. A single street filled with Sendarians having a good time. She had trouble believing these people could be the same unruly, murderous, unethical Sendarians of the Athru?

"Don't drink anything," Darci said. "Remember what I told you about the Khal."

Kenna nodded, even though she was curious.

They were on the outskirts of the festival when Ben rejoined them across the street in a narrow alley. Once everyone was off the road, he asked Zeke, "Why can't we follow the alley to the back side of the buildings? Make our way down the street but out of sight?"

Zeke shook his head. "Not a good idea. There are sensors everywhere."

"Sensors?" Jordi asked, glancing up and down the alley. "What sensors?"

"The kind you can't see and that immediately alert the Athru leaders."

"Which of the three…I mean, two leaders are here?" Ben asked.

Zeke stared at Ben for a long moment before he answered, "Just one," which Kenna thought was odd. The testosterone between these two was getting annoying. A smile broke on the newcomer's face. "Rumor has it you've kept company with Anora."

Ben's face went rigid. He looked over the group, then his gaze briefly drifted along the brick wall of the alley before looking to Kenna. Then, to Zeke, he replied, "I did. But that was a long time ago." There was a pause before he continued. "Is she here?"

Zeke shrugged, nonchalance returning. "Last I heard, she was hiding out here somewhere, but she's not exactly one to flaunt herself around. Anora's an extremely private person."

"Who's Anora?" Kenna asked. The name sounded familiar, and obviously important to Ben, but he'd never mentioned an Anora, so Kenna had no idea who the woman was. Then she recalled something Jordi had recently told her. About a time when Ben was happy—smiling a lot more—because of love.

"You know what, it doesn't matter if she's here," Ben snapped before Zeke could respond. "Stay close, and let's go." He turned and marched out of the alley.

"Okay, come on. Let's not lose him," Jordi said, ushering everyone to follow.

Now, Kenna wanted to know more about this Anora woman and what she meant to Ben. But first things first, they needed to pull off this rescue mission.

27

Meegan didn't like it. This entire plan was crap and felt as if they were walking into a trap, especially with cocky-smirking Zeke taking the lead. She'd wanted to stay close to him—to keep track of him—as they snuck out of the alley toward the festivities, but she'd missed her opportunity when everyone hurried out in a single line, following Ben. She ended up in the back with Jordi.

"After you," he said with a wave of his arm.

Ignoring Jordi's politeness, she hurried to catch up to Liam. She couldn't help but mentally note all the places the Athru could be hiding, scanning every nook or shadowy area they passed. Not too far ahead, Kenna followed Darci, who followed Zeke. At least Meegan could still see him.

The music shifted from a lively tune to one with a heavy beat. The clusters of Sendarians dancing in the street also changed up their movements. Casual swaying and light steps turned euphoric and energetic, matching the drumbeats. The lights crossing above dimmed and turned a soft red, shrouding a seductive veil over the intertwining hands, arms, and swaying bodies.

The second the atmosphere of the party changed, Ben stopped. Meegan eyed him from the back of their procession, unsure of why they'd stopped. She thought he might be weighing their best route to get to the building entrance, but then she spotted the group of Sendarians, not taking part in the festivities. They were standing off to the side, huddled in a group. And they were wearing some kind of military uniforms.

Jordi pushed through, squeezing between their group lined up and the Sendarians' dancing beneath the glow of the red lights. As he shuffled by Meegan, she heard him say, "Oh, that's not good."

Meegan grabbed his arm, and when he pivoted to face her, she asked, "Who are they?"

"Not Rhaltan officers. I can tell you that."

"Is that what you guys are, Rawltan, or however you say it? Is that your military?" Liam asked while standing on his tiptoes, trying to get a better view of the Sendarians in question.

"The Rhaltan are Sendara's enforcing agency." Jordi continued on, shuffling past them, closer to Ben's side.

Meegan gestured with a jut of her chin to the group then leaning in, she said in Liam's ear over the music, "The Rhaltan are their military-slash-police, but not over here in South Sendara."

"So those dudes are like mercenary soldiers?" Liam's body pressed into Meegan as two women bumped into his side.

Together, they said, "Oh, sorry!" their voices laced with giggles, as some of their drinks spilled over the edges of their cups and onto Meegan's arm. Meegan glared at the two women, who laughed and apologized before joining the crowd dancing.

Liam quickly put some distance between himself and Meegan, then pointed to the soldier-like men. "Do you think they're part of the rebel group we're after?"

"There's a good chance they are." Meegan observed the group. They were attentive but in a casual and festive manner. None carried firearms. Instead, they had long staffs strapped to their backs or lashers holstered to their thighs.

Darci stepped away from Kenna and approached Meegan and Liam. "We're going to have to take the long way and avoid those men. Ben and Jordi are—"

"Kenna!" Meegan shouted, pushing past Darci. "Get over here!"

But she was too late. Zeke had Kenna by the hand and was leading her out into the street beneath the soft red glow of lights strung above. He was encouraging Kenna to dance, holding her hands with her back pressed to his chest. His rhythm weren't as energetic as those around them. Instead, he swayed his hips and shoulders, goading Kenna to do the same.

Meegan took a step out into the crowd—to drag her friend's ass back to the group—but the Sendarians in front of her packed in tighter, dancing to the music.

"This isn't good!" Darci shouted, but because of the loud music, Meegan barely heard her.

"Yeah, I know!" Meegan said then called to Ben, waving a hand in the air then pointing to Zeke and Kenna. "Hey! We've got a problem over here!"

The muscles in Ben's jaw tensed. Meegan caught movement from behind him and Jordi. Three of the South Sendarian soldiers were marching toward them. One guy tapped Ben on the arm, and the second he turned, the soldier punched Ben in the jaw. Jordi reacted, unstrapping his lasher from a concealed flap in his pants. He swung, connecting the end of his weapon with the side of the soldier's face.

Meegan was sure the brawl would've stopped the dancing, but it didn't. The music only grew louder. She tugged on Darci's arm and shouted, "This isn't right! I think we've walked into a trap!"

Both girls searched for Kenna while Liam grabbed a large metal plate from a nearby table and started fighting alongside Ben and Jordi.

"Where is she?" Meegan shouted.

"There!" Darci climbed onto a wooden barrel and pointed. "She's across the street with Zeke! And… Oh no…"

"What? What's wrong?" Meegan tried to see over the bopping heads of the Sendarians, who were still grinding and stomping to the rhythm of the music, but they were all too tall. And the red lights weren't helping. With a yell, she asked Darci, "Where is she?"

"Zeke's handing her a cup. And-and, oh no…" Darci crouched on the barrel. "I told her not to drink anything!"

Meegan attempted to push through the dancers again, but they didn't budge. When one of them looked straight at her with a devious smile, Meegan knew this was a trap.

She spun back toward the brawl, which now had twice the number of soldiers surrounding Ben, Jordi, and Liam. She needed to end this so they could help Kenna.

"Meeg! Something's not right!" Darci shouted, overlooking the crowd from on top of the barrel. "He's got Kenna over his shoulder!"

"Enough!" Meegan raised her hands.

"*It is unwise to use your gifts to harm others*," the Eilimintachs warned in her mind.

Ignoring them, Meegan cast the amula. The red glow within the string of lights turned white and intensified until the glass broke with a wave of popping sounds. Violent winds channeled down the center of the street, blowing over tables and chairs, bottles, and decorations. She inhaled, then released the air from her lungs, giving her amula more power—making the wind more forceful in its attack. Nearby windows shattered while front doors swung open, slamming against the side of the building. The South Sendarian men and women dancing in the street struggled to stand, eventually fleeing. The soldiers who had attacked Ben, Jordi, and Liam also fled.

Jordi and Liam got to their feet, catching their breaths as Ben ran by Meegan toward the opposite side of the street, shouting, "What happened? Where did everyone go?"

"Meegan! You can stop!" Darci shouted.

Meegan curled her fingers, drawing in the wind until it had vanished into the night sky. The street was dark except for a few lights untouched by the amula.

Jordi helped Liam regain his composure before they joined the others out in the street. Liam limped while Jordi helped support his weight. "Where's Kenna?"

The entire area had cleared out, leaving the festivities in disarray. They were the only ones left.

"It was a trap!" Meegan barked, rage sparking electric currents from her fingertips.

Darci slowly approached Meegan. "Hey, we'll figure this out. Maybe take some deep breaths or something."

"Don't tell me to calm down!" Meegan yelled. "Come out and fight, you cowards!" she shouted into the night air, toward the buildings.

Jordi's figure stepped in front of Meegan. His kind eyes stared into hers. "We'll find her, but we need to move fast. Are you in control?"

Her body trembled. The energy building inside teetered, and she worried she would lose control. Curling her fingers in, she drew the energy inward. Nodding, she reassured him, "I'm in control. What do we do now?"

"Why would they take Kenna?" Darci asked, circling in one spot, surveying the line of buildings trailing both sides of the street.

"There!" Jordi yelled, pointing toward the end of the main street.

A hundred yards out, past the last building, was Zeke. He was facing them with a caravan of transport vehicles behind him. One by one, they drove away. Zeke stood on the last vehicle's baseboard, holding an exterior handlebar next to the back-seat door. His voice resonated over the music's loudspeaker from the festival. "Anora gives her regards!"

Ben, who'd been checking out the other side of the street, turned and took off running, not waiting for anyone else.

"She also wanted me to tell you," Zeke continued, taunting the group as his vehicle's tires spun in the dirt, "that she's not done with you, and you'll be seeing her soon!" Then he slid into the back seat and slammed the door shut.

Ben ran faster, but not fast enough.

Everyone hurried to catch up with Ben, who was now hunched forward, hands on his knees, breathing heavy. "She's gone."

Meegan stopped next to him, her shoes sliding along the gravel. She held up her hands and called for more winds, hoping to stop the vehicles. After a few seconds, when the taillights grew dimmer, she knew she'd failed. Dropping her hands, she said, "I couldn't stop them."

Darci ran up next to her, breathing heavy. "This is not good!"

With fury in her voice, Meegan pointed out, "You were supposed to stay with her!"

"I... I'm sorry. I..." Darci stuttered.

"We'll get her back," Ben said, standing upright and assessing the town behind them. "But first, let's see if Zeke was lying about the captives."

28

After opening the front door of her home, Gemma turned to face the two Priomh security guards who'd escorted her from Medical. "I'm here. You can leave now."

One guard cocked his chin up. "Our orders are to remain outside your door."

"You being out here will only draw attention." With a hand on her hip, she assured them, "I'm not going anywhere. Breyah should know that."

It was the second guard who answered, "Our orders come from Prince Gerard."

She couldn't argue with that. "Fine. Whatever." Leaving the two to stand out front, she headed inside. "Linc."

"*Yes, Gemma. How can I assist?*" the soothing voice of her Live InterNeural Connection responded.

"Set external glass to sixty-five percent tint."

The windows stretching along the back side of the open living space gradually tinted to the designated percentage. Micah and Xander exited out from within the kitchen alcove.

"It's about time," Micah said with frustration in his tone. His orange eyes glared beneath that stupid Earth baseball hat he'd grown so fond of.

Xander wrapped his arms around her. "Are you okay?"

Holding his embrace for a second longer, they eventually parted. "I'm fine, thank you. Tired and annoyed, but healthy." She sank into the sofa cushion, leaning on the arm. Xander claimed the spot next to her while Micah loomed over them both.

"Holt ran a bio-scan that showed nothing wrong with me, except the fact that I now have two essences."

Micah handed her a glass of water, and asked, "What kind of tech scans essences?"

"The kind that we shouldn't have right now. Her Highness took it upon herself to open all the Reigning Doors."

Blonde brows pinched beneath his cap. "Tell me you're lying?"

Gemma shook her head.

"Why are these doors so important?" Xander asked, looking from Gemma to Micah.

The old Gemma would've verbally attacked him for asking such an ignorant question, but then how would he know anything about Sendara or Isoldesse? Micah returned to the kitchen, remaining within earshot. Gemma faced Xander and explained, "When Isoldesse first arrived to Sendara, our way of life was quite different than it is today. The mainland wasn't always united but divided into regions. Each region was hungry to outshine the others. Isoldesse showed the leaders of the old regions a new way—a way to survive. She used her divine powers to persuade the regional leaders to stop abusing the planet's resources for selfish gain. She convinced them that Sendara would dry up and die within the next few centuries, bringing about the extinction of their people… If they didn't change their ways."

"An actual god revealed herself to your world?" Xander questioned. He ran his hand through his black hair. "That's insane!"

"Let me finish. The story that's told tells of Isoldesse's persuasive personality convincing the region leaders to unite under one land. She remained on Sendara for about a decade rewriting the laws and forming the new royal government. Though, it wasn't only the royal family that ruled Sendara. Isoldesse created the Elemental Council to oversee the planet's resource consumption and the Rhaltan to oversee and enforce security and protection. Anywho, during the ten years she lived among our people, she also wrote out the Anumen Doctrine—laws for Sendara to follow. Our world has been living by the laws written in the Anumen Doctrine since then. Or, well, up to now. The queen has taken it upon herself to rule outside the laws written in the doctrine."

"Like opening the Reigning Doors," Micah added, handing Gemma a small plate of fruit and cheese.

She nodded and accepted the plate. After nibbling on a piece of cheese, she continued, "Beneath the royal palace on Sendara, Isoldesse had the Sendarians build a secure bunker." Xander opened his mouth, but Gemma quickly pressed a finger over his lips before he could ask his question. "Ah-ah-ah, I haven't finished." When she lowered her hand, Xander closed his mouth and let her finish. "This wasn't just any bunker. This was a bunker specifically designed for the royal family. When one ruler steps down and a new ruler comes into power, the new ruler must open the next door inside the bunker."

"How many doors are in the bunker?"

"No one knows," Micah answered. "It's a room, no bigger than this living room."

"There's another door within the room, but it's not to be opened until the next ruling king or queen."

"Okay, that makes sense. So, what's inside the room?" Xander rested his elbows on his knees, engrossed in the story.

"Isoldesse wanted to help our world stay on the path she created even if she couldn't be here. So, she strategically placed gifts in each room to help our world grow."

Xander pinched his eyebrows together, then leaned back on the sofa cushion. "What gifts? And what's the big deal if the queen opened all the doors? Sounds like a good deal to me."

Gemma rolled her eyes. "Of course you would think it's a good deal. You humans are all about more, more, more."

"Nothing wrong with having a little more."

She shot to her feet, almost spilling the hot tea. "That's why your world will end and ours will thrive. You choose more while we choose…" She trailed off, realizing the Athru goal was to destroy everything Isoldesse had worked so hard to establish—the Sendarians' safety from extinction. She whispered while staring out the tinted window, "There has to be a middle ground. A way to have the best of both worlds."

"Yeah, after everything that's happened…" Micah said, coming into the living area with a plate full of food. He leaned against the glass wall that spanned the back side of the house and continued, "Anora might have had good intentions when she, Biryn, and Quaid started the Athru—well, maybe not Quaid—but things have changed. Anora's agenda has changed. But that doesn't mean our agenda has to change. We can still try to take down the queen. We've got Logan and"—he gestured to Xander—"this loggie to help."

"Thanks, jackass," Xander retorted.

Gemma dropped her head into her hand, propped up by an elbow on the arm of the sofa. Rubbing her temple, she slowly lifted her head and said to Micah, "I wish it were that simple. Because it turns out, there are bigger things at play."

"So the queen opened the doors, and now she's got all kinds of gifts she wasn't supposed to have," Xander recapped. "Can't you use that against her? Tell other people about what she's done? Maybe they'll join your cause."

"Well, not such a loggie after all." Micah pushed off the glass wall, bringing his empty plate to the kitchenette. "That might be a workable option."

Gemma sat straight and shook her head. "It doesn't matter anymore. We don't have to do anything because change is coming, regardless. I don't know if it means the queen's reign is over, but it might."

Drying his hands, Micah turned to his sister. "What does that mean?"

"Anora believes the queen secretly started another branch of the Rhaltan to use against Sendara. That's not the case. Well, I mean it's true—but not for the reasons Anora thinks. Queen Adalyss discovered a warning left by Isoldesse behind one of the Reigning Doors."

Micah tossed the towel into the kitchenette nook. "What kind of warning?"

"I don't know. Emmalyn didn't get into specifics, but whatever it was it was enough to spook the queen and have her take extra precautions." Gemma stood, set her plate of food down, and started pacing the length of the living area.

"That explains why she's stockpiling resources against the Elemental Council's orders?" Micah asked.

Gemma nodded. "And it's the reason she's secretly created that extra Rhaltan soldier division. What I can't figure out is what this means for our world. How can we prepare Sendara for something that might never come?"

"Or worse," Micah interjected, "something that might be on its way."

Unsure about how to answer, she inhaled a deep breath. "We need to know more about these Obard beings and the warning Isoldesse left about them."

Just then, the front door opened, and the banished prince strode in. "I think I can help with that. May we come in?" Behind him, the princess and Breyah stood.

"Well, you've already opened the door without knocking, so why the hegah not?" Micah said with a hint of sarcasm, storming off to sit on the stairs on the other side of the open room.

"Ignore him. Yes, please come in," Gemma said, welcoming them over into the main living with a wide sweep of her hand. "I want to hear everything you know about these Obard and how Isoldesse is connected to them."

"Why don't we start with what you know, sister?" Gerard beckoned to Emmalyn.

The princess cleared her throat and stood in front of Gemma, Xander, and Breyah who were all sitting on the sofa. Gerard stared out the rear glass wall, out to the backyard, while Micah remained sitting on the steps. The princess had changed her clothes since Gemma had last seen her in Medical, from a casual white pantsuit to a knee-length, sleeveless white dress. Emmalyn clasped her hands at her waist and explained, "When our mother opened the last room within the Reigning Doors, it only contained a single letter, not addressed to anyone. Whatever was in that letter, our mother burned it the second she'd finished reading it."

"Well, then, how do you know what it said?" Micah asked.

"Because I was there, standing close by."

"You saw what was written?" The second Gemma asked, Isoldesse materialized next to the princess. Gemma's gaze slid to their goddess, who was listening in on the conversation. Her shoulder-length black hair was straight and sleek, not a single dry strand on her head. Isoldesse's focus darted between the royal siblings, and eventually she moved to look over Gerard while the princess continued her story.

"I only saw the words *danger* and *coming* before Mother ripped up the note and ordered the guard to set fire to it before I could see anything else. But those two words, and that every room following that room was empty, ignited her to prepare for something."

Gemma kept an eye on Isoldesse. The Anumen's interest seemed to be centered around the prince.

She was about to tell the others about Isoldesse being present when an urgent message flashed across the glass window lining the back side of the room.

Everyone stood from the sofa, and Breyah moved to the glass. "Linc, accept the incoming call." Immediately, the glass tinted, blocking the afternoon sunlight, and Ben appeared on a large screen. Crossing her arms, she asked, "What's your status?"

Gemma took in the South Sendarian town in the background. She didn't recall hearing any talk about festivities, yet it looked as if there was some kind of celebration.

"The Athru were expecting us. They knew we were coming." Ben shifted the camera view, zooming out to show Meegan talking with Darci and two men, one being younger than the other.

"Where's Kenna?" Gerard asked. The prince crossed his arms over his dark jacket while scanning over the scene.

Ben pursed his lips, inhaling a deep breath through his nose before he answered. "She was taken, Your Highness. By the Athru."

He gasped, then breathed a soft, "No!" heartache lacing his words. In a more stern tone, he berated the Rhaltan officer, "I trusted you with my daughter!"

The older Sendarian talking with the others jogged up to Bennach. He pointed up, then said, "There are Sendarians on the third floor of that building."

Bennach's gaze shifted up.

"It could be another trap," Gemma interjected. "Be cautious."

The two men turned their attention to the video call. Bennach narrowed his orange eyes at her. "And why should we trust your word, Gemma of the Vaudd family? You're a traitor to the queen and Isoldesse for abandoning your position within the Aevo Compendium."

"I trust her." It was Breyah's turn to cut in. "And you've already walked into one trap, so you have to assume they'll expect you."

Hearing her old friend's supporting words reassured her confidence. Then, simultaneously, there was a sense of someone standing close by, yet the space next to her was empty air.

"It wasn't until Isoldesse whispered, *"We need to find Jasper,"* inside Gemma's mind that she flinched. Gemma almost tripped over the low-rise table set between her and the sofa.

The Leadess seemed to be the only one who caught Gemma's sudden shudder. "Are you okay?"

"Yes, sorry. I'm fine." Shaking her head, Gemma regained her balance and focused on the call with Bennach. "It's a trap, but if the Athru are taking cover up in one of the buildings, then you can be sure there's something important Anora wants protected."

That was all Bennach and the man needed to hear before waving for the others to head out. Bennach ran for the building. The video display bounced about, and heavy footsteps pounded the dirt road. When they reached the front door, he looked into the plac and said, "I'll contact you after we've secured the town and found the captives."

"What about Kenna?" Gerard asked. "You cannot leave Sendara without bringing my daughter back to me."

"We'll find her too. I swear it. Breyah, I'll be in touch soon." The display went black, leaving everyone in the room to stare at a dark window.

A somber silence filled the living area of Gemma's home. No one spoke or moved. And when the princess finally broke the silence, her voice was void of her usual cheeriness. "They'll find her. They'll find them all." She then, wrapped one arm around her brother's waist. He didn't hesitate to pull her in for a hug. Gemma couldn't recall the last time she and her siblings had embraced, offering comfort or condolences.

The tint of the exterior glass wall enhanced the overall mood of the room. Breyah took a seat on the sofa. But the second she'd leaned back into the cushion, another urgent call flashed on the glass. "Now what?" Breyah said with a sigh, getting to her feet.

It was Emmalyn who answered the incoming call by pressing a hand to the window, activating the display screen to pop up again. Gemma immediately recognized the royal councilwoman, Shea.

"Princess," the broad-shouldered woman said, eyeing the audience listening in to their call. Her gaze landed and remained on Gemma.

"It's okay. She's helping us."

"Are you sure?"

It was Gerard who answered. "Yes. Now, what is it?"

Shea straightened, tilting her chin up with respect. "Long-range sensors have detected unknown space vessels."

"When did we get long-range—" Gerard stopped himself. "The Reigning Doors, of course."

Emmalyn nodded. "I've actually snuck quite a few things without Mother knowing from her raid behind the doors."

"I don't want to know the details." Gerard shook his head while rubbing his forehead. "Okay"—he lifted his gaze from behind his hand—"what can you tell us about these incoming vessels?"

Shea briefly glanced at Gemma before returning her attention to the royal siblings. "Not much. Only that there are three ships. Each one being at least four times the size of the *Tarais*."

"How long before they reach us?" Breyah rubbed her biceps. Gemma instinctively mimicked her and rubbed the arcstone in the arm cuff. Looking to the royal siblings, Breyah asked, "Why would anyone be traveling to Sendara?"

Gerard rubbed his short beard. "Show us what you found." Shea nodded and split the screen. On one side was an image of three black spheres, like dark planets, flying through space. Gerard tapped the screen, and the image zoomed in. "It has to be them."

"We need to contact the queen," Emmalyn said. Gerard gave her a curt nod, and Emmalyn looked to Shea. "Please contact the queen and update her with everything going on."

"Everything?" the royal councilwoman asked, gaze momentarily flicking to Gemma.

"Everything," Emmalyn answered.

"Very well," Shea replied and bowed her head before disconnecting the call. Half of the screen remained dark, leaving the other half with the image of the incoming spaceships.

"Is it the Obard?" Gemma asked, staring at the image on the screen. Even Micah inched closer to see the ships.

Breyah, Gemma, and Micah waited for confirmation from the two royal siblings. It was Gerard who explained, which was fine by Gemma since the princess tended to veer off topic. He pointed to the image and said, "Yes. It's the Obard. They travel the galaxy, hunting Anumens."

Gemma swallowed, just as Isoldesse appeared. Their goddess stood in front of the image on the glass. Everyone continued talking about these Obard beings while Gemma watched Isoldesse trace one finger over the three spherical vessels.

"Do you know who they are?" Gemma asked. The second she spoke to the thin air beside her the room fell quiet. All eyes were on her. Ignoring them, she approached the Anumen. "Can you tell us what they're coming for?"

Isoldesse didn't respond. She only continued tracing the outline of the ships with her finger, a tear trickling down her cheek.

"Please, help us," Gemma pleaded. It wasn't until she'd rested her hand on Isoldesse's arm that she'd gotten a reaction.

Her confused expression was something between concern and impassiveness. It took Gemma's bonded companion a few moments to offer an answer. "We need to find Jasper," she said, facing Gemma. "Jasper knows how to fix my mistake."

Not wanting to address the part about 'my mistake', Gemma focused on the other hopefully helpful information. "Who is Jasper?"

"I need to know she's safe—I need to know Ulissa is safe."

"Do you know where you are?" Gemma opened her arms out to her sides. "We're on Priomh. Do you remember Priomh?"

The Anumen woman blinked, then looked to the others who were watching them. Eventually looking to Gemma again. "This is not Anuminis. You are Sendarians."

"Yes. You're on Priomh."

"Priomh. The Aevo Compendium research building."

Gemma smiled, happy to hear Isoldesse more lucid. "Yes, except we've moved the research compound, expanded the community."

A small smile emerged. The golden aura shined brighter, highlighting Isoldesse's light brown skin. "That sounds nice." The Anumen woman, brushed one hand down the white sleeve of her jacket while returning her attention to the image on the glass screen. "Your time is running out."

Gemma slowly turned to Breyah. "Isoldesse is here."

"We assumed that." Emmalyn answered instead of the Leadess. "What is she saying?" The princess waved a hand through the air before Gemma.

"Stop that!" Gemma snapped, knocking Emmalyn's hand away. Everyone froze, especially the princess. "I'm sorry. I didn't mean to… I mean, you were hitting Isoldesse!"

"Not to worry." Emmalyn stepped back next to Gerard.

"Ask her if she knows how to stop them." Gerard gestured to the space where he assumed Isoldesse was located.

Gemma nodded, then asked Isoldesse, "How can we stop them?"

Isoldesse drew her finger away from the glass. "What they want, I cannot give to them. So they will come, and they will destroy everything."

Wide-eyed, Gemma snapped, "That's not an option. Now, tell me what the hegah we have to do to stop the end of the world from happening to Sendara!"

Gemma's outburst implied the conversation with the Anumen woman wasn't a good one. Next to Gerard, Emmalyn hugged his arm tighter. Breyah fidgeted her fingers over her arm, where her mother's metal cuff would normally rest. Even Micah looked concerned, holding his baseball cap in his hands, twisting it with a death grip. The only person who didn't look freaked out was Xander.

He'd been standing behind her the whole time, and his expression read more as sorrowful than shocked.

"Are you okay?" she asked him.

"No. I thought we'd have more time together."

Oddly, she thought of the words *Ti amo* and brushed her fingers through his hair. "We will."

"If you give them what they want, there's a chance—" Isoldesse said, her words soft but loud enough for Gemma to hear.

Gemma waved her hands for everyone to stop talking. "What did you say?" She leaned in closer to Isoldesse. "If we give them what they want?"

Isoldesse shivered. Then, blinking several times, she shifted into a frenzy, talking about needing to find Jasper.

"Focus, please! I will help you find Jasper if you tell me how we can stop the Obard from attacking."

Isoldesse's wide brown eyes stared at the ships on the screen. With a shake of her head, she insisted, "You can't give them what they're after. They'll kill her and then turn on you for hiding her!" She crouched low, mumbling, her hands over her head.

Gemma didn't know how to help her so that she'd be more useful in figuring out how to stop the Obard from invading. Normally, she'd snap and slap some sense into whoever pissed her off, but Gemma knew exerting that kind of aggression wouldn't help their situation. Instead, she held Isoldesse's shoulders, and when the woman looked at Gemma, she said, "Why don't you rest? I'll help you find Jasper after you've gotten some sleep."

Isoldesse nodded, then slowly faded away.

"She's resting," Gemma explained to the room. "I don't know if any of that helps, but she said something about not giving 'her' to them." She looked to Gerard, hoping he would understand.

After a long pause, Gerard said, "They want the Fawness. They want Meegan."

29

This couldn't be happening. Not now. Not Kenna. Meegan pressed her back up against the wood shingles of the building. She was having trouble collecting her thoughts—trying to focus on what to do first. The rage and fear building up inside her overwhelmed her to the point that she struggled to focus on what to do next. Meegan had watched her best friend get thrown into a transport vehicle and taken by the same rebels who'd killed Nick.

Ben was assessing the building while Darci and Jordi were trying to track Kenna.

Darci suggested, "Check Liam's location."

Jordi tapped the screen, then faced Liam. "Yup, he's right there."

"But you can't see Kenna?" Darci asked, stepping closer to get a better look at the screen.

Jordi shook his head, then pressed the power button at the top corner. "No. There's nothing. Either it's a malfunction or Zeke deactivated it somehow."

"Or," Meegan added her thoughts, "you weren't tracking her to begin with."

Jordi cocked his head, lowering the plac. "Explain."

"Kenna's wearing a stone around her neck. It's called an arcstone. A powerful stone containing magic from my world. Anyway, the arcstone doesn't work when a person comes in contact with a transessent stone."

"The battery stone powering the bracers?"

She nodded to Jordi. "The transessent stone is an amplifier, not a battery. When the two stones come in contact with a being, energies get blocked. I think that's why you can't track her bracer. We'll have to find a different way to locate her."

"First," Ben barked out, "we find out what's up there. Hopefully, it's the captives. Then, we can focus on finding Kenna."

Meegan wanted to argue, but the words wouldn't form. Her thoughts were too jumbled. Ben didn't wait for Meegan or Jordi to acknowledge or agree, and charged inside the building. Jordi handed Darci the plac, unstrapped his lasher, and ran inside after Ben. Darci slid the plac into her vest pocket, gave Liam the go-ahead nod, then proceeded inside. Meegan inhaled a deep breath, needing to get her head on straight. Footsteps pounded the stairs inside and she knew she needed to move.

Up on the second floor, Meegan heard Ben say, "Priomh Team Leader. We request an immediate extraction. Bring all three vehicles into town and park in front of the three-story black stone building on the north end of the main street."

Silently, Meegan cast an amula for speed. Passing Darci, Liam, and Jordi, she quickly caught up to Ben. He'd been climbing two steps at a time. And when they reached the third floor, Meegan peeked up over the floorboards to see what was waiting for them. The landing opened up to a spacious room. Thick posts were spaced out, stretching up to the rafters above. A single wooden table with two chairs was positioned near a closed door.

Ben didn't stop and the second he'd entered the room, a woman jumped out from behind one of the posts, swinging two daggers, one in each hand. Ben leaned away, barely missing the edge of a dagger. He quickly regained his balance, then confronted the woman, dodging her strikes. A few seconds later, his fist connected with her jawline, knocking her to the floor. More rebels emerged from their hiding spots, all holding weapons—daggers, pipes, lashers, and one guy had a whip.

Jordi rushed past Meegan and joined Ben in the fight. Darci unstrapped her lasher and rushed at an Athru woman who was about to collide with Jordi. The Athru woman had a shaved head and multiple scars trailing her scalp. Meegan couldn't believe this Darci was the same bubbly girl who acted so clueless on Earth. She fought as if she'd been training for battle for years—which, Meegan realized, she probably had been.

Two men with curly red hair, looking like twins, barreled straight for Meegan and Liam.

"Oh, shit!" Liam yelled, stumbling down a few steps from the stairwell.

Her survival instincts kicked in, and instead of retreating, Meegan climbed up the remaining stairs and confronted the two Athru men head-on. With her hands out to her sides, palms open wide, she cast an amula, forcing the two men to collide with one another. Then she thrust her hands forward, throwing them across the room and knocking their bodies into the exposed studs of the wall. Another man advanced at her, and with a wave of her hand, she flung his tall lanky body into the air, then slammed his body against the ceiling. Dust and debris rained over him as he fell to the floor.

"We don't have time for this," Meegan seethed. She spread her arms out to her sides, sending a wave of energy outward. The windows smashed, sending broken glass to the street below. The fighting hadn't ceased. Ben threw punches, Jordi blocked hits with his lasher, Darci wrestled on the floor, and Liam was trying to wiggle his way out of a choke hold. It was her responsibility to save them—at any cost.

Drawing in the winds from outside, she filled the room with powerful streams of air, knocking over wooden chairs and stacked crates. The Athru men and women stumbled against the forceful air rushing them. They blinked rapidly, trying to keep their eyes open to see what was happening.

Liam rolled away from his assailant while Jordi and Darci each grabbed one of the support posts. Ben shouted at Meegan, but the wind overpowered his voice. The amula grew stronger, pulsing through her veins and drawing more air into the room. One by one, she threw a rebel here and tossed a rebel there. They tried to strike her, but they couldn't reach her. She was in control of everything. It was she who decided who lived and who suffered. And these Sendarians didn't deserve mercy.

"*Fawness,*" the Eilimintachs called through her mind.

She ignored them.

"*A Fawness should protect and enlighten those who stray or feel discouraged. Our gift to command the Eilimintach essences around you was not meant to be used to harm others.*"

A *crack* snapped in the air, and Meegan spun around. She faced a man holding a long leather whip. With a quick flick of his wrist, he snapped the whip again, and the tip struck against her thigh.

"You're going to regret that!" She marched toward him while raising her hands up high. The man went to strike her again, but Meegan swooped her arms down and up, commanding the air to lift him off the ground. She pushed her hands forward, and the wind obeyed, throwing the Sendarian backward. His body rolled over a fallen chair. Then, as he stumbled to his feet, she hit him with another burst of air, sending him flying out the broken window behind him.

"*Enough!*" the Eilimintachs' voices boomed in her head.

A powerful force, like the hand of gravity, passed through her from head to toe, pushing out every ounce of power from her body. The room grew quiet as the winds died. The muscles beneath her skin ached, and she had the sudden urge to vomit. She pressed her clenched fists to her stomach, hoping to ease the nausea while gasping shallow breaths. "What's happening?" she cried.

Footsteps pounded on the old wooden floor, and she glanced up to see a Sendarian man the size of an ox looming over her. He grabbed her by the hair, and held her against the wall. Even though her mind was foggy, she tried commanding amula after amula to fight back, but there was nothing. When he drew a fist back, she swore she was done for, but Jordi came in from the side and slammed into the man. They both toppled to the floor. Meegan dropped to the floor too. The two men pounded one another, rolling around inches from her.

Ben and Darci jumped in and restrained the Athru brute. Once the man was secure, they tied up the other Athru members either badly injured or lying unconscious.

Meegan knelt there, unable to do anything but watch. She called on the Eilimintachs, but they responded to her pleas with silence.

"Are you okay?"

Meegan lifted her head and was surprised to see Liam's glamour had vanished. He looked like Liam again.

"Meeg. Are you okay?" Liam repeated.

She shook her head. Tears trickled down her cheeks. "They took it. All of it."

Liam searched the room. "Who took what?"

Holding up her hands, she explained, "The Eilimintachs. They took my power from me."

His gaze dropped to her hands. "What for?"

"In here!" Ben shouted from an adjacent room. Finished securing the last of the Athru, Jordi and Darci hurried off through the open door. Even Liam forgot his conversation with Meegan and hurried to follow the others. Meegan however, was unable to move. Unable to think about what to do now that she was helpless and useless.

"Meegan!" Darci called from the doorway. "You need to see this."

Slowly, Meegan forced herself to get up and put one foot forward in front of the other, until she was standing in the doorway. Liam was crouched next to Julianna while Jordi and Ben helped a bruised-up Sendarian woman.

"Where's Honnah?" Meegan asked, searching the small room.

Ben stepped into the center of the space, addressing the room. "They must've taken her too."

"No," the Sendarian woman said, getting to her feet with Darci's help. Hobbling up to Ben, she explained, "She's working with them."

"Are you sure, Eryn?" Darci asked while looping the woman's arm over her shoulder for support.

Eryn nodded and leaned on her friend.

"There's no way! Kenna's mom wouldn't help the enemy!" Meegan felt a surge of anger, but had no power to accompany it. This was a first—to feel emotions mentally rather than with her powers as a physical sensation.

"It's true," Julianna confirmed, staggering to her feet. "And I don't think Honnah is from Earth."

Well, that Meegan already knew. Kenna had overheard Gerard telling Breyah about that revelation. But why would she be helping the Athru?

"Do you know where they're going?" Ben asked Eryn.

"No. But they took Rian with them." Eryn winced, pressing a hand to her head. "Can we get the hegah out of here?"

That's right, Meegan thought. *The Obard woman was supposed to be here too. What is Honnah up to? And what is she going to do when she sees the Athru have taken Kenna?*

"Can you track Kenna with your powers?" Ben asked, not answering Eryn's question about leaving.

Meegan inhaled deeply, closed her eyes, and searched her mind for the right amula. But her knowledge of the ancient Eilimintach language was gone. She had nothing. "Dammit!" she yelled up to the ceiling. "I need to save Kenna!"

Silence.

She dropped her head into her hands and let the tears fall. Jordi approached her, cupping her shoulder with one hand. "Hey, this isn't your burden to bear. We're all here to save the captives, and that now includes Kenna."

Anger swelled in her core. She might not have power, but she still had muscle. She shoved Jordi's hand away then pushed him. He stumbled a few feet but didn't fight back. A look of shock crossed his face. Everyone stared as she exploded at him. "It is my burden and my burden alone. I'm the only one who could fix the shit we're all in because of that traitor Isoldesse!"

Jordi regained his balance and marched right back up to her, facing off with her. "You're wrong. You don't have to do this alone. We're here with you. We want to help. Let us help."

Meegan was taken aback by his boldness. Tears welled in her eyes because she was supposed to save them. Everyone, even Ben, stood with reassurance, nodding slightly that they had the same goals as Meegan—to put an end to the Athru rebels, find their friends, and get answers. For now, and since she had no other choice, Meegan offered them a single nod. She wasn't ready to let anyone else carry this burden, but because she'd been stripped of her power, she needed them.

"Good," Ben said. "Because I think I may have a way to talk with Kenna."

Wishing she could burn this forsaken land to the ground, Meegan reeled in her anger and listened to what he had to say. "Great. I'm all ears. What's your plan?"

"We'll need to get back to the transport ship. I'll use a stasis chair, and once I'm sedated, all I have to do is wait. She'll come to me."

A small glimmer of hope surfaced inside. She actually liked that plan because she knew exactly what Ben meant, and he was right. Kenna would find him in his dreams.

30

Blinking, Kenna slowly woke from a deep sleep. Her muscles ached with a grogginess she'd only felt after getting her wisdom teeth out. Sitting up, she noted the dim cabin space was too big to belong to a transport vehicle, yet she could hear the hum of an engine. Seats lined both sides of the wide corridor. Black panels curved up the sides and flattened along the ceiling. A thin strip of plastic illuminating a white light stretched down the center, barely giving off any light.

"Where the hell am I?" she said, thinking aloud as she reached for a tender spot along her jawline. The tips of her fingers jabbed into a soft silicone material.

"Best not to touch that," a woman said from across the room. Peering into the darkness, Kenna made out a form, glassy eyes staring at her.

"And you are?"

The woman slid to the center of the long bench. Medium-length locks of blue hair hung over her face, and her pale blue eyes peered at Kenna between matted tendrils. A white tubular plastic thing was wrapped tightly around her neck.

Kenna stood, recognizing Rian the second she came into the dim light, but Rian shook her head. "Don't. Stay there, and don't give them any reason to activate your collar."

Kenna touched the soft silicone of the collar, realizing that hers wasn't inflated like Rian's. "Are you okay?" When Rian raised a blue eyebrow at her, she rephrased her question. "Right. Sorry, obviously neither of us is okay. I guess I meant, are you injured in any way?"

"No, but this collar prevents me from fighting back. Some kind of muscle-controlling mechanism. They've had me sedated, mostly, only waking me during their relocation."

"Where are they taking us?"

"They haven't really clued me in to the details of whatever they're planning. But I know that one of the human captives is helping them."

Unsure of who else the rebels had captured from Earth, Kenna dismissed any thoughts about who was helping the Athru. She was curious to know if Rian had seen her mother. "Do you recall an older woman with long black hair being held with the captives?"

Rian narrowed her eyes. "Who is she to you?"

"My mother."

"Your mother?"

Kenna nodded, then tugged at the edge of the collar. Her neck ached beneath the dang thing.

Heavy footsteps clanked on metal grates from beyond the closed door. Rian slid back to her spot in the shadows. "They're coming. Best to stay quiet and let them do all the talking. And Kenna…" The woman paused as the cabin door clicked, then continued, "Don't trust any of them. Not even—"

The door opened and a tall woman with vibrant red hair sprouting thick curls strolled in. Behind her was a slightly shorter woman with a pixie haircut styled into a faux-hawk. A few men lingered in next but stood at attention by the door. Kenna waited for the two women to say something, but an unexpected third voice caught her off guard. She swallowed hard and turned to see her mother walking in.

"Take that ridiculous thing off her neck!" Honnah protested, coming over and sitting by Kenna. "Hey, sweetie," she said, tucking a loose strand of brown hair behind her daughter's ear.

Kenna reached up and grabbed some of her hair, then stared at the ends. "Oh, no." What had happened to her glamour?

"I like this you better," another familiar voice said, its owner entering the wide corridor. The woman with the faux-hawk sat on the bench, making room for Zeke.

"You piece of shit! You're working with them?" Kenna faced her mother, who didn't appear to be in any danger. "And you! What are you doing, Mom? Are you…helping them?"

"It's a long story, but yes. I am."

"Why?" Tears welled in her eyes. This was not how she expected to find her mother. Working with the enemy.

Honnah stood, slipping her hands into her vest pockets. "Kenna, I've been trying to right the wrongs of Isoldesse for a long time. When this is all over, I'll tell you everything."

"Everything like how you're Anumen and you're not really my mother? Or how you and my father, who is a freaking alien prince, have been lying to me MY ENTIRE LIFE?" She was on her feet now, eyes locked with her mother's. When her mother said nothing, she continued berating Honnah. "Oh, I overheard *Gerard* telling Breyah everything!"

"He's your father."

Kenna spun away, hands flying up as if she didn't know who was who anymore. "And I'm supposed to believe you?"

"He is!"

"I think we've had enough family reunion time," the Sendarian woman with the wild red hair said. "You have your daughter. Now it's your turn."

Honnah nodded. "What you need is being kept safe with the Elemental Council."

"Anora." A shorter man scurried in from the corridor. "There's an incoming message for you regarding the captives."

Anora, Kenna thought. This was the woman Ben had known, possibly had feelings for.

"Cahleen, tell the pilot to set a course for the Elemental Council," Anora barked, then stormed out of the room. The woman with the faux-hawk nodded but didn't exit the same way as Anora. Instead, she walked to the opposite side of the long room and entered a code to unlock the door. It slid open and the second she'd passed through, the door shut with a *swoosh!*

Zeke meandered about the space, not looking at Kenna but instead focused on Honnah. "Anumen, huh?"

Honnah briefly shifted her gaze from Kenna to the young Sendarian man.

Kenna tugged at the collar again. "Zeke, what is this thing? I thought you were helping us?"

He pulled out a rolled-up piece of something that he quickly unlatched and straightened. After he pressed a button at the top corner, the pliable rectangle device morphed into a black piece of glass—a plac. He tapped the screen. Instantly, the tubelike collar around Kenna's neck expanded, tightening against her skin. She gripped the edge of the collar, which was now hard and stiff, limiting her air intake.

She staggered backward, banging into the bench, and fell into a sitting position. "I...I can't...breathe..."

Honnah hurried to aid her daughter, tugging at the collar. "Stop! She can't breathe!"

"Why should I show her any sympathy?" Zeke growled. "She helped kill my brother."

"Your brother?" Kenna gasped. "I...don't know...your..."

"Stop! Please!" Honnah jumped to her feet and faced the Sendarian. "If you don't turn that damn thing off right now, you will join your dead brother!"

He stared at Honnah for a long moment. Meanwhile, Kenna gasped for air, hoping that her mother's threat would convince him to release her. "Fine, but she and her friend will pay." He tapped the screen, and instantly the collar deflated. The tightness subsided, allowing air to flow into her lungs.

Gasping for air, Honnah lowered her hands. "Now you know who I am, so why don't you tell us who you really are?"

Kenna stood, still trying to catch her breath, but eager to hear what Zeke had to say. He cocked his head and with a devious smile, he said, "My name is Biryn. Anora is my sister, and I believe you know Quaid. Or, I should say, knew Quaid." He stepped closer, orange eyes glaring at Kenna. Honnah lifted a ready hand if needed. With a seething tone, he said, "You will pay with blood for his death." Then he stormed out of the room, the door *swooshing* closed behind him.

Slowly, Kenna and Honnah sat again. "I'm so sorry you've been dragged into all this, but I warned your father that we'd all have to face the disaster Isoldesse caused."

"I have so many questions," was all Kenna could say.

"I know. And I will answer every single one of them, but later. Now, we need to finish what I started over fifty years ago, before it's too late. Before *they* find us."

"You mean the Obard?" Kenna asked, leaning into her mother's arms. "Yes."

A voice emerged from behind a netted partition at the other end of the cargo hold. Coming out and sitting on the bench across from them was Rian. "That's what the Anumen girl called me. Obard."

Honnah nodded. "You are Obard, yes. But why you're here is still a mystery."

"We have a way to find out why you're here," Kenna said, moving from her bench over to where Rian sat. "We'll figure things out together."

The Obard woman reached a pale hand to Kenna's arm. "That would be nice. But I don't see how that's going to happen."

Smiling, Kenna explained, "Well, we'll have to go straight to the source and ask her why she brought you here."

Honnah's eyes grew wide. With one hand gripping the netted partition, she eagerly asked her daughter, "You have a way to talk with Isoldesse directly?"

Kenna nodded. "We do."

31

Outside the transport ship, Kenna stood in awe at the view beyond the cliffside they'd landed near. A range of mountains lined the horizon, thin clouds veiling their peaks. Shuffling to the edge, Kenna glanced down the side of the mountain they were on. A lush forest with a mixture of green-and-red-leafed treetops blanketed the valley below.

"I wouldn't get too close."

Scurrying backward, she bumped into someone who grabbed her. She scrambled to free herself from his arms. "Zeke! I could've fallen to my death!" She knew his name wasn't Zeke, but she'd met him as Zeke, not Biryn. Wanting to be anywhere other than near this asshat, she turned and sought out her mother, who was talking with Anora by the cargo hold of the ship.

Careful where she stepped, she wandered over in that direction, away from Zeke. Yet again, she fell for the guy who had no real interest in her—or at least not romantically. It was all a ploy to kidnap her. She hoped that Ben, Meegan, and the others had found the captives and were safe. She didn't want to think about the possibility of never seeing any of them again. Regret filled her with the way she'd left things with Meeg.

"I actually like it when you call me that," Biryn said, jogging over to her, cutting through her thoughts. "Zeke, that is."

Pivoting so he was facing her, dusty rocks crunching beneath her shoes, she grit her teeth and said, "How about *asshole*? Do you like that name?"

He shrugged a shoulder and squinted one side of his face, then shifted into a smirk. "If *asshole* means *handsome, charismatic guy who enchants young women to swoon over him*, then yes. You may call me that too."

Honnah stepped away from Anora before Kenna reached them. Anora turned and walked with Biryn until they were out of sight, heading up the cargo ramp into the ship.

"Mom, what are we doing here?"

With one arm draped over her shoulders, Honnah said, "Stay close to me, okay? Don't wander off or get curious. I know how your brain works."

Kenna's brows pinched. "What does that mean? Why would you think I'd wander off on my own out here? Are you crazy?"

"Do you remember our vacation to Arizona? When we took that desert tour?"

That vacation hadn't been too long ago. Maybe seven years ago, when she was fourteen. Exploring the desert had been what sparked her interest in studying ecosystems beyond Earth. She'd always loved the stars, but it hadn't been until their trip to the desert that she discovered her desire to learn more about how things lived and survived in certain environmental conditions.

Her mother's glare told a different side of the vacation story. "Oh, you mean how I got separated from the tour group?" Kenna asked.

"Yes. It took us hours to find you. The point is, you need to keep that curiosity of yours in check. Okay?"

Kenna nodded.

Halfway up the ship's ramp, Anora waved for everyone to gather around. "Listen up. We go on foot the rest of the way. It's too risky to fly any closer without being detected. This is an in-and-out job. Use your discretion when engaging with the guards. We're not here to kill, but things may turn ugly if we don't get what we came for." With a high wave, gesturing to move out, she stomped off the ramp, leading the small group of Athru rebels along the dirt path trailing the side of the mountain.

"Where are we going, Mom?"

Honnah glanced over her shoulder before leaning close to Kenna. "Remember, stay close."

That didn't tell Kenna anything except that they were heading toward trouble.

After half a day's walk descending a narrow path alongside the lush mountain, they finally entered the forest below. The trees were spaced out and at least four stories tall before sprouting their first branches. Bushels of green and red leaves rustled as peculiar monkey-like creatures leaped from one tree to the next. Every so often, one would release a cry causing the others to answer with a round of strange chittering sounds.

A hand pressed to her back, and she shuddered, quickly turning and stepping away. Biryn raised his hands. "Do you not have woodlands on your world?" Lowering his arms, he lifted his gaze to the sky. "Sendarians tend to prioritize nature over their own comfort, forgoing any luxuries."

She eyed him, trying to decide if the conversation was part of a ruse. A way to win her back over, but she refused to be fooled by his charm a second time.

"I only meant—"

"I actually don't care what you meant," she cut him off.

One of the monkey-like animals scurried across their path. The long body and stubby round heat covered in short gray hair was a blur as it chased a smaller version of itself.

Gesturing for them to continue, Biryn said, "If you stay then you will see what we're trying to do here is for the good of everyone."

Kenna ignored him and kept walking.

"You're not what I expected."

"Expected?"

"For a human," he answered. Lifting a low hanging tree branch, he let Kenna pass under before following. "Are all humans like you?"

She stopped. Glancing behind, she saw they were at the end of their little parade. "We are not friend, and I certainly don't want to learn about Sendara from the likes of you or the Athru." Stepping closer so they were inches from one another, she pointed to his face and said, "You hurt people to get what you want."

His smile hadn't faltered. Wavy red hair hung low over half of his forehead, almost covering one of his orange eyes. "We do what we must to survive."

A bit worried they might lose the others, Kenna said while walking away, "Taking lives for your greater good isn't honorable or right. And I don't want any part of it."

"Well, like it or not you're a part of it."

"Biryn! Up here!" Anora shouted from the front of the group.

He was about to leave her but then said, "You should probably go wait with your mother. Can't have you running off and getting attacked by one of the Giminos." He pointed to the treetops where the monkey-like creatures shadowed them from above. "They won't bother you unless you're alone."

She watched as two furry light gray Giminos jumped from the end of a branch, stretching their lanky arms to grasp the next branch. Their heads were barely noticeable from where she stood. Almost as if they didn't have a neck, their heads sunken into their bodies.

Biryn walked over to Anora and Honnah. As Kenna approached her mother, Biryn led Anora from earshot, to talk more in private.

"Whatever he's telling you, he's lying."

"You're the one who's working with them. Did you know they killed Nick?"

A small gasped escaped Honnah's mouth, and then she sighed. With a slight shake of her head, she said, "I'm sorry. Nick was a good friend. How's Meegan?"

"Not good. Especially since she went full-on Anumen, killing that Quaid guy."

Honnah's shoulders sagged, and she pulled Kenna in for a hug. "Meegan's had a rough life, hiding who she really is an all. It hasn't been easy for any of the Anumen people."

"You should've told me, or her," Kenna said, her face buried in her mother's dark hair. Leaning away, she added, "Do her parents know about you?"

"Yes. But they don't approve of my decision to live separately from the others." Honnah's light brown skin seemed paler to Kenna. Her mother then explained how Bea, the Séara who lives up in North Carolina, was the one that informed Meegan's parents of her existence.

"Meegan mentioned a powerful aunt up in North Carolina."

Zipping the front of her jacket, Honnah smirked. "You do realize that she's not really Meegan's aunt, right?"

"I figured."

Ahead of them, Anora waved over some of the Athru soldiers. Then, after handing them one of those tablet screens and a black bag, she pointed farther down the trail. The three men and one woman took off, leaving everyone to wait.

The two Athru leaders strode over to Kenna and her mother. Anora explained, "We're almost there. Now, I've kept my impatience in check for long enough. You're sure you can convince the Elemental Council to step down? Because if not, then we're going to do it my way."

Holding a hand out, Kenna needed clarification on the matter. "Wait a second. What is your way?"

Anora ignored everyone except for the Anumen. Honnah faced Kenna. "For over a hundred years now, I've been trying to help the Sendarians overthrow their queen and the Elemental Council. I need to make things right after what she did."

"Who? Isoldesse?"

A single tear fell from her mother's eye. "She had no right to interfere with other worlds. If she'd stayed on Anuminis, then none of this would've happened. Our world would still exist, and I'd still have a family."

Anora and Biryn stood by, their attention focused on the mother-and-daughter conversation before them. Kenna ignored their presence because she was getting more pieces to the puzzle. "You lost your family in the invasion?"

"No. I wasn't there during the invasion. I was aboard my *daramum's* ship."

"*Daramum*?" Kenna asked, unsure of the translation.

"It means *grandmother*."

Kenna's eyes grew wide. "Isoldesse is your freaking grandmother?"

Honnah nodded.

"Is this true?" Anora interrupted. "The goddess of Sendara has children?"

"Yes. She's not a goddess, as I've tried to explain numerous times to you."

Her mother's voice along with Anora's and Biryn's grew hazy as Kenna processed the truth of who her mother was. What did this mean for Kenna? Was she a descendant of Isoldesse too? Her father had said something about being so much more than just one race.

"And me? Is Isoldesse my great-grandmother?"

Honnah shook her head. "No, sweetie, you have a different family line."

"Anora!" The Athru woman who had taken off with the others down the dirt path was running back toward them. Three Sendarian men trailed behind her. The woman went directly to Anora and relayed her report. "It's done. We've shut down all communications and encrypted all glass panels, blocking out any commands except yours on this." She returned the glass tablet Anora had initially given the group before they'd left.

Anora glanced over the screen, scrolling through whatever was displayed. "Excellent. Take the others and move into position on the north and south ends of the facility. We'll enter from the east door."

The woman nodded, then waved for the soldiers behind her to follow. Kenna wasn't sure what exactly was going to happen, but she needed to make sure no one else died.

"Mom, please, we have to help these people," she whispered, leaning in closer to Honnah's ear.

"I am."

"No, not the Athru. The Sendarians they're attacking."

With a small smile, she answered, "I'm trying. That's why I told Anora to let me handle the council. Otherwise, her way might turn into a bloodbath."

"Mom. We can't let that happen."

Honnah nodded. Then, with one arm around Kenna's shoulder, she led them to follow Anora and Biryn along the path. "Don't worry, sweetie. I've got everything under control."

32

The Elemental Council facility was nothing like what Kenna had expected. This was supposed to be the place that monitored the consumption of the planet's natural resources. She'd assumed the grounds would be comparable to those of a college campus, with hundreds of Sendarians employed, coming and going. But they were not. This place reminded her of one of those temples hidden deep within a jungle you'd see in a movie, except on a much smaller scale.

Tall trees hugged the stone structure with their massive trunks arching over the top as if trying to hide the structure from anyone flying above. There were no windows within the stone walls, only a pair of wide glass double doors set in the front. For the most part, the aged stones of the exterior were covered in green vines and soft moss. The overall size was comparable to the small-town library a few miles from where Prue lived. Not as grand as she imagined, Kenna wondered how this place was able to monitor and regulate the planet's resource production and consumption.

Sunlight shone through the breaks in the treetops over their path as Kenna, her mother, and the Athru rebels approached the front. One of the glass doors was propped open and it was dark inside.

"Where is everyone?" Kenna asked, clutching her mother's arm tighter.

It was Biryn who answered. "Hopefully all locked up."

She blinked at him, surprised he was being so open and friendly. It confused her, but she didn't complain. The more she knew about what was going on, the better. Playing off his interest in her, she prodded for more details. "And what is it you're hoping to gain by attacking these Sendarians?"

Everyone circled the front entrance. Anora pulled out a plac from her pocket and waved for two of her soldiers to come. Biryn excused himself with a smirk before joining them. Kenna couldn't hear what they were saying, so instead she turned to her mother for answers.

"Seriously, Mom, what are we doing here?"

With a low voice, her mother explained, "In order to get what I need to undo the mess Isoldesse created, I agreed to help them find... Well, find something that will help them take down the queen."

This wasn't right. Kenna knew change was coming for the Sendarians, especially if Meegan had her way. But helping the enemy—the same Sendarians associated with that vile man who killed Nick—seemed wrong.

When the Athru group dispersed, Anora called out, "The site is secure. Let's head in."

Anora led the group inside. Kenna was hesitant to follow, but her mother looped her arm through hers, nudging her to walk.

The inside was dark, barely any lights. One by one, the soldiers turned on their flashlights. Streams of light bounced around the room as they proceeded forward.

Honnah slipped from Kenna's hold and searched the room.

From behind, Biryn whispered to Kenna, "I imagined this place to be much larger than it is."

She was surprised to hear his confession. "You've never been here?"

"The location of the Elemental Council facility is kept secret. But your mother somehow knew."

Honnah called out, "It's over here!" Everyone followed her down a nearby hall, which curved around and around as it descended. Kenna worried they'd end up walking into some desolate crypt or something scary with spiders and rats. But at the bottom of the hall was an oversized wooden door.

The Athru members parted, allowing Anora to approach the glass panel embedded in the door. "It must've deactivated when we disabled the facility's power."

"Let me," Honnah said, holding her hands up in front of her. "*Liida ag Oscii et Glus.*" A splintering sound cracked from behind the door hinges, echoing over the group. Metal clanked, as if gears were being forced to turn. The Athru soldiers shuffled away from Honnah, and even Biryn stepped back. Anora and Kenna were the only two who remained by the Anumen's side as she cast an amula.

"Impressive," Anora said, smirking at Honnah.

It hadn't been the first time Kenna had witnessed Anumen magic, but it was the first time she'd seen her mother cast an amula. Something else she'd have to get used to. Seeing her mother use her abilities reminded Kenna of her bonded companion. She rubbed her arcstone, hoping that Ulissa was doing okay.

With the door popped ajar, Anora called out to her soldiers, "Help me! Without hydraulics the door is heavy. Now, push!"

Kenna stayed back with her mother until the door was open. Bright light filled the small hall they stood in. The stone room beyond was lit only by the giant metal sphere held up by three support posts. The device slowly rotated clockwise while white lights blinked randomly along its surface.

"What is it?" Kenna asked Biryn.

He didn't answer. His focus was glued to the device. It was Honnah who spoke, but not to Kenna. "I've brought you to Sendara's Mainframe Network. Do what you want with it—I don't care. I only need to speak with someone from the Elemental Council."

Anora stepped around the sphere, glancing it over from all sides. When she came back to where Kenna and Honnah stood, she nodded. "I'll keep my end of our deal, but your daughter stays here."

"No!" Kenna exclaimed. "Please let me stay with my mom."

"I'll go with them," Biryn cut in. "You start here. I'm sure whatever she needs from the council won't take long."

Anora nodded, then turned her attention to the sphere, barking out orders to her soldiers. Biryn pointed to the door, and Honnah and Kenna left to find the Elemental Council members.

After heading back up the circling hallway to the main foyer, Biryn led them through the top half of the structure by following a map on his plac. Kenna stayed close to her mom, who stayed close to the Athru man. He held the flashlight, and Kenna was too afraid to wander off in the dark.

"They're in here." He deactivated the plac, then rolled it up and locked it before tucking it into his pocket. The door was another paneled wooden door, but not as large as the one in the basement. The room was filled with ornate furniture. A long table sat with high-back chairs surrounding it. Deep burgundy rugs covered the stone floor. A lively fire thrived inside the fireplace. But there were no Sendarians.

"Where is everyone?"

Biryn shrugged as he turned his flashlight off. "Beannaith!"

After a few moments, an old woman with long gray hair strode out from an adjacent corridor. Two more elderly Sendarians followed from halls across the room. Their silky dresses grazed the stone floor and matched the color of their aging hair. Kenna immediately noticed the golden stone embedded in the headpiece of the first councilwoman. It rested in the center of her forehead, small and round. Kenna knew exactly what it was, and hope sparked inside her core.

It was an arcstone.

"Beannaith." Slowly facing the woman with the headpiece, her mother continued, "My name is Honnah, and I am a descendant of Isoldesse."

"Are you now? Well then. I suppose you are here for the egg?"

"I am."

Biryn leaned closer to Kenna. "What egg?" Shrugging, Kenna ignored him and paid close attention to the conversation.

Honnah approached the woman. "It's the only thing that will put an end to all of this. You and your people can live your lives free from the Anumen Doctrine."

The woman crossed her arms, tucking her hands into the bell sleeves of her dress. "But Sendara is happy. There is peace among the communities. Why would we want to revert back to a time when greed and power clouded our minds, dooming our planet to eventually dry up and die?"

"You are blinded by the old ways!" Biryn snapped at the woman. "You see happiness, but what's really happening is compliance. No one has any free will. A choice to be different, to explore outside of the community assignments and allowances. Sendarians should be allowed to better themselves."

"That sounds a lot like someone hungry for power. Exactly what our goddess wanted to snuff out." The woman raised an eyebrow at the Athru man. "I know who you are, and I know what you're capable of. That's what we do here. We observe and watch over Sendara. And now you want to take all that away?"

Kenna understood both sides, and the truth about Isoldesse weighed on her. Yet, it seemed this council already knew who their goddess really was and where she came from. Curious, Kenna asked the woman, while stepping out from behind her mother, "Is there no way to compromise? To evolve the Anumen Doctrine to allow more freedom to the Sendarians?"

"Only our goddess, the Anumen Isoldesse, has the authority to rewrite our laws."

Oh, geez, Kenna thought. *Maybe they are a bit naïve about who Isoldesse really is.*

Biryn stepped forward, closer to the elder Sendarian, but Honnah held out her arm, stopping him from advancing on the woman. "Please. Tell me where the egg is?"

"It's gone. After the queen opened the remaining Reigning Doors, she ordered us to destroy the egg."

Honnah's expression shifted to one Kenna had seen whenever a delicate museum piece broke or someone lost an important artifact. Something between disappointment and frustration. Kenna also saw a glimmer of something else in the Sendarian's expression. "You're not telling us the entire truth, are you?" she asked.

The woman shook her head. "No. We couldn't destroy the egg. So instead, one of our council members resigned from the council, leaving the grounds with it. She was never heard of again, as we made sure to remove any forms of communication or tracking from her presence. We don't know what became of the egg or whatever was inside."

"So, there's a chance it might still be out there?" Kenna asked, hoping that her mother also realized there was still a chance to find this egg.

"There's no egg here. You got what you needed from these crones, and now we need to get back to Anora." Then, before anyone realized what had happened, three knives were thrown out into the room. One by one, each of the council members dropped to the floor.

Kenna screamed as Honnah rushed to help the woman closest to her. Yellow blood shimmered over the gray fabric of the woman's dress.

"Why?" Kenna screamed at Biryn, realizing his kindness had been another part of his deception.

"They are the shackles holding back the Sendarians from having free will. This isn't your world, Kenna. Though, you do have purpose. So, let's go! You too, Honnah!" With a tight grasp on Kenna's arm, he dragged her out of the room.

Honnah knelt by the old woman's fallen body. Kenna yelled for her to come, "Mom!" Then, stumbling along as Biryn dragged her away, she winced from his grip. He didn't let up and Kenna shouted, "You're a monster!"

"I'm a revolutionist. And sometimes one has to be the other to free the oppressed."

"They're not oppressed!" Honnah yelled from behind, catching up with Biryn and Kenna.

Tears fell from Kenna's eyes as she thought about those women lying on the ground, bleeding out. She wished she could reach Ulissa to ask her for the power to take out Biryn. But she couldn't. Not with the transessent stone still around her wrist.

They quickly returned to the basement. Anora was diligently working with her soldiers to shut down the Sendarian Mainframe Network. Biryn explained the events of upstairs while Honnah stayed close to Kenna. Her mother's embrace didn't help the anger and sadness swelling inside.

Anora turned to Honnah and Kenna. "Once we're done here, it looks like we're taking a trip to Priomh."

Kenna wiped her eyes, unsure of the Athru woman's meaning. It was Honnah who asked, "And what reason do we have to return to Priomh?"

With a wide smile, Anora said, "An associate I thought had betrayed me has taken it upon herself to prove her worth by capturing the princess and our beloved banished prince. I'll admit, I thought this Sendarian had turned on us, but her loyalty to the cause has been true. I never should've doubted her."

"Then to Priomh," Biryn confirmed.

"To Priomh," Anora affirmed. "But first, we finish here."

From behind, one of the soldiers hit Honnah in the head, knocking her to the ground. Kenna screamed, falling to her knees next to her mother. Before she could react, something hard slammed against her head, and blackness took over.

"Hey, wake up. Kenna."

"Ben?"

Slowly the haze clouding her mind cleared, and she opened her eyes to a dark space filled with fog. "Ben?"

"I'm here."

She searched all around but couldn't see him anywhere. "Ben, I can't see you." The cool air swirled with the flow of the fog. "I think I was knocked out." She reached behind her head and rubbed the skin along her neck.

"I'm here," he said, his body fading into view.

Resisting the urge to run into his arms, she choked back her tears. "Another rescue mission gone wrong!" Then, unable to contain her emotions, she let the tears flow.

He rushed to her, not hesitating to embrace her—to console her. "We'll figure this out. Do you know where you are?"

She nodded, her forehead rubbing against his chest. "My mother led the Athru to the Elemental Council people."

"Oh no."

Kenna leaned away, meeting his eyes. "Biryn killed them all."

"Biryn was there?"

"Zeke is Biryn," she explained.

Pulling her in, he held her again. "Okay. I'll contact my superiors and find out the location of the Elemental Council. We'll come there and get you and your mother out."

Stepping away, she shook her head. With a sniffle, she said, "No. Anora said we're going back to Priomh. Something about the princess and my father being held captive."

Ben groaned, briefly closing his eyes. After a short moment, he said more to himself than to Kenna, "Gemma. It must be her."

"Is everyone else, okay? Darci, Liam, Jordi, and Meegan?"

He looked down into her eyes and nodded. "Though your friend seems to have lost her powers."

"How is that possible? Is she hurt?" Kenna wished she could be there for Meegan. To apologize or do whatever it took for Meegan to open up to her again.

"I don't know, and no-well, I don't think so. Not physically." He lifted his hands to the sides of Kenna's face, and told her, "I will find you. I promise. I won't let anything happen to you ever again." Then, just as she smiled, he closed the space between them and pressed his lips to hers.

An explosion of heat erupted inside her, and the second they parted, Ulissa's voice spoke to her from the air around them. "Time is running out. I can feel them coming. You must hurry and find Fawness. She's the only one who can stop them!"

Reading her expression, Ben narrowed his orange eyes. "What is it?"

Kenna swallowed the nerves forming in her voice, wishing she could stay in this moment with Ben for a bit longer. "The Obard. Ulissa says they're coming. We need to get to Priomh."

"I'll tell the others, and we'll find you on Priomh. I swear it." He pulled her in for one last kiss before sleep took Kenna over.

PART

THREE

PRIOMH

33

The second the video call ended with Anora, Gemma moved aside, giving Emmalyn and Gerard room to untie their binds. They'd decided to make the call from Gemma's old home, hoping the background would be noticed. If they were inside the Lead building, Anora might've suspected Gemma was lying. The Athru leader seemed to buy their ploy. Her face had lit up with delight at seeing the two royal siblings tied up and gagged.

"I do want to know the details of how you accomplished capturing them, but I'm tight on time," the Athru leader had said during the video call.

Feeling she'd gained the woman's good graces again, Gemma had asked, "Oh, trouble in South Sendara?"

With a devious smirk, Anora explained, "Thanks to your guest, we've infiltrated the Sendara Mainframe. We're in the process of shutting it down now."

This was big for the Athru. Shutting down the Sendara Network would cause all kinds of chaos. A definite win for the rebel group, but Gemma was concerned that if the Obard attacked, how would they warn Sendara? Not wanting to blow her ruse in luring Anora to Priomh, she played her role. Smiling, she told Anora, "Then you did it! You found a way to force the queen to step down."

Anora shrugged. "We'll see. But having control over the entire planet's communications and information network plus having her two children under our thumb might just be enough to force her to relinquish her title."

"I think you're right." Gemma wished she could share the truth about the queen. That she wasn't stockpiling resources for herself, but for an emergency invasion—one that was getting closer to actually happening. That she'd opened all the Reigning Doors Isoldesse had created not for personal gain but with the hope of finding something to help her get her son back. The whole banished-prince story was still a mystery. Did the queen actually banish him for running away with a non-Sendarian woman? Was it a heat-of-the-moment declaration? Gemma wasn't sure if they'd ever find out the truth, but at least he was here now. The queen would surely be pleased with his return. This new side of Gemma was surprising her more and more each day. She no longer wanted that thrill of power, and desired peace more than anything. After her time with Quaid and finding love with Xander, she didn't want to live on the run or always looking over her shoulder. She wanted to live like her parents—in a quiet home overlooking the ocean.

Before ending their call, she confirmed with Anora, "So, you'll come to Priomh? We can contact the queen together." And hopefully when she came, she'd bring Honnah and Kenna with her.

"We'll wrap up here and then make our way to the old research facility on Priomh. You'll have to keep an eye out for Priomh's Leadess and other security in the meantime. Don't lose our leverage, do you hear me?"

Gemma recalled nodding. She'd done everything according to their pre-orchestrated plan. And it'd worked. Anora said she'd come to Priomh, buying into Gemma's proof of loyalty to the rebel cause.

Breyah and Holt helped release Emmalyn and Gerard from their binds. The Leadess then faced her old friend and praised her for her performance. "That was perfect. You have a talent for politics, you know that, right?"

"You mean a talent for telling people what they want to hear with false intentions," Holt snickered.

"Holt," Breyah said with a sigh.

"Thanks," Gemma said, ignoring the Lead Medic's criticism. Though, she wasn't exactly sure if Breyah was paying her a compliment or poking at her overly dramatic personality. "Tell me again why we need Anora to come here? I'm hoping it's not a way to rescue your wife and daughter," Gemma said, locking eyes with Gerard.

Setting the ropes on the low table in front of the couch, he answered, "Partially, but also because we're going to need Rian's help."

"She's Obard, and she may be able to talk them out of attacking. Especially if Meegan isn't able to use her powers." Emmalyn also set her restraints on the low table. "We need to stop the Obard here, on Priomh. We cannot let them continue on to Sendara."

"That's if Rian is still alive," Gemma said. She crossed her arms, the oversized sweatshirt slipping down over her shoulder. If she recalled correctly, the blue-haired woman wasn't looking so good the last time she'd seen her.

"And how the hegah are we supposed to do that?" Micah asked from the kitchen area. "How are we supposed to stop a fleet of alien spacecraft that have been traveling the galaxy invading and destroying worlds? What weapons do we have that can possibly do that?"

The room fell silent.

"Well, while you all ponder that, I'm going back to Medical. I need to check Prue's vitals along with our emergency medical supplies." Heading for the door, Holt added, "I'll have emergency med packs ready in case we need to evacuate or take shelter."

Breyah caught him by the arm a second before he reached the front door. "Thank you, friend. We'll head up to Medical shortly. I told Bennach to meet us there when they arrive."

With a curt nod, he left, the door slamming behind him.

"Linc, what is the status of the incoming vessels?" Breyah commanded as she approached the glass wall overlooking the backyard. The display area tinted, opening up the long-range sensor image screen. Three large red dots marked where the Obard ships were on the outer edge of Sendara space. They were moments away from passing the farthest and smallest of Sendara's three moons.

Emmalyn pointed to a smaller red dot located above Priomh's compound, in low orbit. "What's this ship?"

Everyone gathered closer, staring at the smaller red dot. Gerard explained, "It's a transport ship, one of ours. But—" His words cut off as something slammed into the glass, startling the group. Gemma stared at the black handle sticking out of the smashed glass window. Sparks ignited from where the curved blade broke through, and the radar display screen flickered momentarily until vanishing completely from the tinted window.

"Well, what do we have here?"

Everyone turned and faced the front door. Gemma opened her eyes to their fullest. Moving past Xander, she took long strides to greet her sister. She grabbed Cahleen's shoulders and led her out the front door. "What are you doing here?"

Cahleen glanced over Gemma's shoulder, looking inside to everyone standing in the living room before returning her attention to her sister. "Anora sent me to bring you back to South Sendara. But then I got a message, like ten minutes ago, telling me there's a change of plans. She wants me to verify your story. To see if you actually captured the prince and princess." Cahleen sidestepped past her sister and entered the house. "And it looks like Anora's instincts were right. You lied, yet again."

"You need to leave." With a tight grasp, Gemma tugged at Cahleen's arm, trying to draw her outside.

The Athru Scout slipped her arm free, spun around while drawing another knife, and then pressed the blade to Gemma's wrist. "Touch me again and you'll lose a hand."

Micah strolled out from the kitchen nook, a sandwich in one hand as he shouted with a mouth full of food, "Cahleen, stop!"

Cahleen's gaze narrowed at their brother. "What are you doing here?"

After swallowing the food, he answered with a smug smile, "Who do you think broke Gemma out?"

"You?" Cahleen lowered the knife. "But why?"

"Because this whole situation has gotten out of control, that's why." Micah glanced between his two sisters, before he explained, "Cahleen, it's not about the Athru mission anymore. The threat is real. You know, the one you and Logan overheard Quaid talking to—those alien beings are en route to Sendara. They're going to destroy everything if we can't figure out a way to stop them." When he said *we*, he gestured to the people in the room.

Gerard held out one hand. "Wait. You've already had contact with the Obard?"

"The who?" Cahleen snarled at the prince. She eyed him as if she were scouting out a target.

He came around from in front of the couch, closer to the front door, but not too close. "The Obard. They travel from one galaxy to another in search of Anumens. They're looking for Isoldesse."

"Oh boy. Here we go." Cahleen rolled her eyes, tucking her dagger into its sheath. "Isoldesse this, Isoldesse that. When are you Sendarians going to move on? Let Sendara evolve and thrive without the word of Isoldesse holding us back."

"Cahleen, please. Just listen to him," Gemma pleaded. Though, she really wanted to yell and tell her sister to grow a brain and think for herself. But she refrained, keeping with her new calmer persona.

As Gerard and Micah explained the situation to Cahleen, Gemma noticed a figure inspecting the broken glass. She left them to their conversation and approached her bonded companion. Isoldesse's hands hovered over the broken display screen.

"What is it?" Gemma asked, trying to look the Anumen woman in the face. It took a few moments, but eventually she acknowledged Gemma.

"Did you locate Jasper?" Isoldesse stood at eye level with Gemma. Her short black hair grazed the white jacket just over her shoulders, a soft golden glow outlining her body.

All eyes were on Gemma now, even Cahleen's.

"No. I'm sorry, we haven't located Jasper yet," she softly said to Isoldesse, knowing everyone was watching her. "Where did you last see him?"

"It doesn't matter." Her solemn expression grew heavier with sadness. "If Jasper cannot be found then we're all doomed."

Slowly, Gemma shuffled in a circle, facing everyone in the room. She explained, "She says we're all doomed because we haven't found this Jasper guy."

"Who are you talking to?" Cahleen asked again, much louder with determination in her voice.

Gemma inhaled a deep breath before she explained, "I was talking to Isoldesse."

Cahleen cracked a smile, then after looking at each person in the room, she asked, "You're kidding, right?"

Shaking her head, Gemma continued, "The other night, my essence was bonded with the essence of the Anumen living in this arcstone." She lifted her arm, showing Cahleen the arm cuff. "We didn't know who was inside, but it turns out it's Isoldesse. And...well, she's a bit confused. Her mind comes and goes only sometimes understanding where she is."

Cahleen stared at her sister for a long breath before flopping her hands in the air, then against her legs. "You sound ridiculous! You know that, right?"

"It's true," Emmalyn pointed out. Standing next to Gemma, she said, "And I did some research. Jasper was Ulissa's partner. But he left with Isoldesse the day of the invasion. They fled and returned to Sendara."

"He's here?" Gerard asked.

The princess shook her head. "No. But there are records of a brown-skinned man living among the Sendarians. He lived in isolation, on a farm with a Sendarian woman. They had one child— adopted—who was also kept out of the public eye."

"What does any of this have to do with our current situation? If Jasper is dead, that does us no good." Dread swelled in her gut. She tried not to think about the outcome if the Obard did invade Sendara. "Is there anything else you can tell us?" Gemma hoped the Anumen would give her something else besides *where is Jasper*.

"The adopted child was a special Sendarian with pale white skin. She also had unusual blue hair, eyes, lips, and nails." Emmalyn pulled up an old image she'd found on Micah's plac. "The Sendarian woman kept a journal. This was the only picture she took of their family."

It was Breyah who took the plac. She stared at the image, then said, "It's Rian. As a child."

Emmalyn nodded. "Yes. And I assume that is Jasper with her."

Isoldesse turned at the sound of her old friend's name. Gemma stayed close as the Anumen woman crossed the room and stood by Breyah. With one hand, she touched the screen. "Jasper."

Gemma asked Breyah for the plac, and when she handed it over, Gemma faced it toward Isoldesse. "This is Jasper?" The woman nodded. Gemma then asked, "And this little girl, she's not a Sendarian, is she?" Isoldesse's nod shifted to a shake. "Is she Obard?"

"I didn't know it was a girl. I thought it was a creature—an animal—like a bird or a dragon. I didn't know it was one of them. They'd left the egg out in the cold…to die. Or so I thought."

Gemma lowered the plac, swallowing the lump in her throat, and told the others what Isoldesse had confessed. "She said she didn't know the egg she took was an Obard. She thought it was an animal. She thought they…the Obard…were killing it."

"That's why they've been hunting Anumens. They want their egg back." Gerard rubbed both hands over his eyes, then up over his head. "They're looking for Rian."

"And these Obard, they're on their way to Sendara?" Cahleen asked, now seeming more interested in the situation.

Emmalyn asked for the plac back, and Gemma handed it over. She tapped the screen to show the same radar image they'd been reviewing before Cahleen had destroyed the window with her blade. "There are three incoming vessels. Estimated arrival is sometime before nightfall."

Stepping away from the group, Cahleen headed to the front door. With a hand on the doorframe, she said, "Then we need to make sure Rian is with Anora on that Athru transport ship. If we give these Obard what they want, then hopefully they'll leave without invading our world. Destroying Sendara is not what the Athru want."

Gemma glanced at Isoldesse, who was slowly fading from view, then back to Cahleen. "Make the call to Anora. Tell her my story is true—that I wasn't lying. And make sure Rian is with her when they come to Priomh."

Cahleen nodded, then exited the house. Gerard instructed everyone to head back to Medical. They needed to begin the evacuation process for everyone in Priomh before the Obard arrived.

"Micah, you and Cahleen stay here with Xander. I'll go with Breyah, Emmalyn, and Gerard. I won't be long. I'm hoping that if Isoldesse sees the facility, it might spark some insight—get her talking some sense rather than all this nonsense about some guy named Jasper."

"I'll let Cahleen know when she returns from her call," Micah said, hugging his sister. It was an odd gesture for them, but she embraced him too.

"Don't die," she quietly added, and slapped the brim of his baseball cap.

Following Gerard, Emmalyn, and Breyah out of the house, Gemma couldn't help but have high hopes they might actually save Sendara.

34

Meegan sat with her back against the wall of the passenger cabin of the transport ship, away from the others. One hand outstretched, she tried to cast a basic amula. Over and over again, she whispered, "*Tarach bach sola.*" But nothing happened.

Doing it again, with a swift flicking motion, she opened her hand, fingers spread wide. She was hoping to create a small ball of light, like the one she'd created after revealing her true identity to Kenna. But again, nothing happened. Her powers were gone. And she'd given up on begging the Eilimintachs. They'd stopped listening to her pleas hours ago.

Darci finished checking Ben's vitals as he slept, reclined in one of the passenger seats, then took a seat next to Meegan on the floor. "Hey, how are you holding up?"

Pulling her knees in close, she dropped her head into her arms, hiding her face from Darci. "I want to be alone."

"I know you do, but now isn't the time to sulk or push everyone away." Draping one arm over Meegan's shoulders, she added, "I'm here for you. Even if you don't want me to be."

The Sendarian liar was the last person she wanted to talk to. Tears welled in her eyes. The one person she did want to talk to had been taken, and how things were left between them killed her inside. Lifting her head, she wiped the tears away with the back of her hand. "Do you think she's dead?"

Darci squeezed Meegan's shoulders. "Who, Kenna? No way. Honnah wouldn't let the Athru hurt her."

Nodding, Meegan stretched her legs out. Her feet almost reached the base of one of the passenger seats. "I need to find a way to get my powers back."

"We'll figure it out, okay? Together." Darci didn't turn away until Meegan looked at her. "I'm serious when I say I'm here for you."

With a small smile, Meegan said, "Thank you."

"He's coming to," Jordi announced to the room. He stood beside one of the passenger chairs, slowly reclining it to a sitting position from a lying one. Ben sat upright mid-incline, swinging his legs over the side. Jordi lowered the plac he was holding. "Those are some interesting sleep readings. What kind of dreams are you having, my old friend?"

"I'll explain later, to which I'd like to hear more about these sleep bio-readings. But first…" Ben looked around the small cabin. Locking eyes with Meegan, he told Jordi, "…go tell the pilot to take off."

"Destination?" Jordi asked.

"Priomh."

Jordi hurried from the passenger cabin, walking by Liam, who stood by Julianna at one of the other passenger seats. Ben made his way over to Meegan and Darci. The two girls got to their feet and waited for the news.

"She's alive."

A rush of relief washed over Meegan. Nodding, she waited for him to continue.

"We briefly spoke. The Athru are taking Kenna and her mother to Priomh. Something about the princess and prince being held against their will." Looking away, he said more to himself, "I'll have to contact Breyah to find out exactly what's going on."

"But she's okay?" Meegan asked.

"I believe so."

She could tell he was holding something back, his pinched expression held longer than Meegan liked. "What is it?"

Shaking his head, he finally responded after a long pause. "It doesn't make sense what Kenna had said about her father and Princess Emmalyn being captured." As he walked away, he said, "I need to find out what's going on. Darci, get everyone ready for deployment. We're leaving in five!"

Before Meegan could ask what else Kenna had said, the Sendarian disappeared down the corridor leading to the ship's bridge.

"Okay, everyone, strap in!" Darci shouted. She helped Eryn strap in and recline her seat. "I'm going to activate sedation mode, okay?" Wearily, the Sendarian woman nodded. When her seat was reclined back to its fullest, Darci slipped a silicone face mask over the woman's head. After tapping the glass panel along the armrest of her friend, Darci looked to Meegan. "She needs the rest."

"I'm sorry about your friend," Meegan said, buckling into her own seat.

Sliding into the seat next to the unconscious woman, Darci reached over to Meegan and squeezed her hand. "Thank you. And don't worry. We'll find Kenna."

Liam secured himself into one of the reclined seats, too, but next to Julianna, who was already under travel sedation. When he was done and comfortable, he told the girls next to him, "No one else is getting hurt or dying."

"Bennach will contact Breyah and find out what the plan is. Everything will work out." Darci placed a hand on top of Meegan's hand. "We have to trust—"

"If you say Isoldesse, I'm going to unbuckle, come over there, and smack you."

"I wasn't going to say Isoldesse. What I was going to say was we have to trust that Breyah, Holt, Emmalyn, and Gerard have a plan. Though, you have to give me some slack when referencing Isoldesse as our goddess. It's all our world has ever known her to be. She's become more of a symbol than an actual being that lived among us all those centuries ago."

More of a symbol.

These words repeated in her mind as the transport ship took off. Maybe Kenna was right. Maybe there was a compromise. She slipped the silicone face mask over her head and let the device soothe her to sleep. When they woke, they'd be on Priomh. And with or without her powers, she'd have to try and help—to try and save Kenna from whatever the Athru were planning to do with her. Maybe if Meegan was lucky, she could convince the Eilimintachs to restore her powers and let her finish the Athru and the Obard once and for all.

35

The combination of her uncomfortable position and the chill of metal beneath her face eventually woke Kenna. Slowly, she cracked her eyes open, and let her vision come into focus. With one hand pressed to her temple, she rolled onto her back, wincing at the pain throbbing in her head. Someone knelt beside her. She glanced up, light illuminating behind the woman's figure.

"Mom?"

"Yes, sweetie. I'm here. Let me help you up." Honnah reached under Kenna's shoulders. "Biryn shouldn't have hit you like that. I told them—"

"He shouldn't have killed those women either," Kenna interrupted. She slowly got to her feet, then shuffled backward until her legs hit the metal bench stretching the length of the cargo hold. Sitting with her hand still at her head, she took in the room. "Is anyone else hurt?"

Honnah shook her head. "Not that I know of. And you're right. There was no need for him to—" Pausing, she swallowed. "To go that far."

Across the cabin, sitting on the opposite bench, was Rian. The collar they'd put on her was active, pinching the pale skin of her neck. Leaning against the metal wall, her eyes closed, the Obard woman acted as if she was either asleep or in deep thought. Kenna felt bad for Rian too.

"Are you okay?" Kenna asked.

It took a long moment before Rian opened her eyes. They looked different. Normally they were a bright blue, but now they appeared faded as if ice coated her irises. Kenna's gaze dipped, taking in the change in her skin color as well. Rian's usual pale skin had turned a shade lighter than her hair, lips, and nails.

Coming out from under Honnah's arm, Kenna crossed the space of the cargo hold to sit next to Rian. "You don't look so good."

The woman's head lulled to one side, resting back against the hull of the ship while her arms crossed tightly over her chest. "I need my injections," she said, voice trembling. "They took my medicine."

Honnah jumped up from the bench, walked to the cabin door, and started banging with her fist. "Anora! Where's Anora?!"

Kenna reached a hand to Rian's, only to immediately withdraw it. "You're so cold!" She searched the area for a blanket or something to put over Rian, but the woman called out to her.

"No. Nothing will help but my medicine. It's inside me." Closing her eyes, she tilted her head back against the wall again. "You need to keep your distance," she whispered. "I don't want to hurt you."

Sliding along the bench, putting some distance between her and Rian, Kenna said, "What do we do if we can't get your medicine?"

Between each exhausted breath, Rian said, "Keep. Your. Distance."

Kenna hurried to her mother's side. "We have to help her."

"I know. I'm trying, but no one is answering this damn door!"

"I need a distraction," Rian said, barely above a whisper. "Breyah would often talk to me, to distract my mind, preventing the change from happening."

The change? Kenna couldn't help but wonder what kind of change. The only thing they knew about the Obard was that they had violent tendencies. But Kenna wanted to know more about who they were. What was their world like? What kind of communities or government or education system did they have? So many things to learn if they could just figure out why the Obard were traveling through space hunting Anumens.

"Mom, what about that egg you were asking those Sendarian women about? The one they no longer had," Kenna hinted with wide eyes, hoping her mother would pick up on the gesture to help distract. Plus, she was curious about why her mother was looking for an egg.

"Yes, of course. A story. That might help. Okay, well…" Honnah lowered herself onto the bench across from Rian. "I discovered my daramum's journals." To clarify to Rian, she explained, "My mother's mother. Anyway, I found her old exploration journals and started reading them. There were so many, hundreds of handwritten notes and logs about every world she visited."

"I still can't believe Isoldesse is your grandmother," Kenna said with a sigh.

Nodding, Honnah continued, "Well, I never met her, but I always felt as if I knew her. Especially after reading so many of her personal thoughts, experiences, and regrets. She was by no means perfect and made mistakes. Her biggest mistake was the day she decided to pay a visit to a dark, cold world."

"The Obard," Kenna said, sorrow in her eyes as she glanced in Rian's direction.

"I am not…" Rian struggled to finish, her body trembling, "them."

A small smile spread on Honnah's face. "I know."

"What happened next?" Kenna asked, urging her mother to continue.

Tucking her black hair behind one ear, Honnah said, "Isoldesse's crew advised against visiting the heavily clouded world, saying the ground conditions weren't like those of any other world they'd visited for the Aevo Compendium project. But my daramum didn't want to disregard an opportunity to help just because their world was different. So, she and a close friend, Jasper, took a transport shuttle to the surface."

"Jasper?" Rian asked, followed by a dry cough. When Honnah nodded, she sat up straight, then asked with a strained effort, "Dark hair with a limp in his left leg?"

"Yes. I believe he was injured during a hike on another world. Do you know him?" Honnah narrowed her gaze at the captive woman sitting across from them.

Rian nodded, wincing from the motion. "Briefly." Ice crystals sprouted from beneath the collar, up Rian's neck. When Kenna stood to help, reaching out a hand, Rian cried, "No! Keep your distance! I can't guarantee that I won't hurt you."

Slowly, Kenna returned to her seat next to her mother.

"Part of the journal-entry page was torn, so I only know that Isoldesse and Jasper wandered a forest that she described as something from a dream. Tall slender trees with barely any leaves on them, spaced out with no undergrowth or greenery on the ground. The only thing they could see along the base of the trees was a dense white fog that came up to their knees. She says they wandered for hours before hearing voices. With caution, they watched from a distance as tall beings with pale skin and blue hair, lips, and nails circled around a podium made of vines, mud, and tiny bulbous-looking mushrooms. Along the top was a small cavity resembling a bowl. She said the beings circled the podium, chanting strange words, the ground glowing blue beneath the dirt. Then, from somewhere off in the distance, loud howling and growling sounds responded to their chants. Whatever beasts they were calling seemed to be getting closer. Jasper warned Isoldesse that they should return to the ship, but she wanted to see what was happening. She ordered Jasper to stay until she'd given the command that it was time to go. Isoldesse noted how something was being passed from the back of the group to the front. When the man closest to the podium was given the oblong object, he placed it on top, the bottom half sitting inside the cavity of the dirt-and-vine podium. One by one, they left, leaving the white-and-blue glass-like egg on display in the middle of the woods. The howling in the distance grew louder, and Isoldesse feared the egg was in danger of being eaten. Once everyone had left, she snuck out from their hiding spot to get a closer look. Supposedly, she examined the oval object while Jasper, who had come up next to her, kept an eye on their surroundings. She noted in her journal his continual comments about returning to the ship and how this whole expedition was a bad idea. But she wanted to know what it was and why those beings left it to the beasts howling in the woods. It wasn't until she saw something moving beneath the glassy surface that her assumption that the object was an egg was confirmed. Then, when the howling sounded as if the beasts were closing in, she feared for the unborn creature, believing it was left as a sacrifice. She lifted the egg from the podium. The blue light stretching up the vines retreated back into the ground, deep below the dirt they were standing on. Jasper protested her actions, but she wasn't going to let the forest beasties devour any living creature."

"What happened next?" Kenna sat completely enveloped in her mother's story. It reminded her of her childhood days when her father would tell her bedtime stories. Though, back then she hadn't realized the stories he was telling her weren't fiction. "Did the Obard discover she took the egg?"

"They did. And they chased her. She cast amulas to help her and Jasper escape to the transport ship."

"And that's when they discovered the Anumens have magical powers."

Honnah nodded. "Yes. Isoldesse didn't know that they also had the capability to travel space."

"They pursued her, didn't they?" Rian coughed, her features slightly returning to normal. The story seemed to ease whatever transition had overcome Rian's body.

Honnah nodded again. "All the way to our home world, where they attacked."

"Why did you ask the old Sendarian women from the Elemental Council about the egg?" Kenna moved closer to Honnah and clasped her mother's hand.

"It was in one of Isoldesse's journals. She mentioned that she needed to hide it somewhere until she could defeat the Obard threat or somehow stop them from hunting Anumens. Only then would she be able to turn her attention to whatever creature resided inside the egg." Standing, Honnah combed her fingers through her hair. "But I don't think they're after Anumens for their power, the arcstones, or the transessent stones. I think they're looking for that damn egg!"

"But the councilwomen don't have it," Kenna said, standing up from her seat.

Tears trickled along Honnah's light brown cheeks. "I know. All these years, living on Earth with you and Gerard, I had a plan—one that solely rested on finding that egg with the Elemental Council. But now—now, all is lost."

36

Exiting the transport ship, Meegan followed the others out onto Priomh's docking station. The extended sleep during their return flight had been a well-needed shutdown. A part of her had hoped that when she woke from her sedation, the Eilimintachs would've reconsidered their decision and returned her powers. But they hadn't. The lingering phantom sensation of the missing piece inside her essence remained empty. She longed to be whole again, and even made silent promises to the Eilimintachs that she'd be better—she'd learn to control her emotions. But her pleas were met with silence.

"Meegan, stay with the group!" Ben called out from the docking station exit.

Lifting her gaze to him from the smooth concrete beneath her shoes, she realized she was the only one left near the ramp of the transport ship. She jogged over to him, apologized, then asked, "Where is everyone?"

He pointed down the windowless corridor. "Everyone is waiting for us by the transit shuttle."

They walked together along the curved tunnel. "No, I mean where is everyone else?"

"Evacuated."

Meegan stopped, the light at the end of tunnel coming into view. "Why have they been evacuated?"

"I'll explain en route to Medical. Breyah and the others are waiting for us there."

He turned and continued, and she followed. Jordi held open the transit doors, letting Ben and Meegan get on before releasing them. Ben went straight to the embedded glass panel next to the sliding doors and tapped at the dark screen.

Darci waved for Liam to come take her place. Once he'd gotten Julianna situated, he sat next to Eryn, letting the injured woman lean on him. Darci then grabbed the wooden bar for support that stretched the length of the transit cabin. "Do we know the Athru ship status?"

Meegan wished she could've helped them sooner. She should've accepted who she was a long time ago—then she could've stopped everything back when Quaid was a threat.

Jordi held out his plac to Darci. "Their ship remains in low orbit. We're hoping they don't change their mind and return to Sendara." The shuttle leaned slightly to the right as the speeding transit curved around a left bend.

"We're almost there," Ben announced.

Meegan glanced over Darci's shoulder to look at the plac while Darci scrolled through the information displayed. "These readings aren't right. They've somehow looped their position," Darci explained, handing the plac back to Jordi. "I mean, I'm not a technical expert, but I think they've somehow pinned the ship's position to those coordinates."

"You think they've already landed?" Meegan asked.

Darci faced Meegan and nodded, but then her nod shifted into a shrug. "I don't know. And I might be wrong, but there's something off about that radar reading. I'll need to access Priomh's main comms system to get a better reading."

Ben finished up with the glass panel in the hull wall before asking, "Can you do that from Medical?"

"I can."

"Good."

Meegan looked around the narrow cabin of the transport shuttle. "Where are the Priomh security guards that came with us to Sendara?"

"They've been ordered to assist with the final round of evacuations." Ben held out his hand, and Jordi placed the plac in it. After a moment, he flipped it, showing the screen to everyone. "Breyah sent this to me while we were in transit from Sendara. There are three vessels heading straight to our location."

Meegan moved closer, her attention glued to the blurry images of three large black spheres. Lifting her hand, she saw the mood ring was a bright turquoise. "No, no, no, no! This can't be happening! Not now! Not when I don't have my powers!" She backed away from everyone, only stopping when she reached the end of the cabin. Arms crossed over her chest, hands rubbing the fabric of her sleeves, she asked, "They're on their way here? Right now?"

Ben flipped the plac over to look at the images. "Do you know who they are?"

Meegan's body trembled. Eyes wide, she nervously shook her head and started shouting, "We have to leave! We've got to get off this planet!" She searched the ceiling for some kind of emergency-stop lever or pulley. Fearful of what they were about to endure, she yelled, "We need to leave before they kill us all!"

Darci grabbed Meegan by the shoulders. "Calm down! No one's going to die, okay? Hey, listen to me!" She urged Meegan to look at her by holding Meegan's face. "We can't leave. Not until we've got Kenna and her mother back, remember?"

Meegan looked up to Ben and Jordi. "How long do we have?"

"A few hours," Jordi answered. "Who are they?"

Tears welled in Meegan's eyes. Her parents' worst nightmare was coming to be, and they weren't here to protect her. And she couldn't protect herself, or her friends. Wiping her eyes, she told them, "They're called the Obard, and they're the ones who invaded and destroyed my home world. They travel the galaxy hunting Anumens, destroying anything and anyone in their path."

Everyone followed Ben and Jordi through the expansive open space Darci called the Centrum. Meegan couldn't think straight. Her mind was all over the place, trying to figure out what to do about the Obard, her powers, and Kenna's safety.

"*Please return my powers*," she silently begged to the Eilimintachs. "*I need to protect everyone. They won't survive against the Obard.*"

Nothing. Just more silence.

Meegan stopped, letting the others walk by. Darci helped Eryn while Liam stayed close to Julianna. Meegan didn't know what to do—how to help. Anger mixed with fear coursed through her. Staring up at the sky through the glass dome, she said in a low, harsh tone, "If everyone here dies…well, that's on you!"

Still, no response from the Eilimintachs.

Darci stopped and turned while supporting her friend's weight. "Meegan, let's go! We need to get to Medical."

Inhaling a deep breath, she continued toward Medical. Ducking her head under Eryn's other arm, she helped carry some of the weight of Darci's friend.

At the end of the skywalk leading to Medical, Jordi held the door for the three. "Everyone's in the Waking Room at the end of the hall."

Once inside the room, Meegan realized why it was called the Waking Room. She remembered waking up in one of the beds that lined the center of the room. She counted, and there was a total of sixteen single-occupancy beds.

"Beannaith, Meegan." Breyah approached her from the window side of the room. Glancing past the Leadess, she saw Gemma talking with Kenna's father and the princess.

Ben greeted Breyah, then said, "Jordi and I are going to search the immediate area for any lingering Sendarians or signs of a threat. We'll return shortly."

"Thank you, and hurry," Breyah said, grazing Ben's arm before pulling away.

"How long before the Obard arrive? And you're sure they're coming here? Maybe they're just passing by?" Meegan swallowed, twisting her mother's mood ring on her finger and hoping Breyah would correct her and say they were mistaken. That their computers malfunctioned and the Obard were nowhere near Sendara space.

But no such luck.

The tall Sendarian Leadess's gaze briefly dipped before she offered an answer. "Sooner than we'd like." Breyah reached a hand to Meegan's shoulder. "Bennach tells me your powers have been blocked?"

With a weak nod, she confirmed. "I'm no help to anyone now."

"That's not true. We still need every able body, and that includes you. Especially because you have the most knowledge of these beings. You can help us figure out a way to stop these *Obard* from attacking Sendara."

"That's simple," Meegan said, stopping Breyah from continuing. "They want me. You don't even have to tell them about Honnah, just send me."

"That's not going to happen," Gerard said, cutting in from behind Breyah. "Besides, we need to try and talk to them first."

Meegan laughed. Not a 'that's funny' kind of laugh, but the hysterical 'you've got to be kidding' kind. Everyone in the room stopped what they were doing and turned their attention to her. "You're kidding, right? Because there's no *talking* to the Obard. They arrive, they invade, they take what they want, they destroy everything else, then leave."

Gerard rubbed the stubble along his chin. Seeing him with orange eyes didn't seem so strange anymore. He waved a hand in

Gemma's direction, and she obliged, joining their conversation. "Gemma, can Isoldesse help?"

It infuriated Meegan that she couldn't confront the Anumen traitor herself. Almost embarrassed, she couldn't make eye contact with the Sendarian woman, knowing that Isoldesse could be there staring at her right now. She imagined Isoldesse laughing or shaking her head in disappointment at how Meegan had disgraced the Fawness name. Brushing aside the annoyance and shameful feelings, she slowly looked at Gemma. She wasn't paying any attention to Meegan, and was talking with Gerard.

"I'll ask. Hold on," Gemma said, then crossed the room to the full-length window that doubled as the exterior wall. The view of the lone mountain off in the distance was beautiful, but that wasn't what Meegan focused on at the moment. She watched as Gemma conversed with the empty air beside her. The traitor was there, inches in front of Gemma—and Meegan had no power to confront Isoldesse. So many unanswered questions—so many lives gone because of what she did. Meegan needed to figure out a way to make sure she paid for her actions.

After a long moment, Gemma returned to Meegan, Gerard, and Breyah. Everyone else in the room resumed helping the injured or quietly talked among themselves. Gemma shook her head. "She's not in her right mind." Then, to Meegan, she said, "Something isn't right with her. Nothing she says makes any sense."

Well, that's just fantastic, Meegan thought. She inhaled an annoyed breath, then asked, "What exactly is the goddess of Sendara saying?"

The Sendarian scowled, narrowing her eyes. "I don't think I like your tone."

"And I could care less," Meegan snapped back.

Gemma balled her hands into fists at her sides. Shifting her weight from one leg to the other, she opened her mouth to counter Meegan's retort. Breyah interjected, "How about we focus on the task at hand? Time isn't on our side."

Shaking his head, Gerard glanced at the plac he held. "No, I'd say we have mere minutes."

"Minutes! What happened to hours?" Meegan exclaimed, wringing her hands. Her fingers found the mood ring, and she twisted the metal band round and round.

Gemma snapped her fingers, drawing everyone's attention to her. "As I was saying"—she shot a narrowed side glance to Meegan before addressing Gerard and Breyah—"she's asking for someone named Jasper. I guess he knows something about the Obard."

Meegan's shoulders dropped, the anger fuming inside settled. "Jasper? As in Ulissa's husband?" Curiosity slid into the forefront of her mind. Why would Isoldesse be asking for Jasper?

"Honnah never mentioned Ulissa was married." Gerard tucked the plac under his arm and glanced toward the exterior glass wall. "Does…or did he even exist?"

"He did." Meegan nodded, pursing her dry lips. "Their union wasn't official," she explained. "They grew up together as friends, then moved to the Black Mountain region on Anuminis—away from Ulissa and Isoldesse's mother, who resided in the Red Umber Forest region. It's all in my parents' journals. The Prinor journals— unofficial logs that are passed down within the Prinor family line— have records of their union."

Shifting in her spot, Breyah looked to Meegan. "Your family, were they rulers of Anuminis?"

"Something like that. Anuminis doesn't have official rulers. Just the Prinor family that mediates and oversees regional activities."

Gemma huffed under her breath. "Sounds like we have another princess in the room."

The anger that had subsided surfaced again, and she wanted to thrust Gemma with a strong burst of air…but she couldn't. And she probably shouldn't.

Breaking the tension between Gemma and Meegan, Gerard asked, "So, Ulissa can tell us more about Jasper?"

She shrugged. It didn't matter, because the only person who could ask Ulissa had been taken by the Athru. The silence weighed on everyone in the room, especially Meegan. Minutes. They had minutes before the Obard would descend upon them and destroy everything.

From the air above, a computer voice spoke over the intercom. "Three incoming vessels have reached Priomh's orbit. One is descending while the other two remain in orbit. Shall I activate the protective barrier wall?"

They didn't even have minutes.

Breyah hurried and followed Gemma over to the window, checking the sky. Gerard and Meegan, and a few others helping the injured behind them, also went to see. Breyah called out, replying to the alert, "Linc, increase the barrier strength to maximum level."

Linc's voice, Meegan thought, sounded so lifelike. She tried to focus on how the Sendarians programmed Linc's audible responses, but her mind wouldn't be distracted from the threat descending upon them. Her mind was a nervous mess of fearful thoughts, one after another.

Behind the group, Liam stayed close to Julianna, who was lying in one of the beds. Holt and Darci stepped away from Eryn, who was also lying in one of the beds, to watch out the window. No one said anything. The eerie silence wasn't helping the anticipation of what was coming.

Then it happened.

Thick white clouds formed from behind the lone mountain, covering it within seconds. The clouds turned dark as they advanced toward the Lead building. Next to Meegan, Princess Emmalyn hooked one arm through her brother's arm. A dark shadow stretched over the treetops, moving at an alarming rate toward the Priomh compound, claiming the land even before the Obard set foot on the ground. A *boom* erupted from the stormy gray sky; thick bolts of lightning flashed as an enormous black sphere broke through the rolling clouds. The second the ship came into view it began to transform, almost as if it were melting mid-descent. The top and bottom drew inward while the sides stretched out until a semiflat disc hovered over the entire Priomh compound.

"It's happening," Meegan whispered, pressing one hand to the glass. "The Obard are here."

37

Isoldesse muttered words Gemma couldn't understand, but the panicked look in her goddess's eyes said enough. Even though she was a pain in the ass, she wished her sister were here. Cahleen would know what to do, or how to fight this kind of threat. Gemma thrived at obtaining intel, as she did for both Breyah and Anora. In the end, a Spiaire's job of spying and befriending people for the benefit of the cause turned out to be no different from what she did for the Athru. Intel was intel.

But Cahleen was the tactical one. Her level of perception and observation extended beyond the best of the best, and her predictions were often spot on.

What would Cahleen do? Gemma silently pondered. *She wouldn't slink away, hoping no one notices, that's for sure. Weapons. She'd want a shitload of weapons.*

Isoldesse's hands clasped tightly at her waist while she stared out the glass wall of the medical exam room. Gemma swore she saw the golden aura surrounding Isoldesse briefly dim. She could feel the Anumen woman's fear rushing through her own body. It was hard not to be scared. The Obard ship hovered over the entire Priomh compound, blocking out the daylight—an attack was imminent and at their doorstep.

Gemma turned to Princess Emmalyn. "We need an exit plan. We are leaving, right?"

"We're not going anywhere without my daughter and Honnah." Gerard stepped in, standing slightly behind the two women.

Neither of the royal siblings could see Isoldesse as she moved to face them. Her gaze trailed over the prince's body, then slid over to Gemma. "He knows Honnah?"

Gemma's gaze darted from Isoldesse to the prince. "Isoldesse wants to know how you know Honnah. I figured you could tell her," Gemma said, tucking one hand under her elbow.

Lifting his chin, he stared out to where he assumed Isoldesse was standing. "Honnah is my wife. We met fifty years ago when she was brought to Priomh as one of Earth's Aevo Compendium subjects. She caught my attention while I was here to visit Breyah." His arm swung out wide, finger pointing to Priomh's Leadess. "She introduced herself to me immediately as an Anumen living among the humans. Then she asked for my help. She needed someone to help her finish an important mission—life-changing for everyone in the universe. I didn't know what to make of it at first, but after a few days of spending more time with Honnah, I knew I needed to help her."

Isoldesse told her bonded companion, "He speaks of new life. The bridge between worlds."

A puzzled expression crossed Gemma's face, and she relayed the message to Gerard. "Uh, she says you're talking about new life. Some bridge between worlds?"

The Sendarian prince nodded, resting both hands over the left side of his chest—over his heart. "She is my pride and joy. I could not love anything more."

"Who are you talking about?" Gemma barked out.

"Kenna," Meegan quietly answered. "Honnah must've been carrying an egg. But the Fawness is the only Anumen able to create eggs and bear children, so I don't understand."

"We had a surrogate mother—a human back on Earth. That is why she's so special. Three races run through my daughter's blood, bones, and everything else that makes her…her. Future generations with her blood will be the bridge to all three worlds."

Meegan stared out to the black ship stretching across the sky, consuming the entire top half of the window's view. The buildings below and the forest beyond were shrouded in a gloomy gray overcast.

"Does the Sendarian man know about Honnah's mother?" Isoldesse asked, sounding more like herself.

Gemma relayed the question to Gerard, who answered, "If you're asking about your daughter, well, she died on Earth, long before I ever met Honnah."

"Honnah is Isoldesse's granddaughter?" Gemma asked, her voice climbing an octave.

Gerard nodded.

The Anumen woman's form briefly faded, and Gemma reacted by trying to grab or support her bonded companion's form. When Gemma's hands passed through Isoldesse's body mid-fade, she leaned away, watching the brief transition. When Isoldesse had fully returned, she nodded and said, "I'm okay. But have you found Jasper? You might check planet Earth for his location. He'll be able to help us."

Rolling her eyes, she grumbled, "Oh, geez. Here we go again." Then, with an exhausted tone, Gemma said to Gerard, Breyah, and Meegan, "She's asking about Jasper again. She thinks he might be on Earth."

Gerard shook his head, leaning back against one of the medical beds. "Honnah has never mentioned a Jasper before, and if she did, I don't remember."

Turning to Isoldesse, Gemma asked, "Why is it so important we find this Jasper guy? How can he help us?"

"We took something from the Obard, he and I. I was hoping if we gave it back, then they would stop hunting our people." Isoldesse slowly circled, facing the window again. The Obard ship loomed overhead.

A loud electrical *zap* hummed through the air. Gemma's attention focused on something off in the distance. A vibrant red light flickered to life along the underside of the ship's outer edge. A wall of red energy extended out from the ship's edge, slamming into the ground below and crushing anything in its path. Fire and smoke erupted along the barrier's borders. Emmalyn shrieked while Breyah whimpered soft words of horror and sorrow. The attack was coming.

"They've trapped us! We can't leave!" Meegan's trembling voice mimicked Gemma's thoughts. She stumbled away from the group. "They're going to kill us all!"

Holt rushed from Eryn and Julianna bedside to the young Anumen. "You need to sit and calm yourself. We're not going to die, not yet at least."

"Has everyone been evacuated?" Breyah asked, her gaze locked onto Gerard.

Sidestepping Emmalyn and Gemma, the prince approached the glass window. He activated a display screen. A two-dimensional rendering of the compound opened up, every building outlined in red. He pointed to their location in the Waking Room of the medical wing, where twelve blue dots were spaced out in the room.

Darci joined them, leaving Eryn to rest. Gemma wished they'd left Eryn and the human captives on the *Tarais* in stasis. The medical bay on the Sendarian ship was fortified and not directly beneath the Obard ship. But what's done was done. They were here, resting in their beds.

"Who are those two?" Darci pointed to the two blue dots in the adjacent room.

"Prue and Ally," Holt explained. "It was too risky to evacuate Prue with the others, especially because the medicine and equipment specific to her biology are here."

Huh, she should've been transported to the Tarias *too! Why keep them here?* Gemma could only assume Holt wasn't thinking straight and hoped Medical was safer than the med bay on Priomh's spaceship.

Slowly, Darci slid her finger, pointing to the room next door to the Centrum. "And those two blue dots?"

Gerard tapped on the Centrum display cameras. A new screen opened, showing Bennach and his Rhaltan companion making their way across the Centrum.

Darci told Breyah, "I'm going to go check on Prue and Ally." The second Breyah nodded her approval, the young Spiaire exited the Waking Room.

A few moments later, Bennach and his Rhaltan friend rushed in. Gemma stayed close to Breyah so she could hear their report. Bennach held a lasher in one hand and told Breyah, "Everyone has been evacuated."

"Good," Breyah answered, looking somewhat relieved. Then she faced Gerard and asked, "How will Anora's ship make it through the Obard's energy barrier?"

"Anora's on her way here?" Bennach asked, blond brows pinched.

"I think they're already here." Gerard refocused the satellite image, concentrating on Gemma's home, isolated on the outskirts of the compound. The home butted up against the Obard's red energy barrier.

Gemma counted the blue dots on the screen. Three of them would've been Cahleen, Micah, and Xander, but there were a total of fourteen dots, two of them guarding the door. "I don't know how or when, but yes—Anora is there."

"Identify them, now," Bennach demanded.

She didn't hesitate, wanting to show them she was there to help. "My sister, Cahleen, and brother, Micah, are there. Along with Xander—he's human—and possibly Logan, a Sendarian friend within the Athru. Logan helped me escape after Anora locked me up for believing I had something to do with Quaid's death."

"And the other ten?" This time it was the accompanying Rhaltan officer next to Bennach asking her the question. "Who are they?"

"I don't know. But if I had to guess, I'd say it was Anora and whoever she brought with her."

"We need to take a closer look," Bennach said to Breyah. "Jordi and I will assess the situation at Gemma's old home and the threat above. You stay here. Lock the door behind us." He waved for Holt. "Get everyone in this room if you can. Stay together."

Holt nodded, then asked Liam and Brody for their assistance in moving Prue. They quickly followed him out of the Waking Room.

"Be careful," Breyah told her brother before he left.

"I'm coming with you," Gerard said. "And before you tell me no, they've got my family, and I can handle myself."

Bennach nodded, then led Jordi and Gerard out of the room. Gemma worried that two Rhaltan officers and one banished prince might not be enough to take down Anora. She was smart and determined, and rarely let her guard down.

"I should be helping them," Meegan said from behind everyone.

As Gemma watched, Isoldesse moved to face the girl and brought her hands to the sides of Meegan's face. "The Eilimintachs are blocking her powers." She faced Gemma. "Tell her I can help her restore them if she wishes, but it's risky and there may be a cost."

Approaching the girl, Gemma snapped her fingers in front of Meegan's face. "Hey! Get your head in the game. You're the most powerful one here out of everyone, even those shitheads up there." She pointed toward the ceiling. "Don't you want to save your friend?"

Meegan narrowed her eyes at Gemma. "Don't you think I would if I could? You think I want to be sitting here…doing absolutely nothing…when I *could* be stopping this whole mess from happening?"

Crossing her arms and giving the Anumen girl a small smile, she said, "Good. That's what I like to hear. Now, if you're up to it and willing to take a risk—and before you ask, I don't know how big the risk is—Isoldesse says she can help you get your powers back. If you want her help."

Meegan's expression twisted, something that would've normally brought joy to Gemma, but now she knew it only meant she'd have to convince this little brat to look past her pride and accept Isoldesse's offer.

"I'd rather die than—"

"Ah, ah, ahhh…" Gemma sang. "Careful what you wish for. Because death is likely to happen for all of us if you don't check yourself and dismiss whatever hate you have for Isoldesse. It's not really an option—you need to accept her help."

They stood there staring at one another for a long moment before Meegan caved. "Fine. But this doesn't mean I forgive her, or that I have to like her. But I will let her help me. For Kenna."

"Good," Isoldesse said from next to Meegan. "Tell her the only way to confront the Eilimintachs is by going to them directly. Meaning, she'll have to ascend her essence. The Eilimintachs *will* come to her in death, especially if she has no heir to continue the Fawness line. It'll give her a chance—*one last chance*—to make her case and get them to restore her powers."

Gemma's gaze darted between Isoldesse and Meegan, finally landing on her goddess. Meegan picked up on the unsettled look crossing Gemma's face and asked, "It's that bad, huh?"

Putting on the best fake smile she could muster, she shook her head. "No. You've got this. Everything will be fine. I promise."

38

Kenna sat up from her slouched position on the couch. Leaning closer to her mom, she said, "I know where we are. This is Gemma's house. If we can somehow sneak out of here, I can get us to the main building to where the others are."

With a slight shake of her head, Honnah looked around the living room. In a discreet whisper, she opposed her daughter's idea with a stern tone. "Sit and be quiet until I can figure out what to do that won't involve getting us killed." Gesturing with her chin to the Obard woman sitting on the floor, she asked, "Do you want a collar around your neck like Rian's?"

Across the room, Rian sat, slumped on her side with her back against the glass wall. Kenna's gaze drifted from Rian to the smashed glass above her head. Something hard had hit the window, creating a narrow hole the length of a finger in the center. Rian stretched her neck, trying to adjust the tight collar.

"No. You're right," she whispered to her mother. "That would only complicate our escape." Kenna shifted her attention from the broken glass to Anora, Biryn, and the woman with the fauxhawk. They kept their voices low, yet it was obvious the woman Kenna didn't know wasn't happy. Her expression was tense, and she kept pointing out the window, as if to emphasize the impending danger from the glowing red threat outside. They'd barely made it inside the house when the red barrier slammed into the ground, causing a powerful shock wave that destroyed the front door.

Yet even after that, it appeared that the two Athru leaders were still in denial.

When Micah walked by, Kenna asked, "What's going on? Why are we still here?"

Turning his back to the couch, he slyly said while pretending to cough into his elbow, "Stay quiet."

"Stay quiet?" Kenna repeated, loud enough to draw the attention of the trio deciding their fate. Kenna stood from the sofa, pointing out the glass wall. "I can tell you exactly what's going on out there!"

Anora narrowed her deep orange eyes while Biryn shifted his feet to face her. Her long braid was disheveled and in need of being redone. She brushed aside loose strands of red hair from her face, and Kenna could see the heated flush beneath the millions of freckles covering her skin. She strode closer, arms crossed, as she said in a taunting tone, "Why don't you enlighten us, because Cahleen here"—she turned and briefly gestured to the woman with the fauxhawk—"thinks we're under attack from some alien threat."

Eyes wide, Kenna exclaimed, "Yes! That's exactly what's happening! I don't know how much she's told you, but they're called the Obard and they're going to kill everyone."

"Why?" Biryn asked, sidestepping into Kenna's view from behind Anora. "What do they want?"

"Quaid made some kind of deal with them," Cahleen answered. "I told you. I overheard him talking with these Obard beings through his ship's comms. Logan was there—he can confirm." Everyone in the room looked to the tall Sendarian man with the scar trailing the side of this neck, disappearing below the collar of his shirt.

Logan, who was standing next to one of the two Athru soldiers watching the front door, turned to the room and nodded. "She's not lying. Quaid was in communication with them. Whoever was on the other end warned Quaid to not be on Priomh when they arrived."

Anora cupped her brother's shoulder and led him away from everyone. They conversed quietly in the corner while everyone stood around waiting.

"That's not why they're here," Kenna whispered.

Honnah replied quietly with an elbow nudge, "They don't need to know."

Jumping to her feet, she called out, "We need to find Breyah and the others." The only acknowledgment she received was a side glare from Biryn.

"Sit down," Honnah scolded, tugging at Kenna's arm. "You need to have patience."

Lowering herself, she told her mother, "Seriously? Now is not the time for patience. If we sit around and wait, soon enough the Obard are going to storm in here and kill us all!" Rubbing her hands up and down her legs, she anxiously said, "What I need to do is get to Meegan before the Obard find her."

In a whisper, Honnah said, "What we need to do is wait until the right moment and then get *Rian* out of here. She's our best hope for stopping the Obard."

"Why? Because she's Obard?"

"Exactly. She might be able to convince them to cease their attack."

"And if she can't?"

Honnah turned her lips in and sucked on the bottom one. Then, shaking her head, she said, "We'll figure something out."

Anora broke away from the private conversation with her brother, waving over some of her Athru soldiers. "You four, come here!"

Two men and two women approached her, while the two brutes standing guard at the door remained at their posts. Anora led the group toward the front door. "I want you to walk the perimeter of this energy barrier. Go in groups of two, and in opposite directions of one another." Biryn handed one of the men a hand-sized plac, and Anora continued, "When you regroup on the other side of Priomh, send word with that." She tapped the plac the man held. "It shouldn't take you long, and I want an update within the hour. Understood?"

All four nodded, then hurried outside. She turned to Micah. "How about you fix some food while we wait?" Rolling his eyes, he moved toward the kitchen. Anora grabbed Xander, who'd been standing against the wall, and pushed him at Cahleen. "Tie this human up with the others."

"Happily," Cahleen answered, taking Xander by the shoulder and shoving him to the couch next to Honnah. "Hold up your hands, loggie."

He did, but not without a grumbled retort. "You always were an asshole, you know that?" She smiled. Then in a low whisper, making sure Anora and Biryn weren't looking, he asked, "You do have a plan, right?"

Kenna didn't miss the wink she gave him before slapping him across the face. "Don't move from that spot, or I'll be forced to use one of these beauties." Cahleen lifted the edge of her dark shirt to show the hilt of a knife tucked in her waistband. "Do I make myself clear?"

With his hands bound, he rubbed the side of his face. "Yeah. Not gonna move."

Cahleen stood straight, turned away, and positioned herself so her body blocked the Athru leaders' line of sight to those sitting on the couch. Honnah leaned over to Xander. "Are you okay?"

He nodded. "Gemma's with the others. She'll come for us. I know it."

"Let's hope so. Because we're going to need a lot of help if we're to face off against the Obard."

Kenna knew her mother was right, and maybe she was right about Rian being a useful ally. But in the end, Kenna knew it was Meegan they'd need to save them all.

Twenty minutes later, Anora, Biryn, and Cahleen emerged from their private meeting upstairs, descending the open staircase set at the rear of the living room. Biryn and Cahleen crossed the room, past the couch, over to where Micah and Logan were conversing. Anora, on the other hand, approached the sofa.

"Get up," she demanded, waving at them.

Slowly, Xander and Honnah rose to their feet. Kenna followed their lead, saying as she stood, "The safest place right now is in the Lead building, where the others will be. And we need to move fast before they find us."

"*They*," Anora said, pointing a finger toward the ceiling and stepping in front of Kenna, "are not here for us. They—whoever they are—will leave us alone."

"Going anywhere but the Lead building is a death sentence. We need to work with the Priomh Sendarians!"

With a wide swing of her arm, Anora slapped Kenna across the face. Kenna fell onto the couch while Anora warned, "Enough! I'm not going to let a *human* tell me what to do!" When Anora walked away, over to Rian, Honnah helped Kenna up from the couch.

"Are you okay?"

Rubbing her cheek, she nodded. "Yeah. Stings, but I'm okay."

"Could you please listen to your mother now? Have some patience."

Kenna sighed and reluctantly nodded.

Across the room, towering over Rian, Anora kicked her hard in the leg. "You, too. Let's go!"

While the Obard woman struggled to her feet, Anora shifted her attention to the two Athru men standing guard at the front door of the home. She whispered something to them, then they nodded in sync before exiting the house.

"There's an escape tunnel on the northeast side of the compound," Anora explained to Micah and Logan. "We'll use it to get the hegah out of here." She picked up one of the backpacks, shouldered it, and stormed out the front door.

Everyone lined up and followed her outside. Biryn stood by the open door, and when Kenna started to walk by him, he grabbed her arm. "Hey, can I talk to you?"

Jerking free, she barked, "Don't touch me!"

"I thought we were good?" The puzzled expression crossing his face seemed sincere, which disgusted Kenna.

"You thought I was *good* with you killing innocent people?"

"Well, not good, but I assumed you knew the risks—the necessary evils one must do in order to achieve change. Sendara needs to evolve, and the only way that's going to happen is through the actions of those willing to do whatever's needed—even kill. You would do the same if your world's freedom was being suppressed."

"But is it?"

"What?"

"Being suppressed?"

Stepping closer, his face inches from hers, he said with an annoyed tenseness, "You've been hanging around that Rhaltan officer too much. Don't presume to know anything about my world."

How had she let herself be fooled by a sweet smile, a toned physique, and that mysterious, luring gaze peeking out beneath wavy reddish-blond hair? Had Liam's and Ben's rejections gotten to her? This guy was a monster—a psycho—beneath his good looks and charm.

"Stay away from me." She backed away. The second she stepped outside, the hum of the electric barrier filled her ears. It was like a million insects buzzing in the air. Covering her ears, she jogged over to where her mother helped Rian while they walked, one arm wrapped around the Obard woman's waist. Kenna almost tripped over broken pieces of tree bark that'd splintered and exploded outward when the barrier came down. It was hard to see, everything shadowed in a dark gray from the black underside of the Obard ship.

But there was enough light to see Ben.

Ben was here.

A surge of joy filled her. Flanking him were Jordi and her dad. The three men stood arm's length from one another as they faced Anora. Glancing back at the front door, Kenna looked for Biryn, but he wasn't there. She searched around the group, but she couldn't find him anywhere. She did see the barrier off to the right, coming from the left side of the house. The soft red glow of the semitransparent field crackled intensely with one energy surge after another. Kenna recalled the vision Ulissa had showed her and Meegan of when the Obard attacked Anuminis. How those who touched or fell against the barrier disintegrated instantly.

When Anora spoke out, Kenna turned her attention from the barrier to watch Anora and Ben's confrontation. "It's been a long time, my love." The tall Sendarian woman swayed her weight from one hip to the other, her long, thick red braid trailing down her back. "Are you out here because you miss me?"

Lips pinched, Ben quickly scanned over everyone standing behind Anora. When he locked eyes with Kenna, his lips parted for a brief second before returning to their pursed position. He narrowed his orange eyes at the Athru leader. "I'm not here for you, Anora. Not today. We're here to rescue Prince Gerard's family and Rian."

"Ah, yes. I did hear a rumor that the banished Prince of Sendara had returned." She clapped her hands and pressed them together beneath her chin. Then, as she spoke again, she spread her hands wide. "How about a trade?"

Stepping forward, Ben raised one hand out to her while lowering the other holding the shortblade. "You know I can't do that." Kenna noted his tone was softer—kinder—than when he confronted Quaid.

Beside Ben, Jordi adjusted his grip on his lasher. His gaze focused off to Kenna's left—on Cahleen. Meanwhile, Gerard had started to slowly shuffle away from his companions. They were subtle steps, but enough for Kenna to notice. She assumed Honnah noticed, too, because her mom was shaking her head ever so slightly while looking to Gerard.

"What is he doing?" Kenna whispered.

"Being stupid," Honnah answered.

Kenna recognized the shortblade Ben had as the weapon he used to fight off the Athru men at the old research facility while Quaid held Kenna at knifepoint. Except this time, there was only one sword and no blue electricity.

"Anora, why all this violence? Why not come to me?" With his sword by his side, he stepped closer. Kenna couldn't see Anora's face, but there was an extended moment of silence lingering in the air between them. She worried that this woman—this horrible woman who had kidnapped and approved the torture and deaths of friends and family—might still have some kind of sway over Ben.

Instinctively, she wanted to intervene and help sever whatever tether Anora held over him. Without thinking, she called out to him, "Ben!"

It took a moment, but he eventually broke away and spotted Kenna among the group. He blinked, the muscles along his jaw momentarily relaxing, before he returned his attention to Anora. "There is no us."

Anora's gaze dipped over her shoulder, but she never fully turned and looked at Kenna. It was clear Anora assumed something between the two from the sly smirk forming. Biryn's words resurfaced in her mind: *You've been hanging around that Rhaltan officer too much.* Somehow, he'd known that Kenna and Ben were acquaintances, which meant Anora knew too.

Moving toward the front of the group, leaving her mom to help Rian, Kenna asked, "How's Meegan? Is she safe?" It was an honest question, because she did want to know how her best friend was doing, but she also wanted to get closer to Ben.

Jordi tightened his grip on his lasher while shouting to Kenna, "Not good. But she's also not telling us much. I think she needs you."

He's right, Kenna thought. *I need to get to her.*

All of a sudden, Gerard charged into one of the Athru men over next to the house. Kenna screamed, hands clasped to her mouth as her dad tripped and fell hard against one of the trees close to the energy barrier. The Athru man wasn't so lucky. He stumbled backward, falling against the barrier. Intense currents of red energy flowed between his body and the barrier. Kenna shuddered and gasped as the man screamed, his body burning so fast from the backside to the front. It was over in a matter of seconds. The charred remnants disintegrated, barely anything left to float off in the air.

Someone retched, and Kenna searched the group until she spotted Xander on his knees, wiping his mouth with the backside of his sleeve. A few feet behind Xander, Micah retreated. The sendarian's eyes were wide beneath his baseball cap. Cahleen, Logan, and Anora, however, didn't move. Their gazes were fixed on the area where the Athru man had died. And where Gerard was getting to his feet.

"Dad!" Kenna cried out. "Watch out!"

But it was too late. The second Athru soldier who'd been guarding the front door charged at the prince.

"No!" She moved her feet, about to run to her father, but Honnah grabbed her around the waist.

"Don't, Kenna!"

"Let me go!"

The Athru man grabbed Gerard by the shoulder, spun him, and punched him in the face. The prince stumbled, then quickly regained his footing, and was about to dodge the blow of the Sendarian man barreling toward him, but he was too slow. The brute rammed his shoulder into Gerard's midsection. The force threw both men backward. Gerard punched at the man's back while the man swung at Gerard's side.

Jordi ran to intercept and to help the prince, but as he darted across the front yard, the Athru man stood straight and grabbed Gerard by the throat, forcing him to scramble backward. Gerard tried to break free, alternating his efforts between slamming his fists against the man's arm and pulling at the man's hand around his neck.

Jordi was about to reach the two men scuffling when the Athru men screamed a deep cry, yelling, "For a better Sendara!"

Trembling, Kenna dropped to her knees as the man overpowered her father, forcing Gerard against the barrier. Then the energy caught him.

A piercing scream erupted next to Kenna. It was Honnah, crying out as she fell to the ground, face huddled in her palms. The world around Kenna seemed to blur. Everyone's shouting voices sounded miles away. Swaying on her knees, she leaned to one side, letting the weight of her body teeter. She caught herself before hitting the ground, still watching the Athru man and her father burn up against the barrier. Their bodies disintegrated like burning paper, until there was nothing left but ash floating in the air.

Her dad was gone.

It was Ben's voice that brought her back, cutting through the haze of grief consuming her. He was yelling at Anora. "You just killed the Prince of Sendara!"

Kenna crawled to her mother and wrapped her arms over Honnah's shoulders. With a tight squeeze, she tried to comfort her mom while watching Ben and Anora.

Anora waved one hand toward the barrier, which sparked red where the men had impacted. "I didn't kill anyone. He caused his own death." The casualness in her tone sickened Kenna.

Jordi, returning to Ben's side, exclaimed, "Your man attacked the prince! You are their leader! Why didn't you stop him?" The Rhaltan man was covered in a thin layer of sweat, dirt, and tears along his face.

"Oh, no! Don't put this on me!" Now Anora raised her voice. "He attacked first!"

On the other side of Honnah, Rian fell to her knees, then eventually onto her side. Kenna tried to reach for the Obard woman, but she didn't want to let go of her mother. Not yet.

"Rian!" Kenna shouted. "Are you okay?"

Eyes squeezed shut, Rian curled into the fetal position. She balled up her fists and pressed them to her chest. The collar had a thick frosty layer that spread up her neck to just under her chin.

Kenna shouted, "Someone help her!"

Micah, Cahleen, and Logan remained together yet distanced themselves from their leader. Xander was the only one who listened and hurried over to Rian. He crouched next to the Obard woman, but when he tried to touch the collar, he jerked his hand back. "Ow!" Looking to Kenna, he said, "It's too cold. I can't… I can't get it off her."

Kenna, still holding her mother, yelled, "Get it off her!"

Cahleen turned to Micah and gave him a subtle nod.

A bright blue light caught Kenna's attention. She looked over to Ben, who had separated the shortblade into two swords. An electric blue current leapt from one sharp edge to the other.

"Are you going to kill me?" Anora asked over the hum of the barrier wall and Ben's electric swords. There was no urgency or fear in her voice. She stood there, still unfazed by the threat surrounding her. She taunted him, saying, "I bet that I can hurt you before you can hurt me."

Kenna could definitely see how this crazy woman was related to that murderer Quaid and that psychopath Biryn. Getting to her feet, Kenna briefly glanced over at the house. Where was Biryn during all of this? Returning her attention to Anora, she saw the woman had pulled out a small handheld object from beneath the backside of her shirt. Kenna wasn't sure what it was, but then she heard the *bang*—a sound she was quite familiar with from watching too many action movies and tv shows. Though, it was so much louder in person.

"No!" She bolted from her mother's side, rushing toward Ben. She slid to her knees next to him. His dark orange eyes were open to their fullest as he stared up at the underside of the Obard ship.

Anora showed off the firearm to the others, and said, "Now, this is a weapon I can get used to. Quite effective."

"And exactly why they're banned from existence on Sendara," Micah retorted.

Tucking the gun into her waistband and ignoring Kenna and Jordi hunched over the fallen Sendarian, she said, "Well, they won't be banned when I'm in control of our new world—the New Sendara." Moving to stand by Ben's feet, she added, "And there'll be some changes within the Rhaltan too. My world will be—"

Her words cut off, and Kenna scooted farther up away from Ben's feet where Anora fell to her knees. The woman's face twisted, mouth gaped and orange eyes trembling. From behind, Rian stood with her hands pressed to the sides of the Athru leader's face. Rian's skin was as blue as her hair, nails, eyes, and lips. Ice crystals emerged from her fingertips and spread along Anora's freckled skin. A long whimper sang out from the Athru leader's mouth as she fell to her knees.

Woven into her desperate cries was her final breath, leaving her body as a white puff of frigid air. Only when the Anora's skin turned a pale yellow and her body froze from within did Rian break free.

Anora remained on her knees, the look of horror preserved like a statue, while Rian stepped away. Kenna closed her gaping mouth, then pursed her lips and nodded to Rian, who breathlessly nodded back. Rian then focused on Ben's wound. He was bleeding out. Shimmering yellow blood soaked through his dark jacket, covering Kenna's hands.

"Ulissa!" Kenna cried out into the open air. She didn't care if people heard her. After several more tries to call her bonded companion, she lowered her head to Ben's hands. She feared Ulissa had given up her life to let Nick's essence remain. She didn't even get to say goodbye. Unable to hold back her tears, she released all the weight of loss and began to cry.

"Let me help," Rian said, lowering herself next to Kenna. Lifting her head and wiping her tears, Kenna noticed the collar was gone from Rian's neck.

Jordi stopped rummaging through his backpack. Then, to Kenna, he said, "Fine, let her try while I try and find a med kit."

With a sniffle, Kenna lifted her hand from Ben's wound, and asked, "What can you do to help him?"

"I can slow his heart, reducing the blood flow. Hopefully, that will keep him alive long enough to get him into surgery with Holt."

"Do it." Kenna silently prayed that whatever Rian was going to do worked, because deep down, she wasn't sure she could handle losing anyone else important to her.

Scooting back, she gave Rian room to work. She glanced over at Cahleen, Micah, and Logan—the only Athru left beside the four Anora sent out to walk the perimeter.

Micah held up his plac. "I let Rian free." He then pointed to Cahleen and Logan. "We're not going to be a problem. We're only here for Gemma. Right?" He nudged the Sendarian woman next to him.

Cahleen hesitated, eyes focused on their dead Athru leader. When Micah elbowed her in the side again, she shook free from her reverie and locked eyes with Kenna. "Yeah. We just want Gemma. I've got no plans to try and be Sendara's next ruler."

For some reason, Kenna believed her. The tough exterior she'd been displaying was gone, replaced with something like fear and self-preservation. The woman's gaze kept flicking from those standing around to the forest to the Obard ship above.

Without thinking, Kenna asked them, "Will you come with us? To find the others?"

Logan, who'd barely said two words since he'd been in Kenna's presence, pointed up and said, "Yes. It appears we'll need to work together if we want to survive this."

Rian placed her hands on Ben's arms. He winced, but only for a second before passing out.

"Linc," Rian called out into the air. "Send word to Holt to prep surgery room one. And tell him to hurry." After a moment, she looked to Kenna and said, "The message has been sent. But we need to hurry and get him to Medical."

Nodding, Kenna moved to help lift Ben, but Jordi intervened. "We've got him. You need to help your mother."

With haste, she nodded and hurried to her mother's side. "We need to go."

"He never listens," she said, tears streaming down her cheeks. "Why didn't he listen?"

"Because he thought he was helping. Now, I can't lose you too, so get up and let's go. Ben needs medical attention."

Everyone climbed into the transport vehicle Ben, Jordi, and Gerard had driven to Gemma's house. When everyone, even the ex-Athru Sendarians, were in, Jordi sped off toward the Centrum. The only one she hadn't seen since their conversation inside the house was Biryn. He was still out there somewhere.

With Ben's head in Kenna's lap, she silently pleaded with him, *Hold on, Ben. Please, hold on.*

39

"**S**o, what you're saying is I have to die?" It was the first thing she'd said in the last ten minutes while Gemma reiterated everything Isoldesse was saying.

"Basically, yeah," Gemma answered, but only after looking to the empty space next to her for confirmation. "She's like ninety-nine percent sure it'll work."

Meegan looked to where Isoldesse was supposedly standing, then back to Gemma. "And how exactly am I supposed to die?" Saying it out loud sounded ridiculous. It did cross her mind that this could be a trap, and that Gemma's loyalty was to the Athru.

She didn't answer right away. Instead, Gemma focused on her bonded companion, then over to where Holt stood. The Lead Medic was tending to Julianna and the other Sendarian woman they'd rescued.

Crossing her arms, Gemma raised an eyebrow at the empty air. "Uh, I highly doubt he'll voluntarily do that." Meegan could only assume the silence that followed was Isoldesse speaking to Gemma.

"What is she saying?" Meegan asked. It was annoying to only hear one side of the conversation. It'd been nice when she had been able to use her powers to hack into Kenna's arcstone, allowing her to hear and see the old Anumen woman.

"Okay, okay. I'll go ask him." Gemma walked away without an explanation. The silence surrounding Meegan felt awkward, especially because she knew the Anumen traitor was there, probably staring at her.

In a low voice, barely above a whisper, she said, "When this is all over, you're going to pay for all the pain and suffering you caused our people. Because you are the reason millions of Anumens are dead. You are the reason our home world no longer exists. You are the reason our kind has to hide, scattered throughout the galaxy, from the Obard. I don't know how, but I promise you that I will find a way to make you pay for it all."

Getting up on one of the twin beds, she watched Gemma talk with Holt at the other end of the row of beds. Whatever she'd said to him, he didn't like it. He shook his head and rubbed his forehead, making gestures that Meegan guessed meant *there's got to be another way* or *I won't do it.*

Eventually, Gemma returned with Holt at her side. "You can't be seriously considering this?"

Meegan shrugged. "It's my only option to try and get my powers back. Besides, I'm not planning on staying dead. Isoldesse has a plan." Her gaze shifted from Holt to Gemma. As did Holt's. They both stared at her, waiting for an acknowledgment that Isoldesse had a plan.

She inhaled deeply, then exhaled. "Yeah. We've got a plan."

"Fine. I'll make the preparations. Just give me a few minutes." He turned and left the Waking Room.

The low point was real. Over the past few days, her boyfriend had been brutally murdered, her best friend had been kidnapped by the Athru, she'd lost her powers, and now according to the Anumen traitor who'd started this whole shitty mess, the only way Meegan could get her powers back was for Meegan to die. What could possibly go wrong?

She hopped off the bed, wanting to hear what Breyah and the princess were quietly talking about over by the glass wall. The view of the lone mountain off in the distance was blocked by the expansive Obard spaceship hovering over the entire Priomh compound. It was the middle of the day, but outside, it looked to be nighttime.

Emmalyn turned to Meegan as she approached. "How are you holding up? Can I get you anything?"

A chuckle escaped. Meegan never imagined a princess would offer to serve anyone anything. "Do you have a paper and pen, or something I could write a note on?"

Breyah pulled out a hand-sized plac that'd been tucked under her arm. "No paper, but you can use this. Come with me." The Leadess turned and walked out of the room, leaving the princess behind. Meegan followed her a short way down the hall, then into a private examination room.

"You won't be disturbed in here." She showed Meegan how to record her video message before leaving, giving her some privacy.

Holding the plac up, she hit the icon that Breyah showed her meant Record and then started talking. "Hey, Kenna. I didn't want to part with you thinking I was angry at you. You're my best friend. No—you're my sister. And I love you. We may not always agree, but I should've done a better job at listening to you—at compromising. I shouldn't have yelled at you on the beach, and I shouldn't have pushed you away. Maybe you wouldn't have gotten so hung up with that Sendarian guide-guy… Zeke? I think that was his name. Anyway, I wanted to tell you that I'm sorry. And that I'm going to try and get my powers back, but there's no guarantee that whatever Gemma and Isoldesse have got planned will work. If I don't make it, then promise me you won't listen to what I said the other day about going back to Earth. Do whatever makes you happy. And if that means staying here—on Priomh or Sendara—then stay. Well, provided that the Obard don't destroy us all first. But you know what I mean. Be happy. That's all I want. For you to be happy. And please tell my parents I love them. Tell them I'm sorry. The last thing I said to my mother was when I was on the phone with her at Prue's house, yelling at her for lying to me about them knowing about Isoldesse leaving Anuminis. Tell them it doesn't matter. None of it matters. What matters is that they…and you…live every moment in the now. Don't dwell on the past or what you could've done differently. Just be happy. All of you. Please. For me."

Wiping her eyes, she ended with, "Until the next life, Iya."

Meegan entered the private patient room. "Hey, guys. I thought Holt was moving you into the Waking Room?"

Ally sat upright in the upholstered chair next to Prue's bed. "I told Holt we'd be fine in here. We're only one room over."

Darci craned her neck out from behind the glass screen attached to the top of the headboard. "You okay?"

With a half-shrug, half-nod, she answered, "Yeah. As good as can be. How's she doing?"

Pointing to the display screen, Darci explained, "Most of the screens are monitoring her vitals and rate of recovery. That one up there monitors the room's environmental conditions. Holt adjusted the room's temp and humidity levels to match those of her home region."

"That explains why it's warmer in here than the other rooms." Meegan pointed to the zoomed in screen. "And that one?"

"This is the one I wanted you to see." Darci traced her finger along the red line, which was fairly straight but pitched every so often. "Something isn't right. I mean, she's healing but every now and then her heart rate spikes along with bursts of adrenaline that reach dangerous levels. Holt's doing everything he can, but…"

Meegan sighed. "She needs to return to Earth."

Darci nodded. "Every medic on Priomh who is assigned to the Aevo Compendium project has been educated in the anatomy of every being from every world we observe. But there's only so much we can do beyond certain points of illnesses or injuries."

"We need to leave, and soon." Ally dropped her sister's hand and moved to the others. "I can't lose her." Fatigue and exhaustion weighed on Ally's posture and expression. When had she eaten last or slept for more than two hours in a bed, and not in that chair?

Meegan stood in front of Ally and held her shoulders. "Are you sure you're okay in here? We don't know when the Obard will attack, and it might be safer with everyone in the Waking Room. Plus, there are extra beds in the Waking Room for you to rest." Ally opened her mouth to most likely object, but Meegan cut her off. "Ah! No, arguing. You're no good to Prue if you're half-asleep, especially if we need to make a quick getaway. You need your energy."

Ally closed her mouth and nodded. "You're right. I'll go get Holt." She hugged Meegan, then left the room.

"You're a good friend, you know that, right?" Darci said without facing Meegan.

"I'm sorry, Darci."

That got Darci's attention. She stopped tapping and monitoring the screens over Prue's headboard and turned to Meegan. "Why are you sorry? I'm the one who should be sorry."

"True, but I shouldn't have taken my anger out on you." She held the plac out to Darci. "Can you do me a favor and give this to Kenna? There's a message on it for her."

Darci stared at the small black device. "No. You can give it to her yourself."

Meegan knew that Kenna missed the old bohemian-styled, chatty Darci from Earth, but she was starting to like this tougher, more soldier-like version of their friend. A small smile cracked at the corner of Meegan's mouth. "I would if I could, but there's something I have to do."

"You're not going out there to face them. Not alone. No way!" Darci shouted while pointing to the window. "We stay in here with everyone else until Kenna, Honnah, and Rian return. Then we'll decide what to do."

Meegan's small smile flattened. "I wish it were that simple. But Isoldesse and Gemma think there's a way I can get my powers back, and I have to try. I can't wait for them to return. This might be my only chance to stop the Obard."

Tears welled in Darci's orange eyes. "Okay, but why give Kenna this message?" Her gaze flicked to the plac Meegan still held out to her.

"It's complicated, and I don't have time to get into the specifics, but there is a chance I won't wake up." Darci's mouth shot open, and before she could argue, Meegan continued, "I understand the risks. We all have to take risks every now and then—trust those we wouldn't normally trust, right?"

Closing her mouth, Darci took the plac. "I'll hold on to it. But you better not die!" Sniffling, and letting the tears fall, Darci wrapped her arms around Meegan. "You are the bravest person I know." After a long embrace, she leaned her shoulders and head back, looking directly into Meegan's eyes, and added, "If we make it out of this, I want to work with you and help you find a new world for the Anumen people. We'll search every world ever visited by the Sendarians—and other worlds too—to find them. I promise."

Now, it was Meegan's turn to tear up. "Promise me you'll do that even if I'm not here. Don't let the Anumen people fade from existence. Turn the Aevo Compendium project into something good, rather than invasive."

"Well, technically we're not hurting anyone—"

But Meegan cut her off. "Darci."

"Right. Not the point. And yes, I will make sure the Aevo Compendium changes its priorities. And helps the Anumen people."

After one last hug, Darci returned to monitoring Prue's vitals, holding Meegan's message. As Meegan made her way to the door, Darci said, "I won't have to give this to her. You'll be fine."

"Let's hope so."

Ally walked into the room again with Holt behind her. He eyed Meegan with a disdainful look. "Let's move Prue first. Once she's settled, we can begin your ascension."

40

Gemma patted the pillow. "Lie back and relax."

"Easy for you to say. You're not the one who's about to die," Meegan said, hesitant to oblige.

True. Old Gemma would've pointed that out too with a sassy comment like, "*Better you than me*." But her perspective on life—and her priorities—had changed. Everything she ever believed in and worked hard for was a lie. Well, not so much a lie but misinterpreted.

Meegan waved a hand, catching Gemma's attention. Then, as she lay back, she asked, "Why do you look like you're the one who's about to meet their maker?"

"Was it all a lie?" Gemma asked, not wanting to make eye contact with Isoldesse.

"Honestly," Meegan answered, resting her hands on her stomach, "I don't know. I mean, the goddess part is obviously a lie. But I read your Anumen Doctrine, and I think your ancestors labeled her a goddess because of her Anumen magic. The guides and laws…

The Reigning Door system she established… She was only trying to help your world survive."

Gemma lifted her gaze, meeting Isoldesse's thoughtful expression.

With soft eyes and a gentle smile, through the golden glow outlining her body, Isoldesse explained, "If I'd known leaving Anuminis to explore the galaxy and help other worlds would lead to the death and destruction of my world, I wouldn't have left."

"What is she saying?" Meegan asked, looking to Gemma, then to the empty air on the other side of the bed, then back to Gemma. "Is something wrong?"

"No. Nothing's wrong."

Meegan adjusted her position and resettled her head on the pillow. "Okay, well… I'm ready. Is it time?"

She decided not to repeat Isoldesse's confession to Meegan about the Anumen woman's regrets. Instead, she nodded. "Yes, it's time."

Holt, who'd been prepping the glass monitoring screen above the headboard, stepped around to where Isoldesse was. The Anumen woman moved aside, even though he couldn't see her.

"Here. Slip this over your head. It should be snug around the top of your head."

Meegan took the silicone face mask. "I remember these from when we first woke up."

"Yes, it'll help me track your vitals." He pointed to the earplugs at the end of the wide headband. "Fit the ends into each ear canal. The bio-filaments won't deploy until after you're asleep."

"Lovely," Meegan mocked.

"Can we get started?" Gemma said, crossing her arms and tapping an impatient finger against her sleeve. "Or do I have to remind you about the hostile aliens that are going to end us all if this one doesn't get her powers back?"

"Right," Holt said, then stepped over to the counter recessed into the wall.

While he was busy preparing whatever he was going to administer, Meegan asked, "So how does this work?"

"Isoldesse explained that after your physical body gives out, your essence lifts from your body and begins to ascend to the Unforeseen World—your second life. But because you're the Fawness, and especially because you don't have an heir—"

"—an heir?" Meegan asked.

"Yeah. You don't have any kids." There was a pause, and then she asked with a raised eyebrow, "You don't have any kids, do you?"

"No! I don't have any kids!"

"Okay, then. Anyway, as I was saying... Isoldesse says the Fawness line will end with your death. So, the Eilimintachs may open communications with you again—to try and save the Fawness line."

Sitting up on her elbows, holding the silicone face mask in one hand, she narrowed her eyes at Gemma before turning to the empty space where Isoldesse stood. "You're not even sure they'll talk to me? We're doing this with the *hope* that they won't want the Fawness line to end?" Pushing herself up to a full sitting position, she shook her head. "Nope. I changed my mind. This isn't going to work."

"It will!" Isoldesse exclaimed, arms outstretched, trying to get Meegan to lie back down, but her hands weren't solid and passed through the girl's body. "Gemma! Tell her, IT WILL WORK!"

"Hey, okay. I know it's not a foolproof plan," Gemma said, coaxing Meegan to stay put by blocking her from getting off the bed. "But it's our only option. And, if this Fawness role is important to the Eilimintachs, then the chances of them reaching out to you are in our favor."

Meegan stared at Gemma for a long moment before sighing and lying back down, begrudgingly slipping the silicone face mask over her head. "Fine."

"Tell her," Isoldesse urged her bonded companion with an eager look, "that if things don't go in our favor, all we have to do is return your essence to your body."

Nodding, Gemma relayed the message to Meegan.

Meegan lifted the edge of the mask and looked at Gemma. Her attitude had shifted to a more agreeable one. "Okay. I'm trusting you."

And as she slipped the face mask back on, Gemma told her, "I will do everything in my power to make sure you come out of this."

With a thumbs-up from Meegan, Holt approached the bedside. He'd been standing behind Gemma, waiting for the situation to calm down. In one hand, he held a slender chrome canister that Gemma thought looked a lot like the injection he gave Rian whenever she had one of her episodes.

They were really doing this. Gemma's heart beat faster as she sidestepped out of the way, letting Holt take her spot next to the bed. "This shouldn't hurt. Close your eyes and take some deep, relaxing breaths." Meegan did as he instructed. He pressed the needle's tip to Meegan's neck and squeezed, activating the transdermal injection. Immediately afterward, he pocketed the pen-sized canister and slipped behind the headboard to monitor the readings on the glass panel.

Gemma returned to her spot next to the bedside. Her hands clasped at her waist as she paid close attention to the Anumen girl's chest. Her deep breaths eventually slowed to shallow ones. And when Meegan took her last breath, darkness fell all around. The only light in the room shone over Meegan, Gemma, and Isoldesse. Holt stood motionless—one finger held up to the glass panel displaying Meegan's vitals.

"It's happening," Isoldesse whispered.

Meegan's entire body began to glow blue. Then, after a few seconds, the light rose, separating itself from the girl's physical form. And when it was completely detached, it drew inward, forming a sphere the size of an apple.

"What's happening?" Gemma asked.

Blue light illuminated Isoldesse's face. "That is her essence." They watched the ball of light draw in the last of Meegan's essence. Slowly, it rose.

"What do I do?"

With a shake of her head, Isoldesse said, "Nothing right now." She reached out and grasped the girl's essence in both hands. Then, to Gemma, she said, "Stay on guard for now. You'll be needed after she's regained her powers, when it's time to return her essence to her body. I cannot, and you must."

Gemma nodded, watching Isoldesse and Meegan's essence fade away.

Slowly, the dark room also faded, and time resumed.

"It appears to have worked on my end," Holt explained, craning his neck around the glass panel, checking his patient. Then he looked to Gemma. "You should do whatever it is you're planning to do. I don't know how long she can remain like this without permanent brain damage."

"It's done," Gemma said, resting a hand on top of Meegan's. "Well, the first part is done."

He came around and inspected the face mask before pressing two fingers to the girl's neck. "There's no pulse."

Gemma swallowed the nervous lump that'd formed in her throat. "Her essence is with Isoldesse. I don't know for how long. I was told to wait… So, I'm waiting. Hopefully when Meegan has her powers back, she'll—"

She was cut off by a large explosion outside. Glass imploded inward, shooting at Gemma and Holt with a force that knocked them over. When she finally opened her eyes, she released a groan. Her vision was blurry, and the room was filled with gray smoke. Wincing with pain—pain from more than one spot—she tried to sit up. The second she lifted her head, the room began to spin. Someone called to her. Isoldesse, she thought. But the pain grew, and her head hurt. She deserved this. This was punishment for everything and everyone she had ever hurt. With no desire to wake up, she let the blackness take over.

41

Multiple explosions erupted around the Lead building. The Obard were firing down on Priomh. The shock wave from the explosion had momentarily lifted the right side of the vehicle, almost causing it to roll. Kenna wasn't sure if it was Jordi's driving skills or a special feature in the transport vehicle that saved them from tipping over, but she was grateful either way.

Jordi slammed on the brakes, sending the vehicle sliding across the front courtyard. It hit hard against a pile of rubble that'd crumbled off the side of a nearby building. Outside, a thin veil of dust curtained the glass windows doming the vehicle, but through it, Kenna could see they were within running distance of the Lead building.

Rian unbuckled herself, then spun in the front passenger seat to face those in the back. "Is everyone okay?" Kenna's heart pounded against her ribs as she gripped Ben's head and shoulders tighter.

"I think we're okay," Xander said, pulling Ben's legs into his lap again.

"Micah's out!" Cahleen shouted from the third row. Kenna turned and glanced over the seatback to see the Sendarian woman unbuckling and moving over to help the unconscious man. Dull yellow blood trickled from beneath his baseball cap along the side of his face.

"How's Ben?" Rian asked, drawing Kenna's attention to the front.

Lifting his chin, she pressed two fingers against his neck. His skin was cold, and after a few seconds, she felt a pulse. It was slow, barely beating, but he was still alive. Looking to Rian, she said, "We need to hurry."

Rian nodded, then told Jordi, "We go the rest of the way on foot." To everyone else, she shouted the same thing but added, "Stay close and move quick." She had one arm stretched across the front and her hand pressed to the top of the driver's seat, and Kenna noticed Rian's skin had returned to its alabaster color. Except the icy-blue crystal that had formed along her hands and arms remained.

Everyone piled out of the transport vehicle. Then, after Rian and Jordi helped unload Ben, Kenna turned to her mother, who'd been sitting between her and Xander, and asked, "Hey, are you ready?"

Staring at her hands, Honnah curled her fingers in and out. "I should've done something. I should've saved him." Then slowly, looking up and meeting Kenna's eyes, tears streaming her cheeks, she asked her daughter, "Why didn't I do anything? Why didn't I try?"

Kenna cupped her mom's hands, squeezed, and said, "No one's to blame, okay? Everything happened so fast." When her mother didn't move, she tugged hard at the woman's shoulder. "Mom! We need to go! The Obard are attacking!"

Another explosion erupted, but this time it hit farther south of their position. Honnah blinked several times before facing her daughter. "I can't do this without him. We were a team."

"I know," she said, letting her grief briefly surface. "But he wouldn't want you to die without a fight. So get your ass out of the truck and help us find the others!"

Wiping her tears, Honnah nodded. Long black strands of hair shifted over her shoulders. Taking Kenna's hand, she climbed out of the transport vehicle. "You're right. I'm sorry."

"There's nothing to be sorry about. Now, come on." Kenna huddled close to Honnah. They followed Jordi and Xander, who were half carrying and half dragging Ben's body. Behind them, Cahleen and Logan did the same for Micah while Rian trailed at the rear, watching for surprise attacks. The one-story and two-story buildings formed lines with wide walking paths rather than roads, in a half-circle sunburst pattern all leading to the Lead building in the center. The back side of the Lead building was all forest. Dark smoke billowed up from the treetops, rushing against the underside of the Obard ship before trailing outward to open air.

The nearby buildings provided some coverage, but not enough. They'd have to run across the open courtyard of the Lead building. They were completely vulnerable as they hurried toward the Centrum.

"Almost there!" Jordi yelled, holding one side of Ben while Xander held the other.

When they rounded the corner and started for the entrance of the Lead building, Kenna noticed thick black smoke rising from the back side. "What is that?" she asked, stopping and shouting back to Rian. "That's closer than the smoke coming from the forest!"

The Obard woman jogged up, her blue eyes focused on the rising smoke. "It's coming from the medical building." Rian's gaze dipped to Kenna. "We need to hurry."

But the second they started climbing the stone steps leading to the entryway's glass doors, the Obard ship launched another attack, striking the front of the building. Kenna's arms flew into the air as her body was lifted off the ground and thrown backward from the powerful blast. She hit the ground hard. Rolling onto her side, she felt the pain of her fall throb along her hip and spine. In her chest, a tightness took hold, preventing her from taking in any air. She coughed, tucking her mouth beneath the collar of her shirt and trying to breathe—but still her lungs wouldn't work.

"Kenna!" Her mother crawled over a large wooden beam. Bright red scratches streaked across the bridge of her nose. When she reached Kenna, she lifted her daughter's head up, slipping her knee underneath to prop up Kenna's shoulders and head. "Hey, you need to relax! You got the wind knocked out of you. Just relax and you'll be able to breathe."

She tried. She really did try, but everything hurt. And the dust wasn't helping. It coated the inside of her mouth and throat. With watery eyes, she shook her head while white-knuckling her mother's arm.

"Kenna! Relax."

From within her core, a familiar warmth spread, followed by a soothing voice. *"Kenna, listen to your mother. Relax and you'll be able to breathe."*

To hear Ulissa's voice and feel the healing power of the arcstone was exactly what she needed to ease her mind and muscles. The dust around them settled, and Kenna coughed while trying to inhale the fresh air. After a long moment of catching her breath, she sat up, still holding her mother's arm. Looking to the woman standing over them, Kenna smiled. Ulissa's golden aura had returned and was brighter than ever.

"Ulissa!" Kenna said while taking in more air. "You're here! You're alive!"

"Iya, my dear. But you're not out of danger. You and your mother need to get up and move, because the Obard are coming." Ulissa stretched one hand out. The golden beads of her dress glinted in the arcstone's glow.

Kenna's gaze followed the old woman's hand, which pointed down a wide stone path. Four shadowy black figures were making their way toward them. Kenna scrambled to her feet, urging her mother to do the same. "They're coming!"

Honnah pivoted to see behind her. Rather than follow Kenna, she hollered into the rubble that surrounded them, "Rian! Where are you?"

Kenna moved to her mother's side. "Mom, we need to get out of here!"

"No! We need to find Rian! Without Meegan here, she's our only chance to stay alive. She might be able to talk to them… Get them to listen!"

Nodding, Kenna agreed. Meegan wasn't here, and if the Obard knew Honnah was Anumen, they would either take her or kill her on the spot. And Kenna wasn't ready to lose two parents in one day.

42

Meegan picked up a red leaf twice the size of a maple leaf, then twisted the stem between her fingers. Unsure of where she was, she followed the dirt path trailing through the forest. Tall trees with rich, dark bark and vibrant red leaves surrounded her from every direction. It felt as if she'd been walking for hours before she finally cleared the forest. Partially obscured by a few stray clouds, the sun shone over the strange land. The dirt path she'd been following split, branching off to the left and right. The right path climbed a steady steep hill, while the left continued through a field of wildflowers. Off in the distance, more trees lined the field. Not wanting to walk through another stretch of woodland, Meegan decided to climb the hillside.

The air was warm. She tried to think about where she'd come from, but a fog cocooned her thoughts, making it hard to remember anything from before. As she reached the top of the hill, a narrow farmhouse came into view on the other side. Long red logs lined the front of the home, adorned with large stones covered in a thick layer of lush moss and lively vines. The thatched roof was mostly brown and dried out, but there were signs of recent repairs with patches of fresh green stalks.

Her gaze drifted to the wood fence across from the farmhouse, lining the open pasture at the bottom of the hill. A woman leaned against the railing, her back to Meegan. The closer she got to the woman, the more she remembered. The haze that'd been clouding her mind slowly dispersed. And when she finally reached the woman, she kept a good ten feet away. "Where are we, Isoldesse?"

Without turning, Isoldesse answered, "This is my childhood home. Well, a memory of it."

Meegan's heart swelled as she realized where she was. This was Anuminis. She looked back over the hillside and out to the red treetops. "The Red Umber Forest."

The Anumen woman slid into Meegan's peripheral, resting her arms along the railing of the log fence. She too stared out to the forest. "There was so much I loved about this home."

"And so much you didn't love," Meegan added, assuming there was more to the woman's memories.

Nodding, Isoldesse explained to Meegan, "You have to understand, our mother wasn't the easiest to live with."

"You mean yours and Ulissa's."

"Yes. She favored me over my older sister because I was born a Creator." Tilting her head slightly, she pointed out, "And I'm sure you know how often Creators are born."

Not very often, she knew that much. She also understood the hype around Creators, especially because there weren't many left in their small community on Earth. As Fawness, Meegan didn't have to worry about being born a Creator or a Bearer, because the Fawness had the ability to create her own seed and bear her own offspring. The downside was she could only have one child during her lifetime.

"That's no reason to treat Ulissa—a Bearer—with any less love than you."

A small chuckle escaped Isoldesse's lips. "Try telling that to our mother. She thought that I was special—that I would be the one to bring back technology." Isoldesse's voice dropped to a whisper when she said, "I tried so hard to live up to her expectations of me."

Before Meegan could respond, Isoldesse asked with a more educator tone, "Do you know the history of the Era of Chaos?"

Meegan nodded. "It lasted hundreds of years."

"More like fifty years."

"Fifty years isn't a long time for our people."

"No, but many died during that stretch of time, and in the end, the Prinor family—your ancestors—decided to ban technology and embrace the gifts from the Eilimintachs."

Meegan shifted her attention to the red treetops again. "What does that have to do with what you did? We could still be here—living peacefully on our own soil."

Next to her, Isoldesse turned away from the forest and stared at the old farmhouse. "Talia, my mum, wanted to bring back technology. She was convinced that if given a second chance, things would be different. And she molded me to be her prime example. With only one pitch to the Prinor family—your ancestors—my mother was given permission to travel to the old-world region. There, where technology rusted and our people's past lay, she and a small team started the Aevo Compendium project. I was blinded by the aspect of helping others. That's all I ever wanted to do—help and teach others."

"Your mother was the one who created the Aevo Compendium project?"

Ignoring Meegan, Isoldesse continued commenting in her reverie, "You know, I had planned on applying to be a teacher at the Amula Academy. To train youthen girls to master their abilities." Inhaling a deep breath, she released the air as a long sigh. Then, turning her back to the farmhouse, she said with resentment, "But our mum had different plans for me."

Off in the distance, a glint of light caught Meegan's attention. At the top of the hill, a coyote-like creature sat. Its silver fur blended in with the sunlight, almost making it invisible. Long pointed ears perked up, as if listening to Meegan and Isoldesse's conversation.

Isoldesse looked to Meegan. "I wanted to apologize to you, and hopefully you can pass on my sincere regrets to our people. I didn't know the extent to my actions. You have to believe me that my intentions were good. I only wanted to help other worlds. To feel like a mother caring for her children, since, well… I'm unable to have children of my own."

It was true that she couldn't bear children as a Creator. Her womb only created seeds that were collected and passed on to those born Bearers. "It doesn't matter. You must pay for your crimes," was all Meegan could say.

Isoldesse nodded. "I know. And I will. And unfortunately, you must carry the burden of saving our people. But to do so, you'll have to convince them." With a wide sweep of her hand, she pointed to the top of the hill.

Meegan's attention shifted to the top of the hill. The doglike creature sat motionless, like a pet waiting for its command to move. Only when it slightly cocked its head did Meegan realize it was a living creature. Leaving Isoldesse behind, Meegan made her way up the hillside. When she was halfway up, the world momentarily shook, like a low-grade earthquake. With both hands out, she steadied herself before continuing on. At the top she moved off the path, following the creature into a soft, grassy spot in the green pasture.

The creature leaned back on its hind legs, ears perked, and said, "You've put us in an uncomfortable situation."

Understanding swept over her. This creature was a vessel from the Eilimintachs, giving them a way to speak to her. Lifting her head, she knew she couldn't blow this opportunity. "I did what I felt needed to be done." But then Kenna slipped into her thoughts, and maybe she hadn't made the best decisions. "Okay, maybe I did let my emotions get the better of me, and I apologize. I only wanted to make those that deserved to pay…pay. "

When the creature didn't respond, only stared at Meegan with those big, round silver eyes, she took it as a sign to continue. "And I guess I could've used my powers in a less aggressive manner. I understand that now."

"And…" The creature's gaze shifted from Meegan to the Anumen woman leaning against the wood fence at the bottom of the hill.

Meegan briefly glanced over her shoulder down the hill toward the farmhouse. "You can't expect me to forgive her, can you? She's the reason this beautiful world"—she opened her arms and looked in every direction—"was destroyed. The reason our people are scattered across the galaxy, hiding from the Obard!"

"But is your world truly gone?"

"What?" She wasn't sure she'd heard the question correctly.

"Anuminis. Are you sure it was destroyed?"

That's impossible, she thought. Yet something in the back of her mind wondered what the world might be like now—centuries after the invasion. "You're telling me that Anuminis may be inhabitable again?"

"We're telling you that it is not wise to assume anything until you've confronted that which is unknown."

The thought of returning to her home world elated her like nothing before. Joy and hope and purpose swelled in her core. With a new outlook, she pleaded with the Eilimintachs, "Please restore my powers. I will not let you down, and I will be the Fawness you need me to be."

Silver eyes stared at her for what seemed like forever, but she stayed quiet, letting the creature deliberate on her plea.

The world around them shook again, more violently this time. The creature got up and approached Meegan. "You promise no more death on your behalf."

"I swear by it."

"And you promise to put aside your emotions, and not use your powers to punish or hurt others. You are only to choose violence as a last resort. And we do mean *absolute* last resort."

Again, Meegan nodded. "I accept my position and duties as Fawness for as long as I'm alive." For a split second, Nick appeared in her thoughts. It was most likely Ulissa had to release his essence, and she understood. It broke her heart to know she'd failed him. She'd forever feel a hole in her heart for his love was like no other. Their love had been everything she'd ever wanted in a life companion. All she could hope was that he was at peace.

Shaking off her grief, she focused on the pressing matter. "I vow to you that going forward I will devote my life to protecting and helping Anumens. I shall find them all and bring them home. I won't let you down."

"And the Obard?" the creature asked, its pointed ears twitching.

"You must understand that I need to protect those who are being threatened by the Obard."

The creature stood up and stretched, its back end rising to the sky while its head dipped to the grass. When it was done, the Eilimintachs said, "Only as a last resort will you use force."

Feeling as if she was on the edge of getting her powers back, she agreed. "Only as a last resort."

The creature approached her and held up its paw. The second she held the soft fur in her palm, the doorway to her powers opened, flooding her essence with the strength and power of the Fawness.

"Then, you shall have one more chance to prove yourself."

43

Wind rushed at Gemma's face. She peeled her eyes open, and the world appeared blurry between strands of red hair tickling her nose. Though her sight was distorted, she could tell the room was filled with smoke. She flinched as sparks of electricity ignited and trickled from the ceiling. Another swift breeze came through, crossing over her and clearing some of the smoke from the room. When she lifted her hand to brush away the strands of hair tickling her nose, her shoulder throbbed as if someone had punched her. Coughing, she covered her mouth. Her eyes adjusted and the room came into focus. She flinched when more sparks of electricity rained down near her head from the damaged ceiling. The exterior wall and parts of the ceiling and floor were gone, destroyed by the explosion. Outside, the black underside of the Obard ship stretched out as far as she could see.

Gemma tried to sit up but cried out the second she moved. A sharp sting stabbed at her leg. She stared in horror at the large piece of glass sticking out of her thigh. Yellow blood pooled around the sliced skin and trickled down her inner thigh beneath the fabric. Everything hurt, and the pain teetered between the glass in her leg and the throb in her head. Rolling onto her good leg, she saw a familiar woman walking through both the debris littering the floor and the dust clouding the air. Isoldesse reached for her, but her hands passed through Gemma. The woman's form flickered briefly from existence. She was trying to say something, but Gemma couldn't hear any words.

She couldn't hear anything but her own muffled heartbeat.

Isoldesse closed her eyes. A sudden warmth sparked inside Gemma's chest. It slowly spread outward, soothing her anxious nerves and easing the pain throbbing in her leg and head. Scooting back, she rested against the bed—the bed Meegan was on. *Oh no*, she thought, hoping the Anumen girl wasn't dead-dead.

Isoldesse waved for Gemma to get up, pointing to the bed. Still, Gemma couldn't hear any sound. "No. I can't… I can't move," she whispered between slow breaths.

Isoldesse's hands waved more vigorously. Her black brows pinched and her lips were pressed into a scowl.

"I said, I can't!" she shouted, pointing to the hand-sized piece of glass sticking up in her thigh.

"Gemma!" A man's voice floated in from the medical room's door, which was now half a door since the other half had suffered from the explosion. "Gemma! There you are!" Xander climbed over a section of the ceiling that had fallen and quickly made his way to her side. "She's in here!" He turned and yelled over his shoulder, "We need a doctor!"

"I have to help Meegan," Gemma groaned, grasping Xander's shirt. "Help me up."

"You're bleeding really bad. I think we should wait for Holt or someone to help."

She shook her head. "No. If I don't help her, we might lose her forever. And we need her if we're going to stop the Obard."

With pursed lips, he crouched and stared at her. She knew he was deliberating what to do.

"Xander!" she croaked.

Quickly, he tore off his shirt and ripped a narrow strip from it. "If I pull this piece of glass out, it might make things worse, especially if it sliced through an artery. So, let's wrap your leg, just above it for now, okay?"

Adjusting her seat, she used her hands to lift her leg. "Hurry!" she cried out, the pain spiking up into her torso as well as down her leg. The arcstone provided some relief, but the glass continued to cut into her flesh with each move she made. Xander moved fast, wrapping his torn shirt around her thigh. When he tied the knot, she screamed.

"I'm sorry, babe."

She felt faint but held on to the conscious world. There wasn't time for passing out. "Help me up," she murmured. He lifted her to her feet without any problem. She knew she was considered on the smaller side for a Sendarian woman, but for him to lift her so easily made her realize how small she truly was.

The second she was up, Isoldesse appeared on the other side of the bed. Getting her bearings, she let Xander hold her up. With his arm wrapped around her waist, she leaned her weight on her good leg. Meegan lay unharmed in the bed, except for a thin layer of dust and debris.

Clearing off the girl, she asked, "Okay, what now?"

Isoldesse motioned with a fist rising from Meegan's chest. Then she reached both hands out and pretended to grab something in the air in front of her.

"Right. I remember that. Meegan's essence rose up, then you grabbed it and disappeared."

Isoldesse smirked and nodded. Then she gestured with another balled-up fist, but this time coming from her chest outward until her hand hovered over Meegan.

"You're going to release the girl's essence?"

The Anumen woman nodded, then quickly held up a finger.

"But..." Gemma narrated as Isoldesse continued to speak through her hand gestures. With one hand balled into a fist, she slowly lifted it higher, directly over Meegan's body. "The girl's essence will rise. So, it'll pick up where it left off." Isoldesse nodded at Gemma's words.

Next, Isoldesse pointed to Gemma, then with her own hands, grabbed at the air over Meegan.

Gemma interpreted and said, "You want me to grab her essence. Stop it from rising up."

Pleased, Isoldesse smiled. Then, with her hands clasped together, pretending to have Meegan's essence, she lowered her hands and spread her fingers out as if to push the essence back into the girl's body.

Gemma understood. After a deep breath, she said, "Okay, let's do it. Let's put her essence back into her body."

Isoldesse closed her eyes and pressed her palms together. When she drew them apart, a glowing white ball of bright light appeared. It was brighter than before and illuminated the entire room. Gemma wasn't sure if Xander could see any of this, but she didn't ask. He was doing his part and holding her up.

Once Isoldesse released the essence over the girl, it immediately resumed its course, rising upward. Gemma didn't wait for a prompt. She quickly reached out and grabbed hold of the ball of light. It was warm, almost hot, but the temperature wasn't the problem. Meegan's essence resisted Gemma's hold. She couldn't pull it down. Her hands lifted higher and higher. Isoldesse waved at her and gestured to pull harder with balled fists as if she were pulling an invisible rope.

Not wanting to disappoint her goddess, she pulled harder.

"You can do this," Xander whispered in her ear. "You are the strongest person I know. You always get what you want, and this is no different! Whatever it is you're trying to do..." He paused, adjusting his arms around her waist. "...you can do it. I believe in you."

His words boosted her confidence. He was right. She wasn't going to let this moment be her downfall. This wasn't a physical task to be won—it was all in her head. Focusing on the warmth in her core, she used the energy of the arcstone to strengthen her mind. And as her thoughts focused on all the good things she planned to do—if they survived—her hands found it easier to hold on to the girl's essence. The resistance also lessened, and she was able to pull the ball of light downward. She'd done it. An overwhelming sense of pride swelled inside her. She glanced over to her bonded companion, who was also smiling. Gemma lowered the ball of light until it reached Meegan's stomach. With one last push, the essence expanded outward, covering Meegan's entire body like a floating blanket. It then slowly descended, returning to its rightful place within the girl.

The warmth in Gemma's core subsided but didn't leave completely. She leaned into Xander. He wrapped both arms around her and carried her weight so she could recover.

Everyone stared at Meegan, waiting for some kind of movement. Anything to tell them she was alive. It felt like forever but was really a minute or two before the girl's eyes fluttered open. Gemma squeezed Xander's shoulders while readjusting her stance.

"You did it," Isoldesse said.

Relief washed over her at Isoldesse's words. "I can hear you!"

Meegan slowly sat up, pressing a hand to her head. Then, after she took in the disarray around her, she asked, "Am I too late?"

Xander answered, "I don't know. Our group got split up. The others are out there somewhere."

Meegan stood from the bed, wafts of dust and bits of debris cascading down her legs. She looked to Isoldesse and said, "Let's finish this."

44

Leaning into her mother, Kenna limped along. During the last explosion, she'd landed on her hip and slammed her spine against something hard. Honnah wasn't in any better condition. Dried blood smudged her forehead. Red blood. She never gave it much thought about what color blood Meegan or her mother had running through their veins, but seeing it now, she wondered what other similarities humans shared with the Anumens and the Sendarians. And why? Why did they all appear so similar? Her mind raced with questions that weren't of any importance at the moment, since the Obard were approaching. But she couldn't help it. Her mind often wandered with curious thoughts, especially when she was nervous.

Staring at the blurry figures growing closer—their forms slowly taking shape—she couldn't help but wonder what would come of Sendara. She and Meegan had been overly concerned with revealing the truth about Isoldesse to the Sendarians, that they never thought to consider what other threats—like the Obard—they needed to worry about. Sendara was completely blind to the threat at their doorstep. Their prince—her father—had come home but only to die before any of them had a chance to celebrate his return. And now it seems they were doomed to share a similar fate.

To what end will they stop? Kenna wondered as she and Honnah picked up their pace, limping and hobbling around the rubble. The pain in her hip and back ached with each step, but falling behind or stopping to rest wasn't an option. They needed to get to the Lead building, where hopefully, everyone else from the transport vehicle had disappeared to.

The smoke cleared from their path, and they came upon what was left of the front entrance to the Lead building. The explosion had ripped a house-sized hole through the glass exterior, exposing sharp edges and splintered beams at the front of the tower. Black smoke streamed upward like thick dark clouds, collecting and spreading out beneath the massive Obard ship. The same for the black smoke still rising from the back side, where the medical wing resided.

Kenna hoped her friends were okay.

"Jordi!" she called out the second she saw the Sendarian man trying to drag Ben up the steps. Ignoring the pain, she tugged her mother to hurry. She wasn't sure at what point she'd started carrying more of her mother's weight than her mother was carrying hers. "Come on, Mom. We need to help Jordi."

When they reached the wide circular steps of the Lead building, she broke away from her mother, stumbling to her hands and knees next to Ben's unconscious body. His lips were pale, and his skin was cold. *Good*, Kenna thought. Whatever Rian had done to lower his body temperature held. His pulse was weak, but he was alive. With a hard tug to Jordi's sleeve, she told him, "I'll stay here with him. You go get help."

"I can't leave him. Not like this, and not with *them* closing in." Jordi shifted his weight to scan the horizon over Kenna's shoulder. She knew exactly what he was looking at, even without turning to see.

"I can protect him." She quickly drew out the arcstone and held it up. "We'll be fine, but you need to hurry and find Holt, or Meegan… Anyone to come and help!"

She didn't actually know if she could protect Ben with the arcstone, but he didn't know that.

As Jordi bolted up the steps and slipped inside, careful not to touch the sharp edges of the broken glass, Ulissa appeared, walking down the front steps of the Lead Building. The old woman's color had returned in her complexion. All traces of exhaustion and sickness were gone. Her aura glowed bright, and Kenna was torn between the joy filling her heart for Ulissa's reinstated health and the piercing ache in her soul knowing that they'd lost Nick.

The Anumen woman's golden beaded dress glinted even without the sun shining down on them. With one hand holding Ben's arm tightly, Kenna pleaded to her bonded companion, "What can we do…to save Ben or stop the Obard?"

Ulissa pursed her lips while taking in the Sendarian man's condition. "Nothing for Ben. The Obard woman did well to slow his heart and buy him some time. Them, on the other hand…" Ulissa lifted her gaze and stared out past Kenna.

Kenna swiveled on her side. Her hip disputed with a bruised ache, but she pushed through it, knowing that in a matter of minutes, it might not matter what hurt. The Obard soldiers were getting closer. They didn't seem to be in a rush, but their focus was directed on Kenna, her mother, and Ben.

"What can we do?" Kenna yelled.

It was Honnah who answered, standing and saying, "I won't let them hurt you." To the approaching threat she yelled, "I won't let you hurt my daughter!" With her hands raised over her head, she muttered words Kenna couldn't understand. But the second the air surrounding them wavered, coming together and forming a tight, solid barrier, she knew exactly what her mother was doing.

"No! Mom!" She staggered to her feet, her hip almost giving out, then steadied herself and grabbed a fistful of Honnah's shirt, tugging hard to get her attention. "Mom, stop! They'll know you're Anumen! They'll kill you!"

Turning her head slightly to her daughter, she whispered, "It's okay. I know what I'm doing."

"This is a bad idea." She knew her mother's determination and stubbornness were not to be questioned. Back on Earth, if Honnah said she was staying at the museum until a problem or situation was resolved, then Kenna and her dad knew that meant they wouldn't see her at home until the task was done.

"If they do break through, then you run." Kenna was about to interrupt, but she continued before her daughter could interject. "You need to save yourself. Staying here to die with Ben and me won't do anyone any good."

Honnah adjusted her stance. Her black hair lifted off her shoulders as she whispered, the words pouring more energy into the barrier protecting them.

The Obard were closing in. Scaly black armor covered their bodies, each pattern of scales slightly different from the next. All four wore identical helmets. Each with a sleek dark faceplate. Icy-blue hair sprouted from the tops of their black helmets, though some had longer strands than others.

They were going to die. Kenna was sure of it.

The soldiers broke formation, one halting and remaining in the rear while the other three continued forward. Then, halfway, the other two stopped, leaving one tall, dark soldier coming for Kenna, Honnah, and Ben.

Kenna feared Honnah would be the primary target.

The Obard soldier towered over them, its sleek faceplate looking down. Honnah spread her fingers wider, whispering an amula to strengthen the dome barrier protecting them.

"There are Anumens on this world?" The Obard pressed one gloved hand to the fortified barrier of air, testing its flexibility. "Interesting."

Honnah ignored him, continuing to chant, repeating the same amula over and over.

The soldier's helmet shifted from Honnah to Kenna.

"Don't you look at her! I'm the one you want!" Honnah snapped, yelling to draw his prowling gaze away from her daughter. Then to Kenna, she said, "Get ready to run."

"No, Mom! I don't think I can!" Tears streamed down her cheeks. Her muscles were frozen as the Obard soldier stood mere feet from them. "I can't run. I can't move!"

"You can," Honnah sternly said. "And you will."

Ulissa appeared behind the enemy. She glanced back at the others before looking to Kenna. "Help your mother. You can strengthen the barrier, like you did with Meegan—when you called for me in the mirror. You might not have known what you were doing, but you possess a powerful spark within your essence, like a transessence stone."

Nodding, Kenna pressed her hands to Honnah's shoulders. Her mother questioned what she was doing but then gasped from the surge of power Kenna passed onto her. "Ulissa says I can help. I'm not leaving you. Or Ben."

The compressed air doming them grew obscure as more air molecules packed in, reinforcing their protection. Though Kenna wasn't sure how long they'd be able to hold the barrier, she hoped help would come soon.

An unfortunate downside was the world outside became distorted, like trying to see through textured glass. They were unable to hear anything either. The silence felt like an eternity. Them standing there and waiting. And when a forceful blow hit the top of their protection barrier, Kenna shuddered and stumbled away from her mother. Without her boost of energy, the obscurity momentarily cleared, allowing them to see the Obard soldier holding his sword over his head. Kenna rushed back to her mother and grasped her shoulders just in time to reinforce their protection as the second blow hit. It was more powerful than the first, and Kenna worried his blade might pierce through.

"You need to run, Kenna! When he breaks through…because he will…you need to run."

There had to be something she could do. Her father had told her she had a destiny to fulfill. It had barely been a week since that day, and she'd done nothing to undo the mess Isoldesse created. She never got the chance to tell the Sendarians about who Isoldesse truly was or what the Aevo Compendium project was about. She never got a chance to figure out if there was a way to keep the idea of Isoldesse as their goddess alive—to retain the hope and peace she brought to all of Sendara. No one expected the Obard to find them so soon.

Another slam of the sword. Kenna held her ground, firmly grasping her mother's shoulders. This time when the blade connected to the barrier, the dome momentarily cleared, allowing them to see the Obard soldier. The haze returned, but Kenna feared their protection wouldn't hold much longer.

As she prepared for another blow, a blinding light shone from outside. The inside of their bubble filled with whiteness.

"Kenna, let go," Honnah instructed, and she did at the same time Honnah dropped her hands. Honnah sank to the ground, head lolling forward and hands catching her from falling over.

"Mom!" Kenna wrapped her arms around her mother and pulled her up, then forced her to move closer to Ben. The two huddled next to the unconscious man, and when the immense white light subsided, Kenna heard her best friend's voice.

"I think you're looking for me! Well, here I am!"

45

Jordi, Darci, and surprisingly Liam followed Meegan out through the wreckage that used to be the front entrance of the Lead building. The three of them veered left, leaving Meegan to deal with the Obard soldier standing over Kenna, Honnah, and Ben.

Two more Obard stood watching the spectacle ten feet back, while a fourth lingered much farther out, neither advancing nor offering assistance to the Obard before her. Jordi and Liam ran to Ben, while Darci went to Kenna and Honnah. The Obard over them sidestepped away, turning its attention to Meegan.

"Hey! It's me you've been hunting the galaxy for, right? The almighty powerful Fawness of the Anumen people! Well, I'm right here!" Meegan strode past Kenna without making eye contact, even though she wanted to stop and apologize for her behavior. She knew that if she broke her gaze from the Obard, it could be mistaken as a sign of weakness. Plus, she wanted to keep the Obard's attention on her so that Jordi and Liam could safely get Ben inside. She didn't know what happened to him, but he wasn't looking too good. His color had drained, and his eyes were closed. Hopefully, he wasn't dead. As much as Meegan wanted to hug her friend and make amends, she had to prioritize their safety.

With both arms raised, palms facing up, she said, *"Teacht luhte tiin sfar."* Two glowing balls of fire materialized above her open hands. The heat radiating from them warmed the air around her as she swept her arms out to her sides. Yelling, *"Liida,"* she swiftly brought her hands forward and launched her arsenal. The fiery balls flew past the Obard soldier closest to Meegan, exploding with a loud boom. The flames formed a barrier wall, dividing the enemy from its companions. The intense heat and light of the flames illuminated the surrounding area, casting flickering shadows on the ground.

The fire continued to spread, until there was no way out. The lone Obard was trapped inside with Meegan and the others. She climbed down the steps, letting Jordi and Liam have more space to carry Ben. Behind them, Darci and Kenna helped Honnah.

Kenna had stopped when they were close enough to Meegan, her arm looped through her mother's arm. She shouted at Meegan, "I'm not leaving you!"

Without turning around, because she didn't want the Obard to attack her, she yelled, "First, get everyone inside! I can hold them off!" She drew two more fireballs with the same amula, then threw them both at the Obard's feet.

It didn't move as the flames engulfed its lower half. Slowly, it walked toward her, leaving the flames burning behind it. The tip of its long black sword dragged along the broken stone of the courtyard.

"You better stay alive!" Kenna said, then continued to help her mother up the broken circular steps.

Now that everyone was out of harm's way, Meegan could concentrate on ending this once and for all. The Obard towered over her, swinging its sword over its head, but before it could strike, she threw out her hands and cast another amula. *"Teacht gohaf luhte garresh."*

The attacker's sword collided against an invisible force. Shiny fractures of condensed air, like hundreds of mirrors, came together and formed a cage around the Obard. It swung again, and again its sword hit the glass-like plates of air. Meegan could see through the unbreakable cage her attacker. Staring directly into the being's faceplate, which was obscured in shadow, she said, "You will know what it feels like to suffer." Despite the helmet hiding her prisoner's expression, Meegan could sense the weight of its gaze on her.

"*Fawness, you made us a promise,*" the Eilimintachs whispered in the back of her mind.

"*And I shall uphold that promise. Trust me. One thing my mother taught me was to not underestimate the power of words.*" She silently explained, "*An empty threat is still a threat to those who believe it's true.*"

"*Your mother is a wise woman.*"

"*No, my mother is a scary woman.*"

Backing away from the contained Obard, Meegan spread her hands wide, momentarily parting the wall of fire and allowing herself to pass through. "It would be wise for you to leave now!"

"Release him!" one of the two Obard soldiers demanded, unsheathing a long black sword from its back. The soldier brandished the weapon above its head, ready to strike. Next to it, the second Obard drew a sword of its own, identical to its companion's, from a sheath at its waist. Both soldiers stood with their swords drawn, slowly advancing toward Meegan.

"Fine. But don't say I didn't warn you."

The power of the Fawness swelled inside her core. The air around her began to swirl, drawing in bits of fire from the nearby flames. She was determined to put an end to the Obard's hunt for the Anumens today. The air intensified, encircling her body closely. Meegan commanded the forceful wind up her arms, and it obeyed, swirling over her skin like elegant gloves. Just as she was about to unleash a storm of air at the Obard soldiers, the third one—standing a few feet behind the other two—suddenly removed her helmet and threw it to the ground.

"Heiress Tiella!" the Obard woman yelled as she sprinted through Meegan's wall of fire. The other two Obard soldiers sheathed their swords and removed their helmets, revealing similar skin tones and blue hair, lips, and eyes. They also both had short light-blue beards.

Meegan lowered her hands but kept the tendrils of stormy air swirling around her arms. If this was a trick, she might not have time to cast another amula. She approached cautiously, lowering the wall of fire to a mere candle's wick. It wasn't until she spotted Kenna helping Rian up the front steps that she sprinted to intercept. With an amula, she increased her speed, reaching Kenna and Rian before the Obard woman.

"Stop!" Meegan shouted, her hands up, blocking the invader from getting any closer. Gray swirls of stormy air wrapped her arms, ready to be thrust outward if needed. Her black hair floated off her shoulders as she searched the Obard's face for any indication of what she was after. But the attacker's blue eyes were wide and tearing up—staring at Rian behind her.

"Tiella!" The Obard woman heeded Meegan's command. "It's true!" She spat, then continued, her voice filled with anger and venom, pointing the tip of her long sword at Meegan. "You have been keeping her from us! Do you not know what you've done?" The woman's face twisted with disgust. She swept her free arm wide, gesturing to everything around them with her hand, while the other gripped her sword. "We will lay waste to everything here and the main world if you do not return what is ours." Drawing her arm in, fist clenched, she narrowed her gaze at Meegan. "You cannot save them all, but if you give us Tiella, we will leave."

Meegan lowered her arms slightly as she glanced over her shoulder to Kenna and Rian, who were now resting on the ground, leaning up against a low stone wall lining the front steps to the Lead building. A thin layer of dust covered Rian's head and shoulders. Beneath her damp blue locks, Meegan saw a thin trail of milky-white blood. Deep scratches marred her cheek, shoulder, and arm, revealing porcelain-colored flesh. Meegan marveled at how the

Obard woman—or any of the Sendarians—believed she was from their world, given that her insides were clearly not like those of the Sendarians. The wounds on her body were a testament to that fact.

"Lower your weapon!" Meegan demanded, lifting her chin and raising her hands again. The Obard woman, who was a full head taller than Meegan, craned her neck to look past her. Her pale blue eyes trembled, as if she were on the verge of tears. When she took a step, Meegan raised her arms. The stormy tendrils swirling around her arms. To emphasize her warning to stay back, Meegan released a burst of energy from withing. White electricity crackled along her skin while the air swirled over her arms. With a pensive expression, the Obard woman shuffled backward and yielded, throwing her sword to the ground with a brash *clank*.

"Who is Tiella?" Kenna asked, loud enough to catch the attention of the approaching two Obard soldiers, who'd been cautiously advancing.

They were muttering words Meegan couldn't decipher, and their gazes were also focused on Kenna and Rian. Wanting answers before they got any closer, Meegan increased the intensity of the power swirling both arms. The stormy air grew darker while the electricity sparking down her arms crackled like lightning.

Meegan then repeated Kenna's question. "Answer her! Who is Tiella?"

The Obard woman looked unsure, leaning her body forward, shoulders arched with gloved hands lingering at her midsection. Her blue gaze darted from Meegan, to Kenna, to Rian, then back to Meegan, and she still didn't answer their question.

"Is she Tiella?" Kenna said, getting to her feet while helping Rian stand. Once they were up, Kenna held most of Rian's weight as they moved closer.

The two approaching Obard soldiers halted but kept a watchful eye on the situation, their swords in one hand and their helmets in the other. The Obard woman, standing before Meegan, raised her arms to the sky and let out a series of shouts in a foreign language. She balled her gloved fists and shook them with conviction, tears streaming down her cheeks as she lowered her hands and fixed her gaze on Meegan. "The day has finally come," she said, her voice trembling with emotion. "We have finally found our Tiella!"

"My name is Rian," she said with a cough, her voice hoarse and ragged from the smoke. As she shuffled closer, aided by Kenna's steadying hands, she stared at the invaders with an almost-sympathetic expression. "I thought I was different. I thought I didn't belong."

"You don't belong here. You belong with us," the Obard woman quickly responded, her cheeks wet from tears of joy. "They," she said while pointing a gloved finger to Meegan, "took you from our world."

Rian nodded in appreciation to Kenna and limped free of her hold, moving closer to Meegan and the woman. She looked to Meegan, reached out through the swirling tendrils of stormy air, and gently lowered Meegan's arms. "It's okay. Let's hear them out."

With a single word, "*Deante*," Meegan released her arsenal, allowing the air and electricity to dissipate from around her arms.

Kenna nudged Meegan's shoulder, and as they turned to face each other, they both reached out at the same time and embraced in a hug. The thought of potentially losing Kenna as well flooded Meegan with a newfound sense of responsibility. "I should have listened to you," Meegan said at the same time that Kenna said, "I'm so sorry."

They leaned away from each other, and Meegan shook her head. "No, I'm sorry. You were being smart, and I was being emotional."

When Rian lost her balance, and fell to her knees, the two girls broke apart and rushed to help Rian, but the Obard soldier got to her first.

"Tiella!" she'd shouted while dropping to one knee next to Rian. The metal of her armor scraped against the broken stone pavers of the courtyard. In a language Meegan didn't know, the woman yelled at the two Obard standing by. One of the Obard men quickly turned and ran. "You need medical attention."

Kenna knelt next to Rian. "Are you okay?"

Meegan circled the outside of the three, moving off to the side. She didn't want Kenna in her path if she needed to react and defend them. It appeared that the threat had subsided, but Meegan wasn't letting her guard down just yet.

The Obard woman cocked her head and stared at Rian. "How long have you been awake?"

Falling to one side, Rian pressed a hand to the ground. She leaned her weight on her arm for support. Taking slow, heavy breaths, she shook her head, damp strands of blue hair swaying across her forehead. "Awake? I don't understand."

"I think she means what's your age—when were you born?" Kenna guessed at the woman's meaning, looking between the two Obard women.

From the wreckage of what used to be the front door, Gemma and Xander made their way outside. He was holding her as she limped along. A piece of fabric was wrapped tight around her thigh.

The moment she'd reached talking distance to Meegan, she asked, "I take it negotiations are underway?"

Meegan pursed her lips, then answered with a curt nod. "Supposedly it's Rian they've been looking for."

"About that." Gemma cracked a smirk. "Isoldesse has a message."

The Obard man standing behind the group straightened, narrowed his blue eyes at Gemma, and lifted his sword. The woman kneeling in front of Rian also stood, all exuberance wiped from her expression. With hardness, she demanded, "Where is she?"

Meegan's insides shifted into alertness, her muscles and nerves humming with anticipation.

"Be wise and patient, Fawness." The Eilimintachs' presence weighed heavy in her mind. *"Their powers are not like ours and come from the core of their planet."*

"Well, that's interesting." Meegan had meant to respond to that information in her head, but let the words unexpectedly slip.

"What's interesting?" Kenna asked, looking up at Meegan. She'd torn off a strip of fabric from the hem of her shirt and was trying to clean up one of Rian's wounds.

"Nothing. It's not important right now."

Kenna continued to help Rian on the ground while Meegan circled behind them.

"Isoldesse died… A long time ago," Gemma explained, standing tall and speaking like an experienced leader handling a difficult situation. Her reply caused the Obard soldiers to stop inching closer. Gemma took a step in their direction, which Meegan thought was brave, and continued, "I'm sure you're aware of the Anumen arcstones, as you've hunted Isoldesse's people for over a century." Holding up her arm, she pointed to the yellow crystal-shaped stone embedded in the center of the arm cuff.

With her chin raised and her gaze inspecting the piece of jewelry, the Obard woman said, "We are familiar with the arcstones. But by stories only."

"Lies!" Meegan abruptly shouted, drawing everyone's gaze to her direction. "You hunt our people *and* our stones!"

No one said anything. Their silence fueled the spark of anger that had reignited inside Meegan from hearing the woman's words, *but by stories only*.

"You invaded my home world, leaving nothing in your wake but desolation and ruin! Then you persistently hunted my kind to either enslave or kill us! You are vile beings that destroy everything in your path—all to satiate your craving for more power!"

Their blank stares carried the truth with their silence, and it was all the acknowledgment Meegan needed. With a wide sweep of both arms into the air, then down in front of her as if she were pushing something into the earth, she made the ground rumble.

Kenna cried out, then screamed when a spike made of jagged rock shot upward from between two of the Priomh buildings. It hit the underside of the ship, crashing into a million pieces that rained down over the compound.

"Meegan, stop! Someone's going to get hurt!" Kenna jumped up and stood in front of her friend. Brushing her hair from her face, she said, "You need to hear them out, okay? Please!"

Meegan stared into Kenna's eyes. She was tired of running from the Obard, but she also knew they were hunters—killing her people and stealing the magic within the stones.

Kenna whispered, "Please, Meeg. Don't do this!"

The Obard woman had crouched down next to Rian, using her arm to shield any falling rocks from hitting Rian. She lowered her arms as the ground grew still.

"They're lying," Meegan huffed. She'd almost let her emotions get the better of her again, but thanks to Kenna, she'd been able to check herself.

From behind Kenna, the Obard man ran toward them, his sword raised high over his head. He was shouting words Meegan didn't understand, but his intent was clear. Shoving Kenna out of the way, Meegan raised her arms. From the corner of her eye, she saw the Obard woman shouting to her companion to stop, but he kept coming. She let go of all the anger and rage she felt for the Obard, and the hurt and betrayal she'd held on to for years, into one powerful burst of energy, which shot out from her hands at the Obard man.

The second she realized she'd let her emotions get the better of her again, it was too late. There was nothing she could do but watch. Time seemed to slow as the stream of white electricity traveled toward its intended target.

A second before contact, someone screamed. It was Rian. Somehow, she'd managed to get to her feet, run, and intercept the spear of energy. But Meegan's wrath didn't hit Rian. Instead, Rian somehow deflected the energy, causing an immense bright light like a giant bubble that expanded outward, blinding everyone in its path.

Even Meegan.

46

"**D**ammit! I can't see anything!" Gemma grumbled, then mumbled a string of curses. "What happened?" She rubbed her eyes, and as the light slowly died, her vision restored to normal. Everything was blurry, then more of a double vision, before finally she could see clearly again. Muttering under her breath, she shouted, "This is ridiculous! What is that foolish girl going to accomplish getting all riled up like this!"

"Don't be so harsh." Isoldesse's voice floated through the air. Glancing to her side, Gemma watched as her bonded companion's body materialized. Her silky black hair was parted at the middle, while the ends curled slightly above her shoulders. Because she wasn't really there, her white pantsuit remained immaculate and pressed sharp along the seams among the dust and debris. "Look," she instructed Gemma. "She's beautiful."

Gemma blinked several times before finding Meegan among the fading fog. The Anumen girl was rubbing her eyes, blinking and trying to see. Looking to Isoldesse, Gemma realized it wasn't

Meegan her goddess was staring at. She craned her neck to see behind Xander, who was still helping her stand, and saw Rian.

"Her skin… It's glowing!" Gemma exclaimed, and shuffled along the stone steps, careful not to trip on the broken pieces from the earlier explosion.

Not only was Rian's pale skin glowing, but her hair and eyes were illuminated with a soft blue glow. The Obard woman, mistaken as a Sendarian her whole life, stood in front of the soldier. The Obard man dropped his sword, which hit the ground with a sharp clatter. He lowered himself to one knee, bowing before Rian.

Rian stood, arms out at her sides. She inspected her hands, then touched her face. She faced the Obard woman, who was hurrying to her side. Rian told her, "I remember! Or at least, I know now who I am…and where I come from."

"I don't understand!" Meegan took a step closer.

The Obard woman whipped out her arm, her sword clutched in her gloved hand. Gemma hadn't seen when the soldier had picked it up again, but she worried Meegan's blood might spill next. "Keep your distance!"

Isoldesse looked to Meegan, raising a hand to the girl. "Please! Don't! Remember your promise to the Eilimintachs!"

Meegan glanced to Isoldesse and nodded. "I should've tried harder. There's just so much anger and hate already there for these beings."

The Obard woman, still pointing her sword at Meegan, said, "I was not lying to you, little Anumen. Yes, we may search out your kind but for information, not for power. Your Isoldesse stole our Tiella from us, and because of that, our world is in chaos."

Gemma looked to Isoldesse. "Did you know?"

Her so-called goddess shook her head. "I thought the egg was to be sacrificed to the beasts of the forest. I thought I was saving a life."

"Your intentions might not have been malicious, but because you did not know the Obard ways, you couldn't have truly known what you were doing. You should've left without interference." It was Rian talking to Isoldesse. "The Obard share a collective mind.

They're able to transmit thoughts and memories from one another through touch. When Isoldesse took the egg—*me*—from the forest podium that day, she disrupted a sacred ceremonial act. Every three generations, an unborn Obard is chosen to carry the memories of the past. I was that chosen one, and the podium acted as the conduit, like a giant download of Obard history."

"You can see her?" Gemma asked at the same time Meegan did.

Isoldesse looked to Rian and the Obard standing nearby. "I didn't know. Please believe me when I tell you I will forever carry this regret with me."

"Yes, you will." Rian then faced everyone else. "My sight goes beyond the many layers present before you all. And it's all thanks to Meegan. Your bolt of energy recharged my essence, allowing me to remember everything."

Gemma, fascinated with the wounds on Rian's body stitching themselves back together, watched with an intense curiosity. The scratches along her cheeks healed, as did the deep cuts scraping her arms and neck. Her strength appeared to be rejuvenated, too, as she stood taller and straightened her shoulders.

"Heiress Tiella! You saved me!" The male Obard lifted his head from his bowed position. He stood tall and told something to the Obard woman, who responded with a nod. He turned on the balls of his feet and marched off.

"Where's he going?" Gemma asked, a little snarkier than she'd meant to be.

Sheathing her sword, the Obard woman answered, "He is going to inform the fleet that we've found Tiella."

Isoldesse descended the last few steps, not caring about the unearthed portions of stone pavers since she was only a projection. When she reached Meegan, she said, "Fawness."

A thin layer of dirt covered her light brown skin. Sticky, sweaty strands of black hair clung to the sides of her face. She gritted her teeth as she half scolded and half whined, "You should be paying for all of this. You're responsible for the destruction of our world just as much as they are."

Unsure of how this confrontation would end, Gemma listened closely. Her curiosity to know more about the Anumen people—to know more about Isoldesse—would be useful in proving her loyalty.

No one spoke, and all eyes were on Meegan. Gemma had no clue how the Anumen arcstone magic worked, and wondered who else could see Isoldesse.

Isoldesse didn't disagree with the Fawness's claims. With an apologetic tone, she said, "I am sorry, but the past is in the past. You will never know the full extent of the regret I carry, and it is mine to bear. I made a mistake. I thought I was saving a life."

From the corner of Gemma's eyes, Rian stepped forward. The glow on her skin subsided, and her wounds healed. "It wasn't right what you did, to interfere with Obard traditions, but every action has a purpose. If Isoldesse hadn't taken the egg—my egg—Kenna would not exist, and neither would your friendship."

Kenna, who was next to Meegan, tucked loose hair from her ponytail behind her ear. "I know it's selfish to say I'm happy we met, because us doing so meant all those lives had to be lost. That horrible day Ulissa showed us back in Prue's guest room had to happen. And I hate that, but I can't imagine a life without knowing you—without you as my best friend."

"We all need to forgive." It was the Obard woman speaking. "This day needs to be the first day of a new era—a peaceful one."

Gemma gestured with a pointed finger that she wanted to say something. Xander helped her down the last few steps to join the others. "We've all done things we regret." Her gaze flicked to Meegan. "Now, we must move forward." Looking to Rian and the Obard soldier, she asked, "But how do we move forward?"

Rian faced the Obard woman. "I will return home with you."

The sharp features of the woman's jawline lifted. Clasping her hands together, the metal scales of her armor rubbing at her sides, she exclaimed, "Balance will be restored!"

Nodding, Rian repeated, "Balance will be restored." Then, to Isoldesse and Gemma, she asked, "And what of you two?"

Before Isoldesse could answer, Gemma said, "We are going to continue the Aevo Compendium, but after we make a few changes. The idea is a good one, but the execution can be tweaked."

Isoldesse met Meegan's gaze. "I'd only agree with Fawness's blessing."

Everyone's attention was on Meegan. Kenna used her arm, still looped through Meegan's, to nudge her friend into giving her blessing. "What do you say? A new start? We can even be a par—"

Shaking free from Kenna's grasp, Meegan backed away. "No! Maybe all of you can forget the past! But it's not that easy for me or the Anumen people." Thunder rolled in from the unseen sky above. Glossy eyes trembled, and her words staggered with unease. "I cannot move forward."

The Obard woman's pale blue brows pinched together as she suggested, "Then return home. Anuminis is not a desolate world like you believe. Yes, we have a scout ship in orbit, but only to notify the fleet if any Anumens return. We needed to find our Heiress."

Dark brown eyes softened, and Meegan shuffled closer. The thunder faded, sounding less volatile. "Anuminis is not destroyed?"

"Anuminis is as it always was."

Meegan's knees went weak, and her body swayed, almost losing her balance, but her friend was there to catch her. Keeping her distance, Gemma could only imagine the joy the two friends were feeling at hearing the news about the Anumen home world.

Kenna tugged her friend's arm and said with joy, "You can return home! You, your parents, and all the Anumens on Earth. Isn't that wonderful news?"

But before Meegan could reply, a man shouted, coming into view from behind a nearby building. One arm raised, Biryn pointed Anora's gun at the group, specifically at Meegan. Gemma's survival instincts kicked in, and she slowly retreated a few steps.

"Punishment is in order! You killed my brother, Quaid"—he aimed the gun at Rian—"and you killed my sister!" He moved closer, then stopped once he'd reached the front courtyard of the Lead building. Most of the pavers around them were cracked, some upturned, and the whole area was sprinkled with debris from the explosion that had hit the front side of the Lead building.

Swinging his arm, he returned his focus to Meegan. "I don't know how you bested my brother, but you shall not get the chance to strike me down!" With his final word, a *bang* rang out, echoing in Gemma's ears.

Gemma knew all about guns from her time as a Spiaire on Earth, so her body shuttered the second the gun went off. Intense fear and sorrow washed over her, but it wasn't her emotions consuming her thoughts. Her gaze turned to Isoldesse. The Anumen woman's hands were clasped over her mouth and nose, her dark brown eyes open to their fullest.

A warrior's cry broke through Gemma's thoughts, and she turned to see the Obard woman lunging forward. The top half of her body stretched outward as she jumped in front of Meegan. She landed on the ground, the sound of metal scraping against cracked stone of the courtyard.

Fawness didn't hesitate. She whispered words Gemma couldn't hear, lifting the Sendarian man into the air. His hands spread wide at his sides, the gun still clutched in one hand. Meanwhile, Rian and Kenna ran to the fallen Obard soldier, turned her over, and assessed the wounds.

Isoldesse also stepped closer, but as an overseer. She turned to Gemma and exclaimed, "We need to help them!"

At first, she shook her head. Then quickly dismissed her fears and ideology about self-preservation and instructed Xander to run and get Holt. She pushed him away, urging him to go.

"He's in surgery, trying to help that officer guy, Ben, remember?" He stepped closer, holding his hands out to keep her steady.

But Gemma swatted at his arms. "No! Xander, go find help! I don't care who it is… Get that Darci girl if you must!"

He nodded and took off running. When he disappeared inside the Lead building, Gemma turned and hobbled toward Kenna and

Rian, who were trying to stop the bleeding at the base of the Obard woman's neck.

"I never got your name," Rian said between sobs.

"Gya. My name…is Gya."

"Biryn, what have you done?" Kenna shouted at him.

White blood spilled out between and around Rian's fingers as she pressed a hand to the woman's neck. "Why did she do that?" Rian cried. "What were you thinking?" she asked, locking eyes with Gya.

Gya was looking everywhere but at those helping her. Her gaze searched past their heads, while one hand clutched Rian's arm. With strangled breaths, she whispered, "They've lost enough… Promise me, you'll…help the girl…find…her people."

"I promise," Rian whispered, tears flowing along her skin.

Meegan, clenched her fist, causing the invisible hold on Biryn to squeeze tighter. He cried out, but that didn't stop Meegan from causing him more pain. "Your brother was a monster. He deserved death." Her words were like venom, aimed at the Athru rebel. "He killed my love and was going to kill my friend!"

"And now you plan to have me share his fate?" Biryn groaned with a snide taunt woven into his tone. He tried to thrash about, probably hoping to break free, but his struggles proved to be worthless. The invisible force Meegan had used to pin him several feet above the ground held strong. He rebuked, spittle dribbling his chin, "I don't fear you!"

"You should," Meegan said with conviction. Gemma worried the Anumen girl might fall victim to her emotions again. With a flick of her fingers, she commanded the air to force Biryn to drop the gun.

Not wanting anyone else to take the weapon, Gemma hobbled over and picked it up. As she examined the components of the primitive device, Biryn tried to grab her from above. Though his fingers were able to move, wriggling to reach Gemma, his hand, arm, and the rest of him was glued to the air that held him.

"Traitor!" he hissed.

With the weapon in hand, Gemma looked up, the black underbelly of the Obard ship as his background, and told him, "Things could've gone differently. You and your siblings could've done better—for Sendara. That's what I was told when I joined the Athru." Then she turned and walked away, Biryn screaming and cursing at her, spit dribbling down his chin.

"That's enough of that," Meegan said and whispered for the air to wrap around his neck.

He gasped and coughed, choking. "No! Wait…!" He tried to plea as the air constricted and cut his words off.

"What would the Eilimintachs say?" Isoldesse asked, speaking out loud the concerns Gemma had. "Spare his life and let him live with his crimes, and of the loss of those he cares for."

With a side glance over her shoulder, Meegan hesitated for a long moment before lowering the Sendarian man to the ground. At first, he fell to his knees, but then he slowly stood. He brushed his hair from his face and stared at the Anumen girl, never moving to advance—just standing there, staring. Meegan said to him, "I made a promise. Even though every part of me wants to rip your essence from your body, I will let the Rhaltan pass judgment on your actions."

Biryn eyed Gemma standing a few feet behind Meegan, his gaze dipped to the weapon in her hand. She clutched the gun tighter, hoping he wasn't stupid enough to lunge for it. His attention turned to Meegan as Kenna approached.

"Gya is dead," she said, one hand on Meegan's forearm. Kenna then faced Biryn but said nothing.

He narrowed his orange eyes from beneath the light red hair hanging over one side of his forehead, then said to Kenna, "I wasn't lying when I said in order for change to happen, one must be willing to do the things others won't." With a wide sweep of his hand, he withdrew a knife from his back pocket and rushed the two girls, his intended target unknown—Kenna or Meegan.

Isoldesse raised a hand, crying out, "No!" next to Gemma.

Everything happened so fast. All Gemma could think was, *He truly is mad!*

Before the tip of the blade reached either girl, a pale hand grabbed his wrist, halting it from connecting to its target. "You killed my kin," Rian said with gritted teeth. Snow-white frost inched outward from beneath her fingers around his wrist, spreading up his arm and down into his hand.

He gasped. Frantic orange eyes watched with horror as his skin, muscles, and blood turned cold. The sound of ice crackling from beneath his sleeve. He opened his mouth and released a string of sharp whimpers. He even tried pulling himself free from Rian's grasp with his other hand, but her strength overpowered him. "No! Stop!" he repeatedly pleaded.

No one stopped her. Not even Isoldesse. Gemma for sure thought her goddess would intervene, but she didn't. No one did. The air was silent except for Biryn's final pleas and painful sobs. *It's torture, what Rian is doing*, Gemma thought as his limb stiffened. Unsure why, she stepped closer and said, "Don't you think that's enough? Let him live without an arm. Let him live so he may never forget."

Kenna's mouth, gaped open from the scene in front of her, slowly shut. "Yes, I agree with Gemma. Rian, you should stop."

"He will only kill again," Rian explained, tightening her hand, encouraging the ice to move faster.

As the tops of his arms crackled like ice splitting on a frozen lake, Meegan reached a hand over Rian's. Gemma for sure thought the girl's hand would succumb to the same fate as Biryn's arm, but it didn't. "We cannot let our emotions control our actions."

It was a long moment, the ice persistent in its course had claimed most of Biryn's right shoulder before Rian finally released her hold. Then, without another word, she spun and walked away to sit by Gya's body.

"He's all yours," Meegan called out.

From behind Gemma, Jordi strode over. "The queen will be most pleased to have one of the Athru leaders alive—to be held accountable for the damage done by the rebel group."

Jordi waved a hand, and to Gemma's surprise, Micah emerged from inside the Lead Building. He carefully climbed over large pieces of stone ruble.

"Where's Cahleen?" Gemma asked as Micah passed by her. He had a bandage wrapped around his head. Though it was strange to see him without his baseball cap, it was also nice to see him awake from his concussion.

"Inside," he answered without stopping. Micah had one of his paralytic neck bands in his hand, offering it over to the Rhaltan officer. "I know these aren't sanctioned, but it's the best we've got to keep him from running away." After securing the device into position, he showed Jordi how to operate the neck band on his plac.

"Yes, this is definitely not a sanctioned device. I will allow its use this one time, but it too must be presented to the queen."

Micah nodded. "I understand and take full responsibility."

"There's holding cells in the training building," Gemma said, limping closer. Her leg had started to bleed again. Her fault for standing on it longer than she should have.

"I can take him there," Darci said jogging down the steps. Jordi thanked the Sendarian and followed her, escorting Biryn into the Lead building.

Micah turned to Gemma. "Cahleen and Logan are gone. They took off through the emergency escape tunnels to the transport ship out by the old research facility. She wanted me to tell you that she'll find you, and talk more later. But for now, she said beannaith." He jogged up the steps toward the once glass entrance to the Lead building. "I'm going to go with the Rhaltan guy to make sure the neck brace works okay." Then he was off.

Gemma turned, away from the Lead building. She was surprised to see Kenna and Meegan facing her. "Thank you," Kenna said. "I think you have good in you. I'm starting to believe that now."

"But I still think you have a lot of growing to do, too," Meegan quickly added. Then to Isoldesse, she said, "You both do."

"Well, we did declare that things are going to change, right?" Gemma said in a slightly sarcastic tone. "I'm all about change nowadays."

The two friends left Gemma and Isoldesse and went to offer Rian their condolences and see if there was anything they could do to help. The three knelt close to Gya's still body, Gemma unable to hear their conversation.

"We should give them some privacy," Isoldesse said, turning and facing the partially demolished Lead building.

Gemma followed suit and turned her back to those grieving. From above, the Obard ship, its black metal glinting like rippling water, released its red energy barrier and freed Priomh from captivity. As it soared upward, its disc-shaped hull began to draw in, the ship's form reshaping into its original sphere structure.

"What happens next?" she softly asked her bonded companion, who was also watching the sky come back into view.

The black sphere faded as it flew farther from Priomh's surface, eventually looking like a distant moon. Isoldesse sighed. "I do not know. But I believe we are entering a new era of peace."

"Sendara's always been a peaceful world," Gemma said, then under her breath added, "Well, sort of."

"Yes, and I think it's time Sendara is given the freedom to evolve however your world sees fit."

Gemma faced Isoldesse. "That's easier said than done. I mean, that's exactly what the Athru originally intended to do, until psychopath Quaid ruined everything."

The elder Anumen woman nodded. "I'm sure you and I can come up with a less aggressive way to approach the queen for a brighter future for all of Sendara."

"I like the sound of that," Gemma answered, thinking of the cottage home they'd stayed in on Earth in the Florida region, and the luxuries the humans had that were restricted on Sendara. "I believe you and I are going to do wonderful things for the future of Sendara."

47

Kenna stared up into the blue sky. The Obard ship was fading, looking more like a distant moon than a spaceship. A hand rested on her arm, redirecting her attention from the sky to her best friend.

"I'm sorry about your dad."

It was hard to imagine never seeing her dad again, never hearing his stories or his jokes about how Mom takes things too seriously. But he was gone. Just like Nick.

"And I'm sorry about Nick."

Meegan tilted her head up, nodding as if holding back tears that should've fallen days ago. After a pause she smiled, looking to Kenna again. "It's going to take a long time for me to let him go, if I even can. But it is what it is. I can't do anything about that."

From behind Meegan, Kenna spotted Darci climbing over a large broken wooden beam. She was waving one hand at them.

"Darci!" Kenna called, meeting the Sendarian halfway. Meegan followed. Rian remained by Gya's body, while Gemma and Isoldesse stood off to the side, staring out at the ruins of Priomh.

"Weren't you showing Jordi the cells to lock Biryn up?" Meegan asked as they reached their Sendarian friend.

"You two should come with me," Darci said, starting to climb back over the beam. "I'm happy to see you're both okay, and yes, well… Breyah found us in the Centrum and offered to show them the rest of the way. She told me to come find you."

Watching her steps, Kenna asked, "Where's my mother? Is she okay? And Ben… Is he okay too?"

Darci held Kenna's hand as she climbed over the beam. "They're both okay. Though, Ben's in surgery with Holt and Ally."

"Ally's helping with surgery?" Meegan scoffed, her brows raised. With a silent amula cast in her mind, she lifted herself over the oversized beam, then landed softly next to Darci and Kenna.

Shaking her head, she said, "No. I mean, she's not performing surgery. Holt is. Ally's assisting since his entire medical team was evacuated with everyone else."

The three girls hurried across the grand space of the Centrum. Pieces of glass, wood, and stone littered the polished floor. Sunlight poured in from a gaping hole in the giant glass dome above the grand room.

As they entered the skywalk at the back of the Centrum, Kenna asked, "And Prue… How's she doing?"

"No change. But Holt thinks once Prue's back on Earth, she'll come to and recover without any permanent damage."

The second they walked through the double doors at the end of the corridor, Princess Emmalyn was there waiting for them. Her eyes were puffy, with a slight tint of pink outlining her lids. She went straight to Kenna and embraced her niece.

"I can't believe he's gone!" she cried into Kenna's shoulder, sniffling and trying to compose herself. "He only just returned. And Mother hadn't seen him—oh, she's going to be destroyed."

Kenna leaned away, holding the princess's shoulders tight. "Then you'll have to be strong for her. She's going to need you now more than ever." If she stopped to think about her father burning up against the energy barrier, she might break down too.

Emmalyn nodded, wiping her cheeks dry. "I always assumed he'd return and take his place as ruler of Sendara. He's the smart and politically savvy one. Not me. But now… Now it'll fall to me."

"It's an honor that you should be excited for. To know that you will help shape the new Sendara." Kenna dipped her head, glancing up at the princess. "Because change is coming for your people, and they'll need a strong leader to guide them through everything."

"Kenna! Meegan!" Ally shouted, running down the corridor toward them. Brown curls bounced free from the rest of her hair pulled back into a tight bun. "You're all right!" She hugged each one tightly before stepping away. "Ben is doing okay. It was a clean shot through. Holt said there were no vital organs hit."

Hearing this eased the worry growing in Kenna's core. She couldn't lose anyone else important to her today.

"So, what now?" Ally asked, looking to each of her friends standing in the corridor.

"The Obard are no longer a threat," Kenna explained. "And Jordi has the last of the Athru leaders in custody."

"So, it's over?" Darci looked to Meegan for an answer. "We're safe and the Anumen people are safe?"

Meegan smiled. "The Obard threat is no more, but the safety of my people is far from assured." She then faced Kenna. "I'll have to return to Earth too. To tell my parents what's happened here." Kenna opened her mouth, but Meegan quickly cut her off. "You should know before you make your decision to return to Earth or stay, that I don't plan on staying on Earth. Rian has offered to take us home— back to Anuminis."

The silence between the four lingered, the weight of Meegan's words sinking in. It was Darci who finally asked, "Like forever?"

A tear trickled from Kenna's eye. She'd not wanted to lose anyone else today, but it seemed she was going to anyway. Her best friend was leaving her.

"Don't give me that look," Meegan said with a smirk. "You were planning on staying here anyway, weren't you?"

"Yeah, but…" Kenna shrugged. "I thought you would too."

"There's nothing here for me except you. And I owe it to my people to bring them home, back to Anuminis. But this doesn't mean goodbye. I mean, there are spaceships traveling the galaxy, for heaven's sake!"

A door opened down the hall. It was Holt. "Ben is recovering. He should be awake shortly." He retreated back from where he came, the door closing behind him.

Darci grazed Kenna's arm. "I should go find Breyah, and then check on Rian. I'll be back, okay?"

"I need to check on Prue," Ally said, then gave both her friends a quick hug before disappearing into a nearby patient room.

"And I need to contact my mother," Emmalyn said from behind. Kenna had forgotten the princess was still there.

Nodding, Kenna said, "I look forward to meeting her."

Hands clasped over Kenna's, she said softly, "And I bet she'll be excited to meet you." The princess turned and headed down the corridor, then out the double doors toward the Centrum.

"We should find your mother," Meegan suggested.

They searched the medical rooms on the side that hadn't been attacked. Some of the lights flickered, but remained lit. They found the room Ben was resting in. He had one of those white silicone masks covering his head, but Kenna knew it was him. Honnah just happened to be in the same room, sitting in a chair, staring out the window.

Kenna hurried to the armchair and crouched to eye level. "Are you hurt?" She scanned her mom's face, turning Honnah's chin so she could see along her neck for any injuries. Honnah didn't respond. Her eyes were glossed over, staring past the two girls. "Mom!"

At her daughter's sharp tone, Honnah blinked and slowly locked eyes with Kenna. "Is it over?" she whispered, sounding more exhausted and defeated than interested.

"It's over." Kenna pulled her mother in for a hug. "I miss him too. But he's gone." Tears fell. "He would've wanted us to stay strong—to be there for one another."

As Kenna pulled away, Honnah's dark brown gaze started to drift from her daughter's, but then she nodded. "You're right. You know, at first"—she faced her daughter—"we didn't love one another. It was a mutual agreement, for the cause of bringing you into this world and setting Isoldesse's mistakes right. But—"

"But then you did." Kenna clasped her mom's hands.

"He wasn't only the love of my life, but he was my best friend too. Something you both"—Honnah glanced at Meegan, then back to her daughter—"should have when finding your life partners."

Meegan rested a hand on Honnah's shoulder. "Well, mission accomplished. Now, everything changes."

A smile broke through Honnah's sorrowful expression. "We've… I mean, I've been waiting a long time for this day."

Kenna released her mom's hand, stood, and faced Ben's bed. "How is he?"

"I don't know. I haven't been… I mean, my mind was preoccupied."

"It's okay." It wasn't her mom's job to nurse him. She'd have to wait to ask about Ben's condition until Holt showed up. Behind her, Meegan sat against the windowsill and wrapped one arm around Honnah while Kenna went to Ben's side. "Hang in there," she whispered, slipping her hand into his.

A procession of soft knocks rapped on the door, followed by Holt immediately entering. "There you two are." He stood behind Ben's bed, reading the screens on the glass panel that stretched from the top of the headboard. "He'll live, but it's going to be a long recovery. And the Rhaltan will most likely give him a desk position or discharge option."

"I can't imagine Ben taking a desk job," Kenna scoffed, looking down at his blond hair peeking out from beneath the silicone mask.

"I can't either," Holt agreed.

She let her fingers slide from Ben's and moved closer to Holt. His navy-blue tunic was tattered along his short sleeves, and dark stains smudged the front. Kenna assumed the stains were blood from Ben's surgery.

"What do you think he'll do?"

"I have no idea. But I do know that he's going to have to take it easy. For how long, I can't say. But the *bull-et*"—he exaggerated the syllables as if he'd never heard of such a word—"tore through his chest muscles, nearly hitting his heart. Two inches lower and Bennach wouldn't be here with us."

Kenna nodded, understanding that she needed to be there for him when he woke. Learning that he wouldn't be a Rhaltan officer anymore might crush him, and she wanted to be there for him. She wanted to spend as much time as she could with him—to get to know him, and possibly fall in love with him. Her feelings were already teetering towards loving this man, but she wasn't the type of person to jump into anything without testing the waters first. Her best friend was right. Kenna was staying.

"Can we talk?" Meegan asked, approaching the end of the bed and throwing a thumb out toward the door.

"Sure. I'll be right back, Mom."

Honnah offered a small smile as acknowledgment. They left the room, leaving Holt to finish up with Ben. Out in the hall, Kenna followed Meegan to the double doors, where she stopped halfway across the skywalk. The sun shone through the glass doming over the stretch of bridge between the Centrum and the medical wing. The heat felt nice—comforting—especially after sleeping on the cold, hard steel cargo-hold floor of the transport ship. Even the company of Anora and Biryn made her skin crawl.

Brushing off the memories of her captivity, she asked, "What's up?"

Meegan's attention shifted from the forest stretching behind the stone wall that surrounded the compound to Kenna. "You know I can't stay, right?"

She did know. After hearing Gya confess the truth about the state of Anuminis, she knew Meegan would want to go home. Her friend had even told Kenna outside that she couldn't stay. That she needed to get back to Earth, tell her parents everything, then with the Obard's help—Rian's help—bring the Anumen people home.

Yet still, she didn't want Meegan to go.

"I know. I wish I could see Anuminis."

Meegan rubbed her hands along Kenna's arms. "Oh, you will. One day. I promise to come back here and take you on vacation to Anuminis."

"That would be a dream come true. To travel the stars and visit worlds."

"Well, I would hope that you and Gemma could work together in giving the Aevo Compendium project new purpose."

Kenna nodded. "I hope so too."

Meegan looked to the forest again. "I miss Nick."

Wrapping an arm around Meegan's shoulders, Kenna said, "I'm sorry you didn't get to say goodbye." From behind Meegan, Ulissa appeared. Her expression mimicked Kenna's apology.

The elder Anumen clasped her hands together. "I couldn't hold on to him. The arcstone's energy had been drastically drained. I was barely conscious."

"It's okay," Meegan answered, facing Ulissa. "It's not your fault. I shouldn't have put you through that strain—you or him."

"Meegan!" Honnah called out, stepping into the skywalk. "I forgot I have something for you." Even though Honnah couldn't see her daughter's bonded companion, she addressed the three of them. "You've all been through so much, and it was sad what happened to Nick. I know how much you loved him." Uncurling her fingers, she held out her hand. "This was on one of the Elemental Council members, and since she no longer needed it, I thought you could use it."

Kenna looked at the familiar yellow stone, embedded in the headpiece the elder woman had worn. The scene replayed in her mind—Biryn throwing his knives and killing the three council members. She shoved the memory from her thoughts and focused on the headpiece her mother held. "Mom, that's an arcstone."

Shaking her head, Meegan declined Honnah's offer. "It's too late. But I appreciate your effort. Nick's already gone."

Honnah grabbed Meegan's hand, turned it over, and pressed the headpiece into her palm. "He's not gone."

Both Meegan's and Kenna's eyes opened to their fullest. Meegan held up the piece. Thin patina strands of metal intertwined like vines, then came together at the front, wrapping around the yellow arcstone. The sun hit the hard angle of the stone, making it glint.

The girls looked to Honnah, but it was Kenna who asked, "How? And when did you put Nick's essence in there?"

"After we returned to the ship from the Elemental facility, when you were asleep. I drew his essence out of your arcstone and transferred it into this one."

"This is wonderful news." Ulissa clapped her hands as she stood behind the girls. Then, with a serious tone, she added, "But remember, young Fawness, an arcstone bond is forever."

"I know." Meegan turned the headpiece over, examining the jewelry. "Though, this won't do. I can't have this thing on my head *all the time*." Closing her eyes, she silently cast an amula. A bright gold light filled the skywalk, and when the light subsided, the metal of the headpiece had morphed into a smaller version that would fit around her wrist. "There. Now, that's better."

"Are you sure?" Kenna asked, already knowing the answer. "Do you think he'll want that? To be bonded to you forever but never living in the real world."

What kind of relationship could they have? What if Meegan wanted children one day? So many questions filled her head that Kenna wasn't so sure this was a good idea.

"Stop listing off questions in that head of yours," Meegan said, smiling at her friend. "You always worry way too much. Besides, I know exactly what's involved and what I'm giving up. He's worth it. And if he decides he wants to move on, then he can continue on to the Unforeseen World and partake in his second life. I would release him."

"Wait, that can be done? Ulissa can leave anytime she wants?" Kenna swallowed, looking to Ulissa, the fear creeping up inside her that one day she might lose her bonded friend.

"It can be done. But I have to choose to go, and that day is far from near. You have nothing to worry about." Ulissa swayed, her gown glinting in the sun shining down through the glass. "You two have much to discuss. I will see you later." The Anumen woman faded from view.

"I will leave you to it," Honnah said, hugging Meegan one last time before exiting the skywalk.

The two girls stood there for the longest moment, staring at the bracelet. With tears welling in her eyes, Meegan smiled at Kenna. Then, as she pinched the small arcstone affixed in the center of the ring, she said, *"Banna idir dufiur et gohdeo."*

EPILOGUE

"How are you doing, dear?" asked Ulissa, her golden dress glinting in the sunlight.

Kenna stood from her seat on a large stone paver that was turned on its side from the attack. Priomh hadn't started cleaning up the areas outside the Lead building. Breyah had only permitted necessary personnel to return—everyone else was on extended leave until further notice.

It had been one day since the *Tarais* left the docking station. Its destination—Earth. Saying goodbye to Ally had been hard. Tears fell and hugs lasted shorter than she would've liked. But Prue needed to return in order to heal properly. Plus, Kenna promised she'd come and visit.

Liam offered to return home with Julianna and make sure Devaney's body was laid to rest and her family notified. She hadn't even gotten to see Priomh or meet the Sendarians due to complications during the Waking. Saying goodbye to Liam was hard too. He had been her close childhood friend. And because she didn't want to leave any hard feelings between them, she told him she was sorry for how she reacted. He apologized too, again. They agreed to always be friends, and she wished him the best of luck with his fiancée back home.

Brody had decided to stay. His time with Matthew while staying at the royal home on the outskirts of Priomh compound had given him time to appreciate this world. Plus, now that Eryn had been rescued and they were able to be together, he wanted nothing more than to stay here with her.

"Well, lookie here. It's my new bestie. I was wondering where you ran off to."

Kenna glanced over her shoulder, the corners of her mouth turning up. "It feels so quiet and empty now that everyone's gone."

Saying goodbye to Meegan was the hardest, but knowing that her friend was returning to Earth with a plan to continue on to Anuminis made it a little easier. A little. It still hurt not knowing when they'd see each other again. It was nice that she got to say goodbye to Nick too. He looked amazing—and happy. Breyah had offered up a plac to each friend, telling them they could stay in contact through these enhanced placs. It was the best parting gift the Sendarian Leadess could give them.

"Are you still sulking about your friends leaving?"

"Aren't you still sulking about your sister disappearing?"

Gemma took a seat on the upturned paver next to Kenna. "Oh, I'm sure we'll have the pleasure of seeing Cahleen again."

"And Micah?"

She looked up to the Lead building. The smoke had stopped, but the exterior was in need of a complete remodel. "Breyah gave him a position as tech support."

"Really?" Kenna's eyebrows lifted. She was surprised he wasn't in a jail cell. "Was that your convincing?" When Gemma didn't answer, but did smile, Kenna asked, "And Xander? Where's that asshat at?"

"Breyah's putting him to work too. Cleanup crew. And that asshat is my betrothed, so he's not going anywhere. Meaning, be nice."

Kenna laughed. She never imagined she'd ever be laughing and joking with the Sendarian woman who kidnapped her mother, Darci, and others as part of the Athru rebel group. But she was happy Gemma had changed her ways.

They let the silence fill the space between them. Gemma closed her eyes and looked to the sky, soaking in the sun. After a long moment, she said, "Isoldesse's head is clear, and she's been more focused since peace was made with the Obard."

"Oh, I forgot!" Kenna got to her feet and held out her hands. "Stand with me and give me your hands."

"Why?"

"Just do it."

Gemma stood and slipped her hands into Kenna's grasp. With the words Meegan had told her to memorize, she cast an amula. *"Olahar dyreac et banna nausc."*

It only took a few seconds, but both Ulissa and Isoldesse appeared. Gemma's mouth gaped open at seeing Kenna's bonded companion, and she almost dropped her hands, but Kenna made sure to hold them tight. "Don't let go."

"Sister!" Ulissa cried, her hands clasped over her mouth, tears welling in her eyes.

Isoldesse lunged forward, grabbed Ulissa's hands, and squeezed. "Oh, I never thought I would see you again!"

The two old women embraced, their auras glowing bright. When they parted, Isoldesse repeatedly begged for her sister's forgiveness.

"It was a long time ago. And you know I could never stay mad at you," Ulissa offered. Kenna thought it was big of her to forgive the woman who had killed her, forced her essence inside an arcstone, and ruined their home world. But she also knew Ulissa was the kindest and most reasonable person she'd ever met.

"Now you can talk whenever you want—with Gemma and I present, of course," Kenna said with a giggle. "But it's better than nothing, right?"

Isoldesse thanked Kenna and asked her to thank Fawness next time they spoke. Then to Ulissa she said, "We have much work to do here. And I would be honored by your council and participation."

"Well, since I go where Kenna goes, I'm here until she leaves. So, I'd be happy to help any way I can." The answer seemed to please Isoldesse as she pulled her sister in for another hug.

Gemma cocked her head toward the Lead building. "We should get back inside. Breyah's calling a meeting with the Leads, and that includes her new Security Lead and—"

"Redesign Lead," Kenna finished. "Though, I have no idea what that entails."

With a shrug, she said, "I guess we'll find out." She shook her hand, letting Kenna know she was going to release her grasp, and they broke their hands apart and watched as Ulissa's and Isoldesse's forms faded from view. "Come on, let's go."

Kenna followed Gemma into the Lead building, where her new life awaited.

ANOTHER WEEK LATER

Ben cringed as he sat down on the blanket next to Kenna. A late-afternoon shadow cast across the field from the nearby forest, but it didn't quite reach their picnic spread.

"I'm supposed to be taking it easy," he said, wincing and rubbing his left shoulder.

"A little fresh air and exercise will do you good." Their picnic had been planned for earlier in the day, but Holt had insisted Bennach stop by for a quick check-in before leaving the grounds.

"How are you adjusting to all this free time?" Kenna worried the question might sour the mood, but she did want to make sure he was okay with his decision to leave the Rhaltan.

His gaze wandered from her to the forest in the background. After a moment, he answered, "It'll take some getting used to. I think I might accept Breyah's offer to work with Gemma, but as Lead Security on the *Tarais*—for away missions."

Kenna placed her hands on his cheeks and turned him to look at her. "Did you do that for me? Because I'll be traveling the stars, collecting research and data for Breyah and the new Aevo Compendium?"

"Maybe," he said, dragging the word out.

"Are you going to be able to work with Gemma?"

He shrugged. "I guess we'll see. Though, I'll only have to work with her regarding security matters while on Priomh."

"And Jordi?"

"Ah, yes. I'm happy Jordi has accepted a security position on Priomh too. He'll probably end up working with Gemma more than I."

She eyed him with an amused glare. "I imagine you set that up so you could keep an eye on her while we're traveling the stars on the *Tarais*."

He gave Kenna a wink, and they both laughed.

She handed Ben a glass bottle filled with water, and he accepted it. Before taking a sip, he said, "I think this is the first day since the attack that we've had no one wanting our attention."

"Besides Holt this morning."

He sipped his water and nodded. "Yes, besides Holt and that ridiculous checkup. I'm fine."

"And by *wanting our attention* you mean my aunt. She's the one who has been glued to my hip whenever I'm not working or learning more about Priomh. I've barely had any solitude or a moment to be alone with you!"

After closing the cap on his water bottle, he leaned closer. "The princess has always been an insistent character. But I think right now, her intention isn't to annoy. She just wants to get to know you better."

"Yes, I know."

Setting the water down, he added, "I do believe this is the first time we've had any alone time, *during the day*." He emphasized the last three words, with a mischievous smile. "That's not to say I haven't enjoyed our late-night encounters."

"Yes, I believe you are correct." Kenna closed the distance and kissed him. When they parted, she could still feel his breath on her lips. "It's been nice getting to know you a bit better, and you've been so patient—such a gentleman."

Kenna had met Ben every single night over the past two weeks in their secret meeting place—in their dreams. And he respected her wishes to wait until they were together for real before taking their relationship to the next level. So, they'd used their midnight meetings to talk and get to know one another better—which ultimately increased their love and devotion.

"I believe I'm officially meeting the queen in the next few days," Kenna said, falling back onto the blanket.

Ben leaned over her, blocking the setting sun from blinding her. He brushed a few strands of dark hair from her forehead. "She's an intense Sendarian, but I've heard rumors that since her son—your father—has passed and the threat of the Obard is no more, she's at peace. The worry that consumed her is gone, allowing her to be the queen she used to be."

"Well, I look forward to meeting her." She brushed her fingers along his smooth chin. "You shaved?"

"Of course. This is a special day. The beginning of something beautiful—the beginning of us."

ACKNOWLEDGMENTS

The story world and characters in this series have been a part of my life for nearly a decade. Creating this series has been a transformative journey, not only as my debut series but also as a writer and publisher. Throughout this process, I have learned valuable lessons about crafting compelling narratives, forging connections with fellow writers and readers, and navigating the complexities of the publishing industry.

I'd like to express my gratitude to the following individuals without whom this book would not have been possible:

Foremost, I want to thank my family, my husband Jim, and our three girls for their unwavering support and encouragement throughout this writing journey. Thank you for always believing in me, even when the road ahead seemed long and uncertain.

I'd like to extend my heartfelt appreciation to Nikki from NAM Editorial for her expert guidance and insightful feedback during the editing process. Her attention to detail and thoughtful suggestions have greatly improved the quality of this book.

I'd also like to thank Aime from Red Leaf Word Services for her careful proofreading and meticulous attention to detail, ensuring that this book is free from errors and typos.

Special thanks to Liz Delton for her invaluable early reader feedback and for proofreading the book's blurb. Her insights and suggestions have been instrumental in shaping this story.

I'm also grateful to Kristin Hilgart for her early reader feedback and for taking on the audiobook production. Her dedication and commitment to bringing this story to life in a new format are greatly appreciated.

If you've visited my author website, then you might've seen some character artwork for the cast of Isoldesse and Fawness. I'd like to thank T.A. Hernandez for her amazing work at bringing these characters to life!

Finally, I want to acknowledge my wonderful friends and family who have supported my dreams over the years. This series is my first completed series, and I'm honored to have so many amazing people in my life who have encouraged and inspired me every step of the way. Thank you all for your encouragement and support.

About the Author

Kimberly Grymes finds herself irresistibly drawn into the realms of science-fiction, fantasy, mystery, and the paranormal. After immersing herself in countless books and on-screen stories, she took the leap to craft and share her own imaginative tales. When she's not weaving narratives, Kimberly enjoys spending time with her family, indulging in movies or TV shows, delving into captivating books, or crafting new designs and products for her Etsy shop.

As a versatile author specializing in young adult fiction, Kimberly's Aevo Compendium Duology introduces readers to a thrilling YA science-fantasy series, while her Three Shades Trilogy offers a darker twist on YA fantasy.

Kimberly and her family reside on the outskirts of Wichita, Kansas, accompanied by their two lively miniature pinschers, Cori and Jubilee.

https://kimberlygrymes.substack.com

Stay Connected
Instagram: @kgrymes.writes